Published by Griffyn Ink

www.griffynink.com

For ordering information or special discounts for bulk purchases, please contact Griffyn Ink at Mail@GriffynInk.com.

This one is for you, readers.

Thank you so much for coming along on this ride with me. I know that paranormal isn't my general genre and it may not be yours either. I'm not even sure where this series quite fits on the spectrum, but I just loved these stories. They needed to be told.

I started by wondering: what would it be like if you really had that kind of skill. It's power, pure and simple, and you could use it for good or ill. I have magicks in the series used all different ways, because—like many other things—it's just a talent or a skill. I hope you enjoyed reading them as much as I enjoyed writing them.

Here's to the Goodman family. And here's to you! Thank you so much.

As always, I cannot thank my team enough. But for this round the biggest applause goes to Eli. This story was in my head for a long time and she waited and helped each time it came back around. Love also to my crew—you guys are the best.

TOUCH OF MAGIC | BOOK FIVE

SHADOW KISS

SAVANNAH KADE

CHAPTER 1

S loan Ellis offered the crowd her best smile. She did not want these people to be able to tell just how nervous she was. She thought she pulled it off for two reasons: first, she had lots of practice trying to look normal while doing things that twitched her anxiety. And second, she'd cast a spell on herself so people would see a calm, confident sister of the bride.

The problem was, she'd screwed it up. She should have cast a spell to make herself *not nervous*. Talk about a swing and a miss.

She took a deep breath and heard it reverberate through the mic so everyone else heard it, too. *Lovely.* Then she spoke. She didn't make any high-pitched screeches, so that was good. She also didn't need to pull the paper out of her pocket where she'd written her ever-so-short toast down.

"So," she dove into the end with gusto. "I would like to wish Rae and Sam good luck on their future together, but I'm not going to. They don't need it. I've seen them in action and they've already proven they have what it takes." She turned to her sister and raised her glass, feeling her heart swell, wishing their mother and father could have been here. "I hope you have sunny days ahead of you, even though I know you two will be fine whatever comes your way. I know Mom and Dad would be so happy for you, Rae, and so ready to welcome you into our family, Sam. Cheers."

She took a sip from her champagne, almost spilling it in her glee at being finished. Ever so carefully, so as not to trip and ruin a toast that had gone as well as she could make it go, she stepped down from the small stage and headed back to her seat.

It was a good day. Sunny, the beach was cooperating with her sister's wedding plans. Rae was beaming and Sam looked like a man who was both ecstatic and thoroughly at peace with his life.

The only downside was that Rae couldn't photograph her own wedding. Sloan had no skills in that area. She'd helped with flowers and picking out a dress and let Rae hand the photo job off to another art photographer she admired. He generally did not do weddings. For Rae and Sam he made an exception.

Settling back into her seat at the head table, Sloan felt a hand on her shoulder. It was Yasmin, her new cousin-in-law and witch extraordinaire. She leaned in and whispered, "Your *Veil* worked perfectly!"

"You can tell?" Sloan blinked up, aside from keeping her voice low, she was ignoring the fact that there was another person who'd gotten up to make a toast. Yasmin could tell she'd cast a spell on herself?

"I can see it," Yasmin whispered out the side of her mouth.

"Who else can see it?" Sloan shot back, not so proud of herself any more.

"Probably Tristan. Definitely Delilah. Maybe a few others? I don't know. Not most people, no worries."

Yup. *No worries*, that's exactly what she was thinking. Because what good was a *Veil* spell to make people think you weren't nervous if they could see that you'd cast the damn spell in the first place? She smiled at Rae's friend Alex as he made another toast to the happy couple. He looked much more comfortable at the mic than she'd been. Probably didn't need a stupid spell either.

She was truly happy for her sister. She almost cried as the crowd sent them off in their convertible. Rae and Sam would drive up the coast, having decided that LAX was no place to start a marriage. Sloan did her part and helped clean up, then begged off partying and said goodnight to everyone she knew.

She drove herself home in the little red Audi that said things about her that weren't true. It was an LA thing to have the best possible car—even if that meant you lived in a terrible neighborhood. She didn't. She had amazing neighbors in her building in West Hollywood. And she'd thought it would be temporary.

Rae had encouraged her to take a job here several years ago. Since her sister was her only immediate family left, she'd come. However, she'd made the arch mistake of thinking that Los Angeles would be full of men. That she'd meet someone and fall in love and...

Do all the things that Rae had done: have a circle of friends, live her dream, find *him*.

So yeah, she was a little jealous. And now she knew she couldn't even cast a spell on herself for it because her new family—Yasmin and Luke—and her new friends down at Blessed Be, their family witchcraft shop, would know exactly what she'd done.

Kicking off her shoes, she dropped onto her very plush sofa and held a solo pity party. She pulled out a bottle of her favorite red wine and poured herself a glass. She only had her own favorites in the house. Because no one else came to drink wine with her. Aaaannnnddd the pity party cranked up a notch.

One glass of wine was enough to convince her to get out of the very pretty dress she'd never have an opportunity to wear again. Even her pajamas said "party of one."

Back on the couch, she refilled her wine, turned on the TV and stared into the distance. It was time for some hard choices.

There were, in fact, tons of men in L.A. However, far too many were workaholics. Many were trust fund babies with no life skills of their own. Actors—she shuddered. Producers or agents—too sharky! And kids. She'd had no second dates for over... a year now. *Ouch.*

So it was time to choose. House? Or Cats? She needed to embrace solo-dom.

She truly liked cats. Yasmin had two. Hex and Voodoo— sweet gray rescues that hung out at the store with her and rode in the car back and forth almost like dogs. Except Yasmin didn't have two cats, *Yasmin and Luke* did. Which kept Yasmin from being a cat lady. She was a happily married woman who only took sips of her champagne at the wedding.

Shit.

Yasmin was pregnant and they hadn't told anyone! Yes, Sloan was putting her money on Delilah's kids getting a cousin soon. And Tristan and Megan would be tying the knot next month. Though they would literally tie the knot in an old pagan ceremony of handfasting. Sloan thought it was a beautiful idea. Then she fought tears. It just wasn't meant to be for everyone.

House.

Right then she decided. She was going to buy a house. Dammit, she had a good job. She had a steady income that could afford more than this apartment and more than the wish that she would find a man and fall in love and everything would fall in line. Clearly, it wasn't going to.

House.

It would be small, but she was only one person. Well, maybe one person and a few cats.

She was halfway through the second glass of wine when she had an epiphany. She couldn't cast on herself, because all her new witchy friends might see it. But she could scry. Thunking

4

the wine glass onto her coffee table with a little too much force, she bolted for the guest room closet. Her pendulum hung there and she reached out for it, frowning as it looked like the small pointed jade piece reached for her, too. *Too much wine,* she told herself, and pulled out her maps.

She set out the map of L.A. then realized she shouldn't be searching for a man if she didn't know yet that he existed. She had two bowls nested on her coffee table. The inside one held potpourri. Lifting it out, she set it aside and pulled her water out of the cabinet. She got a gallon from Blessed Be when she needed it. She'd even joined the circle of witches who blessed the water monthly. That was cool. Pouring it into the bowl she leaned in and almost knocked over her wine.

She looked through the surface and held her question close. *Is there someone out there for me?*

She saw the picture begin to form and she watched with abject fascination. There he was. *Him.* Then the surface rippled and marred the image.

Damn. She couldn't see him. All she could see was dark hair and a tie with little lightning bolts on it. Little, almost cartoony lightning bolts. That was silly. After three tries she gave up. He was there, but she was clearly not allowed to see him. She went to the map to see if this dream man lived in Los Angeles. She got a huge goose egg.

So she'd come out here for nothing. *Great.*

Next, she headed back to the closet to pull out the full US map. She spread it on the table, knocked back the last of her wine and started looking.

It was an arduous task. The wine didn't help. In fact, she must have fallen asleep leaned over the coffee table, because she woke at three a.m. with the side of her face pressed to the map, the fuzz of wine in her mouth, and the little jade pendulum pointing to Chicago.

5

CHAPTER 2

I t was a beautiful day. Green grass, perfect barbecue, and a beautiful woman on a picnic blanket beside him. Well, it should have been a perfect day.

Problem was, none of it was quite right. The barbecue wasn't really a barbeque, it was a catered work event with smiling servers in starched white shirts. There were literally about four hundred people he didn't know milling around. And the woman who was his date had been boring him to tears for about a month.

Max Summerland, corporate raider, deal-closer extraordinaire, and all around guy's guy, was shredding grass for fun. The ladder-climber couldn't remember the names of the last three guys or the hot blonde who came up to ask how he was. Even the ones he knew, he didn't seem to be able to recognize without their stuffy suits and button down shirts.

The girlfriend was an entirely self-made problem, he could admit. Anne Marie, with the perfect brunette curls and wide brown eyes, was surely a very lovely person, but she was waiting for the deal-closer to close the deal. She had been waiting for a ring for about two months now and he knew it.

Right after he had asked his sister what he had done wrong on New Year's in Vegas when he took Anne Marie out to a show and dinner.

His sister was the one who explained the muffled sobs coming from the bathroom. When he got back to the hotel room after his business meeting on the second of January he simply suggested that Anne Marie start packing so they didn't miss their flight, that was when he made the call and found out that he was *supposed* to propose. Never mind that he didn't want to. Never mind that this whole thing had really gone on much longer than it should have. He didn't love her and she didn't love him. He fought off a bout of the willies just thinking about it.

"Something wrong, honey?" Her hand rested on his forearm. Even just that one gesture seemed so contrived.

"No." He lied. He groaned inwardly. It was so much easier to just let things go on, but this was going straight to nowhere. He was considering drinking. It was a bad idea at a work function, but maybe it would make the afternoon pass faster.

With a sigh he brushed the mound of shredded green from the blanket. Anne Marie was talking to some woman with a two-year-old—or maybe a four-year-old, he wasn't sure—clinging to her leg. He smiled a dull, non-committal grin.

"You okay, Max?"

That voice. It was Sheila from accounting. God, she looked different in a T-shirt with a kid stuck to her leg. She looked happy. "Yeah, yeah," he finally found his voice. "I'm okay. I—" He tried again. "I didn't know you had a kid."

"Two actually." She turned and looked over her shoulder. "Here comes my husband with the other one."

It was all Max could do to make nice and shake hands. The contrast between the couple in front of him and the sad lack of anything on his own picnic blanket was striking. Seeing the way this couple looked at each other—after two kids and who knew how many years—it was clear that there never had been anything between him and Anne Marie.

He was turning to say just that when he saw *her*. Dark golden blonde hair, long green dress and a sunhat with a scarf trailing down the back. Wil was keeping step beside her, trying to make her laugh. *She* was trying to look like she was laughing. She was trying to look like she didn't have to try.

Later he would analyze it, that zinging feeling. He'd try to find a way to rationalize it and ignore everything he was feeling. Maybe it was his subconscious's way of pushing him out of his relationship with... with... Anne Marie. For then, he was content to just watch as Wil steered her away. Then he felt the bite of Anne Marie's sharp voice saying she wanted to go home.

With one eye over his shoulder, he reluctantly packed up the blanket and helped a stony Anne Marie to the car. Where he got an earful of how he would never grow up. How she had waited and waited. How all he could do was stare at *that blonde*. How her patience was out and she was finished with him.

Maybe it was better to let Anne Marie think that she was ending things. It would only hurt feelings to say that he agreed. He wanted to feel bad about it, but he couldn't quite muster the guilt. She hadn't been in this for the right reasons either. So he dropped her off at her front door with the promise to leave anything of hers that he found at his place on her doorstep. Anne Marie's mouth had opened then snapped shut. Then she had slammed her front door.

Monday. Monday he would have to find out where *she* worked. Wil probably already knew. But Wil wasn't the right guy. Max *knew*. He'd make her see.

8

CHAPTER 3

S loan's desk was piled high with folders and actual paperwork. That was for HR—who demanded inked signatures. She also had a beautiful Japanese serenity cup on her desk. Her new division-mates had been dropping simcards and microdisks into it to give her hard copies. Sloan was pretty sure that's not what a serenity cup was for.

According to rumor, the guy who had vacated this position had vacated it in soul long before the body quit showing up to work every day. And from the scrolling lists in her inbox, she believed it. She was still getting updates from her old division, too, and she had to get off their email lists first. Actual papers that weren't hers cascaded out of her physical inbox and outbox to the point where she was pretty certain there *wasn't* a point to it. Could she just get rid of the boxes?

Sloan sighed. She had her door open onto the hallway, but couldn't even see beyond her massive monitor, and she had just gotten a call that they wanted to consolidate the position she had been hired for with another in another department and could she move her desk up to fifteen in foreign acquisitions? Sloan thought she'd cry. She wasn't even sure if they meant the stuff or the actual desk. Which she had to say she was quite certain she couldn't lift.

Tomorrow. Tomorrow she would move to fifteen. Today she would cry quietly behind the monitor so no one would see. She thought about telling Rae, but Rae was happy and she didn't want to bring her sister down with reports that the promotion already looked like a massive dud. She didn't want to admit how bad her decision had been.

Tonight when she got in she would call Lisette back home and apologize for waking the kids and listen to Lisette tell her to stick it out. After all, she could always quit and come home later, couldn't she?

After a few good sniffles, she found that she didn't have the energy to work up a solid cry. Instead, she grabbed a manila envelope and made a beeline to the elevator. Unsure whether the envelope she'd picked up even had anything in it, she hit the button for fifteen. She would check out the new digs, and pray that it was decent and that they didn't move her again. She harbored a fear that she would get buried in her inherited files and no one would ever hear from her again.

The elevator was empty. Of course it was. It was five thirty. Everyone in their right mind was going down, not up. The doors opened onto the fifteenth floor right as the front desk was clearing out. The young man at the desk offered brief directions to her new office even as he transferred the phones over to the night service.

This hallway looked exactly the same as all the others. Another sigh escaped her. This appeared to be her fate. Her true love existed, but not in Los Angeles. While it should have given her hope, it had turned her into even more of a workaholic. If he wasn't here, why even go looking?

Though she had a law degree, she also had a complete lack of flair for courtroom drama. So she'd added an MBA—a year of sheer hell online homework. That and an intense ability to focus earned her a decent salary re-working corporate contracts. Finding and deciphering all those words could be like a game, if she was in a good mood.

She sucked in a breath as she turned the corner to her new office. It apparently also earned her an office with a window looking over the next few blocks and a glass wall between her and the hallway. *Ohhh-kayyy.* Maybe she could like it here on fifteen.

Setting the probably empty envelope on a cabinet, she pulled out the chair and settled herself behind the new desk. It was the same desk. Wood and identical to the one she was leaving behind. She was truly excited that this meant that she didn't have to re-organize everything. God, she was boring.

She could see straight down the hall and out into the central area, where there was an actual water cooler. Maybe it hadn't been all talk when Mr. Bernstein hired her. Maybe he was serious about wanting his employees to interact all the time. She'd been surprised to find that the legal people weren't in one clump but dispersed all over the building depending on which team they worked for.

"Hi, Sloan, what are you doing up this way? Come to find me?"

It was Wil, poking his head in the doorway. His overblown personality could have easily been obnoxious, but he accepted that about himself, and it made her smile. "Actually, I just got transferred up here."

"You've worked with the division for a week and you already got a promotion?"

"Promotion? I was certain I was being punished." She grinned at him, happy for the only non-uptight interaction she'd had in a week. But it faded as the face appeared over his shoulder. "Oh, Hi, Max."

He crossed his arms and added his frame beside Wil's effectively blocking the doorway. "You remember me?"

Smiling, she struggled for something to say other than *I haven't been able to shake the thought of you.* So she tapped her temple and said, "Steel trap."

For a moment she remembered his eyes, and the way they'd lit up when they met at the barbecue. Then she remembered the way his girlfriend's eyes had narrowed. She reminded herself that he wasn't free. And her man was waiting in Chicago. The pendulum told her so and it was never wrong. "So what are you two fellas doing in my new office?"

Max turned and pointed. "I'm right down the hall."

Wil grinned, "And I'm over there."

"You guys are the foreign acquisitions team?"

"The best part of it." Max grinned.

God help her.

God help him. She was right down the hall every day. She went to the water cooler and stood directly in his line of sight. Just yesterday he had almost decked Wil, one of his best friends, for sitting on the edge of Max's desk to watch her come and go.

Max had barely managed to hold back. Wil had been making comments for years about all the women who went to the water cooler. The problem was, Max hadn't stopped him before. He didn't think of Wil as a predator or anything worse than a braggart. It felt wrong to stop his friend from being slightly misogynistic over a woman that *he himself* was attracted to. But in reality, it was long past time to stop him. "Hey, shut up, Wil."

Wil had turned and raised an eyebrow as if to ask if Max had thoughts about Miss Sloan.

Max didn't address that. "You cannot be that dumb. I know you think you're only talking to me, but if someone hears you, you're out on your ass. No one's putting up with that shit anymore. Including me."

That really made Wil's eyes go wide.

"You want to be out of a job? That's on you. Don't associate me with it."

"You get a stick up your butt?" Wil asked, genuinely concerned. "Did you hear anything?"

"Yes, I have a stick of human decency up my butt. Those women work for this company the same as you and me. I'm sorry I didn't say anything before, but I never liked the way you talk about them. Honestly, I'm attracted to some of them myself, so I didn't know what to say." He leaned back, not wanting to lose his friend, but still in the process of taking a hard look at his own behavior. "It was never right. It's past time to say so."

Wil nodded.

"Maybe it's why they won't go out with you. Think about it." He knew Wil had already asked Sloan out and she'd apparently shot him straight out of the air.

Max sighed as he watched Sloan through the gap Wil left at his door. She straightened, tugging at her suit jacket before continuing her conversation with Vanessa. He might have the occasional feelings like he was a dog, but he was going to be nothing but professional at work.

He hadn't even managed to flirt with her. How could he? Flirting led to asking a woman out, and he didn't know how to ask. In general, he did. But what did you say to the woman you were suddenly certain you were going to marry? *I don't know your middle name, but I'm positive I'm in love with you.* Or even better *Maybe I could take you out to dinner sometime, then we could drive around and look at real estate. I have enough money saved for the down payment on our house.*

He was certifiable, and he knew it. The slow burning feeling inside him also knew he was *right.*

In the two months since she'd arrived, he hadn't figured out how to speak to her in a personal manner, let alone convince her there could be more between them. So he sat here at his desk, watching her get water every day, and doing nothing. He knew things other people didn't. It was a skill, and it told him they belonged together and they would end up together. The first step was proving to be a doozy though. While love at first sight had cracked him over the head, it seemed cupid hadn't even tapped her on the shoulder. If he wanted her, he would have to go after her.

Max pressed his lips together, deep in thought. He just didn't know how to get her. He hadn't dated anyone since the company picnic. Since he had first seen Sloan. If it hadn't been the real deal, it was way past time for it to have faded. One of his problems was that everything he learned about Sloan convinced him he was right. She really was perfect for him.

But 'perfect for him' meant he had to get off his butt and do something. Sitting here, just watching her as she passed by going down the hall each day, wouldn't cut it.

If he didn't do something soon, she'd meet Mr. Right. Or someone she'd think was right and she'd date him for several years or worse, marry the man and have kids with him while Max watched. He was breaking out in a cold sweat. Time to do something.

CHAPTER 4

S loan had hit a wall in her life. A big, fat, painful brick wall. She saw that it was an immoveable wall, but she seemed to keep running smack into it. She liked her job, really enjoyed the people in her division. But dear God, what else did she have?

Well, that wasn't true. She was becoming a stellar witch. Megan had stepped up, since she also had a natural ability that she'd had to fight to learn to control. Megan was beyond helpful and Sloan could now see things much more at will and much clearer than what she used to be able to do. She got fewer vague hints that would only prove to be true later and more visions that gave her enough of the story to act. So that part was great.

Still, she'd just watched her little sister plan her wedding. She tried to act surprised when Yasmin announced she was pregnant. Megan and Tristan had gotten married in a beautiful ceremony by the sea and they had a house in the hills and even a dog. She had dinners at their homes and invited them to hers. Sloan occasionally hung out with Rae and her friends. She wasn't lost, but she was empty. The truth was, she was jealous. If she'd had a Ouija board, that's what it would have spelled. J E A L O U S.

Yasmin seemed to have picked up on it and even tried to console her with a story of how she'd once thought herself in love with Tristan. That had made Sloan raise her eyebrows and laugh. But the ending of the story was that Yasmin found Luke. Or he found her.

So Sloan went back to her map and re-scryed, wondering if things had changed. Maybe her Dream Man had moved. But it was all the same. He was in Chicago and no, she couldn't see his face.

So she rolled through November. The fun of Halloween was over. She had dumped her costume at Goodwill just yesterday. Even though she loved it, where exactly did one wear a genie costume that was just a little bit daring? She'd worn it to the Halloween party at Sam and Rae's new condo. But it was over and the costume had become useless.

She was caught up on everything at work, even though it took long hours to maintain that state. So she'd been sitting at her desk contemplating what to do next when her boss stuck her head in the door and asked, "Ellis, can I put you on the Farlands/Baskin merger trip?"

Sloan looked up. They'd told her there would be travel, and so far she there'd been decidedly little. Figuring she could be lonely in a hotel room as easily as anywhere else, she'd agreed.

Then she'd gotten the tickets.

Chicago. She was going to Chicago! This had to be it.

She had gone to Madrid with the team last month on her first and only trip. While they were there, she'd spent the evenings watching everyone go out to party and sightsee at night while she did her homework. Reviewing the new contracts the team had drafted. Searching for loopholes. And generally being depressed that she didn't have many friends, even from work, and she certainly wouldn't make any new ones sitting in her hotel room. Then again, losing her job wasn't on her list of things to do either.

But in Chicago, she would not sit in her hotel room. When the plane touched down, she had several versions of each piece of the contract pre-drafted. She could mix and match as needed depending on how the team ended up. They arrived late and in her room—by herself, of course—she fell deeply asleep. The next morning she sent the team in, armed with her wording. When they came out, there were relatively few things to correct. Sloan was ecstatic. The others always asked her to go out with them. This time she would say yes. The contracts would be printed and signed tomorrow and she had the rest of the evening to...

And that was the problem. Damned Chicago had gotten itself snowed in. In the beginning of November. So she was finally ready and no one was going out. She could hit the mini-bar in the corner of her room, though that seemed a little too depressing.

Sloan sighed. *Story of my life. Organize everything and still wind up spending the evening in the hotel by myself.* She opened the mini-bar and looked over the tiny vodkas with the big prices. Prices were probably better down at the actual bar. The one with chairs and a bartender to tell your woes to. Come to think of it, the boys were probably down at the bar, since they couldn't go anywhere either.

And "the boys" would likely include Sheila and Vanessa, so Sloan didn't quite feel like she was walking into a lion's den. Quickly, she shucked off her suit skirt and unbuttoned the white blouse, trading them for the jeans and sweater she had packed for her fabulous sightseeing excursions. Well, she would just sightsee the inside of the hotel and the bar. She might not find her Mr. Right tonight, but she thought she could find her co-workers.

She pulled her hair free of its pins and checked it in the mirror, a little wild, but she didn't much care. Shoving her card key and cash into her back pocket, she thought Lisette would be proud of her. When she had come crying, her best friend had told her that she had to get out a little more. That the only way not to sit at home all the time was to not sit at home all the time. So far, Sloan hadn't signed up for any yoga classes or joined any weird bowling leagues, but tonight she would go to the bar.

Maybe Max would be there. She kicked herself. *And maybe he could tell her all about the ring he was buying for his girlfriend.* The willowy brunette that looked so unlike her own reflection in the mirror that Sloan could be quite certain that she wasn't even his type.

Though he certainly was hers. She had always been a sucker for the guys who were tall and lean and had that laid-back grin. The kind of man who could look at home leaning in a doorway and sweet-talking you. The kind that got you one base further than you had decided to let him go before you were even aware of it. Max had blue eyes and dirty blonde hair and he was definitely *that type.* The same type that had always gotten her into trouble. The same type that was the reason she had taken a job and just moved off to a new city where she didn't know anyone.

Sloan was the kind of woman whose heart always led her astray. The lucky thing now was that it had gone so far around the bend that it was leading her to a man that she *knew* was already committed to someone else. That was a good sign. She would shake her addiction to bad boys. She came here to find a nice, wholesome type. The type that wouldn't be caught in bed with her cousin the week before their wedding. She decided to go one better: the type that wouldn't *be* in bed with her cousin. At all.

The elevator dinged and she sauntered out the doors and through the lobby, trying to look for all the world like she knew where she was going. She considered throwing a Veil so they wouldn't see she was nervous, but she didn't want to go back to her hotel room and cobble together a spell. So she wiped her hands down her jeans and figured the rest of the team would be there waiting for her.

Unfortunately, no one was. And it wasn't like she just didn't spot them. The bar was virtually empty. Almost heartbroken, Sloan weighed her options. She didn't feel like going back to her lonely room, and she didn't want to let the few people in the bar see that she hadn't seen what she wanted. So she slid onto a barstool and waited for the bartender to finish with the guy at the other end.

After a few moments she had a margarita ordered. Rocks, no salt. It was just that kind of night. And when she pushed a five across the bar she heard a voice.

"Sloan, right? So, what would a man need to say to snag the seat next to you at the bar?"

She was so relieved. She wouldn't sit here alone after all. Smiling up at the deep, honey-smooth voice, Sloan almost stopped in her tracks.

Dylan was part of Farland's team for the merger. She'd seen him several times today as they worked. But now he was smiling as he moved toward the seat next to her. He had dark hair and a warm smile that reached all the way to his eyes. Good-looking, but not so good-looking that he likely thought he was God's gift. Just the kind of guy she wanted to fall for. She smiled back, and motioned for him to join her. "What are you doing here?"

"Just looking to see if the rest of the team was still around." It only occurred to her then that Dylan was in Chicago. He worked here, at Farland, which was why her firm had been brought in to handle the merger. Her breath caught as she wondered if he was the man she'd tried so hard to see. Getting her racing heart to slow down, she decided she needed to find out. "But they aren't here. You want to stay?"

Half an hour later she'd finished the margarita and heard all about how Dylan had grown up Urbana. Just far enough from

Chicago to not visit often. Dylan was charming company, and Sloan fought the urge to ask him if he had any dreams or inklings about her the way she did about him. She could barely erase the smile from her face even though she had to pee. "I'm... I've got to go to the ladies room. But I'll be back in just a minute." She ordered another margarita with the bartender before she left and hummed her way off to the bathroom.

She told herself she was having a good time, and there were no HBO movies or mini-bars involved. She was feeling the margarita just a little, and a second wouldn't kill her. But she'd have to stop after this. If Dylan was her dream guy—and didn't he have to be?—she shouldn't stay out all night at the bar with him. They would find their way to each other now that they had actually met. She probably looked like a fool with this grin on her face and she told herself to tone that down, too.

In a few minutes she was back to see Dylan and her margarita waiting for her. The bar had filled a bit since she'd come in. Checking her watch, she saw that it was just now nine. Maybe the others would show up, but she found that now she didn't want them to. Dylan just smiled and picked up where they'd left off.

He even managed to get the story about her fiancé and her cousin out of her. Sloan wasn't even sure why she had told it. She had vowed with every phone call to every wedding guest that his name was not to be mentioned again. Not in polite company anyway. The story certainly didn't show her in a favorable light.

Her head buzzed with the alcohol, and Dylan seemed just the tiniest bit out of phase. The second margarita must have hit her harder than she thought. Glancing at the glass, she saw that it was only about one-third empty. A sigh escaped her. That was what she got when she ordered better liquor. It was smooth enough that she hadn't realized how much the bartender had poured in.

"Dylan." Her mouth drew up in a half smile. "I'm sorry, I'm going to have to go back to my room now. I think this margarita is a little too much for me."

"What about my room?"

Did he really just say that? But she was clearly getting drunk and wasn't even really sure what she had heard.

The look on her face must have explained it. "I just meant that you could come up and watch a movie or something. It's only nine-thirty."

"Gosh, Dylan." Had she said 'gosh'? "I don't think..."

"Come on, Sloan, we could have a good time, you and me."

"No, I..." Why was he so fuzzy? And hadn't she said 'no' already? She wasn't really all that certain. She was growing more certain that she'd blown it. Dylan was *not* her right guy. Shit. She'd wasted this evening with him and he was all wrong!

His hand was on her arm. Her first thought was to punch him. But it must be the liquor, because the Sloan she knew didn't punch people. She had to be misreading the situation anyway, because Dylan was far too nice a guy to mean anything like that. But she really wanted to go back to her own room.

"Hey, Sloan."

"Hmmmm?" She turned and took a moment to place the smile. "Hi, Max."

"Max, hi." Dylan spoke from over her shoulder. "Sloan and I were just headed upstairs."

Huh? More than meaning to do it, she felt her face scrunch up all confused. She *was* going upstairs. She should get up to her room and sleep this off. But Max was already talking. "Is that what she wants? I'm sure Sloan can find her own way up."

Right!

She tried to respond, but each time her mouth opened she was a few sentences behind. The two guys were talking right over top of each other and over her head. She just wasn't fast enough to get into her own conversation apparently.

21

"No reason Sloan and I can't share an elevator. 'Night, Max." Dylan's fingers brushed over hers lightly as he stood and helped her to her feet.

"I—" It came from her own mouth, but she had already forgotten the ending. She frowned, waiting for the rest of the sentence—of her thought—to form, but it didn't.

There was a brief moment of silence, before Max stepped in. "Sloan, it looks like you're getting escorted upstairs. The question is, would you like it to be Dylan or me?"

"That would be great, thank you, Max." Even as she said it she realized that it wasn't quite the answer to the question.

He pointed to her margarita, "Do you want to bring this?"

She nodded once before Max turned to Dylan, who looked a little too peeved for the situation, "Good night, Dylan."

"Good night, Dylan." Her own voice sounded a little too chipper for her own ears, but that was really of no concern. What was concerning was the little tremor of excitement that was running through her at just the thought of going upstairs with Max. They were suddenly standing at the elevator, with that feeling that she was a little unsteady and trying so hard to look like she wasn't. She didn't remember walking over here, but everything seemed normal around her. So she told him, "Thank you."

"You're welcome." He smiled at her, that devastating, wicked grin of his.

Though her *bad boy* sensors went off, she felt her insides melting. She was still a little unsteady and not sure she needed an escort to her room, but Max's hand on her arm was its own reward. Sloan knew that there was something about this that she wasn't supposed to be doing, but her brain refused to let her in on it right now. So she waffled back and forth between wanting to seduce Max and just finishing the margarita because it was so good, before sleeping off her night.

Grateful that she wasn't wearing sky-high heels, she paid a

little too much attention to the crack between the floor and the elevator. She was trying to not appear super-focused on the floor, but she didn't want to trip and look like an idiot either.

"—with the rest of us, right?"

Blinking, she tried to regroup her brain cells and put together the missing sentence, but just couldn't do it. "Hmm?"

"You're on seventeen, too, right?"

She nodded and watched as he punched the button, and swayed a little as the elevator took off.

There was a brief, tense moment of silence then he spoke again. "Do you need any help into your room? You don't look so steady."

CHAPTER 5

Max's eyes fluttered slowly open. There was a wild, high-pitched thrumming in his head. He knew he was happy but wasn't sure why. Trying to remember where he was and what he was doing, he squeezed his eyes shut. Max looked up to see that the awful noise was not, in fact, in his head, but coming from the hotel alarm clock. His brain told him to swing his arm over and he'd hit it off. But his arm was stuck, he couldn't move.

With a gasp, he remembered just why and how his arm was stuck.

Sloan. The heat beside him in the bed was explained. The soft noise of her curled up beside him. The perma-grin he had woken up with.

His eyes were completely open now, the gray fuzz of sleep suddenly evaporated, and he marveled at his amazing turn of luck last night. Thinking he might just close his eyes and inhale her, Max found he couldn't quite bring himself to shut out the vision of her, curled naked in his arms. Her hair flowing over the pillow, her breath an even rhythm against his skin set his heartbeat to a deep, steady rhythm. He hadn't been prepared for all this, but he regretted nothing.

His fiancee. If he'd had any inkling this would happen, he would have gotten the ring a week ago. Max almost laughed. He was pretty sure that she didn't quite believe that he'd picked out a ring for her the last time he'd walked by a jewelry store. Then again, if you had told him a year ago that he'd be ready to buy a ring for a girl he hadn't even asked out, he'd have told you that you were crazy.

He should wake her up. It was going to be a hairy day today with getting the contracts signed and flying home. Everyone was within a few rooms of each other. If this engagement was the first announcement of the day then things would get even more hectic. They had agreed to keep it under wraps until the weekend.

Then, he would shout it to the world.

Sloan stirred beside him. A soft noise, a breath, the brush of her hair as her head turned lightly. The kind of things he looked forward to waking up to every morning from here on out. Feeling lazy and content, he rolled closer to her, running his fingers lightly through her hair.

"Sloan, baby, wake up. We have a huge day to get through and I have to wipe this silly grin off my face before anyone sees it." He kissed her forehead as she stirred more awake, then inhaled her contented sigh, believing that, for once, everything was right in the world.

He believed it right up until Sloan heaved herself backward off the bed as she yelled.

"What?" Startled by her own nakedness, she ripped the sheet from the bed, clutching it to cover herself. "What?" She repeated, though this time her voice shook.

It took a few moments for Max to register the expression on her face. If he had been asked he would have said he couldn't tell. Maybe horror. But that couldn't be right. She was just surprised to be waking up in a strange room. In a moment she'd remember where she was.

But the realization never dawned on her. Her lower lip quivered, her breathing never slowed. Her huge eyes glazed. Finally, she got the full sentence out. "What am I doing here?"

He shook his head, pushing upright in the bed, completely unconcerned with his own nudity, although she eyed him up and down as though it were something completely foreign to her. He tried desperately to formulate an answer. None came. His breathing ratcheted up as he watched her face. Surely, she'd remember it all and then she'd laugh.

But she didn't.

Her terror only grew; her eyes widened. For a moment her mouth moved but no sound came out. When it finally did, it wasn't what he'd hoped for. "Why am I naked?" Her breathing sped up and her voice caught. "Did we—?"

Hell, yes, we did. But he couldn't push the words out of his mouth. Her eyes were too huge, they were wet with unshed tears. Suddenly, his heart slammed into his ribcage. *No.* Slowly his voice formed the words. "Of course, we did. I don't understand."

"No, *I* don't understand. Why am I not in my own room?"

Oh! She's concerned about what everyone will think. Relief washed over him in a welcome tidal wave. His breathing evened out, and he hadn't even finished his thought before he started talking over himself, thankful the answer had been found. "I'll sneak you back to your room." He reached for her waist, "We won't tell until later."

But she only backed away, a jerky movement akin to what a startled rabbit might do. Her voice was nothing more than a harsh whisper, "We slept together?"

"Yes." The earth was slipping out from under his feet, his heart falling into the open cracks. "You don't remember?"

Her tears really did fall now, making slow, fat tracks down her cheeks. "I remember being in the elevator. I remember you kissed me..."

He picked up where she trailed off, hoping to straighten all this out. "*You* kissed *me*. And *we* decided to come back here..."

Slowly, her head moving back and forth, she backed away, until finally she bumped into the wall. It was spoken under her breath, to herself, but he heard it. "I was drunk."

"No! No, you weren't!" He leaped at her, only startling her more. But he saw his world tipping away and he would fight to get it back. "You were fine. You said that you hadn't had too much. You were fine!"

Dammit, he had worried about that, but she had been clear.

Though she'd been practically throwing herself at him— saying she'd had a crush on him for so long...—he'd stopped her once they were inside his room. He'd caught glimpses of something from the corner of his eye. Wondered if he'd smelled it, when she was so close in the elevator. Unable to explain, he'd reached into his suitcase, blocking her view.

Max kept a small set of dowsing rods on him at all times. They were not convenient, not ever, and certainly not now. But he had to ask. "Does she have a spell on her?"

No doubt about it, the rods crossed.

Shit.

He came back to her, and couldn't fight it as she threw her arms around him and asked if he was her "Chicago man"? He'd almost said, "I'm your forever man," but he'd held his tongue. She was possibly drunk, and she'd definitely been cast on. Instead he sank into a kiss that rivaled his dreams before pushing her back. No matter how much he wanted her, this wasn't really Sloan.

"Stand here. Close your eyes."

She did as he asked, giggling the whole time. As he turned away, she tipped precariously and he barely managed to catch her. "Here, sit on the edge of the bed, when I tell you, close your eyes."

"Okay!"

Max headed into the bathroom, turned on the faucet and unscrewed the makeup mirror. This was makeshift at best and he hoped it worked. He was not prepared to cast spells on this trip. He soaped the mirror and used a washcloth to wipe it to a thin layer. Next, he fogged it with the steam from the sink. He hollered out, "Close your eyes, Sloan."

If she saw, he had no idea how in hell he was going to explain what he was doing.

CHAPTER 6

L uckily, Sloan's eyes were closed when he came out of the bathroom holding the mirror. The soap and steam should work, and he noticed the smile sitting on her lips.

It broke his heart. He wanted that smile to be for him, but it wasn't. She was possibly drunk and...He held the mirror up near her. Yes. There were definitely spells on her.

Bad ones.

Black tendrils swirled. Though he could barely make out her form in the foggy mirror, the swirls of the spell were unmistakable. *Shit.*

"Can I open my eyes?" She giggled even as she tipped a little to the right.

With fast hands he dropped the mirror and righted her. "Go ahead."

He needed a minute to figure out how in hell he was going to undo a spell he couldn't quite read, all while in a hotel room in Chicago. If nothing else, he couldn't let her go to work this way the next day. But the truth was, she said she had a crush on him, she'd practically thrown herself at him in the elevator, and he needed to know if that part was real or just an effect of this spell.

It took a minute to gather what he needed. The problem was, it wasn't what he needed. It was makeshift at best. He had a lemon balm that his grandmother made for him with cardamom and musk added, so he could use it like an aftershave. He had witch hazel in his travel pack and... and... shit. That was it. No. He had an amethyst crystal and a small jade chunk that he'd stuck down into the corners of his bag for safety and good luck while traveling. It had been last year, or longer? He dug them out and tried to think of anything else. The soap at the sink claimed to have tea tree oil. He grabbed it.

With everything in his hands, he stood in the bathroom and looked in the mirror at his own reflection. What in the hell was he about to do?

Setting the things down, he decided to get his ducks in a row first. Using the small dowsing rods he went through a series of questions, finally deciding he had enough to try and get the spell off of her.

He emerged from the restroom with his hands full. Sloan looked up at him, her eyes still a little glazed. But she grinned. "What's all that? Are we playing a game? Taking a shower? What?"

Max shook his head, then recanted. "Yes, a game. Here. Hold out your hands."

He put some of the lemon balm into her hands and watched as she smelled it. "It smells like you."

Nodding, he told her to rub it in. Up her arms, down her legs, the nape of her neck, the small of her back. It was the best he could do without asking her to get naked. She was out of it enough to do as she was told.

When she finished, he dabbed the witch hazel on her temples, and she grinned again. "That feels cool."

Making her close her eyes, he set the bar of soap in her lap, though it looked seriously stupid. Then he had her hold the amethyst in one hand and the jade in the other. He poured a small layer of the witch hazel into one of the glasses from the bathroom and with a deep breath and a prayer that Sloan didn't open her eyes, he lit it.

He didn't know how he would explain this to her, or the hotel staff. He was equally worried that someone had cast a seriously bad spell on Sloan, and that he would set off the sprinkler system.

She didn't open her eyes as he held the glass around her and whispered the spell to himself. He wished like hell she couldn't hear him. If he was lucky, she was too spelled to remember. He held the glass of burning fumes in one hand and the soaped and fogged mirror in the other. As he watched, and oh-so-quietly chanted, the black tendrils pulled back.

"Can I open my eyes now?"

Even the tone of her voice had changed and was steadier, more competent, much to his relief. However, he was equally concerned her returning sanity would spell the end of her in his room. And possibly the end of any crush she might have had, if she caught him handing her crystals and waving a burning glass of stinky witch hazel fumes around her. Who would understand that?

The glass was burning his fingers, but he didn't stop. "Not yet. Keep them closed."

His chanting became so quiet it was a sound only heard in his own head, and Max hoped it was enough.

At last, the mirror revealed no more black tendrils. He blew out the burning witch hazel as fast as he could and plopped the glass onto the bedside desk with a thud, shaking his fingers out. Max scooped the soap out of her lap then slid the crystals from her hands. Her soft fingers easily yielded the stones back to him.

"Now?"

"Yes, now." He watched as she opened her eyes. Though he

wanted to run to the bathroom and run his fingertips under cold water, he wanted to see her gaze more.

"I feel better. What did you do?"

He shook his head, unable to come up with even a crappy lie that would work. Her eyes were clear. With a sigh of soul-deep relief, he headed into the bathroom and shoved the pieces down into his travel bag. Running his fingers—finally—under cold water, he thought for a moment about where the night could possibly go from here.

He'd come back out and she'd been lucid, dammit.

She wasn't acting drunk. Not after he managed to erase the spell. She'd also assured him that she was fully in there, not drunk, that she knew what she was doing. *And now this?* It was as if the whole night was erased from her mind. She looked at him like a stranger.

He was in love with her. This couldn't be happening. For a half second he closed his eyes, telling himself that when he opened them things would be okay.

When he looked back at her, Sloan was frantically struggling into her clothes, taking quick glances over her shoulder at him. When he stopped staring like a madman and tried to see beyond his own fear, he recognized the same in her. She looked like a lamb cornered by a wolf. The worst part was that she thought he was that wolf.

Space. She needed space. But when he gave it to her she bolted. Without any input from him, his hand shot out and grabbed her arm and holding her back. She shook, great trembles that wracked her whole body, and the terror on her face made him release her.

It wasn't until she was gone that the shock hit him. His perfect world had shattered. Felled by a sledge hammer blow. She must think he was a criminal. Worse, she believed he had taken serious advantage of her.

That was when he actually collapsed to the floor. The police.

What if she called the police? He couldn't muster the strength to really care about jail time right now. She was gone. But the thought that she believed him capable of that turned him inside out.

For a few minutes he contemplated the weave of the carpet from where he had crumpled. Then wondered if maybe he was, in fact, a deranged stalker. He had thought of no one but her since the day he saw her. He had bided his time, watched her coming and going from work. He'd even picked out an engagement ring. He had simply *known.*

For a moment, he imagined getting questioned by the police. Tears formed in the corners of his eyes as he imagined trying to tell them he saw a spell on her and cleared it. Who would believe that? No one. He wanted to think if he told the police about his grandmother and his mother, and what he could do, they would believe him. But they wouldn't. The fact that the family name was carried through the mothers wasn't proof that he was from a family of witches. That he'd known how to dowse before he could write cursive. That he'd fully believed Sloan was in her full and right mind last night. How had he missed it?

If he was going to be cuffed and hauled away he should at least be dressed. As he pulled on his clothes through the fog of his brain, a loud pounding came at the door. He yelled out, "Just a minute."

He was only slightly encouraged by the fact that no one broke down the door, or yelled at him not to try to get away.

He lifted his gaze slowly from the floor. And that was when he spotted the glass.

CHAPTER 7

S loan showered. She washed her face. She contemplated
calling the police. Then she stopped dead, realizing that
she'd just washed away all the evidence. *Shit!*

Unfortunately, once she thought about what she'd done, her
decision became quick and easy. She didn't want it all hung out
to air. That she was drunk. That she looked like a slut. How her
last relationship had ended. If this went to court, that was
exactly what would happen. Adding to the humiliation, she
didn't even remember last night. There was no proof that
anything had happened to her. She was a lawyer. And a grown
woman. She'd just ruined any evidence she had on her side.
She'd known better, too!

Through all her thoughts, she shook, great violent tremors
that made it virtually impossible to function. She wanted to
believe that it was rage, but she wasn't usually that strong a
woman. She was dull and boring, and she had always trusted the
wrong men. Why should now be any different?

She almost laughed when the memory of her wedding had
crossed her mind. She had believed then that she knew the sting
of violation and betrayal. She had thought she had learned her

lesson. She hadn't gotten any better. Only worse. She wouldn't have thought it could get worse, but here she was.

As there was nothing she could do about any of it, she tried to push all of it out of her mind. She dressed. She curled her hair. She printed the contracts and touched up her nail polish. She had to go out and face the world.

Pulling out her pendulum, she asked it if this was the right thing to do. There was no answer. Of course not. It gave facts from far away, predicted courses, but it couldn't offer moral decisions.

Heading into the bathroom, she filled the sink with water and held the pendulum over it. This time she asked, "Am I on the path to where I want to be?"

Clockwise. *Yes.*

Some kind of calm stole over her.

Sloan breathed a few deep sighs and brushed away a few tears. Really, it was her own fault. She had gone downstairs looking for company and wound up with too much liquor in her. She wasn't the first woman to have done something that she didn't remember, but knew enough to regret.

Sloan clenched her teeth, and double-checked everything. She would not add to this day by publicly humiliating herself by showing up without pants, or having her shirt buttoned wrong, due to her own distraction. Her contracts looked to be in order, but she wouldn't have sworn by it as everything she saw was a little bit blurry. Twice, she made sure that her shoes matched and her clothing was on the right body parts.

The rattles got to her. Things felt loose in her soul and she didn't know how to put them back or even where they belonged. She reminded herself to breathe, and wished to God that she could force herself to be calm. Or at the very least fake it well.

A *veil*!

As she finished the spell, her stomach turned, so she fed it the granola bar that she had stashed in her luggage. It was like dry, crumbly cardboard, and the flavor suited the morning.

Finally, when the big red numbers of the hotel alarm pointed out that there wasn't any way to put it off any longer, she left the room. Her thoughts churned and swirled as she clutched her papers and headed toward the elevator.

In the hallway, Vanessa waved hello, and Sloan waved back forcing a curt smile.

Sheila came up a little closer. "Are you all right?"

"Mmm-hmm." She nodded as the sound came out through clenched teeth and Sloan was smart enough to know she wasn't fooling anyone. Luckily, no one pushed the issue.

Behind her a door clicked and she jumped, turning to face him. But it wasn't Max. It was Wil emerging from Max's room. He gave her the once over, and she *knew*. She knew that he knew. Surely, he heard a different version of the story than hers, but she forced a smile anyway and tried not to die there in the hallway.

Half the team appeared to have already left, so Sloan walked along behind everyone else. Their usual chatter was a mad noise that rushed inside her skull until the silver doors opened on the conference room floor and they quieted. The quiet was more to her liking. Still, she had to perform, and try to look normal. She hoped her *veil* spell held.

If he'd shown up, then maybe she would have been able to assess the situation. But Max was nowhere to be seen. Sloan waited on pins and needles for his appearance. A few moments into the meeting, Wil apologized to everyone at the meeting, stating that Max would join them later.

That bastard! The thought flew through her brain. She had forced herself here, and was trying at least to act normal, and he had the cajones to not show? Again, she fought off the queasiness she felt growing deep inside her.

Zoning out during the presentation was easy. Sloan breathed

deeply and simply let her thoughts take over. She was most angry that he didn't show up. It wasn't fair that he got to take time out from his schedule. She was the violated party, she should have been the one to skip out. Beyond that she was simply disappointed.

The man she'd held up as ideal simply wasn't. Her fantasy of Max was long lost. He didn't exist, and maybe not only was it not Max, maybe her dream man didn't exist at all. That was as hard to swallow as the night she didn't remember. Everyone loved Max and, of course, so had she. But he wasn't what they all thought he was. Not only had he cheated on his girlfriend, he had taken advantage of a drunk girl.

He seemed genuinely surprised. The thought invaded her brain, but she squashed it with a reminder that she had almost believed Joe's story about being caught with her cousin. Almost. She'd vowed she wouldn't be that stupid again.

Her deepest disappointment lay in herself. That one hurt the worst. That she had gotten that drunk and gone off and done what she did. She shouldn't have trusted Max. Clearly, her "better judgment" was just as bad as it had ever been. She was great with real estate, and jobs, and general common sense, but when it came to men, Sloan clearly could not be trusted.

The image of Max softly letting himself into the room appeared just in the corner of her eye. But she would have recognized his walk, the color of his hair, the shape of him, anywhere. Her head jerked up and for a moment she looked over and met his eyes square from across the room.

He looked haggard. Drawn. Out of sorts. His shirt was wrinkled and she didn't think she'd ever seen that before. Then she berated herself for thinking that maybe he was upset, too. He didn't deserve her good graces. Sloan lowered her eyes back to the table top and kept them there for the rest of the meeting.

CHAPTER 8

F or a week Sloan forced herself to get out of bed each
morning. Each day she made a point of not wearing the
outfit she'd draped over her chair from the night before when
she took it off. Normally neat, she now had five suits piled up,
gathering dust and wrinkles.

Stacks of folders littered her desk, her usual neatness gone
like her good mood. Everyone had commented how she was
withdrawn, quiet, not her old self. Sloan didn't respond to them
or to much of anyone. She hadn't even brought herself to call
Lisette and tell her friend about the horrible mistake she had
made.

Lisette would be the easiest to tell. Her best friend from back
home could be told via message or text or even online. Sloan
wouldn't have to face her, but she still couldn't do it. She knew
she should. She needed advice. She'd hit a new low of stupid,
getting that drunk and sleeping with a man. She'd been so
drunk she didn't even remember it, and that was not like her.
Worse, she wasn't even really with him, she was just his side
piece.

Her sister Rae had unknowingly been the other woman

once, and she'd been mad as hell when she found out. But Sloan...Sloan was only mad at herself. She couldn't even remember if she'd been deceived. She was never drinking again.

She sat at her desk and stared at the screen. Though she was leaving early and taking long lunches, all her work was done. Not that anyone would be able to tell. She stayed at her desk, finding new work rather than facing the world or fessing up to her mistakes.

Sighing her way through another contract crossed out and written over—poorly—by an exec, she ticked minutes away, waiting for the moment she could leave. She'd work at home if she needed too. But instead of seeing the contract she saw the pattern in the words.

This was one of Max's. Over the months, she had come to recognize his scrawl. She still believed it to be sexy. The writing itself spoke to her. But it no longer represented a fantasy, now it mocked her for yet another bad choice, this one far worse than any of the others.

Her head and her gaze snapped up as Max appeared in her doorway. Her breath caught. And for a brief moment she truly believed that he was a figment, conjured by her thoughts. He didn't say anything, just stood with his hands loose at his sides, his suit impeccable, and his face blank. He blocked her only way out. It was all she could do to keep from shrinking away from him. Over and over her mind spoke, *Don't let him see that you're still upset.*

Finally, she found her voice. "What do you want?"

His eyes searched hers and, she hoped, found nothing. "Can I close the door?"

With a conscious thought she tried to ease the tension that was growing along her jaw. "I'd rather you didn't."

She didn't trust him and the truth was, she didn't trust herself. Her stupid heart was still attracted to him, even though her brain knew he was twenty kinds of wrong.

Max nodded and came in a little closer, looking like he was acquiescing. But she didn't let the lie of his loose posture fool her. She tried to calculate a way around the desk and past him through the clearance he had left at the doorway. His words penetrated her escape route plans. "It's about Chicago. I thought you might rather keep it private."

Did he do something to me?

It hit her like a ton of bricks. She'd gotten drunk and done something monumentally stupid. On a work trip, too. But had she? She'd drunk one and half margaritas. For the first time, it occurred to her that shouldn't have erased her whole night.

Her body went still with the shock and she tried not to let him see. Had Max done something to her? Would he be here now if he had? Taking a deep breath, she thought, of course she wanted to keep it private, but she wasn't about to close the door or let him have any other power over her ever again. "Maybe *you* would rather keep it private."

With a bone deep sigh, Max dropped his large frame into the seat in front of her desk. He appeared to know that she was extremely uncomfortable, but he didn't seem to care. His head was resting, face down, in his hands, but his words and almost convincing despair carried up to her.

"Listen, I'll bet everyone around here is somewhat aware of what happened. And I also think that everyone thinks I'm some sort of scum. So at this point I really have nothing to hide." It was only then that he lifted his head from his hands.

Sloan's teeth ground. Down at her sides where he couldn't see them, her hands clenched into white-knuckled fists. She held back the spell she wanted to chant. First, because chanting and casting spells at work was a no-no. It wasn't in HR rules specifically, but she didn't cast in front of people who didn't already know. Second, she didn't cast it because it was a curse and Sloan didn't curse people. She still knew the curse spells though!

Was he here to make pretty excuses? It sure didn't sound like he was drumming up an apology. But she kept her mouth shut.

After a moment he spoke again. "I had your margarita glass analyzed."

"What?" The word fell out of her mouth before she even registered anything other than that he hadn't apologized. Or even come close. She waited, staring at him, having no idea what was coming next.

At last he looked up at her, and she was insanely disappointed by how trite he looked. She was such a sucker, and look where it had gotten her.

"That morning, I saw that you'd left your glass on the bedside table. So I called a friend and she suggested a laboratory there in Chicago that does freelance work. I had them analyze the glass and the contents."

"What?"

"You simply weren't that drunk. You behaved normally enough—"

"Close the door," she interrupted him. The command was low and tight and didn't sound like her. It made her even more angry that he knew more about her behavior that night than she did. She still couldn't remember anything past entering his hotel room door.

Rising, he walked the few steps to close them in her office. For once, she was grateful for the glass windows allowing everyone to see in, to see that—despite the closed door— nothing was going on between them. In that short space of movement, she could see that his shoulders weren't squared up the way they used to be. He slouched a little. Max Summerland looked defeated.

Hands jammed in pockets, he turned back to her. "You didn't act very drunk at all. Not after the first half-hour anyway—"

Sloan spotted Sheila coming down the hall and that was the only thing that kept her butt in her chair. "And do you mind refreshing me on what exactly it was that I did that first half-hour?"

He was taken aback. It was the first time he made solid eye contact with her. He was genuinely startled. But he answered quickly, with a certainty she hadn't expected. "We talked."

Still, his words tickled at the back of her brain. She was missing something. There was something he hadn't said. Her heart rolled in her chest. She'd never been normal. She didn't like knowing that someone was lying to her, worse was like now, when she *suspected* it, but didn't know. Rae would know. She would be able to sit here and get some feeling in her brain that would tell her. Sloan needed a pendulum for those kinds of questions, and she couldn't well tell him to wait a minute while she pulled some witchcraft out of her bag and tested him.

She stared right at him. "I thought you said we..." She couldn't even bring herself to finish the sentence.

"That was later." Suddenly the floor had become interesting to him again. "Several hours later."

While she attempted to herd her thoughts together, and tried desperately to remember *anything*, Max gathered himself. At least, most of his old self. "Anyway, I called an old friend who's a doctor now, and she thought I might be right. That you might have been drugged."

Drugged!?

"No." The word rolled out of her, dragging nausea behind it.

Suddenly he was the old Max. He didn't notice that she couldn't really breathe. His posture changed, he leaned forward almost towering over her as he argued his case. The man could sell ice to penguins. "Think about it. You don't remember anything, right?"

She shook her head, thinking that he would try to lead her astray, to convince her to conclude that he had done something other than what he had.

"And you didn't act that drunk. I would never have..."

42

Instead her mind tried desperately to wrap itself around the possibility he presented. With it came a new wave of horror. She had been trying to suppress her feelings of stupidity for about a week. But if she had gotten drunk and been so stupid, then at least it was her own fault. It would be something she could avoid in the future. She already wouldn't ever drink again. But if she had been drugged...

Her initial feeling of violation hit her all over again, but much stronger this time. Sloan dove around him, trying to get out the door. Trying to get to the bathroom where she could throw up what she hadn't eaten at lunch.

As she moved by him, he grabbed her arm. He was simply too strong, there was no way to get past him, and she couldn't speak with her throat and stomach working in reverse. She was cornered, and she was going to lose it. Dropping to her knees, Sloan dry-heaved into the wastebasket. Tears found their way out of her eyes. Her breath rushed in and out of her, while she hugged the edges of the trashcan, squeezing her eyes tight. She was going to cry and she did not want to cry.

After a minute, and a long, deep breath, she realized that Max was kneeling beside her, holding her hair, asking if she was all right.

She slapped at his hands, frantic to make him let go, before she got it together and nodded as she backed away. "I'm sorry."

Sternly, he shook his head at her. "Don't be sorry. It's a lot to take. Even for me, and I can only imagine how you must feel."

With a few blinks of her wet eyes, and a sip of the water he had picked up off her desk and held out to her, Sloan slowly pulled herself together. Just before she was going to speak, Max started again. "The analysis on the liquid in the glass was consistent with GHB. It's a common date rape drug."

Her stomach heaved again, but she managed to curtail it this time. "So there *were* drugs in it?"

"Not really." He shook his head, clearly frustrated. "That's why GHB is so widely used. It breaks down, you can't really detect it—"

"But you said—"

"That the liquid had chemicals in it *consistent* with GHB. There was no way to know that the drug had actually been there at one time. It doesn't *prove* anything, but it very strongly suggests. There's no other understandable reason for those chemicals to have been in your glass. Alyssa, my doctor friend, told me it likely won't hold up in court."

His fingers slid through his hair. Sloan sank into her chair again, sitting for fear that her legs might give out. But Max paced and started talking rapid-fire again. "There were three sets of fingerprints on the glass. Yours and two others."

Her body couldn't take all these shocks. All these pendulum mood swings, from fear to revulsion to anger and back again. "Where did you get my fingerprints?"

Max startled at her question. "From the water glass you had later. My friend told me to keep it and send it."

She didn't remember any water glass, but that didn't mean anything. She felt her eyebrows lift. "You stole a piece of glassware from a hotel?"

"Two pieces." He looked angry about the whole thing and she wondered why he was upset. She was the one who'd been drugged. She was the one who didn't remember. He spoke again. "What else could I do? You hate me and I didn't do anything."

CHAPTER 9

A gain, Sloan wished she had Rae's powers right now instead of her own. She'd grill her sister when she got home tonight. Still, Max went on.

"I'm desperate to make you not hate me. I understand you may never like me, but I want you know I didn't do this."

She'd slept with him. That much had been obvious from the moment she woke up that day and he hadn't denied it. So he'd done *something,* even if it was just talking her out of her undies.

"One of the sets of prints were yours. There were two others, but not mine." This time when he looked at her, she could tell he was waiting for a reaction.

But she couldn't think of anything to say. Finally, when she got tired of him watching her that way, she shrugged. "What does it mean?"

"It means that I didn't touch your glass. Really, Sloan, I'd never do what you think I did."

Her heart ached. Her head hurt. Her ears rang. But Max didn't give up. "Think of everyone who was already there by the time I got to the bar. I have a suspicion, but I don't want to sway you. So who touched your glass? Who would?"

"I don't know." She felt like someone had unscrewed some valve and all her energy had drained out. She wanted Max to go away so she could just curl up under her desk and try to figure out what the hell had happened in Chicago. She'd been supposed to meet her dream man. Instead of being thrilled with a new love on the horizon, she simply wanted to sleep away at least the rest of the week.

"Think, Sloan!"

She shot him a dirty look, and he sank into the chair, clearly feeling chastised. Instead of making her feel better, it made her feel rude. The same thought passed through her head that had passed a thousand times this past week. *If he's guilty, he's sure putting on a great show.*

"Just the bartender and me. No one else.... I think. It gets a little fuzzy into the second margarita."

"You remember the elevator."

"How do you know that?" *And what else did he know?*

"The next morning..." His expression was a cross between sad and sheepish, "You said you remembered it. You remembered that I kissed you. I remember it the other way."

Oh yeah. She had said that. She nodded. "I do remember the elevator. But there are patches missing all the way back to the bar."

"Really?"

Her fingers worked at the hem of her jacket for something to do. She traced the circles of the buttons and wondered if talking to him was the right thing to do. If it wasn't, it sure wouldn't be her first mistake. She nodded.

Softer now than when he had been trying to make her believe, his voice came across the air to her. "What *do* you remember?"

"Some of the bar. I don't remember why I left with *you*. I was supposed to go to *my* room. I remember the elevator, but not how I got there." This was the part that she didn't like, because it laid some of the blame at her own feet. Still, it would be a sin of omission if she didn't include it. "I remember being at your door, and you handing me the keycard to open it...and that's all." *She* had opened his hotel room door. She must have been willing in some way. That memory had only come to her after a dream a few nights ago.

But Max didn't wait for her thoughts to continue. Leaning in, he pushed. "What's the last thing you remember before you start having pieces of missing time?"

"Ordering my second margarita and going to the bathroom."

"Was it waiting when you got back?"

Sloan nodded, only just then seeing where he was going with this.

"Who was there?" Hovering over her now, Max was invading her personal space. Not that he cared.

"Me. The bartender and that nice guy from Farland." She reached up to push him away, but he jumped back before he even noticed.

Furious now, he was almost shouting. "What was his name?"

A quick glance out the glass wall to the main space confirmed her fears.

Forcing a smile she didn't feel onto her face, she waved out to those who were attempting to look like they weren't prying. While Sloan thought she'd done her part making it look like a casual conversation, probably everyone beyond the glass was already aware that it was anything but. "Calm down, people are watching."

He assumed a more relaxed looking pose, but his eyes still burned intensely. "What was his name?"

"I don't remember." It was a lie. She remembered. But if it wasn't Max's fault, did that automatically mean it was Dylan's? She hadn't wound up in Dylan's bed.

"Well, try!"

Two deep breaths. She forced her way through both. With

oxygen came a little of the backbone she was sorely missing. "For all I know, you did this. I won't have you trying to pin it on someone else."

"Listen, Sloan—"

"I *have* been listening! Pretty well, I think, given what you've been telling me." Her jaw ached. She must have been grinding her teeth all along. She needed to go home and fall into her bed and forget the whole thing. There was nothing she could do about it anyway.

He had aged ten years since they had left for Chicago, but maybe so had she. Still he stood before her, pleading with her. "*I* know that it wasn't me. If I can find this guy, maybe I can prove it to you."

"I won't let you do it." This time she stood. She had never faced anyone down like this before. She always just took what came and made the best of it. But she had ceased to care if Max liked her, or what anyone thought of her. The worst that could happen, she decided, was that they would fire her, and then she would be able to go home—all the way back to her parents home in the north—and she would let her friend Lisette take care of her for a while like she really wanted. So Sloan gave Max Summerland a piece of her mind.

"Max, the reason you are so great at what you do, is that you're like a pit bull. You never let go of anything until you've gotten your way. I've seen you do it before and you're doing it now. Why are you here?"

Max Summerland looked like he'd been taken down a peg. "I just thought you should know."

"Well, I can tell you that *I* don't feel any better about the whole thing for knowing. Maybe you came for you."

That 'taken down a peg' look disappeared in a heartbeat. He stood, nose to nose with her across her desk. If she had had time to think, she would have been grateful for the large hunk of wood separating them. His voice rose. "It *is* for me! I know that you've entertained thoughts that I did this. And I don't know any other way to prove that I didn't. I also really want to get this guy."

"Why? For what he stole from *you*?"

For a second, she could have sworn that he was going to say '*yes*,' but that would have been stupid. She was holding the trump card. She was the one who had been drugged, lost her memory. With nerves of steel that she had never known she possessed, she spoke. "You've given me your information, now leave it alone. This is mine. I swear, if you so much as breathe near the guy, I will have legal all over you. Now go."

Max blinked in shock a few times then shoved his hands back down in his pockets before letting himself out the door. Sloan was surprised and disturbed by the fact that he seemed so sexy. Even vulnerable like that. The fact that she could see him that way indicated that a good chunk of her had come around to his way of thinking. She actually believed he was innocent.

She almost wished she had let him handle it, but Dylan wouldn't survive an accusation whether or not it had been him. It was the one thing she had lied about. She remembered Dylan's name.

And, with her new backbone firmly in place, she pulled up her links and looked up Dylan Atterson in Farland's system.

CHAPTER 10

Sloan held the unassuming brown cardboard box in her hands. It had taken a full week to get it here. And that after taking a full week for her to realize that it existed, and to figure out how to get a copy.

With quaking hands she slid the box cutter along the seams, trying not to cut herself with her jerky movements. There were a few bubble bags surrounding the contents. An innocuous looking DVD and a letter in an envelope. Scrawled across the front was her name: *Ms. Sloan Ellis.*

She wanted to watch the video, but she forced her fingers to gently pry open the letter first.

Ms. Ellis,

Enclosed with this letter you will find the DVD copy of our security surveillance as you requested. This disc is yours to keep for your files.

We deeply regret what has happened to your client and offer our sincere hopes that this evidence helps to prove the case one way or another. As with any security system, one hopes one never has need of it. This surveillance is of our front bar, from our Chicago hotel. Footage is from nine P.M. to midnight (the timeframe you requested) on Thursday night, November 12th.

The surveillance camera is located at the wall/ceiling line on the upper right hand side of the bar (to patrons). Most of the occurrences at the bar are caught by this camera. There is no other camera providing footage of this area.

After reviewing the footage, we believe that the bartender, our employee, was not at fault. All of his actions are clearly seen. If you should come to another conclusion, or if you should need to speak to him as a witness, please let us know. We will be glad to cover all his expenses and time.

Please contact us if you find you are in need of any additional information or tapes.

Sincerely,
Gail Withers
Chief of Security
Dalton Hotels

Sloan laid the letter down and turned the disc over in her hands a few times, before she could actually bring herself to insert it into the player and pick up her remote. Her nerves rattled as she waited for the image to appear. But instead of seeing herself at the bar, she saw several other people. The running time read PM 9:00:45. It must have been the wrong night. Hadn't she gone down just about nine?

Resigning herself to all of it being wrong, she pressed the button, speeding up the play rate. Within fifteen minutes of tape-time, the bar had cleared out and the bartender leaned against the racks behind him to while away the time.

The video was definitely not in any kind of HD, and on her big screen, it looked grainy. Still Sloan watched as a dark-haired man appeared and settled at the end of the bar. With a hitch to her breath, Sloan let her finger off the forward button. Then rewound to just before the point where he came in.

Her heart pounded, the only sound in the room given the non-existent audio on the footage. Though her living room was bathed in daylight and it was the middle of a beautiful Saturday afternoon, she felt clammy. The whole thing seemed surreal.

Dylan sat at the bar. He had a beer and was ordering his second as she saw herself walk in. The Sloan image sat at the other end of the bar and ordered her first margarita. Sloan felt her stomach clench. It was difficult to watch herself get taken advantage of this way.

She wished this really had been for a client. She didn't think they would have sent it if she'd told them it was for herself. She paused the video long enough to take a breath and, if not stop the roiling in her stomach, at least get used to it.

She brought her attention to her TV screen again. The Sloan on the screen talked to Dylan. She was surprised how much she used her hands when she spoke. The two of them laughed. She saw herself look around, finish the margarita, and order another. Then, as she watched, she excused herself to the ladies room.

The bartender spoke to Dylan for a minute and didn't begin making her drink until she was already out of frame. Sloan tried to watch the video in slow-mode, but it didn't help, the resolution simply wasn't good enough. Instead, she watched the bartender mix her margarita three different times. She could find nothing wrong unless there was already a drug in one of the bottles within reach. That didn't make sense because Max had told her that it broke down fairly quickly. She had found the same information on the internet as well.

With a quick flash of thought, she rewound and with the same care scrutinized the bartender making her first margarita. Maybe that one had been where the drug was, but she could find no fault there either. After that she wound up with the same conclusion as the Dalton Hotel security people: the bartender wasn't at fault.

That left Dylan or Max. Unfortunately, she'd believed them both to be nice solid men at the beginning of that evening. So here it was. Solid, irrefutable proof that she was a terrible judge of character.

She forwarded to where the bartender made the second drink again. Then watched as his back turned and Dylan took the drink and paid for it. She startled a little. Come to think of it, she didn't remember paying for it. The first of her memory gaps.

While it made her suspect Dylan a little more, buying her a drink wasn't in and of itself a crime. But then, as the bartender turned around to put the cash in the drawer, Dylan's hand reached into his pocket. Sloan gasped into the silence of her apartment and watched as he slid his hand free from his jacket and grabbed her drink at the rim, his hand completely blocking the surface from the camera's view. She couldn't tell if he had pulled anything from his pocket. But he hadn't put anything into the pocket either. So why else go there?

She fought the urge to vomit again. To get up and click off the TV and not watch. Forcing herself to pay close attention, she watched it several more times to be sure. There was no proof. She couldn't see anything going into the drink, or even tell for sure that he had taken anything from his pocket. But it was the only logical conclusion.

Finally, she let the rest of the video play out. She saw herself returning from the ladies room, then sipping at the drink. Dylan talking. Her laughing. Max coming in.

Sloan was surprised by the way Max and Dylan quickly came to words over her head. She wished desperately for a soundtrack as she didn't remember any of this, even after seeing it now. Dylan had placed his hand on her arm possessively while he said something angry to Max. Max argued back. It surprised her that she seemed to be talking to Dylan disapprovingly. What had he done or said to change her mind?

Wasn't he her Chicago Man?

Her heart tumbled. She'd gone to Chicago! She was supposed to find *him*. The one she saw when she scryed. Was her life so fucked up that she made it to his city, and not only didn't find him, but got drugged by another man and spent the night with a co-worker? Could her choice in men be any worse?

She tried for a moment to make it all okay, but she couldn't fit that into the box she so desperately wanted it in. She watched the video again, this time watching how she interacted with Dylan after Max showed up. Then she realized that it didn't really matter. It was another black mark against her first candidate at Dream Man to see that she herself had been upset by her conversation with him. Dylan was clearly not Chicago Man. She'd swung, and not only missed, but had an epic fail.

In the video, she left the bar, unsteady on Max's arm. He pointed and she picked up her margarita, although she didn't remember any of that either. Then Dylan nursed the rest of his drink and got up, exiting the bar without so much as saying hello to the rest of the team as they entered just a few minutes behind her exit.

The video played on with some of her work-mates and other unknown people milling around. She thought she should turn off the set, but she couldn't. Everything she needed was there. No conclusive proof whatsoever. Nothing she could tell the police about. And no bodily evidence on her. She'd showered first thing the next morning, washing away anything that might have helped. Besides, the drugs would have worn off by the time she got up. She had been terrifyingly sober by then. Also, anything they would have found then would only have implicated Max.

That thought quelled the rolling in her gut. At some point she had gone from thinking that Max was such an amazing liar and she was such a poor judge of character that Max had to be the criminal here, to concluding that he had ultimately been as innocent as she.

Sloan began to feel bad. Max, as it appeared on the video, was only trying to help a woman who appeared harassed and was a little too drunk to realize it. From that seemingly decent act, he'd wound up with the entire office thinking he was the scum who had perpetrated the whole thing. To make matters worse, while she hadn't deliberately spread anything, she had made comments that let a few key people know she thought Max was lower than magma. When rumors had swirled behind his back, and a few in front of his face, she'd let him take it and had done nothing to stop any of them no matter how outrageous or untrue they had been.

It was possible that Max had realized she was drunk—or at least not fully sober—and taken advantage of that himself. But none of his actions since then were those of a man who'd done that. He didn't even have the standard 'male' responses to her in general. Wil kept asking her out. One of the bosses called all the women 'honey,' which was only okay because he called all the men 'bud.'

Taking a moment and thinking back, she tried to catalog what she knew of Max without the filter of her massive crush or her anger after Chicago. He'd said, "Oh, Sheila wasn't finished," at one point in a meeting when another colleague had talked right over the other accountant. She'd caught sight of him in a reflection punching Wil in the arm as Wil had checked out her ass. In fact, Max had treated all the women in the office like equals, like respected human beings, all along. Did that hide a predator?

She didn't really think so, but she didn't know. She did know what to do though. She got a glass of wine, thinking alcohol hadn't been her problem and maybe she could enjoy it here by herself. She pulled out the small dish with potpourri and filled her bowl with water from Blessed Be, then she pulled out her pendulum and started asking questions.

Thirty minutes and half the glass of wine later, she picked up the phone.

"Sloan! What's up? I've been worried about you lately."

She sighed. This was her sister. "You were right, I've been in it up to my eyeballs. I'm okay now, but I need you to come over so I can tell you everything. I need your help."

CHAPTER 11

S loan's phone rang at her desk and she reached out almost absently to pick it up. It was very rarely anyone other than Jenny or Netta at the front desk.

"Ellis." She even said her own name without paying attention.

Jenny's voice came through, pert and clear, though Sloan very much suspected the young woman was filing her nails under the desk. "I have a Jeff Landers on the phone. He's in accounting with Farland Enterprises."

She paused. Though she didn't know it, Jenny and the call now had her complete attention. "Okay, put him through."

Jeff Landers came on the line. "I'm just taking over a position and wanted to get in contact because I know this contract is almost complete. I'm just coming in at the end. I didn't want you to be surprised getting a new name on your documents, or not knowing that we'd switched out here."

In another sentence he let her know that it meant what she thought it meant. He was taking Dylan's position due to a sudden resignation.

She pushed her lips back in her best smile, hoping the

expression conveyed itself over the line. "Thank you for calling. I would have been surprised."

Inside her muscles all clenched.

She and Rae had written a letter to Dylan. They'd phrased it just so. They'd referenced legal action. It would have worked by itself, but they hadn't left it at that. They'd laid the letter out on her coffee table altar and put a dozen spells on it. If Dylan Atterson was innocent, the words and the spells would have no effect on him.

If her letter had scared Dylan off, then it meant that he was guilty. She should be getting a correspondence from him soon with his new address. She had threatened to surveil him at a distance and keep him from doing the same thing to anyone else. He likely assumed she was talking about private investigators and cameras—which she could do, Rae had been a P.I. and she knew others in the business. But Sloan was talking about scrying. Despite sometimes wishing she had Rae's skills, her own weren't shabby. She could find him anywhere and if the letter and spell combo had worked, then she had no feelings of guilt about it.

Ten minutes later she and Jeff had hashed out how he fit in as part of the team and his plans to let the merger just go forward as it had been. He'd seen the numbers and said nothing raised flags and everything looked good.

"Thank you for the call," Sloan reiterated as she hung up. She'd been pacing during the call, having popped out of her seat without knowing it. She was trying to hold a reasonable conversation with Jeff Landers while her brain churned about Dylan Atterson. She leaned back against the wall, her breathing started coming faster. Grateful the door was closed, she sank back and gulped a few deep breaths, relieved that it was all as over as it was going to be.

That only lasted a second until she remembered that the wall she was leaning on was glass and everyone could see her sink against it in relief, and probably no one knew why. She could also see out, and a quick look over her shoulder told her that Max was storming right up and throwing open her door. It was like turning the 'mute' button off.

"What the hell was all that?" He wasn't angry at her, but more that she appeared upset.

She didn't understand his reaction, but she filled him in on the details anyway, hoping that might calm him down. "That was Jeff Landers. He called to introduce himself. He's our new accounting guy with Farland since Dylan Atterson suddenly resigned."

There was blinking, and shock, and few other expressions she couldn't quite place. "Atterson resigned?"

She nodded.

"Were you behind that?"

Nodding again, she took deep, even breaths, and realized that she didn't feel quite so hemmed in. Max wasn't a threat to her personal space and, come to think of it, she hadn't felt like that since he'd barged in here with that news about the analysis of her drink glass. Of course, after that the feeling had transferred itself onto Dylan. Even though she hadn't seen Dylan in almost a month, since Chicago, she'd always felt his presence cloying at her. "I wrote him a letter that would disturb him a little if he were innocent but send him packing if he was guilty."

"And he ran."

"Yeah," she offered what smile she could. "You're off the hook."

The relief she expected to see wasn't there. Just a small nod, acknowledging the situation. "You're not going to prosecute?"

Spinning to face him, she let her sudden anger fly. "Why the hell would I do something as stupid as that?"

He started to open his mouth, but she shut him up quickly.

That off-the-handle reaction was not like her. So she toned

it down and tried again, "Look, I have no evidence, and no desire to be held up in court as a slut who wanted what she got!"

Biting his lip, he nodded but tried again. "Sloan, you have plenty of character witnesses here."

Even though he had lost his previous conviction, she still lit in to him. She just needed to let some of it out and he was the handiest target. She wasn't able to stop herself. "I'm sorry, are you a lawyer? What do you know about it? Tell me how I spend my off hours!"

He didn't reply.

"Exactly! You don't know me from Adam when it comes down to it. And I am not about to put my personal life on trial just to lose after everything else." She folded her arms and turned away, silently declaring the conversation finished. The fact of the matter was she was a witch and that was only going to make things worse if anything ever went to court. She'd either have to perjure herself at some point or admit what she was, which would not help her case. She wanted to throw his ass in jail, but she couldn't. It was better this way.

She was reminding herself to accept facts when the soft filter of Max's voice came to her over her shoulder. "Actually, I do know you pretty well."

"How?" She wished she hadn't said it. She wished she could swallow it back. She didn't want to know what she'd told him when she was in bed with him being Wanton Sloan. She didn't want to have to tell him how very much she wasn't that woman.

But he seemed to sense her reluctance and just nodded in response. Waiting for him to leave, she studied him openly. The soft fall of the dark blond hair. The square but lean jaw. The broad shoulders that still looked defeated. Her voice again got the better of her and spoke, unfettered by what her mind wanted. "You would have gotten dragged through the mud, too, you know."

"I'd have done it, if it would have cleared things up for you."

She shrugged. "Things are clear enough. Like I said, you're off the hook."

Again, he didn't leave. His hands found homes in his pockets. It was a gesture showing his discomfort and she hadn't seen him do it around anyone else. Ever. "I'm not concerned with whatever hook I was on. I'm more concerned that you're okay. That you sleep well at night and…all that."

Her lips pressed tightly denying what her voice told him. "I'm fine. But I'm really embarrassed about the whole thing and it would be much easier if you just left."

Her fingers clenched into the wood lip of the desk behind her where she leaned against it and let it support her. Maybe a person could die from embarrassment. She had liked him so much. Part of her still wanted to let her crush on him run wild, but there was no way to clean this up and come out okay. Not to mention that her heart had never chosen well for her in the past. Just because he wasn't a date rapist didn't mean he would be good for her. The very fact that she liked him probably meant he was no good.

He turned, nodding, and headed out to the water cooler. The bands that were wound tight around her chest didn't loosen. The sigh of relief didn't escape. Just when she thought she really would sleep better, she felt worse. But she didn't know why.

CHAPTER 12

Nowhere.

Max was in the middle of nowhere. That's where nine weeks time had gotten him with Sloan. She didn't want to see him—as in, she didn't want to give him a chance and date him. And, literally, she didn't seem to want to even set her gaze upon him.

The one time he had managed to catch her eye, she had looked shocked for one brief moment before she turned and fled as though the sight of him burned.

It had burned. It burned *him*.

She couldn't be that embarrassed, could she? He had tried time and again to explain that what had happened between them wasn't embarrassing at all. It hurt that she didn't remember any of it. It had been the best night of his life until he woke up and it all turned into a nightmare that still hadn't gone away. Instead of getting another chance with her, she told him that she didn't want to know about any of it. Each time he might have had a chance, she had run the other way.

He still watched her at the water cooler. He mostly watched her easy attitude with Sheila. Max was insanely jealous of the accountant, simply because Sloan spoke to her without reserve. Sheila got to be Sloan's friend. So he watched. He watched her laugh and joke. He watched her get stiff in the shoulders when she caught him watching. He would just look away and lament the cruel twist of fate that had left him engaged for almost four hours and vilified for almost three months.

That and the fact that she seemed to be at the water cooler more now. It had been easier when he had been trying to ask her out, than now when he was trying to explain what they had done together and that she really did want to remember it, if only she would listen, and, God, she was walking straight to his door.

Max straightened and felt his heart rate kick up. She hadn't spoken to him in weeks and here she was, coming right to him. Her face poked around the edge of his doorway, and she looked calm, like she swung by to chat about ten times a day instead of never. "Can I come in?"

Like that was even a question. She actually waited until he said "yes."

She breathed deeply as though she needed to think about what to say, but she'd come here and he didn't push. She blinked three times then closed his door behind her and leaned back on it for support.

Finally, Sloan was in his office. Unfortunately, everyone could watch though, luckily, no one could hear. Here he finally was and he couldn't think of a damned thing to say.

Twice, she bit at her lip. Her eyes darted away and then back and Max began getting very worried. What the hell could be wrong?

"I'm pregnant."

He blinked. His heart felt like it stopped. He thought about his breathing. Then moved his head forward, because he was sure he hadn't heard her right.

"I'm pregnant." Her voice was a little stronger this time. Her face a little concerned looking. Maybe because he hadn't responded the first time.

So, he had heard it right. Just those two simple words. And just as he opened his mouth to speak—to say anything—she began to gush.

"I don't expect anything from you. I'll take—"

He had to cut her off. "Well, wait..." It turned out that while he could open his mouth and make words, he wasn't prepared to speak. He had been blindsided and really needed to stop for just half a second and sort things out. So he asked the first thing he thought of. "How far along are you?"

"Thirteen weeks." She stared at him like she was issuing a challenge.

"Three months." He nodded, adding it up. He knew it was his. Somehow his voice sounded so calm and rational, when inside he was so unsure whether he should jump up and down for joy, or scream and bang the walls. It was stupid, and he knew it, but he *had* to ask. "And you want to keep the baby?"

She pulled back as though he had physically hit her. "Of course, I want to keep it. It's too late for an abortion anyway!"

"Whoa! I wasn't suggesting anything like that!" His hands came up in front of him, palms out, as though that would stop all her horrible thoughts about him. If only he could cast a spell on her that would do it. For a moment it was so tempting. "I just wanted to know what you wanted to do. There are so many options. I don't know if you want to raise the baby or if you might put it up for adoption."

"No!" Before he could protest again, she continued on. "I don't expect anything from you. I'll take care of the baby. But I'm about to start showing and I didn't want you to have to come ask."

"No, I'm—...that is—...I want to be involved." He meant that in so many ways that he couldn't even convey.

"You don't have to say that." With a deep breath, she started again. "I have some papers drawn up, if you want we can both sign them. Then you don't have to worry that I'll come after you for money or—"

"What the hell!" Max tried to calm his anger by pushing his fingers through his hair, just to give his hands something to do besides strangling the woman in front of him. Only then did he realize the eyeful that he was giving everyone in the main room. *Screw it.* He closed the blinds, figuring what was really going on was even stranger than anything they might imagine. "I suppose signing these papers would relinquish my rights as the father."

"Yes." It was so soft that he hardly even heard it.

"Why would I do that?" He was shaking his head at her. And at himself. This was getting more complex by the minute. He was still struggling to wrap his head around the basics—Sloan Ellis was pregnant with his child. She also seemed to expect him to just sign away any ties to her or the baby. If he'd had any doubts that she didn't remember their night, this would have sealed the deal. He hated that. With a deep sigh, he looked up at her.

Sloan chewed at her lip again, looking more like a scared child than anything else. But before she could speak he remembered. His body jerked as the memory hit. "How are you even pregnant?"

That just made her anger flare up again. "I don't know! I was hoping maybe you could tell me why you didn't see fit to protect yourself or me!"

He felt like he was being bashed against rocks. She acted as though she truly believed he was so thoughtless a lover as to just have unprotected sex. He had to remind himself that in her head that night never existed. The drugs had wiped it all away. He forced himself to calm down. "Do you even want to hear it?"

"I—"

But as she started to speak he found he didn't care what she intended to say. He was going to tell her. He'd lost a lot to those drugs, too. She might not remember, but he did. Right now, he didn't know which was worse. His anger at the situation was flaring and he came around the desk. He pressed in so close she was almost pinned with her back to the door, his arms outstretched on either side of her head. "I don't travel with condoms. I don't expect to get laid on business trips."

She sniffed, and he continued. "You said we didn't need any anyway, because you couldn't get pregnant. You were sterile from an STD you got in your early college days, from an A-hole boyfriend you had."

"I told you that?" She couldn't even bring herself to look up.

Ducking his head, Max caught her eyes. "Yes!" This time he wasn't so harsh on her. "You told me a lot of things."

Sloan nodded softly, seeming to accept that. It still wasn't as good as if she could just remember. He was so close he could inhale the scent of her shampoo and perfume. She smelled just like he remembered, just like his pillow had smelled that morning, like something musky and sweet, like Sloan. He fought the urge to gather her in his arms, certain she wouldn't take kindly to it. "So, is this some miracle baby?"

She nodded. "It might be my only chance to be a mother. Please, don't feel obligated. I just... I don't want my kid going back and forth between two parents."

"We can work something out." He knew what *he* wanted to work out. He'd just have to find a way to convince her, is all.

"Maybe it isn't yours." She shrugged, which was a risky maneuver with him so close.

But he brushed the statement aside easily. "No, that's my baby. You were very clear that you hadn't been with anyone in a year. Not since you caught your fiance with your cousin."

Her head snapped up to stare at him. "You know that, too?"

"I told you, I know a lot of things."

Her shoulders sagged, and she tugged at his heartstrings. She had borne a heavy load of late. And finally, now, a pregnancy.

Which from the looks of it, made her really excited and really scared all at the same time. He had no way to tell her not to be scared. He didn't know how to not put his arms around her, so he forced himself to step back.

Appearing utterly defeated, Sloan nodded to herself. As she turned to go, she looked back over her shoulder. "I don't know what people will say..." With that parting shot, she was gone, closing the door behind her.

"I don't give a rat's ass what people say." He said it to the air in the now lonely office. "It's not about them, anyway. It's about us." He wished that she had still been there to hear it, because it certainly made things clearer for him.

What he hadn't been able to see was suddenly now obvious. For months he'd been in a fog, but it seemed Sloan had walked into his office and dropped a bomb. When the smoke cleared it left some sense behind.

So he picked up whatever pieces he could and took the rest of the day off.

CHAPTER 13

Sloan had eaten ice cream for dinner the night before. And broccoli.

The ice cream was because she wanted it. She was pregnant and hormonal and it was creamy and sweet and cold. Enough said. The broccoli was because she was pregnant and felt guilty about having only ice cream as a meal.

This morning she had craved waffles for breakfast—the toaster kind. So she'd shoved two into her face like she was starving as she made her way out the door. She had savored her way through an apple this morning at ten. A Granny Smith. Sour, sour, sour. And now a huge ham sandwich with mustard and mayonnaise and two kinds of cheese.

Rae had taken her out for lunch over the weekend and made fun of her for eating a whole foot-long sub—a first for Sloan. Though it was funny, some of the rest of it wasn't. Once she'd finished stuffing her face, Sloan had sat back in the molded sub-shop booth and said, "I really thought you'd be here first and I'd be here...well, probably never."

Reaching out to take her hand, Rae had rolled with the sudden mood change. "I know. And I know how much it upset you when you believed you were infertile, so this really is a miracle."

By then—because her moods swung faster than her pendulum—she was almost in tears. "But it's all backward! I'm supposed to get married first and I don't even have a boyfriend!"

Though Rae still looked at her with something that was awe and pity mixed, Sloan's eyes darted around the shop. Had she said that louder than she intended? For a moment she considered casting a spell on the shop to not hear her. Then she'd have to cast a second spell to make them forget they'd seen her casting spells. Delilah had been adamant about "No *Forget* Spells" though she'd only told Rae and Sloan that they were worse than curses. Luckily, no one was looking. Sloan went back to trying to decipher her sister's expression.

"There is no right order."

"Sure, there is. You did it." She sniffed even though the angst had passed, her body hadn't gotten the message. She really wanted a glass of wine, but they didn't serve it at the sub shop. And, she got no glasses of wine for probably the next year or so, since she was pregnant and all. When Rae didn't grace her idea of a "correct order" with a response, Sloan slid back into despair. "I wasn't prepared for this."

"We never are. I wasn't prepared for Sam."

"Yeah, but that got you *Sam*!"

"And this is going to get you someone you love more than anything, too."

"Yeah," Sloan agreed, though her tone was reluctant. "Still, Sam doesn't spit up on you and wake up screaming for no clear reason in the middle of the night."

Rae laughed, then sobered in relatively quick fashion. "Just so you know, Sam and I decided to start trying."

Sloan sat up straight. "To have a baby? We could be pregnant together?" She'd not heard anything about this. Shocked, she only looked at her younger sister and had a momentary thought that once again, Rae was doing it better than she was. Rae had a husband, Rae might have a baby like Sloan, but she wouldn't be a single mother like Sloan.

"I doubt it's going to happen that fast. But yeah, we decided to throw caution to the wind last month." It was yet another thing Sloan wasn't prepared for.

"You could be pregnant now."

"But I'm not." Rae scrunched her face as Sloan tried to calculate what it would cost her sister to her art and the upward trajectory she was on. Sloan had always out-earned her little sister, who cobbled-together a barely adequate income while she pursued art photography. Then, almost two years ago, Rae's art had taken off. She made thousands of dollars per piece and was getting requests from some big name galleries. She'd even had a piece made into a poster.

Now Rae wanted to get pregnant. On a regular time scale. Planned. With her husband.

How had Sloan turned into the slacker? The one who was cobbling her life together? She tried to smile at her sister but only managed it halfway. Then, begging off due to a headache— she really was getting one—she had Rae drive her home and drop her off at the front of the apartment building.

Looking up at the structure she cursed. She'd been planning on moving out. Getting a house. Or cats. Or probably both. She really needed a house now, but she'd just screwed the pooch on her expendable income.

The thought she'd had while looking up at her building had stuck with her for days, and it pulled away her thoughts worked to stay focused on her job. So she sat at her desk and tried not to think about food and the price of a house in Los Angeles.

It didn't work. Since the nausea of the first trimester had passed her world revolved around food. She hadn't ever before enjoyed the act of eating quite this much. She was practically salivating over the sandwich, even though it wasn't quite lunch time yet. Her mouth was open and the sandwich halfway there when the knock came at her door.

Through the glass she could see that it was Max. *Uh-oh.* But she couldn't just not open the door. So, with a sigh of longing, she set the sandwich aside and let him in, before walking back to her desk and picking up the sandwich again.

"Don't eat that!"

Perturbed, she set it down again. "Don't you dare start doing the Pregnancy Police thing on me. It's ham and whole wheat bread. It's just fine." She didn't mention the gobs of mustard and mayo that she was sure he could see oozing out between the piled-high slices of meat and cheese as she picked it up again.

"I wanted to take you out to lunch."

"Oh." She set it down a third time and shook her head at him. "Trust me, you don't want to feed me. I'm eating everything in sight."

"I do want to feed you. Please."

Please. Nice guys said *please.* But so did guys who wanted you to think they were nice. The one factor all the bad ones had had in common was that Sloan had picked them. Even the celebrities she had crushes on had always been found out later to be cheating on their wives. Or worse. So she spoke the words and smiled that smile that said, "No, thank you."

"Please, it's important."

Important? Everything was important now, she was realizing. "Trust me, this baby isn't coming for another six months. Maybe you should take a little more time to get used to the idea before you make decisions."

He nodded. "You're absolutely right."

She let out her breath thinking she could finally get into that ham sandwich.

Max interrupted the thought again. "But I don't need more time. I really want you to come to lunch with me."

"No." She made one last ditch effort to eat her sandwich, but he covered her hands with his.

"Please, I don't want to do this here."

"Do *what* here?" She sighed at him, realizing she was *never* going to get to eat that sandwich.

He quickly pulled his hands back and jammed them in his pockets. She realized, maybe for the first time, just how much it was bothering Max Summerland, deal-closer, to not have control over his world. "Ask you to marry me."

It was a good thing she hadn't managed to get a bite of the ham sandwich, or she would have choked and died. Instead, she sputtered out, "*Marry* you?" about as ungracefully as she possibly could.

"Yes, marry me." He chewed his bottom lip, but stood his ground, back straight, shoulders square.

Well, he certainly was handling this better than she was. Before thinking, she blurted out a disbelieving, "Why?"

Hey, she was on a roll, why get her shit together now?

"That's our child you're carrying. You said yourself that you don't want him or her going back and forth between two parents. It's less expensive, it'll be easier. You won't have to do it all by yourself."

She suddenly went very still, as though—just for a moment—the whole world had stopped turning. Then she finally managed to make her mouth move. She pushed the words out past the stabbing feeling in her chest that she didn't want to analyze right now. "Those are all very nice arguments, Max—"

"I bought you a ring.... say 'yes'." He quit biting at his lip as he pulled the small black velvet box from his pocket. He looked confident and strong... and *wrong*.

"—but I'm not a deal. Stop trying to close me."

"Sloan—"

"*No.* Please go." Somewhere within her a little black ball had started to form, and she did the only thing she could. She ignored it while she stared at him waiting for him to leave.

It took a moment, but he did. With a small nod, he shoved the little black velvet box back in his pocket. He'd offered it up as proof, she guessed. And, finally, finally, she got to eat her ham sandwich. Even if she was shaking just a little.

She felt the knot growing inside her all afternoon. When she finally made it home that evening, she curled into her big fluffy couch and cried, great tears falling through great heaving sobs. She didn't even know why until later that night, when she woke up, suddenly gulping air, alone in her dark condo.

It was because she had wanted Max Summerland to *want* to marry her. Not for a child, and even though she was well aware that he wasn't what she was looking for. Still she wanted it. She wanted some great guy—anyone really—to want to be with her. That marriage proposal had been anything but that. It had been the modern day equivalent of marrying off the preggo girl to any man so desperate as to take her. In essence, it was a pity-proposal.

Her first proposal had been shit, because Joe had been sleeping with other women. It had looked good and sounded better and had been built on lies. The only thing better about this one was that Max had been honest. He didn't want her, he just wanted a convenience.

Sloan also knew that now, with a child in tow, it would become that much harder to find Mr. Right. Most Mr. Anything's didn't want to raise another man's child. Single mothers were not hot properties.

But this morning, as he stood there with that ring in his hand, for just a moment she'd wanted to believe it was true: that Max Summerland had really wanted to marry her. And not because of their child.

At least, she realized, she wasn't really alone anymore, was she?

CHAPTER 14

G reat. Everything was great.

That was the only way to describe it. Okay, there was that niggling little thought at the back of her mind, that she wanted more to go with it, but what she had was great. Sloan reminded herself of this often. She'd thought she could never carry her own child, yet here she was. It wasn't the way she planned it, but—as Rae had astutely pointed out—what was?

She hadn't planned to move to LA originally, she hadn't planned to change divisions in the company, she hadn't planned to get pregnant. So it was just another happening in a string of things she hadn't planned, and many of them had turned out great!

In fact, she was better suited to be a single mother than most. She had a good income, great benefits, and...well, she needed a house with a yard, but since no one would be walking for about a year or so from now, she had a little time.

So her "great" was maternity clothes that she was just beginning to fit at four months along. She had looked and looked and decided that she didn't need a $90 white shirt that was only going to fit until she was seven months along anyway.

She also wouldn't be needing a maternity ball gown, or sadly, a negligee. Sloan decided the positive outlook was to call that "money saved!" What she did need was some casual wear and suits for work. She remembered Lisette complaining about seven years ago, and in Ohio, about what was available for the pregnant woman with an average-sized budget. Sloan was grateful that LA was full of cool maternity clothes. So she was in a new skirt, new blouse, new jacket and new shoes, just for good measure. She'd piled her closet high, thinking she might save the clothes for the next time she was pregnant. It suddenly occurred to her that she wasn't actually infertile.

She'd pulled out her pendulum and asked it but when she got a "yes" answer she almost smacked her head. Of course, she wasn't infertile, she was freaking pregnant. She'd meant to ask "Could she have more children in the future?" but the universe answered only what you asked. Clearly not in any shape to be asking the universe anything, she'd put the pendulum down and eaten a bagel.

Sloan wondered if anyone would notice that she was pregnant now. She seemed to have gotten noticeably bigger over the weekend. Every day she stopped and waited to feel the flutters she knew were coming.

She had sunshine that seemed to have permeated everything starting in early March and she had little shoots all along the front walk of her apartment building coming up green. They all made her think about her baby. Her thoughts wandered off as she pulled into the parking lot under the building at work. It was dark and chilly with only random slashes of bright light letting on to the outside world, and she let her mind think of babies. Their chubby cheeks, and wide toothless smiles, tiny feet and bright little eyes. She had been having random flashes of thought about these things since the stick had changed color. Every doctor's visit solidified it more, made the thoughts come faster, made her eyes pull towards babies and baby pictures.

The last time she'd gone in, she heard the heartbeat thundering along like a tiny train. Mesmerized by the fact that it was beating inside her, she'd sat for a moment, just listening and marveling that she had a child on the way. She had also, at last, scheduled her first ultrasound. The tech told her they could probably find out the baby's sex. Sloan was anxious to know, but she didn't need an ultrasound to find out. She'd pulled out her bowl and pendulum and asked whether she was having a boy or a girl. Unfortunately, it looked like she would be needing that ultrasound. Her pendulum had gone stubborn and refused to answer. Or rather, it had given every answer in the book.

So she let herself imagine. In her mind her baby was a little boy with blue, blue eyes, and for the first time her excitement didn't cloud her thoughts and she wondered if the baby would have Max's eyes.

She almost shuddered. She wanted the baby to be hers and hers alone. Instead she would have to share her child with a man she really didn't know all that well, but who seemed to have all her old painful secrets in his back pocket. And he could just pull them out and dangle them in front of her whenever he wanted.

She rode the elevator up to her office, squeezing in with other random people from the building and a few she knew as acquaintances. She wondered if anyone noticed that her belly was sticking out more. She had shed her jacket after pushing the fifteenth floor button. Maybe they just thought she was getting fat and no one wanted to say anything. She didn't care.

She walked the hall, wondering if she was starting to get the tell-tale waddle before realizing it was much too soon for that. Then she settled in at her desk, humming lullabies as she scanned copies and struck out phrases and re-worded them before sending out the files. Later, at ten a.m., after a handful of memos and recommendation letters, her phone buzzed.

She picked it up with a smile, as though it were a personal call. "Yes?"

"Hey, Sloan, Mr. Bernstein wants to see you in his office in five minutes." Jenny's cheerful voice rang over the intercom.

Mr. Bernstein?

But Jenny continued. "Oh, and don't worry, he didn't seem upset or anything. Bye!"

God bless Jenny. That was exactly what she'd been thinking, too. "Thanks, Jenny."

Sloan organized the rest of her to-do list for the day and headed out to the elevator, happy as a little clam. Maybe there was a promotion in the works. Nah, it couldn't be. She was just thrilled enough with how things were. The man just probably needed something and she would happily oblige, as she was going to be asking for maternity leave here soon, and a spate of afternoons off for doctors' appointments. Starting in three weeks with that ultrasound appointment.

Janine was at her desk in front of Mr. Bernstein's and waved Sloan in without dropping a beat from the call she was on. With her jacket draped over her arm, Sloan sauntered in, and stopped cold.

Max was sitting in one chair across from Mr. Bernstein and the other guest chair remained empty. *What was this?* The look he shot her clearly said he didn't know either. Bernstein, however, was oblivious to all of this. He just started talking, and Sloan tried desperately to pay attention. She hadn't spoken to Max in nearly a month. Since he hadn't wanted to sign her papers giving up his rights as the father, she had managed to avoid him in the hallways almost completely. She sighed and sank into the unoccupied chair.

"—in Madrid. Now this isn't a sightseeing trip. You'll go, you'll be back three days later. I need you here for the Petersen project. But I trust that the two of you can handle this yourselves."

Blinking, she fought the urge to scream at him *What did you just say?* But she was pretty sure that it involved her and Max traveling to Madrid. Beyond that, she wasn't sure it mattered. Luckily, Max seemed to see that she was out of sorts and he spoke up. "Now let me just clarify to be sure I have everything. Day after tomorrow we fly out, we sign with Delmonico incorporated, and then we're back around three a.m. Sunday."

This time she heard every word. Which was a good thing since she was about to be distracted by Mr. Bernstein staring at her waistband. At least he hadn't asked. She would have told him, but didn't think she'd handle herself very well after this little Madrid bomb dropped. "That's it, you two. Finish up today and spend tomorrow getting ready and Thursday you're off. Janine has papers and info for both of you. Or she will by five tonight. She promised me."

Max nodded and stood, taking Sloan by the arm, looking casual, unbuttoning his jacket as he steered her out of the room. Confused, and hating to be led like cattle, she hissed, "You set this up, didn't you?"

"No, I didn't. But it wouldn't hurt you to have a little bit of faith in me. I'm not asking for a lot of it, though I realize that that's beyond you."

Her jaw dropped open. *How dare he?*

But he seemed one step ahead of her, and he pulled her into a thankfully empty elevator. While she had felt put upon a few moments ago, now she was cornered, literally. Max even went so far as to pull the stop button between floors before he turned and pinned her with that wicked gaze. "You do remember that that's our child you're carrying? Mine, too. And maybe I can't carry it myself, but I can do a lot. If you'd *let me.*"

She opened her mouth to protest but he spoke again before she got the chance. She had the distinct feeling he didn't want to hear what she had to say.

"I don't know why you're so convinced to go it alone. As far as this little trip goes, I did not set it up. I didn't know a thing about it until just now. But it wouldn't kill you to act like maybe you didn't hate me so much." He took only a heartbeat to pause before he railroaded the conversation again. "Unless you think I did it. That whatever proof you had against Dylan wasn't sound."

Her voice was only a whisper even to her own ears. *Shit.* She'd been doing so well at avoiding all this. Now? She wouldn't be able to. "No, I don't think that you did it." But he made her look him in the eyes before he believed her.

"Now, are you okay to fly to Spain? It's a long trip."

"Yes, I'm fine. I just need leg room and a few chances to walk around."

"Listen, if you aren't, I'll think of a way out of it. You won't have to tell him you're pregnant. I'll tell Bernstein that it's because of me and that I want you off the trip."

She wished she had kept her mouth shut a moment earlier, because he was being nice and being concerned about her and the baby. But she couldn't go back and change it, so she shook her head, and at last he pushed in the red button. The elevator started up again with the tiniest of lurches and they rode the rest of the way in silence.

CHAPTER 15

S loan jerked her head up as her brain snapped awake. With a few flutters of her eyelashes she tried to throw off the hazy layer that clung to her from traveling so far. The side of her head was still warm from Max's shoulder, and he turned to look at her now, his hand absently rubbing hers. "Hey sleepyhead, we're here."

She frowned, 'here' was not what she had expected. 'Here' was not a large corporate hotel like all the hotels they had stayed at in every other city the company had flown her to. It was a long, low building with a basic design like many seedy motels back in the states. But the similarities ended at the side by side single rooms with doors opening to the long porch. The charm and upkeep gave away its class.

Max must have seen her frown. "The Delmonico family owns it. It's why they put us here. They're leaving the big buildings to us now."

That's right, she had read that report, too. On the plane right before she passed out. Dear God, she felt like she had spent three full days on a plane and about five hours in a taxi. She stepped out and stood, stretching quietly, not wanting to talk, while Max tipped the cab driver and carried both their carryon-sized bags into the front office. She made a mental note to tip on the trip back out to the airport.

Still in a daze, she followed their hostess under the front overhang, and she smelled the fresh flowers that peeked out of the vines growing up every post and across the rafters. She was finally starting to revive, but she felt grungy. The thought of a shower warmed her until, while Max waited patiently outside, she was shown around her suite. She had everything, including a small kitchenette and loveseat with TV. A polished door led into a separate bedroom and in there, wide sliding glass doors that led out onto a private deck and beyond it to a small pool. The manager said they had heated the water because they were expecting guests. The only other room that was occupied tonight didn't have access to the pool.

That news brought Sloan fully awake. Waving the woman off to take care of Max, she said a quick thank-you and tossed her bag onto the dresser top. She was good at packing for trips, she had a standard list for all occasions, and she hoped it would save her now! Rifling through her stuff, she squealed with glee as she pulled out what she'd been looking for—a bathing suit. Yes!

No. She was four months pregnant with the roundest belly she had ever owned and this was a two piece. She never would have packed it now. It was just in here from all her old trips... this was her standard traveling swimsuit. Right there next to the back-up tampons, just in case. She laughed. Those sure weren't necessary.

Holding the suit up, she eyed it. She really wanted to swim, and she wondered if she might be able to talk herself into it. It *was* a tankini. The tank top should save her from mortal embarrassment if she should be seen and the two pieces would give her belly some much needed room. With a few more self-reassuring words that the other patron at the hotel had no access to the pool and that Max hadn't slept on the flight. She decided to go for it. She should have the pool to herself, in which case it wouldn't matter if she was in a string bikini. She smiled. Mission accomplished. She was going in. Peeling off her cotton knit shirt and the fluid maternity pants that went with it, she climbed into the suit and pulled the towel from the rack in the bathroom. Shower later. Heated pool now.

Shoving aside the sliding glass door out the back of the bedroom, she took only a moment to notice the stars and the warm night sky. The cool night air sent little goosebumps all up her arms and legs, and she ran back inside for the robe she'd seen on the back of the door. The last thing she wanted or needed was to freeze to death when she got out. Emerging again, she saw two tall solid wood fences, about seven feet high, lining either side of her personal patio space. She had two deck chairs and a small Adirondack table. Beyond that there was a slice of pool visible with a strip of cement and tile before cool blue water beckoned to her. She could venture into the pool or stay hidden on her own little patio.

Armed with her robe and towel, she chose the water. Dropping them on the poolside table she let her bare feet sink down into the water as she slowly descended the steps. It was the perfect temperature, a dream begging her to dive under. She went two more steps lower, thanking her lucky stars. She wasn't allowed in hot tubs, her doctor had warned her about the high temperatures, but a heated pool was just fine. She sighed in relief and lowered herself to her shoulders getting the ends of her hair wet, since she'd forgotten to put it up. She simply couldn't muster the energy to care.

With a quick dive she was under water and swimming laps like when she'd been a kid. Layers of travel sloughed away. Her normal breathing rate was returning. She had no idea what time it was, except that it was night. She went three laps, seven, ten.

Setting her feet on the bottom of the pool, she jerked her

head up at a noise. But she scanned the deck area and saw no one. For the first time, she noticed the high walls dividing off each private piece of patio for the whole string of rooms, leaving her with her room behind her and a beautiful view of the mountains out in front of her. Right now, the pool was blessedly private, and she sighed, enjoying it.

Sloan jumped about ten miles high as the water reached up her back. When she spun around, she saw it was just Max, his wet hand on her shoulder blade, and a smile glowing through the rivulets of water running down his face.

"God, you scared me." She tried to steady her breathing, but something about his smile wasn't letting her.

"Didn't mean to." He dove and swam away and so all she could do was continue her laps. She was on the backstroke now and decided to ignore him and just continue.

His voice broke her concentration back at the shallow end. "You're showing."

Again, she put her feet down and nodded that yes, she was. But she didn't know what he wanted. He held his fingers a couple of inches apart. "The baby's about this big now."

She nodded again.

"I've been reading up." His grin was infectious.

"Yeah, what else do you know?"

"That tomatoes are rumored to be good for the baby's brain."

Sloan felt her own smile form as she nodded in agreement, even though she hadn't really intended to. "I've heard that."

"I know that it already looks a lot like a person. It mostly just grows now."

She nodded again and waited.

"I know...that lots of times pregnant women have weird dreams. That you should be able to have an ultrasound soon that will show if it's a boy or a girl, if you want to know." He sounded like a proud school kid reciting his spelling words and knowing he had all of them right.

"I do want to know." She waited for him to ask. Surely he'd want her to tell him when she found out.

Instead he surprised her. "Can I come?"

His smile was caught by her own grin. "Sure." The word had just fallen out of her mouth. She wasn't sure why she'd said it, but she couldn't very well take it back now.

For a moment, his face lit up. Then, just as quickly he turned serious. "I also know that just carrying a baby is an awfully big job, and that it wouldn't hurt you to let me help."

She started to protest that, *yes, it would*, but he didn't let her get the thought out.

He held his wet hands out toward her, palm out, as if he came in peace. "The key word is *let.* I have not, nor would I ever, force myself on you. I am terribly sorry that all this happened to you. I really am. And I'm not the one that made it happen, but I can help you out of it."

"I don't want out!" Her hand flew to her belly, cradling the baby within. Max's baby. Her hand had found a home there a lot lately.

"I'm sorry, I didn't mean it that way. I just meant I can help." He only paused a second. "I also know that within a month, no one will have any doubts that you're pregnant. What do you want to tell them?"

She'd been thinking about that, even if she hadn't come to any hard and fast decisions. It would be wrong to make that decision without Max. "I figured the truth. I think everyone has an inkling about Chicago anyway. You don't have to be an accountant to do the math. And Vanessa and Sheila both know I had sworn off men. Most everyone suspects we spent the night together, and that it wasn't good in the morning."

He nodded at her, but she couldn't tell if he was agreeing with her decision or just her assessment of the facts. She didn't know what he wanted her to say. Since her ears were getting cold, she dove under and resumed her swimming.

Max set up pace beside her for a moment then easily outdistanced her and passed her on the way back before she even reached the end. *Show off.* A few laps later he stood waiting for her at the beginning of the shallows.

He looked her up and down when she stood, and it made her nervous. "What?"

His eyes and his voice were soft. "Can I touch you?"

She let her breath out. "I guess." Feeling more than a little awkward, she took his hand and placed it on her belly. "Although I don't think you'll be able to feel anything. I can't feel anything yet." She wanted to keep yammering, to ignore the warmth of his wet fingers as they spread wide across her stomach. She wanted to ignore that it was his child he wanted to touch.

"Wow." The word seemed to flow out of him, and she tried to force a smile. Sloan tried to ignore her fingers covering his, holding them on her skin, where the tankini refused to cover the swell Max had helped create. His hand slipped from under hers, sliding around the side, making her breath hitch, heading for the small of her back. "I liked that. But it wasn't what I had in mind when I asked if I could touch you."

Her breath didn't hitch as he pulled her closer. There was no protest as his mouth covered hers, sending heat snaking through her entire body. The palms of her hands were on the warmth of his forearms and they slid up his arms and around his neck, pulling her up on her toes. She kissed him back with everything she had.

Because she wanted this. So much. She wanted desperately for it to be *right* this time. She wanted him to actually be a good man. The man for her. Because she wanted to buy into the fantasy. As happy as she was to be having this baby, having a father for her child and a man for herself had been part of the dream, too. She kissed him because the moon and the stars were overhead and he was sinking further into her, hot and wet, his hands skimming her back, and his mouth all over hers.

His lips parted and Sloan let hers follow, wanting—*needing*—the kiss to go deeper. His tongue darted in and met with hers, stealing her breath and her sanity. She couldn't think beyond the right-ness of the feelings surging through her. That this man had already started a baby within her only made her want him more. She pushed up into his arms, moving against him as his hands traced along the laces at the front of her suit, down over her hips, and reverently around the small swell that was their child.

She didn't know how long they stood there trying to devour each other. She pressed against him, chest to thigh, her breasts and her belly molding to the hard heat of him. Shivering when he left her mouth to forge new paths along her skin. He kissed and nipped his way to her ear, down her neck, across her collarbone. His hot mouth left cool trails in the wake of his heat. Her head dipped to one side, giving him better access, while her fingernails grasped for purchase in his shoulders. Hot licks of flame surged up through the core of her.

When he found her mouth again, his fingertips played at the back of her neck, touching lightly, driving her to seek deeper kisses from him, to lightly bite at his lower lip. This time, when his mouth dipped low into the front of her suit, it fell open, his warm fingers pushing it out of the way. "God, Sloan, you're so beautiful."

With a gasp, she covered herself with her arms, glancing around to see who might be watching.

She was quelled by his arms coming protectively around her and his mouth at her ear, whispering, "No one else is here. The pool's private. No one can see you, except me." He pulled her arms away and leaned over to kiss her there. Between her breasts, over her shoulder, down her arm. And then, leaning her back over his arms, to kiss and lick at each nipple. To make her gasp and moan and shiver.

He tugged at the laces still dangling across her torso and barely holding the suit to her. They gave way and he slid the top off completely. Bunching it in one fist, he took her hand in his and led her out of the pool, into the cold night air and a fit of shivers.

He kissed her before her teeth could start chattering, that alone enough to heat her thoroughly. Then he wrapped her in the big fluffy towels she had brought and scooped her up as she gasped in surprise. He kissed her like carrying her was no big deal. Pushing back the sliding glass door, he walked them through his room all the way into the bathroom, and set her feet down in the tub, climbing in with her. He slipped the towels off, dropping them beyond the edge of the tub, completely forgotten as his eyes found her exposed skin again. His hands reached behind him, setting off a spray of the coldest shower she could remember being in.

Even though he blocked most of the water with his body, she dove for the warmest thing nearby—him. Max's arms came around her again and seeped his heat into her. His mouth found hers again, and the water got warmer. It seemed she didn't care how long that took as long as his tongue was stealing her thoughts. He rinsed her hair and his. Then carefully peeled away the bikini bottom she was wearing and dropped it to the tub floor.

Sloan stopped breathing. He had seen her before. *Right?* Though she didn't remember it, she knew it as a fact. But now she was no longer the same. His smile stopped her just before she would have stepped back. His hand clasped hers, leading it to the snap on his khaki shorts and she briefly noticed that it wasn't even a suit he was wearing. Knowing full well what he was asking, she felt her fingers obey his urging. Under her touch, the snap popped and the zipper slid slowly downward.

She could feel him, hard and long, behind the fabric. His eyes heated, showing her what her touch did to him, even through the thick canvas of his pants. Still they didn't slip off him, the water making them cling and mold to his form. Her mouth fell open at the very thought of pushing her hands under the wet cloth and peeling it from him. But she did just that.

The shorts joined her suit at the bottom of the tub, and without warning he reached back and turned off the water. As the chill hit, she dove for him again, seeking out his heat. He reached out of the shower and pulled a huge towel in, first wrapping them both in it together, then standing nude while he rubbed her dry. He encouraged the same from her, and she found herself obliging.

Sloan studied the planes of his chest and his belly. Felt all along his legs and arms vicariously through the towel and even pulled most of the wetness out of his hair. When she dropped the towel, he picked her up again, this time depositing her on the bed, before stretching out beside her.

For a second or two, they looked at each other. But before her thoughts or doubts could creep in, Max leaned in and kissed her again. His touch drugged her, pulling her under, even as his arms pulled her to him. Head to toe, skin on skin. His fingers found her breast, lingering there briefly before they skimmed down her side and traced her hip. He moved against her, his hand grasping at her hip and encouraging her to meet him. She didn't need the encouragement. Her mouth gasped into his even before he pushed her hips away and his hand slid down, between her legs, finding her wet and wanting. He laced their fingers together, silently asking permission with his eyes as he rolled her onto her back and pushed fully inside her.

A small cry escaped her lips, but her eyes stayed locked to his. The feeling of him in her drove her to the edge. And when he started a steady rhythm, sliding in and pulling slowly out of her, and doing it again, Sloan fell over the edge. His mouth covered hers as she came, shattering into a million tiny pieces in his embrace, and through it she heard his voice. She opened her eyes to find that his had never left her. In her haze, she watched him come, his eyes seeing into hers. Probably seeing more than he should.

At last he gave out. His arms buckling as he rolled them to the side, trying to get out words. "I'm too heavy...don't want to hurt...the baby." He curled her into him, where she could feel his heavy breathing at the top of her head and deep in his chest. His arms pulled her tighter to him and she felt small kisses on her forehead. His breathing evened out. Then slowed even more as he fell asleep. At last she did, too.

CHAPTER 16

H er eyes opened in the dark. Sloan was confused about where she was, but the smell and feel of Max next to her set her straight. In the dark, she could feel herself flush as her memories seeped in. But it felt good and safe to be here. It was *right* to be curled in his arms.

His breathing was a sound in her ear as well as a rhythmic rise and fall of his chest against her skin. She tingled all over just being next to him, and she wanted to stay right where she was. Things were going to be okay. Warmth took her over and she curled deeper into him, his arms tightening around her even in his sleep.

Just then, her belly had a small spasm, and as her brows furrowed in confusion she felt another. That was followed immediately by the sensation of someone running a finger along her skin, but inside. In her womb.

She rolled away, her hands flying to her belly. And there in the saturated dark of night her mouth flew open, involuntarily drawing air in. *The baby.* The next tiny spasm she recognized for what it was: a kick. She had been feeling the sensations like tiny bubbles inside for a while now, but hadn't realized what they were. Sloan had shaken them off, thinking she had imagined it. But if they were accompanied by tiny kicks then they were the real thing. Her baby was moving, and she could feel him or her in there.

She lay on her back with her hands spread across her belly, as though she might be able to feel something on the outside. Even though she knew there was no way that would happen at this stage. But she kept her fingers splayed there, just in case. She felt awed by each and every movement and waited, quiet in the dark of night, until her baby decided to calm down before she even began to think.

Finally, the movements stopped and her thoughts pressed in. The voice in the back of her head reiterated what she already knew. It chastised her for past bad decisions and current ones. *Sloan, you've never chosen well before. He could still have a girlfriend. You slept with him and the fact is, you don't even know if he's single.*

You thought you were in love once before, too. And look what the man you chose to marry did.

If it had just been her, she might have gone with it, might have rolled over and given herself again to Max. But it wasn't just her anymore. She *loved* this baby she had never met, and had only just begun to feel, more than she had ever loved anyone.

If Max had been any man besides the baby's father, it might have been different. She might have continued, knowing she could end it when the baby came. The problem was, she was already bound to Max for the next eighteen years at least, and probably on some level for the rest of their lives. A relationship with him would only throw another kink into things. It would only be a way for things to go horribly wrong later.

She sighed into the night. He had proposed. He was crazy, and she could see clearly that he needed to be in control of things. Hadn't she heard that in sales meetings? Always Be Closing, A. B. C. Max was trying to close her. To keep the baby in sight. To his credit, it was his baby, too. And he had a right to have it in sight. Certainly, having him sign away his parental rights hadn't worked, it had only pissed him off, so she hadn't tried again.

Still, she couldn't see herself being what Max needed. Sloan had been learning the hard way all along that she needed someone who needed her. Not someone who needed a lay, like Craig in college. Not sot someone who needed a wife, like Joe. And not a man who needed a mother for the coming baby.

So, as quietly as she could, she rolled out of bed and gathered the pieces of her suit. The top lay wet and cold on the corner table. She found the bottom, also wet and cold, in the tub. Grabbing a towel, she wrapped it around herself before slowly sliding the glass door open and walking through the back, around the tall wooden fence that separated the two rooms. She bit her lip to hold in tears as she made her way across the cold tile to her own room.

The light she had left on when she went for a swim was both a bright beacon and a blinding glare. Inside the room and finding she was fighting tears, Sloan rummaged through her bag for her pajamas. Victoria's Secret. Silk, bought large with room to grow into. When she had first tried them on she had thought the silk felt divine. But it had no heat of its own and offered no comfort compared to Max's arms.

As she climbed into bed, the cold covers set her teeth chattering, and there was nothing she could do about it. As she lay there, she recited a spell to protect herself from Max's advances in the future. She had no herbs, no candles, no scrying bowl. All she had was the old, generic protection spell from her grandmother Ellis's Book of Shadows.

As Sloan saw it, she was a sucker for Max's advances. If he'd been half as smooth in Chicago as he'd been tonight, she could understand why she'd woken up naked in his bed. Clearly, she was a sucker for Max's brand of heat. When she finished the spell, she thought through the facts again.

Max had never asked her out. Not once. She was just someone to sleep with.

The most recent information she had about Max's status was that he had a girlfriend. He'd never said otherwise. Since he and Sloan weren't dating in any sense, there was no reason to believe anything had changed.

Somehow, Max Summerland thought he could ask her to marry him. He'd been clear that it would just be easier. But Sloan knew marriage wasn't easy, and the idea that it was couldn't be anything other than a red flag. Would he break up with his girlfriend if she said yes? The fact that she was asking that question was all she needed to know she couldn't go on like this. She couldn't afford to fall into Max's bed or his arms again.

Out of facts, but fully armed, Sloan hoped the more she recited the spell, the stronger she would make it. So, staring into the darkness of her room, she started her whispered chant again.

An it harm none...

CHAPTER 17

Happy. Max woke up truly happy for the first time in a long time.

With a deep sigh, he inhaled the scents swirling around him —Sloan and sex and whatever the heat between them had smelled like. He smiled and leaned over to gather her close. Finally, he had Sloan in his arms.

Only, he didn't. She wasn't beside him in bed. His hands groped the empty covers and his eyes flew open wide. Towels were still scattered haphazardly across the floor. Surely, she was just in the bathroom. Her suit top was missing off the corner table, but there must be a simple explanation, she likely had it with her. He told himself this several times, as he perked his ears for a sign of life coming from beyond the bedroom door.

But none came.

Sloan didn't emerge.

Max waited, the tendrils of something he didn't want to name snaking up his back. He ignored the coincidences. That it was a work trip. That he had to get up and get to a meeting. That Sloan was staying in the hotel room next to him. Except that she had stayed in his room. He had fallen asleep, naked, with her in his arms.

Hadn't he?

Two dark gold strands of her hair crossed the pillow next to him. *Proof.* He wasn't insane, she had been here. Her head had been on the pillow next to his. But where was she now? Had she woken up too early and gone out for coffee? Maybe she just went back to her room to change? She hadn't wanted to wake him, so she'd snuck out quietly...There were a thousand reasons for her not to be here now, that she didn't leave a note, or wake him to tell him she'd be right back. Surely, she would show up and give him just one good reason.

After an hour passed, he shut off the alarm and convinced himself to get ready for the job they had to do that day. He was less and less able to believe that she was coming back. Pulling the shower curtain aside revealed only his shorts, wet and cold and lonely in the bottom of the tub. That's what finally convinced him that there was only one explanation for her disappearance, and he didn't like it at all.

Max turned on the water, hot drops streaking across his head and down his cheeks. She was gone. Again. Sloan had gotten up and left him in the middle of the night. No word of explanation, no whispered apologies. He wondered if she hadn't voiced her regrets or if she simply didn't have them. Every passing minute dimmed the tiny spot of hope that remained and buried it deeper. Sloan wasn't coming back.

He'd fallen so hard for her within the first few seconds of them meeting. She'd been warm and willing in his arms last night. More than warm and willing, she'd been wanton, free, and giving. This was Sloan, who was carrying his child.

He huffed out his breath and wondered what the hell he was doing. Yes, he'd fallen hard and fast. Something inside him had clicked. He wouldn't have said he believed in love at first sight. He believed other people believed it. He believed some people met and stayed together from that moment on, but he'd chalked that up to luck.

Max paused for moment. What had really happened? He'd seen her and he'd liked the looks of her. Maybe it hadn't been love at first sight. It certainly hadn't been for her. She wouldn't have been able to walk out on him like she did if she felt half of what he did. So the big question was: Was he wrong?

He swore. And swore again. He had been here before, and he had hated it the first time. The first time, fear knotted his gut. The sweet wash of knowing that Sloan was *his* fell away leaving only a deep hole. Just like last time. This wasn't any better. This was maybe even worse.

Because at least last time he had felt sorry for her. Last time, she didn't remember any of it. She had been frightened and vulnerable. She'd been drugged and cast on. She'd likely had almost no idea what she was doing. But this time was different. Or he'd thought it was. This time she had come willingly. She had been talking about their baby, and kissing him back. She had placed his hand over their child and shared that with him. She had given herself to him. And he'd looked for problems. He'd been with her, she hadn't been drinking anything. So she wasn't drugged. He'd surreptitiously cast a small *reveal* on her while she slept on the plane, but she was clean. She'd had no spells on her. She was just Sloan, as herself. But in the end, it made no difference at all.

This time Sloan had *chosen* to leave him, picked up her things and snuck out in the middle of the night. Some part of her made a decision to get up and walk away. Some *rational* part. That made the knife twist and dig deeper.

Drying himself with the towel they had shared, and looking for a way to keep breathing, Max pulled the garment bag out of the closet and pulled the shirt over one damp arm then the other. He slipped into pressed pants, buckled his belt, then knotted his tie. His usual half-Windsor. Over, under, around, and through. All the mundane things, standard in his morning routine, strained him today.

He had to remind himself to breathe. For full minutes at a time, he forgot, until he almost passed out and reminded himself. *In. Out. In.*

Now, his job was to convince himself just how silly the whole thing was. What? He saw her and he just knew? That was ridiculous. He just knew that he wanted to marry her? *Let's be honest here, you barely even know her.* Sure, it would be convenient to marry a woman who was having his child, but clearly the whole thing bothered her. Did he really even want to spend *the rest of his life* with her?

The problem was that the answer was *yes*. An unequivocal *yes*. He *had* known from the moment he saw her. He didn't know how, and 'how' didn't matter, he just did. He wanted to marry her, baby or no baby. He was in love with her. Truly, madly, sadly, in love.

He told himself he was in love with an imaginary woman. He'd had sex with a real one, but the one he'd given his heart to seemed to not exist. So his dream woman had a name—Sloan—and a face—hers—but was just that. A dream. The problem was, his self spoke back to him. It told him that she did exist. That the woman he knew *was* Sloan. The real Sloan. And Max realized that when she'd been here last night, she had been the dream. There had been no moment when he thought, "That was off." She hadn't been bitchy and he'd brushed it off. She'd simply been what he'd known all along.

He would have to find some way to change her mind. Sloan was a practical woman, and she loved their baby already, that much was clear. If he couldn't make her fall in love with him—and last night had been a good kick in the pants telling him that was exactly the case—then he would just have to convince her that *he* was the best thing for her and the baby. That's all.

And he would have to cast a few spells to see what was going on. Casting *on* Sloan was a no-no. His Grandma Summerland would come back and haunt him. But casting *around* Sloan? He thought he could get away with that. He still didn't travel with a good wiccan altar and herb kit, so it would have to wait until they were home. At least he had something to stuff into the hole in his heart and feel as if he were sane for a little bit.

Armed with his new agenda and a deep breath, he turned the knob and left the room.

CHAPTER 18

S loan was shocked at Max's completely unaffected mood. It was as if last night hadn't even happened. She'd planned on sitting him down and talking later, but he was so...blank that she wasn't sure he wouldn't ask her what she was talking about.

Madrid had drawn out for the remaining two days with them acting like co-workers and that was all. Well, she might have acted like a lovesick puppy, looking sidelong at him when he wasn't paying attention and curling up with her pillow at night, wishing it was him. But Max made no move to acknowledge anything that had happened, and Sloan did her best to play along.

Max was not a man who acted as if they'd peeled each other's clothes and come apart in each other's arms. He didn't once ask why she'd gotten up and left in the middle of the night. Probably he was glad that she had. From his lack of response, she wondered if he was relieved—happy even—that she'd turned down his offer of marriage earlier. He would know that he had offered, and to feel he had done the right thing, and he also got to be free.

She couldn't reconcile non-reactive Max with the man who

insisted he wanted to be a real father to the baby. Sloan wanted to scream at the injustice of it all. It wasn't fair for her baby to get Max when she didn't. It also wasn't right to be jealous of her own baby. She was being a bad mother and she wasn't even a mother yet.

"He says he wants to have the baby half the time, not just every other weekend." She spoke into her cell phone, curled into her couch as though it might protect her from a lifetime of wanting a man she couldn't really have. "I'm afraid he's going to demand joint custody."

Lisette sighed from a thousand miles away. "I don't know what to tell you. On the one hand you should be glad that your baby's going to have a good, willing father. Too many kids don't have that. Still, there's never a good solution when the two parents can't communicate."

Those words hit home. Hard. She needed to do a better job communicating with Max. Even if he wasn't communicating with her. "You're very lucky, Lisette, I hope you know that."

"I do know. And thank you for saying so, but right now we have your problems to solve. Mine can wait until next week."

Lisette always made her smile. Lisette always made her envious, too. She didn't like that fact, but if Sloan was serving up honesty, then envy was definitely on the menu. Her best friend had a husband who loved her, and two beautiful kids. Along with the house, the minivan, and all the trappings. Between Lisette and Rae and Sloan's jealousy of both of them, the more she thought about it, the more Sloan disliked herself.

She changed to a safer topic. "Did you get sick with worry before your ultrasound?"

"Oh, god yes! I was petrified the baby was going to have three arms, or a hole somewhere. Or worse..."

Sloan laughed through her relief. "I had actually wondered about the three arms myself. I think I've managed to come up with a hundred far-fetched scenarios." She didn't mention the fact that she'd tried her pendulum and it had gone all over the place. Though she told Lisette a little of what she could do, they didn't really talk about it. Lisette would likely brush off her worry, saying it was just an old wives' tale. So Sloan pushed that thought aside and turned somber again. "I try not to get scared, but what if something *is* wrong..."

"Then you'll get through it." Lisette's voice was soothing, even across the miles. "You're strong. Stronger than you give yourself credit for and stronger than you probably even know."

But that just made the tears fall. She didn't *want* to be strong. She wanted to be *supported*. Sloan tried to hide it in her voice. "But you have a husband, and you know that you can have more kids.... This may be my only chance."

"Oh honey, don't cry."

So much for hiding it. The tears became a full-on sob.

Lisette again came to the rescue, cutting through her—probably hormonal—tear fest. "And then next month when you're all big and round with your baby, you can console me the same way..."

Sloan grabbed the bait. "The same way? You aren't?!"

"I am!"

It was all a jumble. "When are you due?"

"End of September."

Sloan counted. That was only six weeks past her own due date. "How come you didn't tell me before?"

"I didn't know until two weeks ago. I just thought I was eating too much and getting fat. Then I thought maybe it was cancer, because I was so tired."

"I remember. I thought you were just tired of hearing me whine."

The laughter came down the line. Sloan missed this so much. She missed having Lisette face to face. But deep down she knew she'd needed to leave, needed to find a new life for herself and start over. Boy, had she done it with a bang. Now she was going to have a baby, and she needed to be making better decisions about her life.

"Oh honey, you weren't whining. You were legitimately upset. I don't know how I would have handled what you have." Lisette didn't have to go down the whole list. Joe and her cousin. Craig and his STD. Her high-school steady had lost his virginity with some girl from their crowd, *while* he and Sloan had been dating, or so she thought. Come to think of it, she'd had bad taste in men since kindergarten. She had caught Jason Winslow kissing Stephanie Kramer behind the monkey bars in fourth grade, the day after their ice-cream date when she had realized that she was *in love* because he had given her that stupid little jelly bracelet. And now this.

"I think he just wants to build a family, Lis, but I can't be part of that. I need someone who loves me for me. I've decided I'll just become an old maid." Again with the sniffles. Sloan began to wonder if she could dehydrate herself from all her crying jags.

"Oh, Sloan. You won't. Whoever the right man is, he's out there. I know it. He'll love you just as you are. And he'll love your kid."

CHAPTER 19

S loan told herself she was okay, that she was waiting for this magical knight who would love her and her kid to show up. Not that she really expected it anytime soon, but she clung to the idea Lisette had planted, soothing herself with it when loneliness or fear reared an ugly head. She quickly got rounder and let a few buttons out on her maternity skirt. She ate nothing but ham sandwiches for three days straight, and told herself it was okay, because she was pregnant.

She had a nice sit-down with Mr. Bernstein in which she told him she was pregnant, though by then she thought it was pretty obvious. His lack of surprise made her wonder, but he was genial—if not ecstatic—about her new circumstances.

It took a few times of bumping into Max in the hallway and around the office to admit some things to herself. First, she wouldn't recognize her magical knight even if he did show up. She was too swamped in her own feelings for Max. Two, If Max could be her knight that would be okay. Except for the problem that she wouldn't believe it. And given the fact that she only fell for the wrong guys, she was convinced of the logical conclusion:

that the right guy might come along, but she wouldn't fall in love with him even if he was right in front of her. Even if she no longer had feelings for Max. No matter what she did, she was destined to miss the right one and find all the wrong ones.

Speaking of right in front of her, the wrong guy was headed straight to her door. She'd made it four days since returning from Madrid without speaking to him. So much for making it to five.

Max leaned in her doorway, his crossed arms showing off his broad shoulders and making her stupid stomach flip. "Hey, Sloan. I was hoping you'd join me for lunch."

"I don't know." She did have a ham sandwich stashed in her drawer. Not that a wheat-bread sandwich was her reason for waffling, but she tried to convince herself it was.

"I packed a picnic. You know: short walk, long lunch, a few ants.... Please?"

Good lord, Max Summerland asking her *please*. That was going to do her in one of these days.

She opened her mouth to turn him down, but Max beat her at getting words out. "I wanted to keep up on the goings on with the baby."

Well, shit. He had an absolute right to that. She had to play nice or the whole thing could go to hell. Then, she reminded herself he was a deal-closer and she was his holy grail deal to close. At least this time it was only for lunch. He was coming after her using the baby and her hunger as bait. Though Sloan saw exactly what he was doing, she caved. She was such a sucker.

"Okay, five minutes?" She wanted to be mad at herself but he said he had food. The baby needed food!

Four minutes later, she was sorting the last files into 'done' and 'to do' when he showed up again, this time with an actual wicker basket in the crook of his arm. She sighed a swear word.

If the others in the office hadn't already started putting two and two and two together and getting "baby," then this was a huge neon flashing sign. This looked just like a real date. The very thought made her heart flutter, but her head wondered what explanation she could offer her co-workers if they asked. *No, no, it's not a date, we're just going out to discuss my baby, who is also his baby.* Yeah, that was worse.

She wanted to cast a spell so no one would see them walking out together with her belly and his picnic basket. She wanted to cast a spell so they forgot about rumors that she'd woken in his bed in Chicago. But *forget* spells were nasty little things. Delilah said they always seemed reasonable, and they always left a trail of destruction in their path. Sloan trusted Delilah.

Sloan and Rae's mother had been run out of their old Italian village after using her skills to find a missing person. Though that kind of skill ran rampant through the family, Sloan's mother had said it was only her and left town, rather than have her whole family be banished from the farm and the only home they'd known. They'd called her a witch. And here Sloan was, becoming one. But the spells she'd contemplated might deserve the treatment her mother had gotten.

She pushed the thought aside and followed Max out her office door and down the hallway. It seemed everyone watched them go by as they practically paraded out. They even ran into an abnormally high number of people from other departments on the way down, just to be sure that the whole company knew.

When they at last made it a good three blocks away, they settled on a spot in the soft sun on a block of deep green grass at the small park. Max set the basket aside and pulled out a huge piece of sheet plastic.

Classy. Okay, so she was being sarcastic, but she had expected a little better effort from Max than a plastic picnic mat. Then he pulled a beautiful woven blanket out and laid it over the plastic. "I just didn't want the blanket to get wet, you know, if the grass was damp or something."

Sloan mentally kicked herself and was glad that she'd held her tongue.

Reaching for her hand, Max helped her lower her increasingly awkward frame and get comfortable on the blanket, before sitting himself down. This he did with his knees touching hers, near enough that she would be able to feel his heat and just detect the scent of him. He stayed far enough away to not invade her personal space. Just enough that she couldn't accuse him of any indecency. Still, they must look like a couple to everyone who passed by, and her swollen belly only confirming that idea.

He overwhelmed her whether he meant to or not, and there was nothing she could do about the jolt that went through her every time they touched. Just a simple gesture, his hand brushing the back of hers by accident, or to get her attention, and she must have flushed. How could she not, with what she'd been thinking? When his fingertips slid along the palm of her hand, it had taken her right back to that night in Madrid, in the pool. And on his bed.

She'd seen next to nothing of Spain or the city of Madrid. Between the work and her infatuation with Max, she'd barely looked up. Sloan remembered the airport, where he carried her bags. They had driven around a lot getting from place to place, but she didn't remember the views they passed, just a standard limo interior and Max's thigh pressed next to hers, sending shivers up her whole body. It was better when she avoided him entirely. But right now, he was talking to her, giving her a fresh new blush.

"I made sandwiches." He pulled a few fat, lush-looking hoagies out, stacking them next to the picnic basket. "Boarshead ham and turkey, one chicken." He pointed as he spoke. "Rye, and that's a Hawaiian seven grain."

He must have seen her eyebrows go up. "Hey, I make a mean picnic and I can cook, too."

She smiled, although it was a little forced. He was closing the deal, always closing. She wished for a second that things could be different. That he *was* the right guy. That if she leaned a little forward, his hand would come around her neck and he would pull her close and kiss her deeply. Later he would hand feed her the grapes he was pulling from the depths of the basket. In her imagination, a shining gold band circled her left ring finger.

But her finger was bare. And he was offering her bottled water, served without a kiss. She accepted. The sandwich was heavenly. He had beaten her ham on whole wheat twelve ways to Sunday. For a short time while they ate, the sunlight filtered through the leaves and an easy silence settled around them.

When Max did finally speak, she got the distinct impression that he had purposely waited until her mouth was full before he started. "Listen, I don't know what happened in Madrid."

She swallowed, struggling to speak. Although to say what, she wasn't sure. He didn't know what happened? Did he need to repeat seventh grade sex ed classes?

But he held his hand up. "I'm not sure I want to know."

Sloan just nodded, not sure she wanted to tell him either. "If you decide that you do, I'll tell you."

"I'll keep that in mind."

Was she disappointed that he didn't want to know? If she had to judge by the weight in her chest, she was. Since he brought it up but clearly didn't want to talk about it, she didn't know what to say, so she took another bite, and let Max continue. "I just want us to start over. We have a baby coming. And as much as you might like to get rid of me, I'm not going anywhere. I always wanted a family of my own."

She nodded, but again he didn't let her speak. Dismissing the past and turning the topic more to the present, he changed direction on her. "When is your ultrasound appointment? You said I could come."

Why had she said that? Wiggling like a fish on a hook, she blurted out the words that popped into her head. "Maybe you could watch a video of it later."

His face fell. He looked like a boy whose puppy she had just kicked. Still, he sucked it up, even if he visibly bit back what he wanted to say. When he did speak his words were conciliatory. "If you'd be more comfortable that way, I'll deal."

No. He wouldn't. She felt like a terrible person just for suggesting he not come. All evidence said Dylan Atterson was entirely at fault for all this. While Max might not have been drugged, he'd been a victim of a bad circumstance, too. Even though she wanted to say he should have worn a condom if he really didn't want to be in this situation, she couldn't do it. She was glad to be having this baby! And she probably had the word 'sucker' tattooed across her heart in a beautiful flowing cursive. If she ever had a chest x-ray they'd see it. "No, it's okay, you can come. I said you could."

Though he shook his head, his voice accepted. "Only if you're sure."

Holding back the sigh with all she was worth, she assured him, "I am."

It *was* his baby, too. She wouldn't be pregnant without him. He had every right to be there. God, that puppy dog look lit his face up. Yup, s.u.c.k.e.r.

"When is it?"

"Next Tuesday, ten a.m. One fifty medical plaza at UCLA. Suite 300."

"You remember the day and time and address?" He pulled his day planner out and input the appointment.

She heard the giggle escape her throat. That was the problem with Max: as uptight as she was around him, he always made her laugh and smile. "Are you kidding? I am so excited I'm going to blow a gasket. I don't think I've been this excited since my seventh birthday and my pink huffy bike."

He laughed, too, causing her a brief pang of anger at herself for telling him 'no' the first time. He shouldn't have had to wear her down to come with her. He didn't seem to notice any of the thoughts in her head though. "You're right. I think I'm gonna bust. What do you want, boy or girl?"

Shrugging, she looked skyward. "Happy and healthy, otherwise I don't care."

"If you could chose?"

"I don't know. I think I'd relate better to a girl, but I think boys don't have as many issues." She stopped herself. Wow, one turkey sandwich and she was blabbering stereotypes about boys and girls.

But he didn't press. "I have visions of teaching my son how to play ball, but then again you always hear about Daddy's girls. I mean you can teach any kid how to throw a ball, and any kid can tell me they'd rather wear princess dresses than do a sport. So I guess I don't know either." His smile was warm and sweet and sucking her in. She didn't need that. His voice was almost conspiratorial, "I guess we'll take what we get."

We? When had they become a *we*? *Probably when you made a baby together*, Sloan told herself.

"I can pick you up and drive us in, if you'd like."

She had visions of him at her doorstep. She didn't need that, either. Or the fact that a ride in would mean a ride home at the end of the day. "I want to get some work in that morning before I go."

"I can drive from the office."

With a low sigh, she gave in to that one, too. As usual, he had neatly cornered her. "Okay."

How many more concessions was she going to make? And if she kept backing down, how was she going to keep the wall around her heart?

Suddenly she was incredibly grateful that she and Rae had found their cousin Luke. She was even more grateful that Luke was married to a bona fide witch. Sloan was never going to be able to resist Max and his onslaught on her own. She was going to need some magic.

CHAPTER 20

Max was torn. The picnic in the park had been a fantastic first date. He wasn't even certain if she'd known it was supposed to be romantic. And it wasn't like any other date he'd ever been on, what with his date being four months along with his baby, but it had been wonderful.

Under the tree on the picnic blanket, Sloan had laughed. She'd smiled real smiles at him. He knew some of the things he was asking were things she didn't want to give up easily, but he'd pushed—just a little—and she'd caved. Surely, she would have held her ground more firmly if she really hadn't wanted him there. He looked at her face and wished he could pull out a dowsing L-rod and ask the universe to double check her answers. He'd saved that for later. He'd back out of the appointment if any of his spells or readings said she really didn't want him along.

Later that night, in his apartment, he'd finally pulled out the dowsing rods and checked all her answers. Though he'd held his breath the whole time, ultimately he'd been pleased that she wasn't lying. That part was good. It was the things he saw when he wasn't looking that bothered him.

His Grandma Summerland had taught him to look with 'the side of his eye,' as she called it. His peripheral vision saw things the conscious brain missed. In the park, when he'd leaned over to get the sandwiches, he'd caught a glimpse of something. Naturally, it escaped him when he looked directly at her and he chalked it up as a dust mote.

But when he'd fallowed her pointing finger to a bird in the tree above them, he'd seen it again. So while they ate, he stayed quiet and was grateful when she did, too. If she thought anything of him looking away and admiring the scenery, she didn't say anything. What he was doing was looking at her, with the side of his eye, like his grandmother had taught him.

It was definitely there.

Smoky tendrils of grey and white, curling around Sloan as though they owned her. Somehow, she'd gotten another spell on her.

It had taken him a while to wrap his head around it. It was a legitimate question: Who got spells cast on them? It could happen. Maybe she'd run into a witch and they cast on her for whatever reason. The first time he'd seen it, she'd been cast on at the hotel bar. Dylan Atterson had hit her with GHB and a *forget* and *desire* spell combined.

But Max had removed it.

He'd double checked. That spell was gone long before he and Sloan even pulled their shirts off. Also, that one had a black glint. It had been a nasty little fucker, intended to hurt or use the victim.

As he watched this one, the grey and white pieces snaked and moved around her. Max had hardly been able to look at Sloan, let alone speak. So he'd eaten his sandwich and tried to figure out what she might have gotten herself into.

The best he could figure was that Atterson had cast on her again. Sloan said she'd written him a letter. It was probably full of legal threats that may or may not have carried any weight. Hitting her back with another spell would earn that ass his revenge and someone like Sloan would likely never even know she'd been spelled, let alone tie it back to that little weasel.

Normal people didn't think in terms of spells and casting. When things were wrong, they didn't fog their mirrors and look for tendrils in the air around them. They didn't grab a pendulum and ask if they'd been cast on. But whatever this one was, it was strong enough for him to get a glimpse of it while they were in the park.

Though he'd had a great time, he'd spent most of the meal and the rest of the afternoon worried. Atterson was the only one Max could think of who would do it. There were witches everywhere, not in high numbers certainly, and few who'd been raised in the craft like him, so it didn't have to be that piece of shit Dylan Atterson. Still, that was his first, best bet.

While Max wanted to sit down and remove the spell, the best he could do would be a general *removal*. It would be better if he knew what he was removing specifically. But first he had another more tangible message.

At home, he logged into the company information and pulled up his old files. He had a contact number for everyone who'd attended the Chicago meeting. Pulling up his cell phone, Max hoped that Atterson had maintained the same cell number. The work line would likely be dead or would lead to the new Jeff Landers guy.

It rang and rang. *Shit!* Atterson wouldn't answer if he recognized Max's number and he likely also wouldn't if the number showed up as "unknown." Max hung up and called back. He waited five rings, then hung up and called back again. The little asshat would know it was important. Just as Max was trying to decide what kind of threat would work best on voicemail, the line clicked.

"Who is this?" The voice was gruff and irritated. And though he'd only heard it for a short while several months ago, Max recognized it. *Bingo.*

"This is Max Summerland from Bernstein." He let the idea that it was a business call hang for a second, then he slashed that to the ground. "I know what you did to Sloan Ellis. I have evidence and I can prosecute you."

"Look, I—"

Max knew that Sloan had already threatened him, but she hadn't understood she'd been cast on. Max was going to add another layer.

"Shut up. I know Sloan wrote to you and I know she decided not to prosecute. But if you do anything to her again, you'll wish she had thrown you in jail. What I can do to you will be a thousand times worse."

"Look man. She said she was single. It's not my fault you had a crush on your co-worker..." the tone was mealy and condescending, that of a man who was used to getting away with certain things. Of course he was, he was using magic and probably no one suspected him, but Max was putting an end to it.

"That's not what this is about. Let's discuss the fact that you put GHB in her drink."

"That shit breaks down. I don't know what her proof is, but you can't trace it..." There was an air of superiority and Max felt his blood boil at the almost-admission of guilt. He wanted to reach through the phone line and strangle the little fucker. But he couldn't, so he played a better card.

"That may be true, but you didn't count on running into someone who can spot the spell you placed on her, did you?"

Silence held for a minute. Anyone who hadn't put a spell on Sloan would have started in about Max being off his rocker. That Atterson waited him out was practically a confession. *Son of a bitch!*

Max waited until Atterson spoke. "Look, I—"

Then he cut the little bastard off. "I also know that you cast another spell on her since you got fired—"

"I didn't! I swear. I mean I bought that crap off the internet!"

Max didn't believe him. Or if the asshat had bought it off the internet he clearly hadn't quit doing it. "I don't care how you got it. I can see it. I took the first one off her. I'm taking this one off her, too. If another one shows up—and I don't care from where—you're going down."

He paused for effect. "If you tell anyone about this conversation, I'll deny it. And then I'll make your life a living hell, and no one will believe you. I can and will turn your world upside down in the worst way possible. We need to be crystal clear about this. Do. You. Understand. Me?"

"Yes." The answer was only the one syllable. It sounded as though the words were gulped, which made Max happy. Finally.

"I'm watching Sloan. I'm watching you. If you come near her in any way shape or form again, you'll regret it." As he said it, he realized it was possible that Dylan Atterson had been recording the conversation. With no further words, Max hung up.

Shit.

His only consolation was that he could probably make the man lose the recording. There were spells to make tech go awry. Maybe he just needed to add that to his to-do list tonight. After what the other man had done to Sloan—and what he'd probably intended to do that night had Max not intervened—he found he had no compunction with making Dylan Atterson's phone suddenly crap out on him.

Max looked around his apartment. It was six-thirty. He'd called as soon as he'd walked in the door. If he hightailed it, he could pick up what he needed before everything closed.

Still in his business suit, he turned and headed right out the door. He cast small spells along the way to turn the lights green and clear the traffic. With a snap of his fingers he cast one last spell to open up a parking spot in front of the store. Two minutes until seven, he pushed the door open, relieved that he'd made it.

The place was hopping, and it looked like they wouldn't close for a little bit. Letting his tension out, he picked up a basket and started gathering what he was missing. In just a moment, a voice came to him, "Let me know if you need help."

Max looked up. "Oh, hey Tristan. I'm just refilling what I've run out of."

"Looks kind of specific..." Tristan eyed the basket. Though Max had his Grandma Summerland teaching him, Tristan had been raised in a family of witches and was not only incredibly powerful, he also made Max feel comfortable here at Blessed Be. Max wondered if Tristan had cast a spell so no one from work would ever recognize who was coming or going. No one wanted to explain to their co-workers why they might have been seen entering a magic shop.

"I have a general spell removal to do..." he told Tristan, because while he'd managed to threaten Atterson pretty well, he'd forgotten to ask what exactly had been cast on Sloan. Though if the little dirtbag had gotten it off the internet, then even he may not know. Max wasn't going to call back. "And I also need a *scrambler* spell."

Tristan eyed him, but the two guys went way back. Max had no problem explaining what Dylan had done and, once he did, Tristan had no problem hooking him up with the best *scrambler* spell they could create.

CHAPTER 21

All her atoms were bouncing around at superspeed. Sloan could feel it, and it was driving her crazy. In case that didn't make her feel weird enough, she was afraid the adrenaline in her system was going to hurt the baby. Even Max hadn't been able to hold her in a conversation on the short drive from the office to the doctor's.

Everything was nuts. She'd cast a *relaxation* spell on herself a handful of days before, but it seemed to have disappeared. And that *resist*—the one that was supposed to keep her from falling for Max?—it was turning out to be pure crap. She'd called Yasmin and asked if her powers failed her during pregnancy, too. But *nooooo*. Not Yasmin. She felt stronger than ever. Sloan wanted to believe it was because Yasmin had been at this much longer than she had.

Despite *seeing* things from her very early childhood, Sloan's scrying and spellwork had come about only recently. Despite being naturally skilled, she was still a relative newbie. Yasmin seemed to think that could easily get thrown off track by pregnancy, but it didn't make Sloan feel any better. Come to think of it, her skills had been messed up when she was trying to do something as simple as tell if her baby was a boy or a girl. Midwives with no witchcraft skills had successfully been doing that one for hundreds of years. Just not Sloan. At least today she was relying on technology, not witchcraft. Maybe the tech would work okay, she told herself.

She looked down to see Max's hand snake across the gearshift, maybe in search of hers. But she had clasped her own hands tightly together in her lap to ward him off. Or maybe so she didn't have to find out that her hand wasn't what his hand had been searching for.

They parked in the garage, about a billion miles away from the elevator, and for a disturbingly high fee, too. The med center should have tram service for that kind of money. She almost quipped that to Max, but didn't think that she was capable of pulling off 'funny' when she was so nervous.

The elevator took way too long to get down to P-2 as well, further ratcheting her nerves. She was a mess and wondered if she'd burst into tears before they made it to the offices. She was ready to run the stairs, but since they were still fifteen minutes early, and Max said he didn't think she should be running stairs anyway, they waited the short eternity.

At least once the elevators came she was actually making some kind of progress. When they arrived at the offices the clean, starched-white feel helped put her at ease. Still, today was unusual. Sloan wouldn't be seeing Dr. Lee today. Instead, they were going straight to the office ultrasound specialist. Signing in with a nervous hand, Sloan sipped at her ever-present water bottle and slipped away to pee in the cup for the nurse. Then she went back to fidget in the waiting room next to Max, who was desperately trying to look absorbed in a *Your Baby Now* magazine.

Her heart pounded out the minutes. Max's foot tapped to a tune that only he could hear. And she chewed off most of her lipstick trying to stay calm.

Finally, she heard her name. Max squeezed her hand, and Sloan was startled to find that she didn't even realize they'd been holding hands. Looking down, she saw his fingers were laced through hers and they didn't let go as Sloan followed the nurse back through the hallways to a cramped room with a patient bed and a wheeled ultrasound machine.

She watched as the nurse placed the chart in the pocket just outside the door and then typed a few things into the machine before wishing them luck and closing them in. The small space left Sloan and Max alone with barely enough room to stand. She extricated her fingers from his and hopped up on the bed just to get a little more distance between them, maybe enough that she could draw air.

"You don't have to get undressed or anything, do you?"

Sloan decided not to take it as an insult, and she shook her head. "I just have to pull up my shirt. I'm ready."

His fingers twitched beneath the white cuffs of his shirt, and he nervously pushed his sleeves back, revealing strong muscled arms that moved in time to his growing anxiety. "Are they going to leave us waiting in here for forever, too?"

With a nervous giggle she nodded. "Probably, they're very busy. And when they aren't...well, they never aren't."

At last, the nurse, Suzie, returned with a man in a lab coat. Sloan wanted to protest that he was way too young to be doing this, but she kept her mouth closed and simply shook his hand. His name was Dr. McNeill and he spoke directly to Sloan, but tilted his head indicating Max. "Is this the Dad?"

She nodded and was hard pressed to ignore the bright smile that spread across Max's face.

"Well then, let's get down to business." Dr. McNeill plopped onto the round stool and began firing off questions without pulling his nose out of her chart. Due date? How was she feeling? Had all her tests come back all right? Sloan rattled her answers off, wondering why he didn't already know if her tests had come back all right and growing more jittery by the second. So far, she'd managed to stave off her nerves by thinking that it was all in the future and there was nothing she could do. But now it was here.

"Do you want to find out the sex?"

Sloan turned to Max, who was, of course, looking expectantly at her. "I do. Do you?"

He nodded almost too vigorously.

"All right, lay back and pull up your shirt." Dr. McNeill finally looked at her before tucking a wide paper drape at her waistband while he talked. "Now I can't guarantee that I can find out the sex, and I can't promise that I'll be right, but I'm pretty good at this."

Sloan nodded and bit her tongue to keep from yelling at the poor man, *Get on with it already!* Taking a deep breath, hoping for some zen she wasn't finding, her hand snaked up to where Max was standing near her head. His fingers were already there, waiting for hers. Clutching at him for dear life, Sloan hoped she might be able to steal something—some shred of sanity—from him. They clung together like war survivors, scared and excited, waiting to see what came.

In a few seconds, the doctor had squirted a warm blue goo across her exposed belly and smeared it around with the paddle. He did this almost absently, while his left hand rolled a paddleball installed on the machine then typed in a few key words on the keypad. At last he smiled at her. "Ready?"

She nodded again instead of shouting, *I've been ready!* and lay quietly while he held the paddle still against her belly and flipped a switch. A jumble of black and white popped up in an arc on the screen. Sloan stared at it, literally trying to make heads or tails of what she was seeing, until Dr. McNeill frowned.

Her heart sped up and Max's fingers tightened on hers. *Oh*

God. Why was he frowning. That could not be good. Her heart sank and she braced for the worst.

"Have you had an ultrasound before?"

"No." It was soft and sad even to her own ears, and she took a deep breath and steeled herself for the bad news, even as she heard Max doing the same.

"Well," He turned the computer screen to face her and Max. *Oh God Oh God Oh God.* She almost didn't want to look. But he pointed at the screen, traced a white shape, and watched their faces with a small smile. "There's your baby."

Her whole body trembled. "Is everything okay?"

The doctor nodded and she could feel her breath let out and her fingers let loose a little of their death grip in Max's hand. The doctor finally saw her tension and gave a wider smile, probably just to make her feel better. It worked. He pointed again as he spoke. "You can see arms here. Here's the head. I don't see a prehensile tail..." He must have thought he was funny. Sloan only nodded in all seriousness. No tail. That was good.

The doctor realized his idea of a joke had fallen flat with them and he headed back into neutral territory. "So far so good. I have measurements and such to take. Give me a minute."

This time it was Max that frowned, but that didn't worry her anywhere near as much. He pointed to the black and white jumble that she was already in love with. "Then what's that?"

Her heart lurched, even as Dr. McNeill smiled. "Good catch, Dad. That's your *other* baby."

"*What?*" She almost jumped up off the table.

"Congratulations, you're having twins."

"But..." She couldn't form sentences. Her head fell back against the paper-covered pillow with a crunchy thud. Her brain scrambled again. "But I heard the heartbeat. There was only one..."

"Must've missed it. Honestly, that happens all the time." He turned his attention back to the screen as though it was no big deal. "The baby on the left," he pointed to the screen then her belly, "looks like maybe a boy, and I can't tell at all about the one on the right."

He continued moving the paddle around, and rolling his little mouse and clicking on things.

She couldn't breathe. She must be breathing, she was alive. *Twins? Dear God.*

When Sloan finally raised her eyes to look at Max, his gaze locked on hers, and his smile was so wide and genuine that he looked like a candidate for the mental ward. When he glanced away Sloan followed his gaze, looking at what he saw, down to their intertwined fingers. For the first time that morning, she could feel the heat of him there. It seeped along her arm and into her heart, cementing him there. The very crazy thought ran through her head that she would be all right. Because she had Max.

CHAPTER 22

Max trailed slightly behind Sloan as she paced a short path around her office, his hands gripping the open book. He read out loud from two steps back. *"Twins, while not twice as much work as one baby, are considerably more work than a singleton.* Blah, blah, blah. *If you are single you should consider having your help live with you. Being a single parent is difficult, but it is multiplied when there is more than one baby. The stress of single parenthood can be overwhelming, but it's even more so when there are two babies to care for. Use any support system you have."*

"Max..." She was sure there was a warning tone in her voice, but he just as surely didn't seem to hear it.

"That's me. And you. We're each other's support systems."

"Max..." Sloan tried again. She had work to do. It had only been three days. She had stuff to catch up on, because both of them had walked around in a daze all through the remainder of Tuesday. She hadn't been much better use on Wednesday either. She wasn't sure she was being of any value today either, but she had to try, and she couldn't do that with Max following her around her office and telling her how much she needed him. She turned to face him down and shake him off.

He smiled. "I'm buying a house."

"What?" Okay, he had her attention now.

"I'm buying us a house."

"*Us?*" Oh gosh, he really was crazy. And she hated that it sounded so very good to her ears.

"I'd like your input." He stood still now, the book folded closed by his side, his finger marking the place as though he might start reading to her again at any minute. At least he was looking right at her, paying attention to only her. She hoped that meant he understood the enormity of what he'd just said, and maybe that he wasn't clinically insane.

"Max, *we* aren't buying a house." *As much as I would like that,* but she didn't say that part out loud.

"I know, *I* am." He looked her square in the eye. He was flat out serious. *Oh, God.*

She finally pulled her ace out. She'd been holding back, wanting to know but not wanting to either. So she sucked in a breath and pushed out the words, then braced for the answer. "What does your girlfriend think of all this?"

"What girlfriend?" He tilted his head, frowned, and generally looked at her like she wasn't speaking English.

She let out a deep sigh. She deserved this, she supposed, for thinking she held some trump card over him. "The dark haired one." She felt herself digging the hole deeper, but kept her eyes trained on him.

"We broke up last May." Then, in the blink of an eye, he flashed into boiling anger. "For God's sakes, Sloan! You thought I had a *girlfriend* all this time? What do you think I am?" He only paused a second. But it was long enough to see the pain she caused. Without intending to, she had seriously wounded him. His jaw clenched, and his eyes flared again. "Don't answer that. I really don't want to hear it."

Realizing that she might as well have just called him a heartless bastard, she felt the shame creep up her neck, and she started to apologize, but he was having none of it. He shut down that part of the conversation and steered things where he wanted them. But he spoke through clenched jaws that told her he hadn't let it go. "I think the kids should have a yard to play in."

That burned, but she tried not to let it show. Of course, she wanted her kids to have a yard, but despite working on her budget, she didn't have that kind of money. She hadn't been with Bernstein as long as he had. She had spent her first working years in a small town without a foreign acquisitions department. And she bet he didn't have a wedding to pay off either. "That's fine. Get a house."

She was bitter. She could either have a baby or a house. The house she'd been able to afford would have fit one person. It might have fit two. But three? She didn't think so. And the cost of diapers and baby food and clothes that now *two* babies would outgrow faster than she could buy new ones was more than she could risk. She could maybe do it if she budgeted down to the penny. But likely no one would give her the home loan with two more mouths on the way. God forbid, either kid got an ear infection, she'd have to make a decision about food, the house, or the baby.

Max broke through her irritated thoughts. "Should it be near your condo?"

She laced her arm through his and led him toward the door. "Whatever you want."

Then she pushed him through and closed the door behind him. Turning away, she tried to hide her face, hoping no one would see through the glass that she was fighting tears.

Luckily—or horribly—Max didn't come back.

CHAPTER 23

His head popped up. Max new she was coming. He had some weird Sloan-sense. Sure enough, he could see she was emerging from her office, but that alone didn't mean anything. It was the fact that she was heading straight for him that made his heart race, his breathing falter.

It shouldn't. He should shake this, whatever it was. His feelings for her were entirely misplaced. She clearly didn't want to be with him. She didn't want him involved with her baby —*their* baby—even going so far as to offer him a chance to sign away all his rights. When he'd been dense about it, she blindsided him with that insulting question about his girlfriend. God only knew what she really thought of him that she *hadn't* said.

He had to catch a clue. She was throwing them at his head at high speed. He'd just been ducking and thinking he'd win her over. He was an idiot. She didn't want him. And he should stop wanting her.

The problem was, no matter what she did or what his head knew, his heart *did* beat faster, his breathing *did* falter. And, in spite of the times she had turned away, he was still crazy in love with her. That one lightning strike the very first time they had touched had been the end of his old life. In his heart, he had no option but to wait and see where the road led. He couldn't push. He wasn't going to stalk her when she'd made her point clear. But through no fault of either of theirs, they had two children on the way. He was going to be involved there. If he couldn't be a good husband or lover, he was at least going to be a good dad to his twins.

That always made him take a deep breath. Two babies. Even if *she* didn't want *him* around, he sure didn't want to go it alone with two tiny babies for a whole weekend. That thought made him shudder. What if he did something wrong? He'd never been around babies and figured he was pretty much guaranteed to do *something* wrong. The thought petrified him.

He didn't get to dwell on any of it for long, because there she was, in his doorway, nervously fidgeting with the knob, and finally entering and shutting the door behind her.

Wanting to tell her how beautiful she looked, Max bit his tongue. He was sure she didn't want to hear it. She never wanted to hear it. She just tried to avoid him. Her normal aversion made him very curious why she was seeking him out now. The last time she came in here and closed the door behind herself, she'd laid her pregnancy on him like a mic drop. So what was she up to now?

Her words gushed out. "About what I said about you having a girlfriend..." But after the initial burst, she trailed off.

Max crossed his arms and didn't get up from his seat, still pissed about that. If she wanted to bring it back up, so would he. "Oh, forget about it. I'm sure I seem like the kind of guy who sleeps around behind his girlfriend's back all the time." That came out ruder than he meant, but he had been thoroughly insulted.

"I'm sorry."

"Don't worry about it." He turned the chair around and

began working at the small table behind him. If that was all she had come for, then she could leave.

"I do worry about it."

"Don't." He tried again to wave her away without looking at her.

But she didn't give up easily enough. "I wanted to apologize for a lot of things."

At last, he turned slowly around and looked at her. This he wanted to hear. Maybe things were looking up. However, in the past, his hopes hadn't served him all that well where Sloan was concerned. So he reined them in and waited.

"I'm sorry about that remark about you having a girlfriend and I'm sorry for way back in Chicago…that I suspected you."

Leaning his seat back, he crossed his arms again and tried to be nonchalant and forgiving. "Not a big deal. I would have suspected me, too, given the circumstances."

Her eyes searched until she held his gaze, and he didn't like it. It felt like she could see into his soul. Clearly, she couldn't, because she would have answered what she saw. She would have said either *I love you, too* or *I don't love you, so please stop trying*. But she said neither of those things. She just looked sad. "I let everyone think that maybe you had. There were rumors. I never heard them directly, but I know they were around. I got Sheila to cough up a few things she had heard. And I should have told them that it wasn't you."

"You could tell them now."

"I already did. A while ago. I gave serious information to a few key gossips. They spread the word. No one thinks it was you anymore. They haven't for a while." She managed the smile only on one side of her mouth.

He dug, hoping for more. "What exactly did you tell them?"

"That you didn't do anything to me, that it was all Dylan. That I was confused. I went back and told them that this is your baby, and that it's twins." As he watched her hand fluttered and strayed, calming only when it found a home against her belly. She still hadn't moved from where she leaned against the closed door. "It ought to feed the rumor mill for a while."

"Wow." *That was a lot to digest.* She would keep the gossip flowing for months with all that. He pushed his fingers through his hair. *It must be standing on end. Now what?*

"Oh God, I'm sorry, I didn't think." She was nearly in tears. *Tears?*

"Didn't think what?"

"That you might not want everyone to know that these are your babies. Maybe you wanted to see someone else or..."

Now he was around his desk, his hands on her shoulders and he wanted nothing more than to hold her against him and let her cry about whatever she was crying about. "There isn't anyone else. And I'm proud that this is mine." His hand, too, found a place flat against her stomach. "I'm glad we're having twins. You didn't say anything wrong."

She leaned toward him just the slightest amount and that was all he needed. His breath fell out of him and she was there, in his arms, where she should be. He held her close enough to feel her everywhere, wondering at the weight that always seemed to find a welcome home inside him whenever she was touching him. It was only part of how he knew she was *the one.* He felt grounded—fully *here*—when she was with him. He wondered if she felt even part of that, or if it was all in him. "I don't know how to convince you that I'm a nice guy—"

"I know you are." She sniffled.

"Because you don't seem that convinced."

Sloan blinked back a few stray tears and smiled up at him. "It took me a while to figure it out. I never pick the right guy."

"I know. You told me." His fingers found her temples, and his thumbs pushed back her hair revealing luminous, wet, blue eyes that pulled him under every time.

"Huh?... Oh, Chicago."

"Yeah." He tucked her head under his chin and inhaled the mixed scents of her shampoo and perfume. Her arms circled around his waist, and he hadn't felt anything so good in too long. "I'm not Joe, or Craig, or even Jason Winsomething from third grade."

"Fourth." She looked up. "You know about Jason?"

"Yeah." He wanted to tell her about the house. That she could have her own room if that's what it took to get her there. Max wanted her to know about his plans, for the house, for a swing set, and ultimately a beautiful blond wife named Sloan. But that was probably too much to dump on her right now. So he toned it down. "I just want you to know that I won't run away or run around. I'll take care of you."

She buried her face deeper into his chest and hugged him closer. It was the opening he needed. "I'll marry you."

Well, that was like throwing ice on it.

She jerked back. She glared daggers, furious for some reason he couldn't fathom. "I can't marry you, Max. Stop asking."

She shoved at his chest, catching him off guard and making him stumble back a few feet. With that, she was out the door, gone before it had even stopped its swing. And the front of him, where she had been pressed just moments before, had gone cold.

CHAPTER 24

"He asked me again!" She wailed into the phone. Tears rolled down her cheeks. "Rae, I can't handle this."

"Can I suggest something stupid?" her sister asked and even understood when Sloan sniffled a nodded answer. "Maybe you marry him. Maybe he's the one." When Rae said it, it sounded so very real. Reasonable even. Like Sloan could just waltz back in and say *I made a mistake when I said no, I meant to say yes.*

But that would never work. "Why would I do that? I don't want to spend the rest of my life in love with a man who doesn't love me back." Sloan sniffed. "He doesn't really want *me*, he just doesn't want his kids going back and forth between two parents. If I'm being honest, that just makes me want him more."

"It will all be okay. You can handle it." It seemed that she had heard that line a lot from Rae and Lisette lately. Usually, it made her feel better, but not today.

She railed against fate some more. "I finally fall for a nice guy, a good man, and he doesn't love me."

"I think my plan is actually really solid." Sloan could hear her sister's fingers snap over the telephone line and she wondered if her sister was casting a small spell. But Rae's voice came

131

through again before Sloan could ask. "Marry him, seduce him. End of story, happily ever after."

"Seduce him?" That was the worst idea she had ever heard. She wailed. "I'm huge!"

"He slept with you in Madrid. I know you. He'll fall in love with you. He will. I have no doubt you can pull this off."

"I was only *very* large then. You wouldn't believe how fast I am getting bigger."

"I can only imagine, but the thing is: *he keeps asking*. If it was only about convenience, he would have come up with another idea by now. You said he's smart. But he keeps asking the same thing. You can do this. Marry him."

"And when he realizes that he can't fake it anymore and cheats on me?"

"Then you divorce him, take half of everything he has, and sleep with every hot hunk who comes along on the weekends he has the kids."

Sloan couldn't help it. She bust out laughing, loud guffaws that cracked her up, until—without warning—they turned into tears. Just the thought of Max telling her he'd never loved her and he'd just done it for the kids was heart breaking. She tried to brush it off. "I'm just more emotional now."

"No joke. I am a basket case, and I only went off my birth control." She heard Rae talking to Sam in the background. "No, I'm fine, really." Then back into the receiver "See? I'm crying for you right now, and Sam's all worried."

Of course. Because Rae had someone who loved her, someone there to worry about her. No wonder she thought Sloan should just marry Max, to Rae it had become unfathomable not to have that kind of love.

But Sloan knew what it was to not have it, to know that you'd never had it. And to know that, given your track record, you probably never would. "You don't know what I did, Rae."

"Uh-oh. What was that?"

She told her sister how she'd scryed about her perfect man. She wasn't proud that she'd sunk low enough to look him up, but she had to confess. "He's in Chicago, Rae! And I'm stuck here in L.A. tied to Max for the next twenty years. Oh, and I have such a huge crush on Max that I probably wouldn't know my dream man if he walked up to me and told me he was the one. So how am I supposed to find him?"

Sloan was practically wailing again by the time she finished her confession-slash-diatribe. But it was the silence on the other end of the line that made her stop. "Rae? What are you thinking but not telling me?"

"Sloan, you found Max in Chicago..."

"No, Rae, he's from *here*."

"And you know as well as I do that 'Chicago' doesn't mean he lives there or grew up there or any of that stuff. It just means that 'Chicago' is related to finding this guy."

This time it was Sloan that was quiet. She hadn't thought of that. Still, as she turned it over, tried to remember what *exactly* she'd scryed for, she tried to make it make sense. Could Max be the guy?

"I don't think so, Rae. I work with Max all the time. Why wouldn't I have found him here?"

"You did. You fell for him before that trip."

"Then the scrying wouldn't have said 'Chicago.'" Her heart was tripping along, missing beats. Could Rae be right? Could it be Max?

"You did get together with him in Chicago. Maybe the answer you got was about the event, not where he was from. It sure changed everything." Rae's voice sighed through the information, washing over Sloan as a possibility she hadn't considered. "I can't say this idea is right, but I'm not convinced I'm wrong either, Sloan. Maybe you just found him in the most unconventional way. You certainly do have feelings for him. I can feel them from here!"

There was a smile in Rae's voice on that last line and it put a matching one on Sloan's. They had the same smile. She decided to consider it. She could scry again, get out her pendulum, ask more specific questions. But she wasn't ready to deal with the answers tonight. As happened so often since she got pregnant, she was quickly overtaken with exhaustion. "I've got to go, Rae. I am sooo tired. I feel like lead!" She tried to sound casual. Like she wasn't on the verge of way too many tears.

They said goodbyes without Sloan giving herself away. At least she hoped she'd pulled it off. Sometimes Rae let her get away with it, sometimes her sister called bullshit. Luckily, Rae just told her goodnight and to sleep well.

Trudging up to her bedroom, fighting to keep the tears from falling yet again, she did what she had decided she wouldn't do. She admitted to herself that she was in love with Max Summerland. Whole heart. Whole soul.

She was so screwed.

Sloan lay down on the bed and stopped fighting it. Fat tears fell until the pillow was soaked. There was nothing she could do about any of it.

CHAPTER 25

F lats. Sloan needed to remember to wear flats. "Thank you again, guys!"

Sheila and Vanessa had picked up the tab for lunch. Sloan wouldn't have ordered so much if she'd known they were going to do that, but she had to admit she'd finally been worth the cost. For the first time in her life she could eat the entire portion of seafood pasta at Gino's. However, she could no longer walk the four blocks back to the office without her feet hurting. She'd tried not to show it, smiling and chatting all the way back, not wanting her coworkers to feel guilty about her own error.

At last she made it the final few steps into her office, flipped the blinds closed, and kicked off the so-painful shoes. As she put her feet up, she could almost feel the sound of relief slip out of her. *Ahhhhhhh.* But she quickly groaned and dropped her feet back under the desk as the unwelcome knock came at the door. *Argh!* "Come in."

"Hey." Max's head peeked around the door, then he let himself in, casually closing it behind him. "I saw you going by.

You know, you're five months pregnant, you shouldn't be wearing heels."

"Trust me, I am painfully aware of that fact now. It was a miscalculation that I won't be making again."

"Are you okay?"

When she shrugged and offered only, "I will be," he lowered himself onto the stool she had been using to support her feet.

"Here." Reaching down, he pulled both her feet up into his lap, despite her protests. Gently tugging her wheeled office chair closer, he moved her until he held each foot in one hand, and began rubbing his thumbs along the arches of her feet.

"Ohhhhh. Oh. My. God." Her head tilted back and it felt so good it almost hurt.

He smiled. A slow, soft, sweet, too-sexy-for-my-own-good, Max Summerland smile. Sloan melted right there in her swivel chair. In her head she let out a series of moans...followed by curse words. She just couldn't afford to get in this deep with this guy.

"Feel better?" He kept rubbing, and Sloan nodded as she kept her eyes closed. Strong fingers found her ankle bones and pushed against the soles of her tired feet.

"Mmmmmm hmmmmm." Rae's words sprang to her mind. *Marry him.* She could have this all the time. *Right?*

But she couldn't. In hear head, she could see the look on his face—the one she imagined—when he's realized that she's truly in love with him, and he thinks she's pitiful. Or worse, because there would come a time when Max would come home smelling like another woman. Sloan could almost feel her heart break, just from her imaginary scene when Max would tell her he's fallen in love. With someone else. When he never loved her. No thank you.

"I found a few houses."

That snapped her eyes open, but she tried to sound unconcerned. "Oh?"

"I'd like you to come look at them with me." His thumbs kept an even pace back and forth across her feet, dulling her thoughts.

"Max," She couldn't really lean forward for that 'piece-of-my-mind' look she was going for, not with her feet in his hands. She wasn't about to give that up, she could feel it everywhere, and it felt *sooooo* good. "It's your house, Max. You don't need me to see it."

"I'd like you to." His hands snaked around her ankles again, applying gentle pressure and releasing the stress there. "Your children will live there. You should be concerned."

"I am concerned." Sloan took a deep breath and even the tone of the words conveyed almost the exact opposite of concern. How was she supposed to think when her crush was rubbing her feet? And even if she wasn't being lulled by a massage, how was she to explain that she'd like nothing better than to go house hunting with him? For a house for *their* family. But not like this. They weren't a family. Not the way she wanted. "But it's *your* house. It really isn't any of my business."

With a nod he again moved his hands a little higher on her calves. "I see. So if you don't come, then you are almost saying that I don't have any right to see your place, or to be concerned about it."

She didn't even have to nod in response to that one. He couldn't come to her place. Not unless he was moving into the other side of her queen-sized bed. She had a wiccan altar and spell set in her second bedroom closet. She was going to have to move that and make that room into a nursery. *Shit.* There was a literal Pandora's box in there. She wanted to keep the lid on her thoughts and her newfound religion. But her voice had been run off by the feel of his fingers on her feet. She quickly shut the lid on that.

His tone was pleading. "Please. Come see the houses. I assume that your place is fine. I'm not going to weasel my way in. But I've got to move somewhere larger and I could really use some help."

Did he really think she would fall for that old *help-me* line? Wow. She must have seemed dumb.

He smiled again. "Sloan, really. I have no idea how to go about buying a house to raise kids in—"

"Just get what you would have liked to have as a kid." What kind of brush-off did the guy require? It was like she was diabetic and he kept offering her candy and cake. If he kept at this, she'd tumble one day, head over heels, then where would she be?

But Max completely missed the cues on her inner turmoil. He just laughed and kept feeling up her feet. Something about way he touched her skin made her feel like he was enjoying it as much as she was. She had to be making that up though. It was horribly difficult to pay attention to the words coming out of his mouth. "I don't think anyone is selling houses with hidden passages and firepoles that slide from the bedroom right down to breakfast."

Sloan couldn't help but giggle and join him. "Your firepole went to breakfast? Mine went to the pool in the basement. I had a trampoline in my dream living room, too."

"Even if they sold that house, I couldn't afford it. Please come. If you don't, my mother will insist on flying out and helping." He was practically begging.

Her chest expanded in a deep sigh. "All right." Damn him, he had hooked her. But what could she do? Sloan stood no chance against him normally, and here she'd been wooed by humor and a good foot massage.

And that was that. She knew when she'd been closed. He told her that he already had an appointment with his real estate agent on Sunday, and that he could move it if she needed. Of course, he already had an appointment. He'd probably already told the agent to expect her. Done deal. She couldn't back out now. So, she told him Sunday was fine, and assured him that she would wear flats.

It seemed, just like that, the foot massage was over, Max gently placed her feet back onto the floor, and before she could move out of the way, he leaned over and kissed her forehead. It felt far better than it should have. "I'm sure that you have work to do, so I'm heading back to my office."

All she could do was nod. Done deal.

But halfway out the door he stuck his head back in. "And I'll be right here at five thirty to walk you to your car."

What? "I don't need to be walked to my car. I'm fine, really." She turned back to the papers on her desk, trying to both end the conversation and mask the disappointment she felt.

"You're right, you don't. But I think you do need someone making sure you leave at five thirty, and that you don't hang around until seven or eight to finish up a few things."

"Uh!" She looked up, righteously offended.

"Yeah, I heard about last week!" He raised his eyebrows at her. "And you'll be leaving at five-thirty every day from here on out."

With that, she stood as fast as she could. "Let's get one thing straight here, Max."

His head snapped back, and he looked startled for the first time since she'd met him. She'd seen him surprised, shocked, and even angry or ecstatic, but this time her stern expression caught him off guard. This time it was Sloan who closed the deal. "You do not get to come in here and tell me when I'll be leaving. I'm a grown ass woman. I may not make the choices you like, but I don't tell you when you will and won't leave the premises. And you'll do well to remember you don't tell me the same."

He looked at her for a minute. Then he managed to get the first part of his sentence out. "But that's my child you're carrying—"

"Yeah, it is. I'm carrying your DNA to personhood. I'm doing it. Inside my body. Do not get any stupid ideas that you have any jurisdiction over what I say, do, or eat. I've got enough shit on my plate without a man trying to tell me what to do." She didn't move, just stared him down.

When he didn't say anything. Sloan continued. "Maybe just think about how stupid it would sound if I'd said that to you."

This time, he nodded slowly. "I was just worried that—"

She held her hand up. "You're allowed to be worried. You're allowed to say so. You're allowed to make suggestions. But you just issued an order like I was your child or something. Don't do it again."

Holy shit. Where had that backbone come from? She hadn't even cast a spell on herself for it. And that was probably a good thing, since none of her spells had seemed to work of late. But maybe Lisette had been right and Sloan was stronger than she thought.

"I'm sorry." His words were soft and they sounded sincere. All traces of Max-the-closer had fled. "I shouldn't have said it that way. I'm worried you'll work yourself into the ground or be here alone late and get hurt."

She wanted to tell him she accepted his apology—she apparently had a new backbone, but she wasn't a bitch—but that last line changed it. "Max...you're worried about the babies."

"No!" Now he was angry. Could they not have a civil foot-rub and conversation? Apparently not. "You're right that I shouldn't tell you what to do, but don't you put words in my mouth. I'm. Worried. About. *You.*"

They stared at each other for a minute, and this time she did manage a nod in acknowledgment. Then she sighed. "Look, I'm not dumb—"

"I didn't say you were."

"—I had no idea I'd be walking anywhere other than around the office today. I'll be better prepared tomorrow. And you're right about working late, too. I don't know a way around it. I get twelve weeks of maternity leave, so I have twelve extra weeks of work to do before I have twins on some random future date that I can't quite prepare for." She'd worked herself up as she was talking.

Max looked at her with squinted eyes. "I don't think that's how leave works. I think you're supposed to actually leave the work to someone else."

Sloan tipped her head. "Is that what you're going to do?"

"I'm taking leave when the babies come. They'll need both of us!"

"How much?" she challenged him. How had this turned? She'd been getting a foot massage for Pete's sake, and now she was standing on her tired feet and arguing. And not getting her work done.

Sloan watched as a dull red color climbed up his neck. "Four weeks."

"Uh-huh. Just four?" He didn't respond and she pushed on. "And you're going to leave every project behind in someone else's hands for those four weeks? Not call in? Not work from home?"

Her raised eyebrows led to a sheepish look from Max before his eyes darted to the suddenly interesting design in the carpet. Sloan kept going. Holy Backbone, Batman! "And Bernstein hasn't asked you if you plan to continue working once the babies are born? Because he asked me. I told him I'd be back, but he made sure to talk me through what to do if I change my mind. Did you get that talk?"

Max shook his head still studying the carpet. Then his shoulders slumped. "Did he really do that?"

"Of course, he did, Max! I've got you on one side, telling me when I can and can't leave the office, and my boss on the other, suggesting that I'm not committed to my job because I got myself knocked up on a work trip! You're just as much going to be a parent as me, right? But you're not getting this shit." She barely took a breath. "We work for the same company, so it's not that there are different policies in place. So yes, Max, I was going to do it anyway because—just like you—I don't like other people coming in and dicking up my work. But also because it's been made very clear to me that my boss thinks I don't know my own mind just because I'm pregnant."

She stared at him, hating the feeling of tears in the corners of her eyes. Fucking hormones. She would not let the drops fall, so she stared hard at Max.

This time, he looked her right in the face. "You're right. I was totally out of line. Please understand my intentions were good." He paused and she watched as he visibly tried to rearrange his words. "I'd like to stay and walk you to your car each night. It's not about you, it's about the fact that you're not as stable on your feet as you were and if you get stuck and don't eat, it's worse than if it was just you in there." He waved his hand up and down her body clearly having run out of his good words. "You tell me when you're ready, and if it's okay with you, I'll walk you down to your car. Okay?"

She nodded once. "I'm not dumb. You're right, too. I'm working too hard. My body is making people and I'm trying to do almost twice my normal workload here and be psychic about what to get ready for when I'm out. I don't know that it's humanly possible." Though she did add another scrying to her to-do list. Maybe she could psychically figure out what to prep!

"Okay," Max agreed, nodded, and turned away. Before she could say anything else, he was gone, and her mouth was just open with nothing to do. That was Max, say his peace and leave. At least she'd gotten him to—hopefully—stop bossing her around. His subtle bribery was hard enough to deal with, she wouldn't put up with being treated like a child. And how had he heard that she was staying late anyway?

Fine. The stupid thing was, that he was right. She did need to stop staying late. If he wanted to stay and walk her to her car that was all well and good. The rest of it she'd just have to deal with. Despite his claims of taking paternity leave, Max didn't have to worry about it. His boss didn't suspect he'd quit because he was having a kid. Max wasn't the one at greater risk of needing a C-section because they were having twins. Which, of course, meant a longer recovery time. And he probably wouldn't cry when he had to come back to work.

She sighed again. Her prattling, even if it was only in her head, wasn't making the unread emails in her inbox any shorter. And she needed to get cracking if she was going to make it out of here any time close to five-thirty. With sheer force of will Sloan clicked on the new folder and opened it. *I must not think about Max or cute babies that have Max's eyes. I must not...*

CHAPTER 26

Sloan pushed the door to her sedan open and began the task of getting herself out of it. It was Sunday and she hadn't come up with a good excuse not to come, so here she was, meeting Max and the agent at the real estate office. All to go hunting for a house that she wouldn't live in.

But her children would live there at least every other weekend, and probably more the way Max kept talking. He was right, she should see the place, she should have some input. He should also get a tour of her condo. Just not now, not until she had her wiccan stuff out of the way. Surely he'd find out about her later, but it should be years down the road when he knew he could trust her. There was already way too much on her plate; she couldn't deal with that conversation anytime in the near future. She admitted that sometime soon they would need to sit down and have a discussion about everything else though. They needed to know how they each planned on raising these children, whose religion the twins would follow, and how they could be shuffled back and forth between never married parents with minimal emotional damage. Sloan didn't even want to begin to deal with all that, so she told herself to take baby steps, one at a time, and the first baby step was helping Max find a house.

Locking the car, she turned to find Max and the agent emerging from the office. Her lungs locked and her ribcage took a hit. The woman was a willowy brunette with that hair that just fell in perfect waves. She had a gorgeous face, and she wasn't at all pregnant or fat. And, of course, she was wearing the best heels and laughing that stupid, flirty laugh that Sloan had been guilty of herself a few times. And she looked a lot like the girlfriend Max was with when they'd met. Was she his type?

That pinching in her chest...it was jealousy and she knew it. So Sloan bit her lip and stood, leaning against her car, waiting to be noticed. She tried desperately—desperately—not to look down at her own weekend maternity outfit. They didn't see her, and she failed. She looked down to be reminded she was in white canvas sneakers and maternity jeans—that had to be about three steps below mom-jeans, right? Her red and white striped shirt didn't begin to hide the bulge of her belly, in fact it accentuated it. She'd chosen the shirt for just that reason, thinking it was cute. She was cute, rolly polly round and adorable. It would have felt great if Miss Slim and Perfect Realtor hadn't shown up.

Sloan sighed. She should just climb back in and drive away. She could go home and eat a carton of ice cream while simultaneously pretending this had never happened. If Max even remembered she was supposed to be here, she'd claim she didn't feel well or something. She was turning away and deciding which flavor of ice cream to buy, when she heard him.

"Hey, are you okay?"

Busted. Sloan stepped back out of the car with something in her grasp. "Yeah, I was just getting my—" She looked at her open hand. "—lotion."

The beautiful agent held her manicured hand out, "I'm Laura. You must be Sloan. I've heard so much about you."

I've heard that line before. It had turned out to be from one of the women that Joe had been sleeping with. Sloan forced an imperfect smile. "Nice to meet you."

With that, Ann apparently considered her fully initiated into the world of homebuying. "Max and I have been looking at the numbers, and we've come up with a good list for today." She smiled that smile, that deal-closing smile. "And if you don't see anything you like we can get another list ready for next weekend. There will be new houses on the market by then I'm sure." She and Max spoke the same language, and Sloan hated her just a little bit more. "My car is over here."

Of course, it was a BMW. Laura the real estate agent probably wasn't paying off a failed wedding either.

"Sloan's in the back." Max held the door open even as he informed Laura of his seating choice. *Great, he was stuffing her out of the way. Why had he even invited her?* His voice overrode her thoughts, "It's safer there. Do you mind if I ride in the back with her?"

Then he looked stricken and leaned in close. "I'm sorry. Do you want to ride up front?"

"No. I'm fine." Her face heated. He *was* a nice guy. And, of course Laura didn't mind. Sloan just wanted to disappear, but that was an impossibility. She forced another smile and realized that she'd had two of those in two minutes. Not a good rate. Max held out her seatbelt, bragged about the twins, and showed Sloan the list of houses and stats, some complete with tiny xeroxed pictures.

Laura ran them through a drive-thru, buying them all drinks before heading off to see the first home on the list. Sloan didn't like it, the roof was too dark and the front lawn wrapped all the way around the corner lot letting almost all the yard be seen by people driving by on the street. Not that she would be having dinner on the patio to care. But the swing-set shouldn't be in full view, right?

She kept it to herself as they wandered through the split-level rambler. No two bedrooms were together. She would want that proximity, for the parent to be near the babies. Though she wanted them in her room to start, her plans were to have them in the nursery sometime around six months. Plans changed, but they couldn't in this house.

Max checked each and every room, trying out closets, looking for squeaks in the hardwood flooring. Finally, he turned to her, hands in his pockets. "So, what do you think?"

"It really matters what you think. I'm sure it's fine."

"You don't like it do you?"

"Not really." She shook her head just a little and, before she could say anything else, Laura was behind her.

"What don't you like?"

Oh no, what had she gotten herself into? Why had she expressed an opinion on a house she would never live in in the first place? "I'm sure it's not important... I—"

Laura smiled. "I don't care if you love this house or hate it like a Kardashian. I'm not the owner and they aren't here. I just want to help you find the right place."

As much as the agent was being nice, Sloan didn't really want to like her anyway and decided to go for broke. "But don't you have to sell us a house or you don't make any money?"

Laura smiled again, with no recognition of anything other than a sincere question. "I've found that the cutthroat agents make great money and have no friends at the end of the day. I do just fine taking good care of people. And I've had a number of people not buy, but they often refer me to people who do."

Well, what she said sounded good. So Sloan spoke again, wondering why Max wasn't the one doing the talking. Didn't he have questions? "Well, there's no way to put the babies' room next to the parent's."

"Good point, I hadn't thought of that." The first comment from Max.

She continued. "It's split level, there's nowhere to set up a spare changing table... you'll always have to carry a child up or down stairs to change them. And there are steps and a breezeway between the house and the garage, that will make things harder to get a baby into a car, let alone two." Then she decided it was time to shut up.

"It just didn't seem like the right place to me, but Sloan's right." Max's smile was infectious and it caught all the way up to his eyes. Sloan had to look away.

Laura pulled out her list, laying it on the counter in the empty kitchen, and chewed the end of her pen for a moment. "Okay, cross off 13486 Hutchence St. And on page two get rid of the first three."

"Oh, no!" Sloan protested. "I didn't mean to—"

"Hey, why show you houses that won't work for you?" Laura started leading them out to the garage.

Max walked right beside her, marking notes on his copy. "I liked the first one on the second page."

"Sure, we can see it if you still want. But the garage is the basement floor. You'll have to go up a full flight of steps every time you come in."

Max nodded. "Did I say I liked it? No, that was dumb." He looked at it again, "I guess it doesn't look like there's much flat yard for a swing set."

"No, there's not."

And they were off again. Of the next four houses, two got crossed off the list and two got left as maybes. Max and Laura kept their heads together for quite a bit of it, causing the little green monster inside Sloan to start gnawing at her periodically. Somehow in the midst of all that, Max managed to get himself invited along to her next doctor visit.

On the way to the last place he asked if he could pick her up for work the next morning.

Pick her up? "Oh, I can still drive myself."

"You've been going in early."

He knew about that? "So?"

"So, you aren't supposed to work extra hours. I'm volunteering to drive, so you can work in the car. You'll get your work done during the commute, but not have to put in the extra time. I'll pick you up and take you home."

"I—"

"Please, let me."

How could she argue? He made sense. Her commute was sometimes forty-five minutes. She could get in an extra hour and a half of work each day if she didn't have to do the driving herself. The man was a gold mine and he was harder and harder to resist.

She loved him and she hated him. He was a good dad, only trying to do what was best for his babies. Babies that he wasn't feeding or growing or doing anything for right now except watching over their mother. The problem was she didn't even want him to do that. Even though he was asking rather than demanding, it was still stifling to be watched over. She would lose her private time in the car. She would lose her radio show or audiobook. But that wasn't on him. She was just losing those things. Or she'd lost them when she got pregnant. Moms didn't get to listen to steamy romance audiobooks in the car. They didn't get to wake up when they wanted. They had to do what was best for their children. And the fact was, she was exhausted by the time she got home. Rae had taken pity and helped her clean the place last weekend, though in the end, Rae had done over three-quarters of it after making Sloan stop and put her feet up. Her big, puffy, feet. *Ugh.*

In the end, she consented. Max was right, and he was offering her a good solution to a serious problem. She bit back her affected sighs until they pulled up at the last house and everything else washed away.

With a creamy yellow color with sage trim, and a lush lawn

surrounded by a picket fence, it caught her attention right away. Maybe it was awful inside. Sloan kept repeating that idea to herself. It was the only way not to be bowled over and want to put her own offer on it. *Maybe it's awful*, she tried again.

Then she found herself inside. Leaving the others, she wandered from room to room. It was simply perfect. Long, deep closets hid behind sliding doors. Nice trim lined the floors and ceilings. The rooms were all in the proper order. Mostly, the house just evoked some weird knee-jerk reaction. This would be a *home*. She could see furniture in it—her furniture would look perfect. She wanted to cook in the kitchen and look out over two little kids playing in this backyard.

At that moment, she truly hated Joe. For the first time in a long time, she was seriously mad that she was still paying off that stupid wedding. Though she had a good job, she'd taken a cost of living hit by moving to L.A. She could have paid the bills faster if she'd stayed put. But Joe was there, with her cousin. Or his new girl. It pissed her off that she still had to pay most of the fees to the caterers, because they had already retained servers and bought the food. Had she caught him earlier, she might have gotten some of the deposits back. But no, Joe went out screwing the night before. No deposits returned that late. Sloan had a very expensive dress that hung in a bag in her mother's closet. No one wanted to buy an unused wedding dress from a girl who found her future husband cheating. That was just plain bad luck. Her credit card bills showed it, too.

She didn't hear Max come up behind her, and she jumped at the sound of his voice. "Do you like it?"

She couldn't just burst into tears and say *yes, but don't buy it, I want it.* Unfortunately, there was no way she could afford to buy it out from under him either, so Sloan shrugged. "It's nice. Good layout." And she turned away to... check out the laundry room or something, before her tears made an unwanted appearance.

She sucked it up for the rest of the tour, just barely

managing to keep it together. She could blame it on the spare hormones, right? Max dogged her every step of the way, making it that much harder to fight off her reaction to the place. Sunshine poured through the wide windows in the living room, making it feel warm and welcoming. It had French doors to the back patio, for goodness sake. What idiots had left this amazing house on the market?

After a good half hour testing out every door and cabinet Max was still noncommittal. So Laura smiled and asked if next Sunday afternoon would be good, same time?

Sloan couldn't take it. She wouldn't survive walking through the next house that she wouldn't own. So she pulled out her day-planner and, standing a few feet away, stared at her blank page labeled "Saturday and Sunday". She shook her head. "I can't, I'm booked the whole weekend. You two should just go ahead without me." She closed the book and smiled up at both of them, offering up yet another forced smile. She prayed for a quick trip back.

CHAPTER 27

They had been quiet most of the drive home—Max in his own world and Sloan on the outside looking in. That was pretty normal for them. She tried not to resent that her work was getting curtailed. She knew it was for the best, that her babies needed her off her feet as much as possible, but didn't they also need a mother who had a job? One who could put food on their table? So, like most days, she let him drive—which meant he often decided when they would go in, and when they would leave. Like most days, she set her thoughts to simmer and watched him while he seemed happily oblivious over there on the driver's side of the car.

But today, halfway to her place, he burst. "I bought a house."

"*You did?*" That was a shock, he hadn't said anything about it after that first day when she had bowed out.

"Yeah, this one just spoke to me that it was the right one. So, I made the down payment and I get to move in three weeks from today." He was beaming.

"Laura must have been a great help." Even as she said it, Sloan kicked herself for still dragging that ugly jealousy around with her. "You make it sound so easy."

"Well it was. I just signed thick stacks of all kinds of papers that say I can't sue anyone for anything ever. That it might burn down or blow up or flood and I'm responsible for all of it. There were five pages specifically dedicated to me stating that I understand I'm in an earthquake zone..." He shook his head at that one and then sighed deeply. "I get to do all the upgrades and repairs. Then I wrote an insanely huge check that represented way too much of my life's savings. So, yes, it was easy. And I have an ulcer now, I'm sure."

She started to laugh, even as he spoke again. "And I just now realized that I am insanely stupid. So stupid, in fact, that I didn't even see it until now."

"What?"

"I'm an idiot, because you're a contract lawyer and I was signing about three inches worth of contracts. There I was, selling my soul to the devil and not sure if I was getting a good deal for it. I should have called you."

"I would have been glad to help."

"Part of me wants to go get the papers and have you read over them, while I still might have a chance of backing out." He ran his fingers through his hair, and carefully took the next turn, as though jostling her might harm their babies.

"And the other part?"

"Doesn't want you to see what I signed like an idiot, when I didn't pay attention to all the little details." He shook his head a little. "I know I'm supposed to read things before I sign them, but I'd have missed the whole week of work just to get through them all. So at some point, I just started john Hancock-ing everything without even looking."

"I'm sure you did just fine. But I'll read them through if you want." She smiled, glad to help him for once. "When did you sign?"

"Last night."

"Wow." Just last night while she had been on the couch

reading a magazine, Max had been getting their children a better future. And apparently sweating buckets to do it, too.

"Of course, it was just last night." He smiled at her. "If I had done it any sooner, I would have told you before now. There just wasn't time this morning."

There hadn't been, she thought back on the mad rush they had, especially once she got hungry on the way in and Max pulled into a drive-thru to appease her.

But she didn't get to think more. He was looking at her while they were pulled up to the last stoplight before her place. "I was hoping we could have dinner tonight to celebrate. I wanted to take you out, but I think you're not supposed to be on your feet anymore today."

In the pit of her stomach, Sloan felt both excited that he wanted to share it with her and warm that he was paying attention. She *was* tired though, so it looked like the final consensus was *no dinner*. She tamped down the disappointment and topped it with a small smile.

"I still would love to have dinner to celebrate," he offered as he hit the gas and just made it through the light.

She hated her traitorous little heart for lifting. "You don't have to. I can read the contracts tonight." She didn't mean it to sound as guilt inducing as it came out.

But Max just laughed. "I *want* to have dinner to celebrate. If it will make you feel better I will also bring the house papers, too."

She had been bad, the way she had said it. So she gave him one more chance to back out. "I really am too tired to go out. It was a big day."

"No kidding, Bernstein sapped the energy from me at that meeting this afternoon, too." His hand snaked across the gearshift and his fingers found hers and toyed with them lightly, as he pulled up in front of her place. "I could go grab the contracts, and a few things, and come back and put dinner together while you read."

She chewed her lip. She didn't need time to think about it. She needed to be someone else. Someone who could stop and just enjoy the feeling of his fingers in hers. Someone who didn't have to worry about her kids' future, and their Dad.

"Would that be okay?" He prompted.

"Yes. It would be great." She managed to smile, looking directly in his eyes, unsure what it was she was seeing and still wishing it was something more. Then she put her hand behind her and released the door, turning and climbing out as best she could with her awkward shape.

Sloan waved him away, then climbed the stairs and unlocked her front door.

Why had she said yes? She had absolutely no issues about going over the house contracts he had signed, but she was only just now realizing that he intended to come back here for that dinner. *Here.* Her eyes scanned her living room from the open front door.

With a sigh, she swung the door closed behind her, and was glad that she was tired all the time. She hadn't been up and around enough to make too much of a mess out of Rae's cleaning job. All she needed to do was straighten a few magazines here and there, wipe down the kitchen, and clear the counter in the bathroom. She knew her cosmetics were all over the place.

Sloan almost groaned. She was already tired. Climbing the stairs had almost been too much. She looked down at her swollen belly. Gosh, had she really thought the words 'all she needed to do'? How stupid was that? Just straightening the living room was a major chore these days.

Still she took a moment to lean back against the door and slip out of her flats. First things first, get out of this suit. Maternity suits were nice for daytime, but nowhere near comfortable enough for evening lounging. So she got into fluid pants and a cotton maternity tee shirt and set to work.

Forty minutes later she was breathing heavier and had just finished the bathroom. The surfaces were wiped down and the underwear and shirt she had crawled out of this morning for her shower needed to be thrown in the wash. With them wadded in her hand, she headed for the bedroom, and decided that she had just enough energy and time left to pull up the covers and get her shoes out of the floor and onto the rack where they belonged.

Turned out she was right. Just as she had made the bed and laid back on the pillows, the doorbell rang. Sloan inhaled and pushed up to sitting, reminding herself that he was bringing dinner and these days any guest bringing dinner was welcome.

She greeted him in her bare feet, her pedicured toes peeking from beneath the long hem of the pants. Ooooops, she'd forgotten shoes, but it was too late now, and it was her house anyway. Not knowing what to do with herself, she just stood there while he looked her up and down, never letting her know if he'd found any flaws.

Surely he'd found some. He was used to seeing her in suits, with her hair done and, at least up until recently, heels. This was hardly the Sloan he would recognize. But his voice held none of the snobbery she'd braced herself for, "I'm so glad you changed. I did, too."

Finally, she snapped out of it and actually looked at him, seeming much more comfortable in his jeans and thin sweater. Unfortunately, it more served the purpose of making her *less* comfortable. The jeans hugged his butt, and the sweater clung, molding to him everywhere she wanted to touch. Emphasizing his shoulders and chest and abs. Yup, she *sure* wanted to read house contracts. She watched him pass by into the living room and had to remind herself of exactly that thought.

He had a grocery bag tucked in each arm, and refused her

help making his way straight back to the kitchen. The first thing he pulled from the bag was a stack of legal size xeroxes straining the black binder clip that fought to hold them. His muscles flexed holding the stack out to her.

"Wow, you weren't kidding. This really is about three inches thick."

He nodded. "I think Bernstein can buy international companies with less paperwork."

"We can." Her laughter bubbled up as she took the pages and turned back to the living room to start thumbing through. He did need these checked over. This could easily be a nightmare. No wonder he was talking about getting an ulcer. Even more important, she needed to get away from those tight jeans and the sinful thoughts of what she couldn't have.

Sloan started wading through the documents, her eyes scanning every word if not truly *reading* it. She knew what they were supposed to say and her brain was looking for deviations more than anything else. She kept searching, spotting a signature here, a notary seal there. She found a page marking the down payment he had placed on the house, and held back her gasp with a few rapid blinks. At least he couldn't hear her facial expression from the kitchen.

Except he was Max, so he was standing over her with her spatula in his hand at the exact moment after she saw that page. "Yeah, it hurt. Trust me, that took a while to save."

Still she managed to rein in her expressions. "What were you saving for?" Right after she asked it, she realized that she didn't want to know. Whatever it was, her pregnancy had surely stolen it from him.

Not letting her concern or her question get in his way, Max handed her a drink.

"What's this?"

"Mocktail!" He smiled as though that explained everything, and he stood and watched while she took a sip.

"Oh, that's good. Thank you." She waited a beat, but he still didn't answer. For some reason, she couldn't let it go. Sloan asked again, "What were you saving it for?"

"Trip to Spain."

"You could have gone a couple of times with that chunk."

He raised his eyebrows. "Remember the brunette?"

Sloan nodded but held her tongue, *all too well.*

"Well she wanted to go. She also wanted a BMW, and a house."

"I'm sorry. About Anne Marie."

He looked startled. "Why?"

Wasn't that obvious? But it seemed she'd be forced to say it. Pointing at her belly, "It seems we got in the way of your romance." She flinched even though she had tried so hard not to. It wasn't like she'd seduced him. Well... on second thought she didn't know that one for sure.

"I broke up with her long before Chicago. Don't worry yourself on that account." His head tilted as though he knew something she didn't, and Sloan wondered what that was. "She wasn't the right one for me."

"So you were just sitting on it until you thought of what you wanted?" She still felt that clenching in her heart. The one she had tried so hard to steel herself against. She and these babies had taken so much from him, and he hadn't complained. He'd even stepped up to the plate and was there for her. Forget *there for her*, he was *here*, right now. Making her dinner. She really didn't deserve this.

"Hey." Max sat next to her and put his arm around her shoulders. "I *did* find what I wanted to spend the money on. I'm so excited I can't see straight. And I'll take you over to the new house once I've got my stuff moved in."

"Okay."

But he had already hopped back up to tend the food in the kitchen, leaving her with the remaining inch of legal papers.

Her focus was flagging but she wanted to be useful. So she used a little focus spell she'd been doing at work a lot lately. With her finger in the condensation from her mocktail, she traced a small circle on the table top and mentally repeated *Clear mind, bright eyes, laser focus.* It took about three tries before she felt it.

With another sip of the very tasty mocktail, she turned her newly sharpened attention back to his contracts. So far, she'd seen no red flags, not in the papers anyway. It seemed there were red flags in her life, everywhere she looked. But there wasn't anything she could do about them. So, trying her hardest to ignore them, Sloan kept her attention on the stack of papers.

CHAPTER 28

Max hummed slightly to cover the small spell he was casting on the chicken. It was not cooking evenly. Normally, he was a passable chef, but tonight, that would not be good enough.

Two minutes later, he checked again, lifting the pieces and being sure the pan side of the chicken was a crispy brown before he served it onto the nice white china he found in the cabinets. Sloan didn't seem to have any plastic or colored plates, so he was grateful this didn't have gold edging or anything that would suggest it was her fine china. He hoped it would do, because he'd just maxed out his knowledge of dinnerware.

It turned out that chicken marsala wasn't going to be his greatest kitchen triumph, as it didn't look all that good. His spell said it would taste great, but mushrooms were swimming in the sauce and sliding off the chicken to pool on the sides of the plate. They wouldn't make a nice presentation, and he frowned for a moment trying to figure out a spell for making mushrooms stay on top of the chicken. Then he realized it would be decidedly weird if she pushed them off and they went right back up there. Then he would wind up telling all well before he was ready. Witchcraft was definitely a late in the game reveal. Sometime after you might mention that you were divorced and only maybe before something like you'd grown up in a cult. He consoled himself that it would taste heavenly.

Taking another sip from the mocktail he'd looked up online before coming over, he ran down a checklist. Salad from a kit and bottled dressing. Broccoli he'd steamed himself—at least he could do that. He was ready to get another round of mocktails for dinner. Her pregnancy was making him get creative. He couldn't just bring a bottle of wine.

Max had desperately wanted to take her out, but she'd looked so tired, like the day had simply taken the shine off her. Going somewhere else would have added stress rather than reducing it. He was not going to do that to her, as much as he'd wanted to sit and talk with her instead of being in here cooking while she was in the living room going over his papers. At least his credit report wasn't in there or copies of his bank statements. He felt very exposed, but also safer in her hands. Why he hadn't thought of her reading the documents before, he didn't know. He knew she could save him his terrible blunders.

"Well," She called from the living room, the sound of her voice indicating that she had gotten up and was coming his way, "It looks to be all on the up and up. Only thing is that I can't tell if you paid anywhere near market value on this place. And they have you sewed in tight on the price. So don't look it up. There's nothing you can do about it now unless you completely back out."

He smiled, warmed head to toe at her solid appraisal of the papers. He took the stack from her hand and slipped it back into the grocery bag, leaving her with only dinner to worry about. "The price was fine with me. I really liked this house. I would have paid all of what they asked. And dinner's ready."

Holding up the two plates he'd prepared, he watched her eyebrows rise. She licked her lips, just a tiny unconscious movement, but he wanted to rewind the scene and present the plates again and again, just to watch her tongue flick out like that.

Sloan pulled silverware from drawers and big thick paper napkins from a cabinet, before asking if he wanted a beer. He hadn't planned on drinking, especially since she couldn't. But that little flick of her tongue got him to thinking that he wouldn't be able to sit through this evening without it. He pushed one of the mocktails aside and took her up on her offer.

He was pretty sure she had no idea she was so sexy. Sloan seemed to think she was just pregnant and there was nothing more to her than that now. She still had that tight butt and lean legs. She still had those sloe blue eyes that slayed him from the first time he'd seen her. She was far more dangerous to him now that he knew what those eyes looked like when she was staring up, naked underneath him.

The new-to-him thing was that the belly was sexy, too. He'd seen plenty of pregnant women and none of them had turned him on before, but that belly was *his*. He felt a surge of testosterone just knowing that he had caused it, and that, no matter how much she thought otherwise, she was marked as *his* to every other male who passed her. Despite having hauled his ass into the new century, and despite truly believing the women in his office were ultimately just people like the men, there was something different about Sloan. And he could admit that he liked when other people thought of her as his. Max longed to tell her just what he was thinking.

That passing thought convinced him fully that a beer was exactly what he needed, because with him, beer made him tighter lipped. He would know that he'd been drinking and he wouldn't feel that he was formulating the right way to tell her, so he'd more likely keep his big fat mouth closed. He might succeed at not asking this woman who didn't want him to marry him.

So he set about the mundane tasks of putting out the food and holding her chair for her and worrying that she wouldn't like it. "Don't worry, it tastes better than it looks."

"Well, it smells fabulous." As she took the first bite, Sloan let out a small moan, a sound that made him not want to eat his own dinner, but just sit and watch her eat hers. Which he knew would be quite impolite.

Instead he made small talk, "Good?"

"Oh, it's great."

"You look more alert than late this afternoon." Aaack, foot in mouth. *You don't say that to any woman, let alone a pregnant one.*

Luckily, she didn't seem to acknowledge his blunder. "Oh, I am. Today sapped me, but reading contracts actually makes me feel lighter."

He had to question that one. He felt his expression change with his thoughts. *More beer.* He tipped it up as she answered his silent question.

"No, really. It does." And there wasn't a lull in the conversation until they had put the dishes away and he polished off his beer.

Oh, crap. But he had no sooner thought it than she pointed to his beer.

"You shouldn't drive for a while." Sloan wiped a towel across her hands, and didn't seem to blame him for that one. "Besides, I think I owe you a tour."

"You don't owe me anything. I—"

Her head cocked to one side. "Do you want the tour or not?"

"Yes, ma'am!" Taking the towel from her, he set it on the counter and motioned for her to lead the way out of the kitchen. This place screamed *Sloan*. He would have known it was hers whether she'd brought him here or not. Floral patterning on the sofa, matching stitched coasters that she must have done in some spare time somewhere. The TV must be in the cabinet across from the couch and stuffed chairs. It certainly wasn't looming big and black like his was. He wanted to see it all. To get ideas. Not that he would be able to pull off any of this without her help.

"Okay, you've seen the kitchen and dining *area*. My aspirations are to have a real dining *room* someday." He filed that away, not mentioning that the new house had one. He had no clue what to do with it, but Sloan would.

"That door leads out in front of the garages, although I have no clue why it exists. I just go down the inside flight of stairs and out the garage door when I want to get there."

He followed her cute backside through the living room, watching the stripes on the pants swing with the sway of her hips. He imagined other men looked at this when he was with her in public, and not trailing behind her. Deep in his soul, Max enjoyed being out where all the strangers assumed that they were married, or at least that they were together. He only wished she felt the same. Then he forced his mind back to the present. "Are all these stairs good for you?"

Pausing at the top, she turned. "Yup, it's great exercise and not taxing... This is my den. It's a mess now, and it usually is. I'm thinking I'll turn it into a nursery and put the computer downstairs." She propped her hip in the doorway and continued talking, lamenting the size.

He wanted to tell her that the new house had a room that would make a nice, big nursery. It could even have an office and would easily hold all four of them, *if* she would share a bedroom with him. But that was such a big 'if' that he held his tongue. He wasn't sure he could achieve it without casting spells on her, and he'd live his whole life alone before manipulating her that way.

As she turned away to head to the next stop on her small tour, Max slid his head to the side and hoped she didn't notice.

From the side of his eye, he didn't see the remnants of spells anymore. His breath eased out and he hoped she didn't see. He'd been worried about removing the spell remotely, which was even harder when he didn't know what it was. Luckily, Tristan at Blessed Be had set him up with a great one. It should keep her spell free for a while. Not that Atterson even could cast on her anymore. Max had not only scrambled his tech, he'd done a *binding* on the guy. He had to focus; Sloan was talking again.

"This is the upstairs bathroom. And this is why I rented this place." She pulled back the shower doors to reveal a deep, shiny oval tub. He cringed. He couldn't match that. Not at the new house or his current apartment. In fact, he hadn't thought of bathtubs at all except to note that he had to step over the side to use the shower.

"And that's my bedroom." She pointed to a closed door as she walked to it. "They'll sleep in there with me for a few months. That's why I haven't painted the nursery or anything yet."

She walked in and sat on the edge of the bed, her motions clearly showing she was still just a little worn down from her big day. That was probably another good reason that she hadn't painted the nursery yet. And he didn't want her breathing in those paint fumes either.

Max considered jumping in to volunteer, but knew she wouldn't appreciate the gesture, even if she understood that he wasn't trying to take over her life. Instead he turned to face her. "You're always telling Doctor Lee that you can feel the babies move. Could I feel them from the outside now?"

"Oh God, yes, they're little savages in there!" And with no hesitation she grabbed his hand and placed his palm firmly on her belly.

For a few long seconds he stood, silent, in front of her. But he didn't feel anything. Finally, he shrugged and gave up. "I'm not feeling anything."

Her smile was bright, almost ignoring his look of failure.

"Well you have to wait a few minutes sometimes. If you want you can sit down and wait."

So he did as he had been told and sat beside her, unsure what to do or say. As he did, he wished all this away. She didn't love him. If she loved him, then he wouldn't be this nervous, his blunders would be forgiven, he would already know how to feel the babies growing inside her.

She shook her head at him.

Yup, blunder number one, coming right up.

"You need to sit with your hand on my belly while you wait. Otherwise you might miss it."

"Oh," He started to reach across, and noticed that she had her hands behinds her on the bed. "Are you comfortable?"

With a wry smirk, she answered. "I don't think I remember comfortable. Everything is squinched up in there, and then it gets kicked at. But I'm okay."

The dark wood headboard called to him. He desperately wanted to feel his babies move, but not at Sloan's expense. So, he kicked off his shoes, and crawled up to fluff a few pillows, then asked her if that would be better.

With a nod she turned and crawled toward him and the head of the bed. It wasn't the slinky sexy crawl he'd seen once before, long ago. In fact, it was the result of that night. This was slower, more precise, more of a woman who was thinking of her future, not the present. And he had done that to her, but he couldn't find it in him to regret it.

Waiting patiently while she positioned herself, Max watched as she squirmed and settled, then squirmed and settled again. He wished he could think of something to make her more comfortable, but he couldn't, and he began regretting his testosterone-fueled joy at having done this to her. There wasn't room for her in her own body. He almost opened his mouth to apologize, then she took his hand and placed it softly on her belly, palm down. "There. Just give it a couple of minutes. I guarantee one or the other of them will roll or kick or something."

For a few seconds he was quiet, but then he put voice to the thoughts that had been passing through him while he waited to feel something under his hand. "I wanted to tell you that I'm sorry for any..." *any what? inconveniences?* "—troubles this has caused you."

"Don't be." She shook her head and her smile was faraway. "It hasn't been textbook, and there are... *issues*, I guess. But I wouldn't change it for the world."

He started to speak, but she kept going, and he let her, desperate to hear anything thing she might tell him.

"I thought I could never carry my own child. This might be the only shot I get at it. So I'm more than excited about having these twins. And I didn't get a chance to thank you—"

"You did." He assured her. *She was thanking him?* Her thanking him was the craziest thing he'd ever heard. She had gone with him up to his room in Chicago and he had dumped all his feelings at her feet. She had responded in kind and he, being sober, should have recognized that she wasn't. Not truly. He'd failed to recognize that his feelings for her were insane, no matter how much he liked or wanted her. He should have known there was no way that night was real. Yet here she was apologizing to him. He tried again to shut her apology down. "And besides, you shouldn't."

"I should. I started to say so before, but I didn't get through all of it last time." She took a deep breath. Whatever it was it was big, so he waited. It just took her a few seconds to gather her thoughts. "You kept me out of *his* hands."

She meant Dylan.

"He might have beaten me up, or... God, I hear stories, who knows."

"It's okay. It didn't happen." The thought had scared him, too, and he had wondered if she ever thought about it. But now he saw that she did sometimes think about what could have happened, and he wished she hadn't.

But she continued, almost as if he hadn't spoken. "Clearly, I was fertile then. I could be carrying *his* babies. With no one to help. Their father would have been..." She finished the thought with a small shudder. Her fingers crept up to under her eyes, where she brushed at tears that hadn't yet formed. "I might have had to chose whether or not to keep them. I—"

She took a deep breath again, but he could read her. He could see she wasn't finished.

"I don't think I could have made that choice, but I don't know if I could have raised children who were fathered by—"

His hand slipped from her belly as he moved to hold her. "It's all okay, you don't have to make those choices. It didn't happen."

"I know it didn't. And I have you to thank for that." A few stray tears escaped and she wiped them away, before retuning his hand to her stomach to wait.

After a moment, he broke the silence. "This is amazing Sloan. I mean, I'm amazed that I get to have children. I know most men run screaming in terror from kids, but I always wanted it. For me, it was always just a matter of *when*."

She started to protest, he felt it coming.

But instead of stopping her, he jumped. A knot had formed beneath his hand, then disappeared. She was nodding when he managed to look at her face. "Pretty wild, huh?"

Rolling instantly to his knees, he spread both his hands wide across her stomach and waited quietly in awe. All of three seconds passed before it happened again. This time the knot formed then traveled a short distance before disappearing. Then a few seconds later, the baby on her right just rolled, then produced another quick jab.

His face must have given him away.

She laughed. "That was a foot. The earlier movements were elbows."

"You can tell?"

She laughed again, nodding. "Yeah, you learn after a while, and now of course, you can *see* them moving."

"See them?" Still he didn't move his hands.

CHAPTER 29

S loan scooted down on the bed. "If you promise not to laugh..."

"Why would I laugh?"

"Because it's this horrible huge belly." She scrunched her face.

He shook his head. "Maybe men *should* bear the children. They'd all be drinking beer and admiring their guts. Okay, so the beer part is clearly bad. But Sloan, it's a huge, amazing belly with my children in it."

Still she held out until he said it.

"I promise, no laughing."

He waited while she slowly lowered herself onto her back and lifted her shirt from where it covered her stomach. "Wait. You'll see them."

He was looking at her face, and that would never do. "You have to watch my belly, or you'll miss it."

As he stared, she sent up a silent prayer, thankful that she hadn't gotten any stretch marks yet. She tried desperately not to squirm under his gaze, so she started talking again. "I think I want to paint the nursery yellow. Not too bright, not too primary, and probably put little animals around."

"What kind of animals?"

"I have no idea. What do you think?"

His eyes were still trained on her belly, but he answered right away. "Lions and tigers and bears—"

"Oh, my." She giggled. "What if they're girls?"

"So? Their Daddy's going to teach them how to throw a ball and fight and—"

"What! How to *fight?*"

"Yes, fight." He nodded almost to himself. "How else will I be able to send them off to kindergarten? What if there are bullies? What if my daughter has to teach some boy to respect women?"

Sloan felt her giggles bubble to the surface even as she fought down images of Max seeing his small blonde daughters off to school with reminders of karate moves. "Trust me, the little boys won't be all over them in kindergarten."

"Trust me, they will." And he looked her square in the eyes. "I've seen their mother."

She blushed, she could feel it, but he didn't break eye contact. Just then, the babies saved her. "Look!" She pointed to her belly and, in a flash, he wasn't looking in her eyes any more.

"Oh, my gosh."

She knew he was seeing bumps form and move across her belly. The little aliens were in there, and she had moments where it was almost scary that you could see so much movement beneath her skin.

"Yeah." She nodded. Still feeling the one on the left turning, and finally kicking a few times to settle down. She winced when one of the kicks landed somewhere in the vicinity of her liver.

"Are you okay?" He wasn't looking at her belly anymore. "Maybe we should stop this."

"I'm fine. I got kicked in the guts is all," He started to protest but she spoke over him. "I'm going to get kicked regardless, you might as well get to see them move."

"If you're sure..." He trailed off.

"I'm sure." The babies had settled down for a moment, so she started prattling again. "I think I'm going to put them in a cradle here beside the bed for the first few months."

"One cradle or two?"

"Just one, I've been reading this—ow, kick—book I have on twins, and—"

"It says that they often sleep better and get on the same schedule if they're in the same bed as long as possible," he finished.

"You've been doing your homework." She was impressed. But then again, with this man, when was she not?

Sloan watched, frozen, as he moved up beside her, and stretched out, his head propped on one hand. He wasn't watching her belly anymore, he was peering into her soul. She desperately wanted to squirm away, but his gaze had her pinned. Barely breathing, she felt rather than saw his other hand come to rest, skin to skin, on her belly. Slowly it slid across to the other side, leaving her wrapped in his embrace, nerves tingling in his wake.

Her whole body felt like a live wire as his head moved toward her. And her muscles turned traitor, leaning toward him, waiting to accept his kiss. It was just the lightest of feather brushes at first. Then he did it again, and this time he pushed deeper.

This wasn't an accident or anything she could easily explain away. She knew now that he wasn't hiding a girlfriend somewhere. Though she knew it wasn't wise, she gave in. His tongue played at her lips until she opened for him, and his response was heavenly. Her mouth accepted him in a way her brain couldn't and gave back, kissing with want and hope that she dared not speak.

His hands slid up her body, while her lungs let go of all their air. Softly, his fingers burrowed in her loose hair, holding her to him while he kissed her. His lips worked magic, like she was tipsy or buzzed from a spell, as they moved over hers. For a moment he pulled away, and she opened her eyes to find him looking into hers. The blaze there left no doubt that he wasn't interested in stopping things. She felt her mouth turn up to meet him for more.

This time when his tongue sought hers out, she opened immediately to him and offered no resistance whatsoever. Her hands snaked around him, feeling the strength of him first in his arms, then his shoulders. His fingers trailed down the side of her face, her neck, tracing a path down over her breast, and along her side until he wrapped his fingers at her hip. Pulling her flush against him, he deepened their kiss, tongue probing, hand moving again.

But he pulled away and didn't come back when she moved toward him. Briefly, she felt bereft of his warmth, but she started telling herself that this was for the best, she shouldn't get too tangled up with him anyway, her heart couldn't afford it.

But Max didn't go anywhere. Instead, he just reached across her and looked for the switch to the lamp beside the bed, the only one on in the room. "How does this..."

"You just touch it, anywhere that it's metal." She started babbling. "My friend Lisette sent it, it's for old people, but it's great when you don't want to have to get out of bed."

"Like now." His voice was low, and he'd done as she instructed and the room was dark. There was some light coming in from the hall, but not the glare that had been there moments before. Her brain ran away on tracks it didn't belong on, wondering why he'd had to turn out the light as soon as he'd started kissing her.

He slid down beside her, growing icy slivers in her as he went. When he was lined up eye to eye, he cocked his head, curious at her expression before his hand came up to cup her face again. When she would have looked away, he gently held her in place, "It's not that I don't want to see you. I desperately want to see all of you, but it was glaring in my eyes. I can see you better now."

The icicles melted completely away as he kissed her again. She wondered if he really could see her or if he just saw into her. Her breathing became ragged as he kissed the tip of her nose, and then left a small trail with his lips up the side of her cheekbone. He held her in place while he lavished his way across her jaw and wrested a gasp from her as he suckled gently on her ear.

When his hand slid lower to cup her breast, she pressed into him like she wanted to, then pulled away like she knew she should. The soft whisper of her voice spilled into the darkness. "Max, I can't."

"I know." His sighed words were full of regret. His mouth found her forehead and kissed each eyebrow. The hand on her breast slipped around her and searched for the edge of the covers, at last wresting them down under her, and up and over both of them.

Legs intertwined, they lay still for just a moment, until he kissed her again, squarely on the mouth. Soft and sweet, it had none of the appetite of his earlier kisses, though it lingered long enough to make her wish. "So, roll over, and talk to me."

Sloan rolled and his arms followed, pulling her back snug against him, his hands resting on her belly. *Talk to him?* She couldn't form words. It was all she could do to burrow deeper into him and pray. Pray that it lasted beyond tonight. And try to forget that it wouldn't.

She felt his words at her neck in the brush of air as they went by. "What do you want to name them?"

"Um,..." His lips found her neck and sent little shivers up and down her. "I don't know."

"I like Sloan."

"For a name?" His hands roved, up her arms, down her sides, along her spine. She felt her breath seep out of her.

"Mmmm hmmmm." Again, his mouth found her nape, just before his fingers traced the underside of her chin. The soft tickles made her head fall back and he stole the opportunity to kiss her mouth. His lips finding hers somewhere between soft tenderness and screaming passion.

When he let her breathe again, she responded, certain that she had held the thread of the conversation so tightly because it was her only lifeline. "I absolutely refuse to name one of my children Sloan. They need their own names."

His sigh was one of great dejection. "Well there goes my Sloan and Sloan vote."

She swatted at his arm where it wrapped around her. It was the only thing she could get to. She tried to ignore that the arm pulled her tighter against him, and his breath came at the back of her neck again. "One of them is probably a boy. He'll get beat up in kindergarten with a name like Sloan. What do you like, really?"

"I do like Sloan, but it's already taken, you're right.... Lindsey?"

She mulled it over for a minute. "Possibly. Remember, as it stands right now we need two girl's names and two boy's names. Just in case."

"Mmmmm hmmmm." He kissed her neck again, cementing the smile that was on her face. They continued that way for a while, his mouth periodically moving against her exposed skin, making her breath hitch and her muscles clench. They threw names back and forth when she could find words to speak, yes to some, a definite no to others. Slowly, Sloan felt herself lulled into sleep.

It had been so long since she'd been comfortable. But his

steady breathing and her sense of belonging here in his arms weighed her down in the best way possible.

His voice came to her through fog. "What last name do you think they should have?"

Her mouth didn't work well, she was already half dreaming, happy in a place where there was a sense of home, and the weight of small children in her arms. "I don't really care."

The fog was thicker, her concern less, but she heard it, even if she couldn't react at all.

"Me either. I don't care if it's Smith, but I would most love if all four of us had the same last name."

But she couldn't pull herself out to respond. She was too far under.

CHAPTER 30

M ax blinked several times and turned again to fall asleep in the thick fluffy floral comforter. The next time, his eyes popped open and stayed that way. He didn't own a thick, fluffy, floral comforter, but Sloan did. And she wasn't here. Surely, she was just around the corner. She had fallen asleep in his arms last night. Though they'd been clothed and he wished they'd been naked, it had still all been so right. The soft weight of her nestled back against him had made him stop thinking of changing her mind. The smell of her hair from where her head rested on his shoulder made him think the moment was pretty damn good.

Max was snuggled down into a massive tangle of plump pillows. And after a moment, when Sloan didn't magically appear to explain her absence, he started to investigate. His heart, which had beat so contentedly in his chest, began banging against his ribcage, demanding escape from the hell he was getting more and more certain she'd sent him back to.

No, she wasn't coming back, she hadn't even slept here. The pillows were snuggled around him, not a space for her at all.

There was no dent from her body, and no room for her to have slept. He was square in the middle of the bed.

Had he been a horrible bed hog? It wasn't like him, but maybe he'd done it. So, he flung back the covers and stood, his clothes horribly wrinkled except for his shoes still waiting patiently at the end of the bed.

His heart knew, with all the rattling it was doing in there, it knew something was wrong. Max certainly had his suspicions. She'd done it before—left him in his bed while he slept. Unable, or unwilling, to stay the night. So with leaden weight inside him, he took a fortifying breath and headed down the stairs to find his answer.

Maybe she rose early and was having herbal tea or such. There were so many acceptable possibilities, so much he still didn't know about her. But he did know that she would curl into him as if she felt what he felt. He knew that she would kiss him back with a passion he'd never had from anyone else. To her that same passion must have been found commonplace or even lacking, because she didn't even stay the night. Max was certain that the answer to where she'd gone, and why, was already before him.

Sloan wasn't downstairs.

The kitchen showed no evidence of breakfast.

She wasn't in the garage.

But the two-person table in her dining *area* held a small lavender square of paper, with her neat, loopy script. Usually his heart leapt at the notes she left, but he dreaded even the simple act of leaning over and picking this one up. She would only leave a note if...

Max,

Out for my morning walk. See you Monday.

Sloan

A clear and succinct good-bye. A *please don't be here when I get back* kind of a Dear John letter. His teeth clenched, holding back the slow burn of dismissal. It shot straight through him, surprising in its force, even though he had seen it coming from a mile away. After a few deep breaths, the square of scented paper escaped his fingertips and wafted down to the tabletop to rest almost in its starting place.

See you Monday.

He turned away to...to not look at the note. To try to pretend for one brief second that she hadn't left him. Again. But he couldn't pull it off. Faking his way out of a knife twisted that deep just wasn't in him.

But as he turned he saw the couch. Two pillows that matched the bed were propped together in one corner and a throw blanket was tossed nearby. She must have just vacated it. It looked like she had slept the entire night here, propped upright.

For the briefest of seconds, his heart soared with the hope that she had been uncomfortable and had been forced to sleep on the couch. His mother had told him that one, sharing her pregnancy stories to fill in the gaps of information Sloan wasn't giving him.

But that wasn't it. Sloan hadn't folded her blanket. The fact that he could tell that she had slept there at all meant that she had beat a pretty hasty retreat. An unfolded blanket went against all Sloan-logic. She had wanted to be sure that she missed him when he got up.

Angry now, more at himself than anything, he trotted up the stairs and put his shoes back on. He had been so stupid to believe... In fact, she was probably just around the corner, watching the front of the little townhouse, waiting for his car to leave. He was keeping her out of her own place every second he lingered.

So his shoes smacked their way back down the polished wood stairs, and he flipped over the little lavender square before slamming his way around a few drawers looking for a pen. He scribbled, *Thanks for looking over the house papers, Max* and couldn't think of anything else that wasn't just him lashing out one way or another. He double checked it and saw what he said was perfectly simple and to the point. No emotion involved. Clearly, the way she wanted it.

Grabbing his bag with the documents in it a little more harshly than it deserved, he slung his jacket on as he left down the front walkway, praying that she saw him leave. The papers slid across to the passenger seat as his fingers curled into his pocket for his keys. In the process they brushed against the small blue velvet box that he'd brought with him last night, just in case he found a moment and got the chance.

Then he heard his own voice in a deep acid laugh. He should just throw the ring out the window.

CHAPTER 31

The drive in to work had been quiet and uneventful. Sloan wanted to apologize, but really, for what? *Max, I'm sorry I fled the scene the other night. I just...* just what? Can you say *I'm just so in love with you and I had to get out of there?*

No. You couldn't. Not when she couldn't leave or even simply avoid him. It was bad enough that she felt this way—that she couldn't have what she wanted of him—but she had to continue to deal with him. He would be at the birth. They would raise children together. At a bare minimum she would see him two or three times a week to swap kids until the twins were old enough to drive themselves.

No, she couldn't say anything. Telling him how she felt would only create more problems than they already had. No doubt about it. So she sat quietly in the passenger seat. She let him drop her off at the front of the building and tried not to be disappointed as she found her own space in the elevator.

What was she hoping for? That he would walk up with her, hand in hand? That he would scoot people aside and keep everyone from crowding too close around his pregnant what?...*wife?*

Exactly. *Not going to happen.* She wasn't his wife. Despite his kisses, he hadn't even suggested boyfriend/girlfriend status. All he'd asked for was a marriage that would save them both on the mortgage. So even if she did become his wife, it would only make things worse. She could easily envision them being married. Him protecting her, taking care of her, helping her through the birth, and then saying a polite 'thank you' when it was over. After that, he would want his time with their children and she would be of no use to him anymore.

He was Max, she knew he wouldn't just discard her like an old cardboard box, but she also didn't harbor illusions about what this was. It was a one night stand that had turned into more than either of them bargained for. So if they were married, he would love his babies, but not her. Sloan refused to go through her life being insanely jealous of her own children, and that was already at risk without being married to him. He could offer, but saying 'yes' would just compound the heartbreak when it was all over. Sloan swore to herself she wasn't sending these two kids through a divorce when she had the power to prevent it.

Sitting down at her desk, she started sorting through the latest set of contracts, not really seeing the pages before her. She just wished he would give up. She'd feel more...justi-fied...vindicated...*right*. But she was the un-closable deal and it would be a while before Max gave up and turned his attention to another challenge.

Her door was closed, so Sloan decided it was safe and picked up the phone to call Rae. "Can you pick me up for class tonight?"

"You still want to go?" Rae's skeptical sound didn't give Sloan any extra confidence. Her sister didn't know that she'd slept half the night before in the arms of the man she was in love with. When Sloan didn't answer, Rae commented again. "You haven't been having the best of luck lately."

Sadly, that was true. The one thing she'd really been doing and growing at before all this was witchcraft. She'd been good at it, too, but these past several weeks, her skills felt like they'd just slipped away. None of her spells stuck. She and Rae had graduated from the beginner's class, and then from intermediates, rising up quickly with their natural skills. Sloan had been better than even her sister, and Rae was good.

But last week, the advanced class was doing *light* spells. The classes naturally dwindled in size as the level went higher. Megan could pack thirty people into the Monday night beginner's classes these days. But as time went on attendees flunked themselves out or had other life obligations, so by the time the advanced classes came around, the group was decidedly smaller. Though she wouldn't touch the beginner's level stuff, Delilah did teach some of the more advanced classes. She was Tristan's sister and, together with Yasmin, the three of them owned the store, though Yasmin and Tristan ran it.

So Sloan had followed Delilah's instructions to a T. It hadn't worked. Three of the five students had produced light on the first try. Sloan was one of the two that hadn't. Delilah encouraged her to mess with the spell a bit, try her own spin on in. That had worked! Sloan had been so excited for a moment, especially after the previous week's *smoke* spell had been merely half successful as well. But her excitement at her light was short lived. It blinked out quickly and she never managed to bring it back for more than a few seconds at a time.

Delilah had brought muffins from the Cake and Cauldron— her bakery in Hollywood. She'd put candles in them, encouraging the students to light them with their new spell before eating them. In the end, Rae had to light Sloan's and the only consolation was that Delilah let her keep the decadent treat as a pity muffin. So Sloan was anxious to go back and get something right. *Anything.*

"I have to go *because* of my bad luck, Rae. I have to get my skills back." She sighed up at the ceiling. "If tonight goes horribly, I'm requesting a *mojo* spell for next week. Those exist, right?"

Rae laughed, at least lightening the mood. "One can hope. I'll come get you. Though I love that you're having loverboy drop you at home so I can pick you up there instead of just having him drop you at the shop."

"Are you serious? Rae, think about how much it took you to tell Sam the truth. And if it had blown up and he hated it, you could have walked away. I can't. Not for *eighteen years!*" She heard her voice getting higher. "I know you and I don't think there's anything wrong with it, but the general public would take my kids from me if he went into court and just said, *their mother thinks she's a witch.*"

If the jury didn't believe her, they'd take her kids away claiming she was mentally ill. If they did believe her, they might still take her kids away, claiming she was a danger and casting spells on everyone around them.

She loved Max, she wanted to be with Max, but their mother had lost her entire family and hometown over one incident with her *skills*. The difference had been that it happened before her mother met her father. There had been no children involved. Her mother made a choice for herself and left everyone and everything she knew behind. Sloan had to make a different choice. If she didn't, she could have her children ripped from her if Max—or anyone in general—found out what she could do. So she would certainly have Max drop her off at home and have Rae pick her up and head back the same direction, thank you very much.

Rae suggested dinner, a throwback to the old days when they'd been starting their witchcraft classes and they'd both been single. Now Rae had shiny rings on her finger and a schedule that didn't allow for dinners with her sister as much.

Also, Sloan now had an appetite for three. *How things changed when you weren't looking*, she thought.

The morning ticked by slowly, with only a snack and, later, a visit from Vanessa to break the mood. Making her way downstairs, Sloan traipsed across the street to enjoy the sunshine and a book with her bag lunch. She had been reading so much lately. Still, it beat most of what was on TV and it didn't go on without her if she fell asleep in the middle of it. Which was a good thing.

She had switched to an ereader after noticing marks on her belly one night where she'd propped the book, leading her to probably unfounded fears about babies with book dents in their heads. So now she mostly held the device up as she read, her arms growing heavy until she just passed out, smacking herself in the face with the tech. At least the new stuff was very lightweight. Still, even books were getting dangerous.

She polished off her sandwich and carrots and apple and three girl scout cookies. Sloan figured that there were three of them living in this body and they each deserved a cookie. When she checked her watch, she realized that she should limit herself to finishing this chapter then head back in to the office and her remaining work. Even though it felt great out in the sunlight.

The building felt positively dreary in comparison, and she blinked a few times to adjust to the lack of light as she headed in toward the center of the building and the elevators. But in a few minutes she was at her desk, and she frowned. The envelope wasn't where she'd left it.

Turning it over didn't tell her anything about why or how it had been moved. So she looked back at the pile of papers on the corner of her desk and spotted the gift. Wrapped in yellow paper with tiny blocks spelling b-a-b-y, and a soft yellow bow, it had been waiting, hiding out of sight under the folder.

Who would hide a present? And why?

She wasn't sure, but slowly she turned it over and examined

it. A heavy box, no clues there. Best just open it, it was for her anyway, no one else around here was having a baby, and certainly no one else sat at her desk. She slid the bow off the end and peeled back the paper, before flipping over the little kraft brown box and lifting the lid.

A book.

A paperback.

40,000 Baby Names.

Max.

Her shoulders slumped, even as her heart leapt, just a little. Without her permission, her fingers found the edges of the book and began flipping through it. Dog-eared here and there, Max's neat scrawl circled, checked, underlined, and made notes, "sounds manly" "sweet" "reminds me of you."

He was trying to kill her. That had to be it. She wondered if the jury would catch on to murder-by-false-hope. Probably not. Standing up, she flipped the blinds that would shield her office from the hallway. It was weird, but she was pregnant. No one would question her.

She pulled the small, fat, white candle from the bottom of her drawer and reached for the ribbon that was next to it. She'd been prepared to say she'd kept it from a baby gift if anyone had asked. They hadn't. No one cared about a candle and a ribbon. Using a lighter, so the room didn't smell like a match head, she lit the candle and tried again to do a spell to put a wall around her heart. She had to get over this.

He kissed her and turned her on, but he was a nice guy with good intentions toward their children. He was stuck with a pregnant not-even-a-girlfriend and he was being decent about it, so he probably wasn't getting any. It made sense to get your rocks off with the woman who'd already handed herself over once before. Twice before, Sloan corrected herself.

Twice. The man had every reason to believe she'd put out,

and it was her own fault. So she had to stand firm and even cast a *shelter* spell on herself, if that's what it took.

Holding up the candle as it burned, she chanted her spell softly three times through. Then she wound the ribbon around it, blew out the flame with intent, and put it into the drawer. It probably wouldn't work any better than any of the other crap she'd been casting lately, but at least she'd tried.

She kicked off her shoes, to look like she'd been doing something pregnancy related like stretching or rubbing her feet, and then popped the blinds back open. No one was around anyway. She needn't have worried. So she sat back down at her desk and ignored her files as she thumbed through the book for the next hour. Finally grabbing a pen and adding her own notes.

CHAPTER 32

M ax had woken to the best feeling that morning. In his dream, he'd woken up in heaven. In a big sunny room, on a big fluffy bed, all by himself. One of those days where you just wake up and there's no alarm, and you aren't tired. His dream self stretched and wandered through the house to the living room, where Sloan was curled up in front of the couch watching TV. She smiled and he looked across the room to see two little blonde heads bobbing toward him for a smile and a hug. "I thought I'd let you sleep in." She pointed over his shoulder to where his alarm was buzzing mercilessly.

Unfortunately, the only parts of the dream that had been real were that the alarm *was* making a terrible racket and he *had* slept in. Sure, he was sleeping in a little later than usual because they weren't going straight to work, the doctor's appointment was at nine-thirty, but he had overslept the snooze alarm, even.

So, he had scrambled to get out the door. He had to dig clothes from the boxes he'd moved them in. He slapped open drawers desperately trying to remember where he decided was the logical place for his brush. Max couldn't find anything and he didn't have time to cast a *find*, either.

He'd been close to getting out the door, when his home phone rang. For some inane reason he went out to check the caller ID display and even picked up the phone. "Hi, Dad. Why are you calling from work? I thought Mom said you were going to retire."

"Because I didn't want your Mother to hear." His father sounded weary and Max knew that was never a good sign. "We need to have a talk, Son."

Well, that wasn't good. The problem was, Max actually didn't have time for it right now. He would have to call his father back and get whatever lecture was coming about how he was living his life wrong later. He was opening his mouth, but his father must have seen it across the miles. His mother was from the family of witches, but no one could get one over on his dad. Not even now when he was a grown-ass man and he was running late.

"Your mother may tell you that it's okay that you aren't married to this girl who's having our grandkids, but she's worried sick."

The talk. Max shoved his fingers into his hair and pulled his other shirtsleeve on. There would be no cutting this call short. True to form, the man didn't even wait for any acknowledgment that he had been heard. He just plowed ahead. "Well, you won't get that from me. It *isn't* okay that you're not married. And it sure isn't okay that you don't care—"

"Dad." The man had always had a way of getting right to the quick of things. "I know it isn't—"

"Your mother told me about the unusual circumstances as to how it happened, but you slept with a woman you hardly knew and you're going to have to be a man about it. I thought I taught you better than that."

"Dad." He sighed the word out, desperately wanting to explain. Still he gave up trying to button his shirt. "I've asked her to marry me. She said 'no.'"

"Try again." God bless his father and the 'if it doesn't work just give another try' theory. These days that was called sexual harassment. And on top of that, Max didn't want to bully Sloan into marrying him. His father was going to have to learn to deal. But he didn't have time to put that horse back in the barn this morning.

"I am trying." It was *a truth* if not *the truth*.

"That's not what you told your mother."

He felt seventeen again, and he wanted to yell that his father didn't *want* to hear. But he wasn't seventeen, and he lived under his own roof now, and he could be calmer. "I didn't want her getting her hopes up."

"Well, you'll just have to try harder." At least the older man's tone wasn't so harsh. "You just make that girl understand she's got a good thing with you and don't worry about your mother. I'll handle her."

He begged off the rest of the call, explaining that he would be late to pick up Sloan. That yes, he did get the present his mother had sent for the babies. And he went off to finish getting ready, now in even more of a rush and irritated to boot.

He continued to shake his head at his father's antiquated notions of 'handling' his mother. Sloan couldn't be 'handled,' couldn't be 'sold' on his ideas. She had to be won, and he was doing a poor job from the response he was getting.

Today was their seven-month check. Seven months to the day from Chicago, and where had it gotten him? Excited and terrified. Moved into a new house that needed some paint and a little remodeling. In debt up to his eyeballs. His parents down his throat. And Sloan still turning away from his every offer.

He was considering getting the doctor to put the ultrasound on *his* stomach and seeing just what size ulcer he was working up. But as usual, there wasn't time. He slung his tie around his neck as he bolted through the door to the garage. No steps. Strollers would glide right through.

Waiting impatiently for the garage door to chug its way up, he slapped his seatbelt across his waist then peeled out of the driveway. Not a good show to the new neighbors, he was sure.

He couldn't be late. Sloan would just hop in her car and go without him. It seemed almost that she was doing him the favor by letting him pick her up and drop her off each day. Not that she was rude about it, but it was clear that she would rather drive herself and set her own hours. Coming in early and working long into the night, all the while mumbling that he didn't understand about her career and maternity leave.

Sadly, she was right. He'd gone into Bernstein and said he wanted the full twelve weeks of paternity leave that the company offered him. Bernstein had looked at him like he was nuts, but he'd signed the papers and handed them back. That was it. No questions about his loyalty to the job. No talk about what to do if he decided he wanted to be a stay-at-home-Dad instead. Sloan had nailed it. Max had walked out with his signed papers and a huge dilemma about how to either turn in the president and owner of the company for gender-based discrimination or talk to the man. He pushed that thought aside, too. It was a headache he wouldn't be able to deal with today.

The lights were all against him, and he suffered through each. First tugging his tie over his head and tossing it into the backseat, then rolling up the cuffs on his sleeves. The whole suit could wait until he made it to the office. It was a little warm for wearing it out and about. By the time he pulled up in front of Sloan's, he had the top few buttons of his shirt undone as well. He was just getting a little warm, right?

Sure enough, Sloan was nowhere to be seen. He'd look for her car, but suspected that if she was still here it would be in her garage. He opened the car door, already pushing it to make the appointment on time, and slowly climbed the steps. It was just a formality. His father had drilled it into him that you didn't quit until you had checked everything, just to be sure.

Just as he was raising his hand to knock on her front door, his cell phone buzzed in his pocket, making him jump. "Hello?"

"Max. Where are you? Are you okay?" It was Sloan and she actually sounded concerned. That alone was enough to make him smile. He'd meet up with her.

"Well, actually I'm on—"

Just then the door opened and Sloan stuck her head out to look around, nearly burying her nose in his chest. A nanosecond before they would have collided she jumped back and let out a little yelp. The sound traveled louder through the cell phone causing him to wince. "—your doorstep."

"Sorry." She turned off the cordless phone and set it on the small table just inside the door. "I was beginning to get worried, that's all."

Tucking his cell phone back in his pocket, Max laced his fingers through hers. "It's okay. I was running late, I'm sorry."

Her hand felt warm and soft in his and his father's words came to mind. *Try harder.* He would just have to show her how he felt. But that was hardly an option right at this moment. They had a doctor's appointment to keep. And since they hadn't been able to find out the gender of either baby for certain last time they were both on pins and needles even without the added drama of being late.

Max walked a few steps in front of Sloan holding her hand and guiding her down the steps from the front of her townhouse. From the layout that he could see, the garage was on the bottom level and she had a flight of stairs to get to her main floor. Clearly, she hadn't been thinking of having kids when she moved in here.

Come to think of it, he hadn't even thought about these front stairs before. With the lush foliage all but hiding them from the street and the fact that she was always at the bottom waiting for him every morning he had never given it a second thought. But now, as he handed her in the passenger door of his coupe, he realized that he didn't like her navigating those stairs alone every morning. Especially given that she couldn't see her own feet.

With only a few words while his mind raced about what to do about that problem, he took off toward the doctor's office. He could simply ask her to wait at the top, but that would likely offend her practical nature. He knew that much. Maybe he could simply show up earlier and walk her down each morning. Maybe...

Well, he had all day to think about it. At the next light he turned to his silent companion. "Are you excited?"

Her smile was small. "I'm trying not to be." She shrugged.

"Why? I'm am."

"Well, I hear it's often difficult to tell with any certainty what the sex is in the case of twins. Even if you do get a solid answer it's usually only about one of them. So I don't want to get my hopes up that we'll know. I just don't want to wind up disappointed."

He nodded. A logical answer from her. The way she had been for quite a while now. Every question, every idea, met with a logical rebuttal. Where was the woman who'd told him that she wanted to follow her heart this time and not get hurt?

Right now, he had other problems. Like it was ten minutes to ten with no parking in sight. He dropped Sloan off at the back entrance to the building, and went in search of a space. By the time he caught up to her she was in the office, already checked-in, sitting with a magazine, looking all calm and collected, except for a slight case of nerves given away only by her eyes.

Max dropped into the seat beside her and once again laced his fingers with hers, her grip telling him that he'd been right about the nervous shimmer in her eyes. But his mind wandered off to the conversation he'd had with his father earlier. *Try harder.*

Yes, he wanted Sloan to marry him. She didn't know it, but he always had that little blue velvet box with the ring on him, just in case. He was armed with a thousand ways to ask. He was ready should any viable situation present itself. But when he got down to it, what he really wanted was for Sloan to love him back.

He wanted the house, the kids, the minivan. *And* the loving wife. The problem was that it was all so close, except for one thing. She didn't want him and that was a doozy. In the meantime, he would have to take care of that pesky minivan problem. Okay, maybe an SUV and a dog. But already Sloan was having a harder time getting in and out of his coupe. One way or another, it had to go.

He just couldn't figure out why she didn't love him. She wasn't in love with someone else, at least as far as he could tell. She believed she always chose the wrong men, but he'd been here at every turn. He'd worked so hard to be the right man. Then there was that lightning bolt between them the first time they'd touched. He had simply *known*. Why hadn't she? He'd done nothing in his life to warrant such a nasty trick of karma.

For a moment, he sat and watched her from the corner of his eye. Wondering if he was doomed to love her for the rest of his life, while she brushed him off over and over again. If all he would ever get was the beginning of a night, but never the end. He wondered how long he would keep it up before he got kicked enough to learn, because right now he didn't see that end point.

Then the nurse popped her head out the door, and nearly everyone in the waiting room looked up expectantly. But this time she said, "Sloan Ellis." And so they stood up as Max shook off his thoughts, and followed her to the back rooms.

After an eternal wait, with Sloan getting more and more wound up every minute, Dr. McNeill walked in, reviewing the folder. "Hello again, Ellis and Summerland family. We're going to do some measurements, but first let's see if these babies will tell us what they are." With no further ado he cued up the machine and set to work looking around.

He moved the paddle this way and that and clicked and rolled his little rollerball. Finally, when Max thought he would bust from seeing grainy black and white images that he didn't really understand, the doctor spoke, "Look at this." He pushed the screen around to face them and pointed with his pen tip.

Dr. McNeill carefully encircled a portion of the image and smiled.

Max didn't get it, and from the looks of it, neither did Sloan. Just when he was getting ready to admit his ignorance, the doctor saved him. "No doubt about it, that's a boy."

Sloan lit up. Her smile infectious and pulling him in to that world where she was supremely happy. "Are you sure?"

"Very....Now let's see what we can find out about baby B." He wiggled the paddle around for a few more moments, while Sloan cocked her head at an unnatural angle just to see the screen. Max wanted to tell her that he'd let her know if anything interesting popped up, but it wouldn't change what she was doing, so he kept quiet.

"Hmmm." The doctor spoke to himself or to the baby, Max wasn't sure which. "Roll over, squirt." then, "I think it's another boy.... come on, roll this way..."

Sloan gripped his hand. "He rolled! What is he?"

The tech frowned. "He did roll. The wrong way. I've got a head here." He traced some lines on the screen and Max could see the tiny nose and mouth in profile. His heart melted right then. This was his child. Later it would call him 'Daddy' and Sloan 'Mommy'. And... oh dear God, when he actually thought about it, the whole thing was petrifying.

After a few more minutes and a few shakes of his head, Dr, McNeill called it quits. "Maybe we'll get a better look next time, but don't get your hopes too high. You're lucky to get this much.

But so far, the measurements are on target and they both look very healthy. Congratulations." He shook their hands nodding at each of them separately and disappeared out the door telling them to wait right there, he wanted to show the doctor something.

So Max held her hand while she sat up and smoothed her shirt over her belly. He wanted to tell her that his mother had sent her a present. But he didn't want her suggesting that he bring it in to work. He wanted to keep his excuse for taking her by the house. He wanted to show her the master bedroom, the only room he had already painted. He'd found some creamy color that looked even better on the walls and added a soft white trim. That's what they had told him at the paint store would be beautiful and go with anything she picked. They didn't add that it would also soothe his wishful thinking. They didn't know.

He was brought back to the scene at hand as Sloan tugged her fingers away from him. He only just them realized that he had been running his thumb across the back of her hand. He started to smile and tried to think of something to say, but the regular doctor came in in her lab coat and sat down. "Hi guys." She turned directly to Sloan. "How are you feeling?"

"Fine." Max watched as her throat clenched, and saw the alarm rising even before she choked out the words. "He said the babies were fine."

"They are." The doctor thumbed through the file even as she offered a sincere smile. "But your amniotic fluid is low, and that could lead to problems."

"Low?" He jumped in. "How does it get low? Where would it go? Did her water break?" He tried desperately to tamp down the panic that was crawling slowly up inside.

"No, it didn't." The doctor smiled again. "These things just happen, and like most things, they happen more often with twins. What we need to do now, is make sure that things stay okay."

"How do we do that?" He could hear the relief in Sloan's voice.

"Bed rest."

His own sigh of relief escaped him. Bed-rest was easy.

"*Bed-rest?*" Sloan wailed. And when he looked at her she had this horrified expression on her face.

"Sloan, what is it?"

But she didn't answer him, instead she spoke directly to doctor Lee. "There has to be another way. I can't go on bed rest."

"There isn't. Not unless they're born early." She thumbed her way through the chart again. "You're at thirty-one weeks today, you need to keep them in there until at least thirty-six. That's five weeks."

"Then what?" Sloan demanded. "Then I get one week to heal and recover before going back to work!"

"What!?" Where had she gotten that atrocious math?

Even the doctor frowned. "You should have twelve weeks of maternity leave. So that gives you at least seven."

His head whirled. Seven weeks? He'd just set his own leave up to twelve weeks. Max figured he'd need it just to adjust. He had not calculated Sloan having to count some of her leave *before* the babies came.

Sloan's shoulders slumped, and she was fighting back tears. "When do I have to start?"

"Now."

Now?

"I want you in the car with your feet up, then in bed with your feet up for the remainder of the day. From here on out, you'll only get out to see me. You don't scrub the floors or do the dishes." The doctor made a pointed look at Max to be sure that he understood. He nodded vigorously while she continued. "You go to the bathroom and the kitchen to get food. You keep your phone on you all the time. No running to get it. No needing it and not having it at hand. You can go into the living room to watch TV or read but be sure that your feet are up and that you aren't constantly up and down."

She sized up Sloan's reaction before continuing. "If you don't do this, you'll put your babies in jeopardy. You'll wind up on tighter restrictions—" Sloan looked incredulous, "Or even in the hospital. Do you understand?"

Near tears, Sloan nodded. It was all he could do to keep from holding her to him and just letting her cry. Instead, he helped her off the tiny padded table and held her hand and elbow as they made their way out to the front. "I'm going to walk you to the door, then drive around to get you."

Doctor Lee was standing right behind them. "Good, that's the way it should be."

"Don't worry," He knew his smile was watery and doubted he inspired much confidence, but he spoke anyway. "I'll take care of her."

Then they were at the front and he ran around to get the car, after sitting Sloan on a bench to wait. What had gone wrong? He'd cast a spell to keep her and the babies safe. So he told himself they *were* safe. And that maybe he should have cast a spell that nothing at all go wrong. He drove up the ramp from underground parking and had a horrid thought. He'd wanted Sloan to need him. Had he inadvertently added that intention when he was removing the other spells and keeping her safe? Had he made this happen?

He didn't even know how to confess what he'd done. So he just tried to make the sharp curves and not hit anything as he looked for her at the front of the building. As he pulled up, he got a good look at her expression. It was like she'd lost a family member. His heart ached for her, but he could only help her into the low car and then take her home.

She was in full blown tears before they were halfway there

and didn't even notice that he had changed his mind, that he wasn't following the right route. He was taking her to his home. It should be hers anyway. He followed the roads carefully, not quite having lived there himself for long enough to drive it automatically.

Sloan was in a terrible state by the time they reached the place. She didn't look out the windows or comment or anything. Just let him help her climb out of the car and then lift her off her feet.

With her feet dangling over his arm, she rested her head against his shoulder, and let Max carry her into the master bedroom. It would have been very romantic had she not been crying and angry at the world. So he tried not to think about carrying her over the threshold as he laid her out on pillows he fluffed, and then tucked the covers up around her.

She was miserable, and he didn't really understand any of it. He was thinking about work-arounds. Maybe she had to go back five weeks earlier than planned, but he'd be home with them. Maybe she was reacting more because of hormones. But that didn't seem like it. Instead, it seemed she just knew something terrible that he didn't. He'd have to find out what it was. Then do his level best to fix it.

In the meantime, she burrowed deep into the covers, shaking with small sobs as she tipped over the edge to an uneasy sleep. But he loved her there, nestled in the same blankets he'd thrown off just a few hours ago, in the room painted cream and white just for her.

If she would agree, he'd keep her here. He'd take care of her, just like he'd promised the doctor, and Sloan, and himself. She wouldn't want him to, he knew it. She'd want to be independent, but right now she wasn't allowed to be. So there were suddenly a thousand arguments as to why she should stay, and he knew them all.

CHAPTER 33

Sloan woke for a moment in the sweetest cloud. Surrounded by the soft haze of comfort and the knowledge that everything was fine, she snuggled deeper into the fluffy blankets just before the harsh wind of reality blew it all away. The bed was unfamiliar. With that odd realization, the knowledge that she was stuck on bed rest came crashing back to her.

Dear God. Her chest constricted as she thought about it. She would have to take all twelve weeks of maternity leave. Unpaid. How would she cover the rent? How would she enjoy her children? She still needed a few more weeks of work to build up to the amount of savings that she needed just to get by. That account was nowhere near as full as she had wanted it to be. And now, well *now* the account wouldn't only stop growing, it would already start depleting.

Sloan fought off the tears that were pushing their way out from the backs of her eyes. Surely these babies could feel their mother's stress. She tried to shake all the doom and gloom and force some logic and balance into her system; she tried to think of some solution. But she was already far too frustrated to come up with anything. Nothing besides *note to self, win lottery.* That was unlikely, since she didn't have Yasmin's way with lotto tickets. A few thousand right now would go a long way. She reminded herself that even if she did have Yasmin's touch, she *still* couldn't win the lotto, because she was no longer allowed to go to the corner store to buy a ticket.

She realized then that she was not only fretting but sitting up, and she wasn't supposed to be. She would have to find a way to fix things while lying down, because doing anything less than everything for these babies wasn't an option.

Sinking back into the sweetness of the bed, it again occurred to her that it was unfamiliar. Luckily, it was too soft and warm and smelled too good to be threatening. She just had no earthly idea where she was. The walls were a beautiful soft cream color, freshly painted, with eggshell trim. But otherwise the place was pretty bare. A lone dresser stood in the corner, the bare wood stark with straight masculine lines against the softness of the walls. She decided that she liked the contrast of the look.

Glancing up, she saw that the bed had no headboard. It was just a mattress on box springs and a frame, all pushed against the wall. With a small frown, she wondered again where she was.

"Hi, Sleepyhead." Her answer stood in the doorway holding a steaming mug. Sloan pushed herself upright to face Max, certain that she looked a mess. He didn't sip at whatever he held, and for a moment she wondered at the expression on his face. Then she figured out that he was standing there wondering what she was thinking. The last she remembered was crying her way home in the passenger side of his coupe. Taking a deep breath of resolve, she looked up and met his eyes.

She wanted the tea or coffee or whatever it was that he was holding. On a better day, she might have wrested it away from him. Instead she pled her case. "I'm doing better now, you can take me home."

But he ignored her request. "I made you some tea." He approached with the mug and set it on the bedside table.

"Thanks, but I can't. Too much caffeine."

"It's herbal...*something*. No caffeine."

Of course, it was. He was paying as much attention to her pregnancy as she was. Maybe more. She eyed him but propped herself on her elbow and attacked the hot liquid anyway. It smelled heavenly. After a few sips with him watching, she spoke again. "I'd like to go home now, please."

He eased onto the bed beside her, and Sloan knew it wasn't a good sign.

"You should stay here."

"I should go home." She countered.

She waited for his argument, but it didn't come. Instead he said, "Okay, but tell me why you were crying so hard. I'm sure it wasn't just hormones."

Even as she started to take the way out he had laid at her feet, he spoke again. "I wouldn't want to leave you alone if your hormones were going to get the better of you like that. So what was it?"

She took a deep breath, amazed at just how easily he had maneuvered her, and just how much she needed to say.

But Max jumped in again. "Is it money? I know this can't be easy on you financially."

The fury hit her so fast she almost jumped off the bed. "How do you know that?"

He looked taken aback, like she had hit him. "You told me."

"I did *not*—"

"In Chicago."

"Did I tell you my entire fucking life story in Chicago?"

At the prompt of her incredulous stare he continued. "You told me about the wedding and how you had gotten left holding most of the responsibility to pay it off after he bailed. That you'd be paying down your credit cards for a while."

The knot in her chest sank a little lower. He could only know that if *she* had told him. She wasn't even sure Rae knew the extent of the debt of that wedding. She and Joe were supposed to pay it off together. His parents said they'd help. But they'd only helped their poor son weasel out of it.

"If you don't want to stay here, maybe you could just stay until someone else can come take care of you." His finger traced a fold in the comforter, and he didn't meet her eyes.

She looked down, too. "My Mom and Dad are gone. I have Rae, but she's a newlywed. I don't want to impose."

"You have a new cousin..." he prompted. He was trying, she had to give him that.

She almost snorted. "Yeah, and their first baby was due three days ago." Jeez, Yasmin could have had the baby while she slept away the morning. Though Delilah had promised a psychic as well as mobile alert when Yasmin went into labor. Apparently, Delilah could push thoughts like that. Sloan had wondered if she could pull other thoughts out...

When she thought about it, she didn't know where she'd go. Maybe that was why she hadn't thought about it before. She didn't like the answers she knew she'd get.

"I know."

He knew that, too? "What else do you know?"

"A lot of things." His voice was soft and gentle and he smelled... just like the bed. Like him. "What about your friend back home?"

"Lisette?" He did know a lot. "She would come in a heartbeat—"

"Good—"

"But she's pregnant, too."

"Oh, that must be neat. Except that she can't come." His hand reached out and covered hers. Her own hands were shaking, as evidenced by the ripples across the hot tea. "I think you're stuck with me."

"I—I, I can't." Max waiting on her while she got bigger and bigger. She couldn't take the thought, let alone the actuality. "I'll hire someone."

"Please." She couldn't make out his tone. "And run your credit cards even higher? It's that you lost your paycheck, isn't it?"

That was the simplified version. So she nodded.

His hand reached up and cupped her face, gently coaxing her to look at him. Sloan managed to hold back from leaning into his touch, but she didn't pull away either. "You have me, and we have my paycheck."

"Max, I—"

He cut her off. "You're giving me the greatest gift I've ever been given. Let me do this. I can cook and clean and I hear I'm a great conversationalist."

She managed a little laugh, but contrary to his last words, he ended the conversation they were having by getting up and walking away. He stopped in the doorframe and turned back to look at her again. "Is there anything you won't eat?"

Sloan gave him her wryest look, as she motioned to her belly. This time she made him laugh and she tried to ignore the warmth spreading through her. Just now, she realized that the light was starting to fade beyond the windows.

Max smiled, as though somehow he knew just what she'd been thinking. "I called in for the both of us today. But only for today. I figured you'd want to handle the whole shebang tomorrow in your own way."

She nodded. She should have told him thank you, but her mouth couldn't form the words.

Still he didn't leave. "What would you have done if I wasn't here?"

Half her mouth pulled up in a sour grin. "Given up and gone back north I guess."

"With my babies?" He looked so incredulous. As though she had said she would knife him in the back if given a chance.

"If I had been truly alone, yes, but that wouldn't have happened. I'm not alone. You're you."

Max nodded and finally headed out to fix dinner, leaving her there with the things she had just said. *If she had been truly alone...* She had known all along that she wasn't. Max would be here for her. Whether she could handle that or not.

Sloan admitted a few things to herself while she polished off the hot tea. She was keeping Max at arm's length out of fear for her heart. But she couldn't afford that kind of distance now. Her babies couldn't either. Despite needing to hide a few things—could she do spells from in bed? Or in front of the TV?—she would have to throw in. And she might as well go whole hog. It wasn't as if her heart could be protected at this point. She had it seriously bad for Max Summerland. Her pendulum might know her Dream Man was in Chicago, but Sloan's heart was here.

The next big thing she admitted to herself was that she'd consciously chosen to ignore how she was going to handle two babies alone, or how she was going to explain to them when they were older why Daddy didn't love Mommy back.

She knew that she couldn't just move. She needed to be here. Her children needed their father, too. Giving up all hope of the independence that had defined her since her parents had died, she accepted that she needed to be taken care of for a while. Then she let it sink in that Max was the only one to do it. Setting down the mug with a great sigh, she slid deeper into the soft blankets, thinking how exhausting a day of nothing had become. And that the sheets smelled just like Max.

CHAPTER 34

The next morning, Sloan woke to the sensation of having to pee. Seriously, though, when did she not these days? Looking around she saw only three sets of doors in the room. One set clearly led to closet space. This was an older house and the closet doors slid across each other. They'd also recently been framed out in that eggshell trim. The one door led to the hallway, so the last one must be to a bathroom, right?

Testing her feet on the floor, Sloan paused for a moment to get her bearings. She hadn't had any issues sitting up in bed the night before when Max brought her dinner, but suddenly standing appeared to become an issue. One day off her feet and already her head was woozy. She took deep even breaths and waited for it to pass.

Her eyes blinked a few times as the room came into sharper focus, and she stood, teetering for just a moment as her misplaced weight pulled at her. She was alone here, so she snapped her fingers casting a small *balance* spell to keep her upright, then headed off to the mystery door. Turning the knob, she discovered that sure enough, it was a bathroom and this was the only door to it. That brought a surge of relief as well as something else. The knowledge that he had tucked her into the master bedroom. His own room. *Shit.* She sighed. Her happy thought turned grim. He'd vacated his own room for her without the slightest cringe or comment.

Sloan washed her hands and checked out her reflection in the mirror that ran the full length of the wall, trimmed again with molding in that eggshell paint. Yup, an older house, even the mirror was trimmed. Something nagged at her in the back of her head. But her reflection nagged more, winning out. The dark circles under her eyes only irritated her.

What? She wasn't getting enough *rest*? And, of course, she was pestered by the disturbing thought that she didn't even know where she was. Well, she was in the same clothes as yesterday and at Max's new house, but where was that?

He'd left her here alone. He had come in with hot tea and a TV and her cell phone before he'd headed into work. So she'd drunk the tea for sustenance and then called Mr. Bernstein directly, waiting on hold for a full seven minutes according to the red alarm clock at her side. Then she had shakily explained the situation to the older man, trying all the while to sound confident and positive about her situation and attitude. Every last tone and chipper response of it a lie.

Bernstein shocked her. He offered her a part-time, remote position that would give her partial pay for the next handful of weeks. It meant she didn't have to start her leave until her babies were born. He didn't give her any crap about how she might change her mind and even transferred her through to his secretary. Next, Sloan was given an intro to a group who was job-sharing, in case she didn't want to come back full time. It was something Sloan had never considered. It was allowed only brief consideration this time, too. Although it was a great idea in theory, job sharing meant paycheck sharing, and she couldn't afford that.

Shoving the thoughts away, she tried to wipe her memory

clean and settled into a rousing morning of watching crap on the television and drifting in and out of sleep because it was all just soooooo boring and the bed was just so fluffy.

She needed books and for that she needed an actual book. She could see what Max had if she could get out of this bed. She also needed food. All of which required that she leave the room. Trying not to be so excited about finally having a good excuse, Sloan threw off the covers and wandered into the hallway. The paint here was off-white and looked only a few weeks older than the bedroom paint. Her brows pulled together as she turned through the open doorway into the living room.

A deep dark leather sofa sat under a bank of windows with absolutely no curtains, shades, or even sheers to cover them. A blink and a glance in the other direction revealed a bank of black technical components. A huge TV, DVD player, an Xbox or something, and a sound system that, on closer inspection, was wired to speakers placed strategically all over the room. A man's living room. The windows were bare, but he already had his surround sound up. She shook her head to herself.

She had been in her own place just over two years, and she'd owned all the pieces from day one, but her surround sound still hadn't been hooked up. Such a girl's girl.

She stepped further into the room and took in a circular sweep, reminding herself that she was looking for the kitchen, that's why it was okay to be up and exploring. From the formal dining room, which was nearly bare except for a freestanding cabinet, she could see into the kitchen. There was a small table already pushed back into the eating nook. It, at least, looked like it might have seen a few meals.

Again, she frowned. Turning back to look at the living room from this side, it clicked. French doors, just beyond the couch, led to the patio out back.

No!

Max had bought the house. *The* house. The one she wanted.

Now she would never have it. Her heart sank. Her lip quivered and she bit at it to stop the motion. Doing her best, she reminded herself all the while that she should be happy. She couldn't have afforded it anyway. Now her children would at least get to grow up here. That was what she wanted, wasn't it?

No. She wanted so much more. But that didn't stop her eyes from blinking at the tears pushing up from the back. He had bought *this* house.

It doesn't matter, Sloan repeated that thought to herself as she went to the fridge to scrounge up lunch.

Again, evidence of the testosterone in his system was right before her. The fridge was spotless. She could see every corner. A few takeout containers were there along with mustard, bread, and peanut butter. Who kept bread and peanut butter in the fridge? Men. Men living alone. That's who.

It was a shame that she was off her feet, or she really could have contributed, paid him back. Kept his fridge stocked, made or bought him curtains, and...

Then again, if she'd been on her feet to do all those things, she wouldn't be here as a guest in her dream house anyway. So she came up with a half dozen little single-serving packets of restaurant jelly from one of the fridge drawers and made herself a very cold peanut butter and jelly sandwich. Then wound up with a room temperature glass of water because she couldn't find any ice.

Finally, shaking her head at the fare, she sank into the large sofa and picked up the remote. First, she blasted herself with sound from a very loud, very hard metal radio station. *He liked metal?* She cringed until she located the volume button and got it down to a decent noise level. She didn't want to change his station. Judging from the array of remotes laid out on the side table she'd never get it back anyway.

After a few minutes of random button-pushing, she found the remote for the TV, and a few minutes later she managed to figure out how to not have to watch the extremely violent movie that she was stuck with on Showtime. Sloan polished off the sandwich and urged herself through every last drop of the glass of water, while she watched the same stuff on the very large TV as she had on the smaller one in the master bedroom.

She considered ordering books online, they could be here tomorrow. But where, exactly, was *here?* She thought she could give adequate directions but didn't believe any online store would accept that. Probably there was no blank for that either. *If current address is unknown, use the following space to provide relatively accurate directions.* Nope, not going to happen. Then there was the whole billing address on the card not matching the delivery address.

She remembered a junk drawer in the kitchen. It wasn't full of junk yet; he hadn't lived her long enough. But he was getting a good start on it. Even so, it was still relatively organized, which meant she knew exactly where there was a pen—okay, a marker—and a pad of paper—well, post-its. But that was adequate to make a list.

Giving herself permission to get off the couch, Sloan waddled her way to the kitchen, glad that no one was watching. She returned ready to scribble and this time reclined fully and started jotting everything down that she needed. She had four notes, fully of her scribbles, stuck along the arm of the couch before she began to slow down. *List-girl strikes again.* At this rate, it would feel like home in no time.

"Why are you on the couch?"

She jumped. "Max! Don't startle me like that. It can't be good for the babies."

"I'm sorry, and don't try to sidetrack me, missy." He wagged a finger at her. "Why are you out here?"

"I got hungry." She shrugged, "There was nothing on TV."

"Then there's nothing on TV out here either. It's hooked up to the same dish." He grabbed up the remote and clicked the set off, before turning back to look at her. "I came home to make you lunch."

"Unnecessary. Lunch has already been eaten." She smiled and pointed at the empty paper-towel where the sandwich had been. Sloan moved to sit up, but was interrupted.

"No, don't move—"

"Sorry, habit."

"—I think you've already moved around enough today."

She laid back while he came up and plucked a sticky note from the arm. "I'll bet this says that I need curtains, right?"

"Nope, things I need from home." Even looking up at him from this angle he was still insanely good-looking. What was she going to do? Sloan grinned. "You don't need curtains. They're too heavy for this. You just need sheers that you can open and close easily. It's the back yard, no one will be looking in."

CHAPTER 35

"No, no, and *no!*" Max was finally angry at her. Though she tried her best to look contrite, she really had pushed too far. He let loose though, since a contrite look from her wasn't enough. "I let you go along to your house because I thought you were right, that a list wasn't going to be good enough. But you made me hover over you to keep you off your feet the whole time. And now, you are *not* going to hang this stuff up yourself. In the bed now, missy!"

She started to comply as she heard him muttering, "I'm going to put in a request to transfer you to sales when you get back to work, you could sell a buck knife to a fish. I swear."

Sloan tried to keep it in, really she did, but the laughter just bubbled out of her. When Max saw her and joined in, she couldn't hold it back anymore. It only took a moment until the movement made her ribs hurt. As she grabbed at her sides, it brought him to her like a magnet.

"Are you okay?"

"Yeah, it just hurts to laugh. There's not enough room for everyone in here." She pointed at her belly, while he nodded. His mouth was so close to hers, and God help her, she remembered every night in her dreams just how it felt to kiss him and to be in his arms.

She changed the subject. "You shouldn't have stayed home today."

"Sloan, it's Friday, and I was already out yesterday. I didn't feel like going in." He held up a fistful of hangers strewn with her maternity clothes. "Now just tell me where you want these."

She raised her eyebrows. "In the other bedroom."

"No, you're staying in here. The bathroom is closer and the other room isn't ready for anyone."

"Then you shouldn't be in there, either. This is your house."

He faced her square. "If you aren't saying that you want me in here with you, then be quiet about it and tell me where you want these hung."

She snapped her mouth together. *Dammit.* She did want him in here with her. She'd let him help. She knew there was no protecting her heart, but some part of her still thought it was better this way. When she opened her mouth again, she made sure to let out only the phrase. "Over on the left, please."

She couldn't have him in here every night. She would go mad, playing house like that. This was already too much. Max hanging her clothes in his closet. Smoothing them. Asking if he could put the folded things into a drawer. And pulling open the second drawer, spotlessly empty, when she protested.

Leaving was going to be hell. Especially when she added the consideration that she would be leaving her babies behind, at least sometimes. He would want his time... And she would leave. She was so grateful, but still angry.

On the way to her place, he'd asked her about working from home.

"How do you know about that?" She'd been puzzled, but he hadn't even answered her before she put it together. "*You* put Bernstein up to that! You intervened on my behalf. Max! That's not your place."

The man had a tendency to run roughshod over her and it was really starting to piss her off.

"I was just trying—"

"Stop! Stop trying." She turned to face him, and he'd been about to say something about her anger and the babies and she'd had enough of all this shit. "No, Max, don't make excuses. Stop forcing your help on me. I *do* need help. You were right about that, but you're not right about everything."

"Don't you like that you won't have to take your leave until it's actually time? Don't you like that you'll have a paycheck until then? I get that it's smaller but it's not zero and that's important."

She wanted to swallow all of it. "Max, you're missing the point. It doesn't matter if you're right. It matters that you're trying to make decisions for me without asking how I feel about them. Maybe it's a great idea but I wanted to make it myself."

"What does it matter who says it?" He stopped at a light and turned and looked at her with a truly puzzled frown.

"Oh, dear God. Have you *ever* had a girlfriend or a woman in your life who was her own person?" She'd been trying to make him think about his mother or something, to think about how he was treating her. But his prolonged silence as he seemed to need to think about it made her want to crawl out of the car. "Are you living in a cave? Do you not understand that when you suggest it, the message you are sending to Bernstein is that I can't handle it myself? That the men will take care of it? It's *my* job."

His voice was small as he pseudo-apologized. "I was trying to make things easier for you."

"You did. You made this one thing easier and you made everything down the road harder. I can't be taken seriously if I don't speak for myself." She huffed out another sigh. She really did believe his heart was in the right place. "I get it. Biologically, I'm hindered by this pregnancy and you aren't. You're trying to be helpful. But you need to remember that I didn't just become a piece of baby Tupperware that you need to control—"

"I'm not trying to control you, Sloan!" He was almost angry.

So was she. "Could've fooled me." Then she held up her hand, not wanting to get into an actual fight. "Imagine it this way: you get sick. You're home for a week and in that week, I've rearranged your desk at work to be more organized and signed your documents for you. I agreed to new cases and called your clients. Told Bernstein you wouldn't be back for *another* week. Just trying to be helpful." She swung that last sentence upward at the end to put a cheery tone on it.

Max was silent for a minute, then he made the last turn and nodded. Parking in front of her house, he walked around the front of the car and held out his hand as she climbed out. "I'm sorry. I get it now. I didn't mean to step on your toes."

"Can't see them anyway," she muttered and he laughed, the tension broken.

"I really am sorry, Sloan. You're right."

She nodded. "I will stay with you. I do need help, but you need to make suggestions rather than just *doing* these things. I need you to ask first. And I need you to consider that I need you to ask first even more because there are suddenly so many things I can't do and it's driving me fucking nuts! I need to be able to still make whatever decisions I can. I can't go to work and see my friends. I haven't had any human contact except you for the last forty-eight hours." She was griping and she knew it.

As she talked, his face and shoulders fell a little and he nodded. But he seemed to get the point and once they were inside the apartment, he let her direct his every move. The one move of his that she didn't have control over was the one where he burrowed even further inside her heart. Barely an hour later, they made it back to his place.

Sloan sighed deeply and shoved what she could from her mind, not bothering to correct him when he took it for exhaustion, and made her lay back down. So she watched while he unpacked, mortified when he handled her underthings, and relieved when he let it pass without comment.

He asked which books she wanted by the bed. She'd been too embarrassed to bring the romance novels, so she chose a mystery with what looked like a good love plot and tried to forget the half-read paperback with the half-naked man on the front.

"Oh, I found this by your bed and brought it, too. It had a bookmark in it." He held something just beyond her range of vision.

Rolling, she turned to see what it was. Of course, it was the borderline erotica romance novel. Half of it clearly well read, the second half as yet untouched. She grinned. "Oh thanks." *Oh yes, bring on the humiliation.*

"You read that stuff?" His hands were on his hips, and he stared down, head tilted, and waited.

She could be ashamed, or defensive or... "Of course, I read it. *Everybody* does! *And* her name is Sloan, so how could I not?"

Taking the book back from her, he now examined the steamy scene on the cover with fresh eyes. He pointed, "Is this Max?"

The half-clothed, black-eyed lover was Max's opposite in so many ways. She stifled a giggle. "No, that's Storm Wind."

"Bummer. Max is a much better name."

"For an Apache?"

His eyebrows rose. "Of course. Max is Apache for *Manly Warrior.*"

Now she really did giggle. A little too much. "Ouch." A few deep breaths and she'd be fine.

His reaction was a little less severe now. After just twenty-four hours it already felt comfortable to be here with him.

His voice cut into her thoughts. "What do you want for dinner?"

Sloan cocked her head, a bemused smile playing at her lips. "What could you possibly make me with bread, mustard, and cold peanut butter? Never mind, I don't want to know. Despite being pregnant, I won't eat it."

"How about chicken lasagna?"

"You are kidding me. From the freezer, right?" She was leaning up on her elbows, the fictional Sloan and Storm Wind almost forgotten, dangling from her fingers.

Max approached her, his form putting Storm Wind to shame. The reality and smell of him was far better than her fantasy of another man. He plumped another pillow and pushed it behind her, then pulled her elbows out taking the weight off them. "From scratch, in about an hour and a half. How about some carrots and juice in the meantime?"

Her mouth watered, and she could easily think of more than one reason why.

CHAPTER 36

"I'm sorry," Sloan apologized again. "I'm whining."

It was bad enough that she was miserable most of the time and only fairly miserable the rest. She was honest enough to admit that she wouldn't want to be around her either.

"It's okay. I can't begin to imagine what you're going through." Max sat next to her and stabbed a sausage link from his plate next to hers on the bed tray.

She couldn't pull the tray in close the way it was meant to be used. At best she got it as close as knee distance. "Don't get me wrong. It really is amazing and I really am excited, I'm just...."

"More uncomfortable than you've ever been in your entire life?"

She nodded and scooped another mouthful of fluffy omelet. The man had not been kidding about being able to cook.

"Dr. Lee's instructions basically keep you chained to the bed. I can't imagine that myself. I just have to be up and around to stay sane."

"Me, too. Except when people threaten my unborn children." Sloan nodded again. "I've now read more in the past two weeks than in the entire rest of my life combined." Next bite, hash browns, crispy and a little salty, just like she liked him. If she hadn't measured about as big around as an ancient redwood she would have thought she was living the dream.

A little knot formed in the center of her chest. He was silent, for the moment just eating in her company. "Thank you."

His blue eyes found hers, and he fixed her with a solid stare. "Stop thanking me. I—"

After a moment, when it became clear that he wasn't going to finish the statement, she spoke again. "You've gone above and beyond the call of duty, Max."

He smiled. "I know. I wanted to."

"I'm sorry I got so mad about you talking to Mr. Bernstein." Contrite. That was the word for the knot in her chest. "I should have just trusted you had the right intentions, you've been nothing but good to me."

That earned her a genuine smile. The kind she was seeing more and more lately. The kind that reached all the way to his eyes, that she could see in his posture. The kind that spread heat throughout her whole system in a way that she would have to deal with later. But right now, sitting in his bed, eating breakfast on a Sunday morning, pregnant with his twins, she would ignore the inevitable and sink deeper into the feeling.

"You were right. I wasn't paying attention to how I did it. I would have been upset with me, too."

Blinking a few times Sloan hauled herself out of dreamland and back to the conversation at hand.

"So you know, I originally went in to tell him I was considering filing a complaint about how differently he'd treated you and me about taking the full twelve weeks of leave."

Sloan felt the shocked expression plaster itself on her face. "What did he say?"

"That I was right, and that he needed to rethink what he was saying. He added that women are more likely to leave. I told him maybe it was because he kept *suggesting* it to them! So that part time thing was somewhat his idea to make it up to you. But we did cook it up together without you." He took a deep breath and got serious. "Tell me honestly, are you all right with the outcome?"

"Ohmigod, yes." She had used the offer to finagle herself a deal. Three-quarter-time pay, plus benefits, no loss of maternity time, and work to do in bed. Contracts to review from home. And Max was providing courier service. She got to talk shop on the phone a few times a day to others in the office. She had an excuse to call Max at work. "I have *something to do*. And I'm earning some money. I'm really not sure how you managed to tell Bernstein you were going to write him up and managed to turn that into a benefit to me."

"It's what I do." He held up his orange juice and clinked it against her glass. "Cheers."

He emptied his plate while she was still eating, and sat, just watching her, for a few moments before he spoke softly. "Should we pack your hospital bags today?"

"Oh, no! It's still way too early." She could feel her whole body pause, deathly still.

"Sloan—"

"It's too early." She picked up her fork and started to eat again. She was done with this conversation.

But his hand reached out and claimed hers, stilling the movement. Even though her eyes stayed squeezed shut, he was looking at her, she knew.

"Sloan..." Like cold water, his voice smoothed past her. "We have to do this. Dr. Lee said we should have done it last week, just in case."

"I can't."

"Then I will."

"No!" She grabbed for his hand, catching it even with her eyes still closed and stopping his rise from the bed.

"I don't understand. Please, tell me why."

"It can't be done." Her voice was barely a whisper. And having said it she opened her eyes.

He saw. The sheer terror there, what she couldn't hide. Instantly he was at her side, arms around her, his lips soft at her temple, her cheek, her mouth. "Tell me." But he was kissing her again. "What's so scary about having these babies?"

Again, his mouth against hers, and his hands tangled in her hair had the power to pull the tension out of her, to convince her to confess, to believe that it wasn't so terrifying after all.

When at last he pulled back enough for her to speak, it still took a moment to gather her breath and the words. "I'm not scared of having them."

"Then what?" He hadn't let go of her face and held her still, eye to eye, while he waited her out.

"I'm scared of *not* having them."

A few blinks from him, then understanding. But the dam had been breached, and the words came flooding out. "They're already in danger of being early because they're twins. The problems that put me on bed rest in the first place triple that chance. If they come too early, I'll have to go home from the hospital without my babies." The flood came now in tears, too.

"They won't come too early. We're taking good care of you. You've done a great job of staying in bed and staying unstressed. I have faith that it will all be fine."

The fear boiled again in her. "Everybody does! Everybody does their best, but it still happens. It has to happen to somebody, there's no cosmic law that says it can't be me!"

"Us," he corrected, his arms tight and warm around her. "I know. It's occurred to me that everyone else gets a newborn. But we'll get two, and probably preemies."

"What if we only get one?" The barest of whispers, her voice seeped between her sobs. "What if we have to come home and leave them at the hospital?"

"That's not happening." He let her tighten her around him

this time, let her leach some of the faith from him. "There are two of us. We won't leave them at the hospital. We'll stay. We'll find a way. And we'll cross that bridge when we come to it."

She nodded as he pushed her hair back out of her face and brushed the fallen tears from her cheeks. His kiss absorbed most of her panic, her frantic fear.

"Sloan, packing that bag does not give the universe permission to do this to us. It's just one less thing to take care of later."

"Okay." She tried to buy it, really, she did.

"And, more importantly—on the off chance that it does happen—we need to give these babies every opportunity. That means no running around like chickens with our heads cut off. We grab the bag and go. We have to be ready."

He was right. He made sense, and when she admitted it, she really didn't. "Okay, let's just do this so I can forget about it."

Max nodded and found a small suitcase and the list of *what to take* from one of his pregnancy books. While Sloan directed, he told her how he set his cell phone to Dr. Lee's number every night just before he went to sleep, so all he had to do was press "Call." He actually slept better, he said, knowing he had taken as many details off his shoulders as he could.

She smiled. Then it turned to bafflement as he opened the bottom drawer of the bureau. "I hid these right under your nose. I hope you like them." And without much flourish he handed the small pile to her. The top pieces were matching peach satin, clearly from a pricey lingerie store. Matching pajamas, with lacey edging, and a drawstring waist. She fingered the fine material. "Max—"

He interrupted, "I know they're larger than what you usually wear, and I'm sure they'll be too big really soon, but I thought you should have something nice to wear at the hospital, since we'll be there at least a few days." He was nervous, shifting from one foot to another, turning back to his job of packing. He added travel packs of shampoos and toothpastes to the suitcase as well as a few changes of clothing for him.

"It's beyond nice, it's beautiful." She laid the clothing out across her knees and spread the sleeves out flat. It was gorgeous, and it had been resting on something soft. When she opened up the powder blue confection it was a bathrobe, short and fleecy and thick. "Max! You didn't have to—"

"I wanted to."

Her voice found its way. "Thank you."

Before she got both words out, he was sitting on the bed next to her, all but a few items packed, his hands on her again. His mouth sought hers and she offered no resistance. She had none to give.

With one arm, he tucked himself up alongside her, holding her where his lips and tongue could taste little bits of her jaw, her ear, her eye. While she let out tiny sighs as she melted into him, his free hand pulled the gifts from the coverlet, letting them drop onto the open bag he had left beside the bed.

Her neck was sampled while he lifted the coverlet and slid in beside her, lifting her legs to drape over his. He turned off the lamp, not letting up on his assault and folded her neatly into him.

When he had her where he wanted her, and when Sloan was sure he would settle into deep breathing, his fingers trailed up her arm, until at last they turned her face to him again.

"Sloan." It asked everything and answered nothing, as did the deep searching kisses he dulled her senses with.

CHAPTER 37

M ax held her hand. He did it to keep her steady, not just because he liked it, right? He smiled, because it was a beautiful day, and not because he had slept curled next to her each of the past three nights. More importantly, he'd woken up with her in his arms the past three mornings. No empty beds, no notes, just Sloan. Each Morning, she'd been pressed against him, once sprawled halfway across his chest, her hair trailing along his shoulder and her breath against his neck a sweet enough pleasure that he had gladly been late to work. She let him run his fingers through her hair and didn't protest.

The second night, Max crawled in after she was already asleep, but last night he'd come in earlier and found her reading. An open arm was all the invitation necessary for her to scoot over and tuck herself alongside him. She had read while he had turned his face into her hair and pressed tiny kisses along her temple.

Tonight, he was praying for long, deep soul kisses and missing shirts and searching hands. It felt like she had finally given in to the inevitable—that they belonged together. Nothing had ever meant as much. He intended to do everything he could to keep her with him. So, fingers laced through hers, he pulled her along to the garage and opened the door with no fanfare.

She gasped. "Ohmigod. Is this yours?" Her eyes were wide as she turned to face him.

He somewhat nodded. "Ours." He wasn't going to propose again. That always seemed to wind up with her upset and saying 'no.' The doctor said they needed to minimize her stress. So no more proposals. At least not until after the babies were home. For now, he wasn't above making moves. Getting her into his arms at night. Tying her shoes if necessary. Touching her whenever possible.

And he wanted to touch her. She looked amazing in her short jeans, and white linen blouse, sneakers laced, hair loose, and eyes wide. "You bought a minivan?"

"You can't get car seats into a sports car, nor should you." He opened the door and helped her up into the seat.

"But where's the coupe?"

"Traded it in." He closed her door then walked around and climbed behind the wheel. He still wasn't used to it. It was like driving a big hulk of metal after years spent in one sleek mini-coupe after another. However, that was exactly what he wanted wrapped around his kids. And his wife.

"Oh, you didn't."

"Yes...Yes, I did," He grinned, wide and silly and sure. If there was one thing he wanted to be positive of, it was that she would never mistake his emotion for feeling hemmed in or simply doing-the-right-thing. Sloan might not know it yet, but she was going to marry him. Her curling into him at night had given him a new outlook on things. He had at least another forty rounds in him yet.

"Wow." She twisted, looking down the length of the car. "They aren't even born yet, and already you're vying for father of the year."

"Why thank you—" He stopped himself just short of adding

Mrs. Summerland to the end of that thought. He was stopping himself a lot these days, but that one was a first. With his mouth clamped firmly shut lest something fall out of it, Max pulled out of the driveway and headed to her weekly appointment with Dr. Lee. Somehow, they made the drive in complete silence.

Well, there was silence in the car. In his head he heard nothing but the roar of his thoughts. *Mrs. Summerland. Mrs. Max Summerland. Mrs. Sloan Summerland.* It all sounded good to him. He liked the ring of it, the way it would feel on his tongue. But why didn't she?

Sloan Ellis continued to baffle him. She just kept saying 'no.'

Not that he thought he was so irresistible—he wasn't that hung up on himself. He was okay in the looks department, the income department, the chivalry code. Probably not stellar at any of them, he knew.

It was that he felt in every cell that Sloan had been made just for him. He had felt that lightning bolt hit him that first time they'd met. It had been both animalistic lust and something much deeper and more profound at the same time. His mother had once told him he would know when he found "it." Max couldn't say he'd taken her comment to heart. Now that it had happened, he understood. He'd just *known*. How was he supposed to convince Sloan that generations of witchcraft in his family had given him the ability to see that they belonged together? That was doubly hard since he hadn't even yet broached the subject of having generations of witches in his family. He still hadn't even told her he'd pulled spells off her. She seemed blissfully unaware of any of it.

One day, he'd have to tell her all of it, but not today. Most people had no real comprehension of what it was to be a witch. So telling her what he could do would likely stress her out. His confession was off the menu for a while. Still, every minute they were together just proved it more to him. She understood him.

She made him better. She made him laugh. She wanted him. She loved him. Why didn't she know that?

At one point she had.

He still wasn't convinced, like she was, that she hadn't been herself in Chicago. She couldn't have been anybody else. None of what she'd said or done had been un-Sloan-like in any way. She had been shy, and surprised, when he confessed his feelings to her. Offering only little bits and pieces, and finally, oh so carefully, opening her heart. She'd told him about her past. About Craig. About Joe. About how scared she was to be wrong again. And how this was different.

He had told her about the ring. How he had picked it out for her the day after they had met. Max remembered at that moment he'd been so afraid that would send her screaming, making her think he was truly insane. Instead, she'd smiled, been surprised and flattered, and she'd said 'yes.' She said that she was sure about him and them. It was only after that, that their clothes had melted away and she had thrown his universe off kilter again.

His memory of that night was a huge part of why he couldn't seem to accept that she didn't want him. Because she did. She had. He had to have that back. Whatever it took. Even if what it took was patience. Max knew that whatever he was or wasn't, he prided himself on not being stupid. If he threw away what they found that night would be stupid.

Luckily, she was sitting in the cushy seat beside him, somewhere between two to six weeks from turning his world upside down again. And he couldn't wait.

So he held her hand in the parking garage, and sat flush up against her while they waited for Dr. Lee. He laughed and stole a few kisses when the ultrasound looked like Baby B just might be a girl.

When Sloan inquired softly about ice cream, he pulled in to

the nearest specialty shop and ordered up two sundaes. Then he got jealous of her plastic spoon.

He couldn't cast a spell to make her love him. Well, he *could*, but it was wrong and it wouldn't be real. No, he had to actually win her over. Max contemplated what he could do to remind her of what she'd said in Chicago, or maybe, if she couldn't remember, he could duplicate it.

Later, he had to leave her at the house and head back to work. If she was being good, she napped. And he planned.

CHAPTER 38

"Are you dressed?"

Sloan's head snapped up as she slipped her feet into her shoes. "Yes, come in."

"Ready to go?" He held his hand out, and she put a little pressure into the grasp, allowing him to help pull her to standing.

With a small smile, she nodded. An *outing*!

Rae had come and stayed with her when possible. They'd played an epic game of Monopoly one day. Another time, Sloan had worked with Rae out at the dining room table, doing her own job. But she brought food and stayed in the bedroom for a TV show or two. Yasmin brought a scrying bowl one afternoon and they'd tried to see the babies, though it hadn't come clear. Luke had stayed home with their own new infant and Yasmin had spent much of the time showing off baby pictures. Sloan had begged to see more.

The dark haired baby girl managed to look like the perfect mix of Yasmin and Luke. Megan had come once, so had Luke, and so had Delilah. Sloan had them come during the day when she was most prone to boredom, or would most discover something she needed to get out of bed for.

But none of them had crossed paths with Max. With Yasmin and Megan and Delilah, it made sense. They wouldn't have hidden the scrying bowl. Delilah would have said hello in their living room while waving her burning sage and just looked at Max as though he was the odd one. On the upside, Sloan could have brushed them off as her crazy friends, but she hadn't wanted to even get into it. They didn't have children...yet. So they didn't have a custody arrangement yet either. Sloan was not willing to play with that at all.

But as she got ready to go out, she realized she always told Max when someone had come over; he'd even encouraged it. Still, none of her friends—even Rae—had ever crossed paths with Max. Had she unconsciously done that on purpose? Kept them separated? She couldn't say for sure, but she didn't really have time to think about it. She had to get ready to leave this house.

Glorious day, she was getting out. Even if it was to work. Dear God, she never thought she'd see the day when she would be just so excited to see the building. But she could talk face-to-face with everyone, and maybe sit at her desk and pretend her life wasn't upside down.

In her original plan, she would have worked right up until she went into labor. Of course, that was when she had thought she was only having one. That was before she understood the need for bed rest. Before she'd become someone for Max to take care of. Sloan had expected a lot of things that hadn't come to pass. Still, now she was simply excited to be back in the new minivan, cruising along.

She wanted to like it, and really she did. She had wondered how Max thought he was going to get any car seat into the back of that sports car, let alone two. The problem was that he hadn't simply traded up a level, he'd gone for the minivan. He'd bought the house. He'd even taken care of her. Max had outdone her at every turn.

Sloan was coming to grips with the fact that Mommy would never measure up to Daddy in their kids' eyes. Worse, how was she going to leave? What if she caved? She wouldn't. All she had to do was imagine putting her kids through a divorce when Daddy found the right woman.

"You're quiet today."

She smiled, just a little. "I've got a lot on my mind."

"Care to share?"

No. "I'm happy to see everybody and all, but *the day* just keeps getting closer, and I have no real idea what to expect. And no one can tell me. And..." She let the sigh she had been holding back escape. Now that she had voiced it, all the things were true. Yet none of them had been what she was actually worrying over.

"Overwhelmed?"

She nodded, glad that he had accepted her answer at face value.

"We're in this together, Sloan." His smile beseeched her to let him be 'in this' with her. What he didn't realize what that 'together' was the problem, not the solution. Giving only a tight nod in response, she was thankful when he let it drop.

Finally, he pulled into the parking structure, eliciting a scared gasp from her as the top of the minivan came precariously close to the ceiling beams of the parking level. Sloan cringed waiting for the grind of metal. Then craned her neck to look.

Max just laughed. "Yeah, it still freaks me out, too. Every time I pull into one of these things I think the top is going open like a sardine can. But it hasn't happened yet."

True to his prediction, the car and the parking structure remained intact, and he pulled the beast of a car smoothly into a spot near the door.

It was all familiar, but certainly not the same. Max was carrying all her binders, for one. He didn't dare let anyone crowd her on the elevator, just like she had hoped they wouldn't. Only no one really tried. Lord, the way they were staring at her and backing away, they must have thought she was going to go into labor right then and there. Like she would ask one of them to deliver the baby.

The more she thought about it, the more she understood. With twins, she must look about ten months pregnant. No wonder they all looked at her with worried faces. Max didn't seem to notice the looks they were getting. He just laced his fingers through hers and kept close.

Finally, after several stops of people looking relieved to get off, the doors opened on fifteen. And Sloan was surprised to find herself staring at an empty front desk topped by a pastel banner that read "Congratulations Sloan and Max."

She blinked a few times, but the words remained hanging there across the paneling behind the front desk. This was not her imagination. Slowly she turned. "Did you know about this?"

From the dazed expression on his face, he was just as surprised as she. Max shook his head and walked into the main room, trailing Sloan behind, fingers still laced together. He looked shocked to find decorations and a cake. By his expression, he hadn't figured out as the elevator doors opened that it was a baby shower.

Vanessa came up and put her arms around Sloan's shoulders. "We didn't think jumping out and yelling *surprise* was really a wise thing to do in this case."

Sloan laughed. "Thank you."

In seconds they had her with her feet up in a chair that had been wheeled into the center of the common area. They had set out punch and cake, and then they tormented her and Max with silly baby shower games. They started by cutting strings each person thought would exactly go around Sloan's belly. The women had no issues with finding out if their strings were the right distance around the pregnant lady. The guys however, couldn't deal.

"I know I won't win." Holding up his string, Neil approached. Sloan just laughed. It must have been all of twenty-five inches.

"Neil wins!" She exclaimed. When everyone raised their eyebrows at her, she rescinded. "Well, he has my vote anyway. Did you really think I was that small?"

He shrugged, looking thoroughly embarrassed by the whole thing. He made his way back to where the guys had huddled in the corner, as if they might protect Max from the brouhaha and baby vibes. Periodically, he looked up and met her gaze, making sure she was okay, checking in without words to see if she needed anything. Even from across the room he waited on her.

But he didn't have to, Sloan got fawned over. She almost cried, the way they all seemed so excited for her. To her eternal gratitude, not a single one asked about her and Max. How she was living in his house. In his bed. Why she didn't have a ring.

Finally, they did make her cry. When they sat Max on the floor next to her chair and made him let her open all but a few of the gifts. Slowly the mountain of small fluffy things grew. Blankets and little teddy bears. Sleepers, footies, diaper genies, and a few big things. Swings. A dual stroller.

Of course, those were from the guys, who had simply taken up a collection and thrown the money at Vanessa and told her to get something good and not too ruffly. Only Wil came up with his own present and he handed it to Max. "Here you go, bud."

He turned back to the group and spoke up, as sure of himself as any man could be at a baby shower. "I happen to know that this guy right here—" He pointed down to where Max sat, "is really looking forward to all this. He's excited about becoming a dad. And to that I say 'why!?'" Wil shook his head in shame. "And we didn't even get to give him a bachelor party."

He addressed the rest of it directly to Max. "I couldn't in good conscience get you anything that had to do with diapers or drool or crying. But I hope that you enjoy this anyway."

So Max opened the huge box to find tiny baseball caps and matching shirts with small training bats and child sized mitts and even a tee. He held up each piece, grinning and showing it off proudly to the group. Suddenly, Sloan was hit with a certain vision of the future. It gripped her, both in her heart and her brain. She knew it was real, maybe the same way Rae knew her feelings were real. In her mind's eye, she saw Max in that backyard with two small kids who could barely walk—

She didn't dare let the vision go any further. Luckily, Jenna broke into her thoughts. "What if they're girls?"

Wil looked exasperated. He grabbed one of the tiny caps and gestured with it. "That is just the kind of sexist thinking that's holding women back. The hats have a place to put your ponytail through. Good lord."

Sloan smiled before Wil turned back to Max, looking for all the world like he was sending his best friend off to World War Two Normandy. "Good luck, buddy." He sighed.

CHAPTER 39

Her whole body felt heavy. Her arms were weighted down, her back was stiff, and her legs just wanted to curl around the body pillow and lay in the big, fluffy bed that was her home for way too many hours of the day. She was rarely allowed to leave it, even though she wanted to. The last doctor's appointment had revealed that her amniotic fluid remained low. The good new was that as the babies got bigger, they got healthier and more able to survive an early delivery. They also got more likely to come early.

Usually she hated the bed. It had become a comfy, fluffy prison. But right now she was tired. Snuggling back in, she decided she wanted to enjoy one of the few moments when she actually wanted to be here.

Rolling over, Sloan stared at the ceiling. It wasn't to be. She simply could not sleep. There was only a thin stream of light coming from under the door, not the glaze of sunshine that met her in the early morning hours. At least when the babies came and demanded to be fed at all hours, she would already be plenty used to getting up all hours of the night.

She shuffled a little, careful not to wake Max, as he still had to get up and go to work the next morning. She stared at the ceiling some more, walked her way through a fantasy of meeting Max on the beach instead of Joe. Wondering if they would have even liked each other back then, she finally managed to get tired again.

Well, that had been the plan anyway. With a great effort, Sloan rolled to look at the clock on the side table. 3:27. All of sixteen minutes since she had last looked at it. Why was she still awake? With a quiet sigh, she shifted under the covers, again taking the best care not to disturb the sleeping man beside her. He had to be awake at six thirty to get to work on time.

Instantly, she missed his heat. Very quickly, she'd gotten used to having him here, next to her, holding her at night. She wondered what she would do after the babies came and she was in her own bed again. Alone. She shoved the thought away. There was nothing she could do about it now. So through heavy lids she made out the bathroom door and pushed herself upright, yawning as she went. As carefully as she could, she slipped through the door into the moonlit master bath, cringing as she clicked the door shut behind her.

God she felt heavy. All this bed-rest was making her weak. Through the haze of half-sleep and half-exhaustion she couldn't even tell if she had to pee or not. Sloan tried to force her eyes open a little, to get a better look at herself in the mirror. She'd left the light off, knowing that her eyes would never fully adjust to it, and that she didn't really want to push herself all the way to awake. She looked a mess. Her hair wound round her head and aimed sleepy corkscrews in every direction. Her eyes looked like she had just enough gin in her to try for a good sultry look and miss the mark. Her lips looked puffy, and she chewed on them just for a minute, before realizing any effort was useless and she really should go back to bed.

She blinked the blink of the undead a few times and took a faulty step backward, only upon lifting her foot did she realize that she had stepped in something wet. She cursed the need for actual thought as she leaned over a bit, trying to determine what had made the dark stain on the carpet. Who knew?

But as she stood back up, she found out. Fluid gushed from between her legs, making a second dark patch on the bathroom floor. The words ran through her brain. Surely her water had broken. It had to have. That was the only logical explanation. But it couldn't have. She was still five weeks from her due date. It was too early. That was when the panic set in.

"Max." It was no louder than a whispered croak.

So she bit her lip, causing enough pain to focus herself, and she yelled. To wake the dead. To screech out all the fear she felt. "Max!"

Her eyes finally opening all the way, she watched, in slow motion, as he pushed the bathroom door open, eyes wide, "Sloan!"

Her lips quivered and she heard no sound. She imagined she only mouthed the words, "My water broke."

He followed her pointed finger to the soaked spots on the floor, taking in the wet front of her gown. "Oh god."

Immediately Max launched into action, turning to put their plan into action. The bag, the car, his pants. At the last moment, he stopped for a second, turned back, and grabbed the sides of her head. Pulling her to him, he kissed her, lightning fast, but with all the fluid force of a hurricane, and he smiled, "Let's go do this."

Sloan breathed in deep, and then she flipped out. Max made normal motions. He'd been sleeping in solid color pajama pants. Clearly deciding this was perfectly acceptable for the maternity ward, he pulled on a T-shirt and slipped on sneakers, and was standing, hair all askew but packed bags in hand as she emerged from the bathroom.

"I'm not dressed." It was the only thing she could think of to say. Her brain wasn't working.

As his hands simply opened, the bags dropped and hit the floor. "Okay." He popped open a drawer and pulled out a pair of comfy pants and a maternity T-shirt and held them out to her. Then he stood there, waiting.

"Go away."

"What?" He seemed truly perplexed, like he should just stand there while she climbed her rotund self out of her wet gown and horrible maternity underwear.

"Go away." When he didn't move, she added, "Now."

He hustled, grabbing both bags, and heading out of the room. As Sloan peeled her sodden clothes and looked around for some way to dry off, she heard the beep of the car alarm being unlocked out in the garage. She found underwear and grabbed a towel in case her *other* water broke, and she laughed out loud at the ridiculousness of it all. Then she started crying.

Luckily, she was as fast as him, and she was dressed and running a brush through her hair by the time he came rushing back in, grinning until he saw her tears. "Baby..."

"I'm so scared. It's still too early."

"I know. They'll be fine. I just know it. Let's go." He gently took the brush from her hand and then hauled her behind him out the door to the garage.

Max was looking at her with a funny expression as she spent a moment spreading out the towel on the minivan's passenger seat. "I don't want to ruin your car. Oh!... I should get some plastic. The towel could soak right through. I..."

"Shut up and get in the car." He was suddenly behind her, his hands at her waist, and he was 'helping' her to climb in when the first one hit.

"Owww."

Instantly his hands released her. "I'm sorry, I..."

Sloan couldn't speak. The air had been suddenly sucked from her lungs with the pain gathering in her abdomen. It had to be a contraction. God, it hurt like a... She only shook her head and pointed to her belly. He understood what that meant, and it spurred him into action again. Reaching across her waist, he buckled her in then closed her door, watching for her fingers and toes the way he would with a child. Then he bolted around the car, climbing in, starting the ignition, and throwing the car into reverse all in one motion. By the time she could breathe again, they were already past the first light. Taking a breath, she gave her first instruction. "Call doctor Lee."

"Already did." He waved his cell phone at her, before he pocketed it and laced his fingers through hers. Then they were careening through the predawn streets. Max, the simple, straightforward man, was in a panic, and was trying desperately not to show it.

A smile burst across her face and she knew, from somewhere deep, that she loved him. Some part of her wanted to tell him that. But the fact was, none of that mattered now. She had a job to do. She had two healthy babies to deliver. Right then, another contraction hit.

"Here!" Max flicked his watch off and deposited it on what was passing for her lap these days. "Time them."

She nodded and wished she'd paid more attention. But Max seemed to understand that, too.

"Little breaths in and out, in and out."

Sloan found it was more work than expected to just not hyperventilate. If it hadn't hurt so much she would have laughed about the whole thing. A thought suddenly occurred as the pain ended. "Max, we're going to get to see their faces."

"I know." He grinned at her until she waved desperately at the road he wasn't watching. At least it was empty this time of night. Then the minivan was racing through the parking structure at the hospital, a little too fast for her taste, but before she could comment on his driving she was deposited on a bench by the door and the guard was called to bring a wheelchair as Max raced away.

For the briefest of moments she worried he'd simply abandoned her in a fit of hysteria. *What if he doesn't come back?* The thought was brief enough to be cut off by the squeal of his tires as he found a spot just beyond the row of handicapped parking. Max came racing up on foot, looking like a crazed lunatic, or a man about to become a father for the first time, just about the time the guard arrived with the wheelchair.

"Okay baby, climb in." Max tossed the duffel bag over his shoulder and helped her to the chair.

Finally finding some of her own calm, she tugged at his hand. "I'd like to walk."

"But you can't."

"Why? Because I might send myself into labor?"

Max tugged harder. "Because they might be able to stop it."

Well, damn. He made sense. Though Sloan had told herself that most babies born five weeks early turned out fine, if they could keep them in another week or so, it would help them. Unable to argue, she sat obediently, and let him wheel her up to maternity where they were expected.

Inside of ten minutes she had been stripped, gowned, injected, and tied to wires and monitors. Two heartbeats were chugging like tiny trains, echoing through the labor room. On the TV set mounted in the far upper corner of the room, they could watch the lines as little heart rates changed. On another monitor, they watched as her contractions came and went. Other mothers in labor were monitored on the screen, too. But it was the code of their own little babies that had them both transfixed. The noises of the steady little hearts were soothing to her own heart. They sounded stable, and the numbers said both rhythms hovered around one hundred and fifty beats per minute. She'd done her reading and knew that was a good number. So far, there didn't seem to be anything too drastic to worry about.

Before she knew it, Doctor Lee had arrived and was

delivering news before even getting a 'hello' out. "Well, Sloan, it looks like the Terbutyline didn't work. You're going to have these babies this morning."

They talked a little, then Max followed Dr. Lee into the hall, leaving her alone for a moment and feeling quite a bit left out. There was nothing she could do about it; she was tied to the bed and held under threat of hurting her babies. She was left to sit and wait patiently and feel the tiny creatures in her rolling and getting ready to come out.

Sloan looked up as Max came back into the room. "What did you talk about?"

"I asked what we were in for."

"Oh." She wasn't sure that she really wanted to hear, but he spoke anyway.

"She said that she thinks they'll be okay. A lot of babies are born this early nowadays and they survive just fine." He took a deep breath, and plunged his fingers into his hair. It was now standing straight off his head, but Sloan didn't have time to care. "She said that they'll be small, and they'll be in an incubator for a while, and they'll have oxygen in their noses and monitors and wires everywhere, and maybe IVs, but that in a few months no one will ever be able to tell." Finally he looked at her to gauge her reaction.

"Okay." Taking a deep breath, Sloan reminded herself she could handle anything as long as her babies would be okay.

CHAPTER 40

"Can you move your toes?"

Sloan concentrated as hard as she ever had on anything. Still, her toes didn't move. She just grinned like a maniac and answered "Nope, try again later."

She felt remarkably well for having been sliced open after seven hours of labor. How could she not? She was in a room painted with vines and done in horribly trite mauve accents. She was now in a different bed, one that had a button to raise her head and feet, and it was surely the only way she was going to get her toes to move right now. But there was a large incubator beside her bed with two tiny red creatures in knit hats and the smallest diapers she had ever seen. They were both passed out from exhaustion from their ordeal, but Sloan couldn't summon the ability to sleep.

She knew she should. It was two in the afternoon and she hadn't slept since three a.m. Max had finally run off to find food, but he'd barely stepped out the door when he was back again. "They're going to deliver my meal and bring you a juice with ice."

"Okay, thanks." She only spared a second to look away from her babies at him.

"Will it bother you if I eat in front of you?"

"Oh, no." She grinned at him. She must look like a wild banshee, but she really didn't care. "The anesthetic hasn't even begun to wear off. I can't feel my stomach, I have absolutely no idea if I'm hungry or not."

So Max perched on the edge of the bed and joined her staring into the plastic enclosure where two very tiny chests rose and fell in almost perfect rhythm.

Max's food arrived and he made her sip her juice. She held it with only her right hand so that her left would stay warm, so that she could reach in through the hand hole and touch a little foot or hand. Max was just putting his food into his mouth when a nurse knocked on the door.

"Your sister is here..." She let the end trail up to make a question.

"Oh! Let them in." For the first time, Sloan wondered about her face, if she was still puffy from having morphine, if her hair looked as wild as her most recent adventure would indicate. Rae wouldn't care, but *visitors*, dammit.

She didn't have time to think it through before the nurse was back showing Sam and Rae in through the door. Though Sloan would have thought she was going to get a hug first, both Rae and Sam leaned over the clear incubator and peered in.

It was probably a full minute, where Max and Sloan looked at each other and didn't ask. Comparatively, they were chopped liver. Then Rae turned first and engulfed Sloan in a huge hug. "I have a niece and a nephew! Oh, my God, Sloan. They are amazing."

She watched as her sister turned and held out her hand to the father of Sloan's children. It was the first time the two had met face to face. She wasn't worried about Rae outing her as a witch, but it was odd to realize Rae had met the babies before she'd met the babies' father.

Max seemed to realize it at that moment, too. Sloan wondered if he thought she'd been holding out on him. It didn't matter, there wasn't much she could do at this point. So she stayed silent as Rae held out a hand.

"Max, nice to finally meet you."

"Same to you, Aunt Rae." He grinned as he said it, the oddness of the moment broken and brushed away.

Rae returned his smile and stepped in to hug him. Luckily, Max took it easily. Sloan heard the whispered words between them.

"Thank you for taking care of my sister."

"Thank you for taking care of the mother of my children."

Shit. She should have had them meet before now. Though she couldn't quite put her finger on what it was, she knew something had just changed.

Stepping back for a moment, Max went to scrub his hands. When he came back, he put one hand into the not-quite-sealed hole on the side of the incubator. They watched him reach in, around tiny wire thermometers and several tubes. The heart and temperature monitors were held onto tiny chests with shiny stickers that reflected the light at different angles as the babies breathed.

As Max's skin brushed against one tiny little hand, it moved and curled around his finger, barely covering the first knuckle, and leading Sloan to imagine a day when the little hand would be larger, but still small enough to fit within his grasp.

His voice broke her reverie. "Did we ever decide on names?"

Rae and Sam looked back at her, too as a few blinks fluttered their way across her face. Sloan couldn't hide her shock as she realized she'd believed there was still time to decide. "You liked Lindsey."

He nodded, but never took his eyes off the tiny pair.

"Lindsey March after my grandmother, then. March was her maiden name. If that's all right."

She looked to Rae to see if claiming a family name was alright and was rewarded with a smile and nod.

"I like it." Max shifted his gaze. "And Michael, right?"

"Okay. Michael what?"

"Michael Lennon after my grandmother. Sound good?"

As she was nodding, a tiny wail erupted, and her breath pulled in of its own accord. Michael's voice was small but angry and in the next heartbeat he found out that his little sister would give him a run for his money.

Max looked at her in complete panic. "What do we do?"

"Call the nurse!" She was fumbling for the call button wanting to laugh at herself. Here her child was crying, and she was calling someone else to tell her what to do. What a start at being parents.

But even as she tried to hit the button a nurse came in and looked the new parents up and down. "Looks like I arrived at just the right time."

With an insane efficiency that Sloan knew she would never master, the nurse first shuffled Rae and Sam out of the room. There was no time for hugs as the nurse checked diapers and changed one, all the while never actually looking at the babies she was caring for. She introduced herself as Marybeth and diapered away, explaining how the babies were too young for store-bought wipes. Alcohol and all those additives, you know.

Sloan paid rapt attention, but Marybeth leveled her gaze at Max. "Okay, Dad, this is your job. Watch the first time." She pulled a striped blanket from the warmer under the incubator and laid it out at an angle before flipping one corner down. She then proceeded to open the incubator and remove Michael, laying his squalling little self in the middle. Within five seconds she had him wrapped up tight with just his face and hat showing. He immediately calmed down, and looked, wide-eyed, at the new world around him.

Sloan barely had time to wonder at the marvel of a warm blanket than Marybeth had nestled her tiny baby into his mother's arms and handed another blanket to Max and said "Okay, now it's your turn."

Baby Michael looked up at her, blinking. His little bow mouth formed an 'o' as though he knew what was going on and wasn't sure he approved. Sloan divided her time between gazing down at Michael and looking, worried, at his father.

Poor Max seemed flustered beyond belief. Like he hadn't known he was going to be tested on it. He carefully laid out the soft woven blankie, taking longer for that one step than Marybeth had taken for the whole procedure. Finally, he looked up. "Okay."

Clearly, he hadn't expected to be handed the baby. He held little Lindsey like he thought she would just shatter at any moment. Even Sloan had to comment. "She won't break, Max."

Gently he laid the screaming girl on the center of the blanket and did, or tried to do, exactly as Marybeth instructed. When he was finished, Lindsey wasn't quiet or calm. If anything, she seemed madder. In far less time than it had taken for Max to step back to admire his handiwork, she had flailed her way out of it. His smile fled.

Marybeth's just grew in response. "That's okay, she was way too low in the blanket anyway. Did you see how her eyes were just barely peeking out? You want her whole face to show so she can eat or get her binky."

She proceeded to open the baby back up and help Daddy through it another time. Then she started for a third, at which time Max protested. "Please, can you do it? At this point, I'm just torturing her."

But Marybeth laughed again. "She's fine. She knows you love her. Babies can tell that kind of thing." By the time she had finished soothing the baby's father, she had the baby in a little bundle and being held out to Max.

With a look that combined awe and terror, he took her then let Marybeth hand him what she had declared a "preemie" binky and scoot them off to the next bed. She pulled the drapes around Sloan just far enough to block her view of Max. "Now your chart says you're breastfeeding, is that right?"

Sloan nodded and was purely focused as she and Michael were walked through their first breastfeeding lesson. When all the fumbling was through, they were given a lesson on burping then he was placed back in the incubator and Marybeth went around the drape to fetch Lindsey back.

She chuckled as she handed over the alert baby. "Her Daddy's out cold." Then Marybeth insisted she stay through the second round of breastfeeding, because early babies sometimes didn't want to suck and that was a problem.

It turned out to be a problem that neither of her babies had, Sloan thought. Just as they finished, and she realized that she was the only one still awake, another woman entered the room. She introduced herself and explained that she was there to process the birth certificates.

Sloan calmly answered all the questions. Spelling out each first, last and middle name and reciting Max's address for mailing and both their full names. An eternity later the woman got up to excuse herself and Sloan didn't even see her reach the door before her own head hit the pillow. *Ah, Bliss*, was the last conscious thought that passed through her head.

CHAPTER 41

M ax felt his heart leap into his throat.

Sloan was healthy, whole, and physically ready to go home. But the babies weren't. Not only was it going to be heartbreaking to leave them here, it was exactly what Sloan had been afraid of. While her sister and all her friends had shown up and would help, it still wouldn't get the babies home.

Luckily Dr. Lee took pity on them. "You *do* look a little peaked, Sloan. I can sign you through for one more day. But I don't think I can medically justify much longer than that."

He watched Sloan nod and thank the petite doctor, even though he could tell she was near tears. His hand snaked out and stroked her hair. He hadn't given it permission to do that, but he found he didn't mind when she leaned into his hand. Her voice was tinny. "I can't leave the hospital without them. I... can't..."

"I know." He wanted to say they would do just that if that's what it came down to, because they were strong enough to handle it. But this was not the time to tell her they would suck it up and deal, especially since he didn't know how to deal with it himself. He was trying to be strong, but he was just as panicked as she was.

Max had been home just a couple of times in the past few days, so he'd had a few hours away from the hospital and the babies, though Sloan hadn't. He'd told her he was picking up supplies they had missed. That he was going to shower. He'd done those things, but he'd also pulled out the small altar he'd stashed in the back of the guest room closet and set a spell on both his new children.

It had taken a while and he could only hope Sloan wouldn't call him on the time he was gone. He could claim traffic—he had hit some—but he didn't know how to tell her he'd cast *health* and *safety* spells on their newborn children.

When he returned, he was sweating what she might ask him. But Sloan was waiting in the pretty satin pajamas that he'd gotten for her, the fluffy robe draped over the closet door handle. She'd left it hanging there this morning after her painstakingly slow sojourn to the shower across the hall. Though Max volunteered to help, she insisted that he stay behind. She didn't want the babies to wake up alone.

Max had to admit to himself that while the thought of having twins only made him even more nervous about being a first time parent, he was now insanely glad neither of them was in the incubator alone. It was hard on both him and Sloan that they weren't allowed to cuddle the babies like they wanted. Neither of the twins was holding their temperature like the pediatricians needed to see before they went home. And the dream of Sloan and him walking out of the hospital with babies in arms on a normal time schedule was quickly fading.

Lindsey and Michael would need incubators for what looked like at least another week, as well as round the clock medical attention. When they'd gotten that news, Sloan simply curled into him, just needing comfort, just needing to cry. He held her in his arms, feeling the tiny tremors go through her. With a quick glance around the room he took stock of the situation and decided that he hadn't bargained for any of this.

After he met her, when he had fantasized his future with her, it had involved dating and romance. He envisioned a proposal, a ring, and a 'yes' answer. Children came later—after he and Sloan had time to be themselves—and were born healthy. Also, he had to admit, in his imagination they had come only one at a time. He hadn't fantasized about hospital rooms, and fear, and repeated 'no's.

Still, he couldn't trade any of it away. He loved her and he loved his kids. He just had to figure out a way to fix things. Unfortunately, he didn't know if his next announcement would help things or not. He took a deep breath to get himself started, but Sloan wailed. "How are we going to do this?"

"Well, we'll stay here. We'll go home just for little short whiles, and we'll rotate shifts with them. We'll get comfy chairs and hang out like the other parents in the NICU do. We'll read a lot and work in our easy chairs and hold our kids whenever possible."

It seemed intense but workable. Though before he could finish, she wailed again. "I can't go home! I won't leave them alone and I can't drive for three weeks!"

The aftercare of a C-section, he thought. "We'll get you home. Actually, my mother called yesterday evening..." Sloan looked up at him, tear-streaked face waiting, "From the airport."

Sloan blinked.

"She should be here in about three hours."

"Your Mom?"

He nodded, anxiously waiting for her response. The truth was, Max had no clue what she was thinking. There was a spell for that, but not time nor room to cast it. He was stuck watching her face like any other man.

"Why?"

"Because her grandbabies are in the hospital." *Because her son can't get the mother of her grandbabies to marry him,* but he didn't give voice to that one. That last thing they needed at this point was another 'no' hanging between them.

"She's coming here?"

He nodded even as Sloan's hands flew to her face, her hair. "Oh god, I can't meet her like this!"

Slowly, so slowly that it was painful for him to watch, she climbed out of the bed, using her arms for support, shooing away his attempts to help. She shuffled to the bathroom and grabbed her brush, tediously pulling it through her hair.

He jumped up right behind her. "Hey, calm down. Let me?"

With a smooth motion he removed the brush from her hand and began running it through her hair. Just that act calmed him down if not her. He stopped thinking for a moment to enjoy the soft blonde strands trailing through his fingers. He caught her reflection in the mirror, thinking that even with the tear tracks and her wet blue eyes she was beautiful. He smiled at her reflection. "My mom is coming to help. And I know she can be a bit of a busybody, but you say 'Mom, I need you to do this' or that, and she'll make sure it gets done. The house will be spotless, and you'll have a chauffeur whenever you want."

"I can't do that. I can't call her 'Mom'." Her pink lips turned under and tucked between her teeth. His gut pulled, wishing it was his teeth tugging at her lips, and knowing that she didn't want to hear it.

So he laughed, remembering high school and how everyone all through college had called her Mom. "You should call her Mom, she'll love you forever for it."

"Really?"

"Yeah." If she called his mother 'Mom' it would help the woman believe that Sloan really was a part of his family. It would give him hope that she might make it legal one of these days. He handed back the brush and smoothed her hair beneath his fingers. A tiny squall caught both their attention and he beat

Sloan to the incubator and pulled out a warm squirming body. Lindsey needed changing, and he didn't need a nurse to do it for him anymore.

In a few minutes, his brand new daughter was in a fresh diaper and bundled into a warm towel, one that was tight enough that she couldn't squirm out of it. She screamed some more, a sound that was still charming and magical to her parents' ears. So he handed her off to Sloan. And, as usual, Sloan turned away from him, hiding herself as she breastfed the baby.

She was still turning away from him, still acting like they were separate units. At night, she curled into him as if they were one, but not during the day. He wanted her all the time. Max believed he'd seen their future, but he'd never imagined it would take so long to get here.

A single word kept racing through his mind. *When?*

CHAPTER 42

M rs. Summerland was a godsend. She was also apparently the origin of both the twins' sandy brown hair. The sweet woman with the sweet smile had a sweet disposition, too. A firm grasp on God and a solid foot on terra firma made Sloan like her right away. How could she not? The very first thing the woman had done when she arrived was rush past her own son to hug Sloan and tell her that it would all be all right.

Then Mrs. Summerland spent a good hour just admiring her grandbabies. She once referred to them as Sloan's 'handiwork,' and she thanked them both so much for giving her such beautiful grandchildren that even Max got embarrassed. She praised Sloan for staying on bedrest for so long and keeping them as healthy as possible. Just when Sloan was certain she couldn't be complimented on another thing—for something she was certain she'd actually failed at—Sloan heard her praises sung for being so calm and collected.

Then the woman insisted on being called 'Mom.'

Despite all this, Mrs. Summerland managed to not preach at all, she just helped. There seemed to be only two things that made the woman frown. The subject of Max and Sloan's lack of a marriage, which produced a fleeting look that skittered across her face and was gone. The second thing was when the hospital staff told her it was time to put the babies back in the incubator. She would do it without a fuss if one of their temperatures had dropped too low. Otherwise she was a mother bear, telling the staff that babies needed to be held, and homes didn't have visiting hours. Then she blatantly disregarded the posted visiting hours and dared the staff to drag a sweet little old lady away. She managed to frighten off most of the nurses.

Sloan was okay with all of that. Her children got to be held all the time, and visiting hours didn't apply to their Grandma. Mrs. Summerland brought steaming hot portions of casseroles that friends had dropped off so that Max and Sloan could eat without leaving the hospital. She drove Sloan home for a shower and a nap in the big fluffy bed. She cleaned the house, then hired a masseuse to come to the hospital and give all the parents shoulder massages. This evening the woman insisted that she babysit while the two of them went out to dinner and a movie.

Sloan desperately wanted to call and check on the babies. So did Max, she could tell. He had 'new father' written all over his face. His fingers pranced nervously across the surface of the cell phone he had turned to vibrate only. Sloan had hers in her hand as well. They had made idiots out of themselves making certain Mom Summerland knew both numbers by heart, even quizzing her before they left. But neither of the phones had rung. Things were okay.

With her heart in her throat for so many reason, Sloan found herself on her first real date with Max. It had only taken nine months to get one real date with her dream guy. Nine months, two children, a lost memory, a lost house...the list was too big to count. As she sat next to him in the theater, her mind wandered. Had Rae set this up? Had she cast a *together* on them?

Lord knew Sloan's own spells were just sloughing off everything. *Nothing* stuck. Rae could have done this, and it would be just like her. If not Rae then Yasmin, or even Megan. Sloan had no idea, and it wasn't as if she could just call them up with Max standing right here and demand they tell if they'd cast on her.

In the purely normal realm, Sloan also had no idea whether his mother knew this was actually their first date. Had Max said they were dating? Together? Had he just mentioned that Sloan was having his children and let them assume what they would? She had no clue and her brain wandered aimlessly until his hand snaked across the movie chair armrest and twined through her fingers. The heat of it soaked quickly through her entire body and replaced the usual theater chill with a sexual heat. She kept her fingers locked with his, even knowing it was a bad idea to get so attached. But it was difficult to continually turn away what she so desperately wanted.

One word kept running through her head. *Soon.*

She had a reprieve here, while the babies were so small and needed everything all the time. It was a chance to stay in his arms a little bit longer, but she would have to pry herself free soon. Her heart was breaking at the mere thought. And she knew it would break even further when she left. Sloan kept asking herself how would she possibly survive. If she was in too deep and it couldn't possibly hurt worse than it already would, then why not stay and wait for things to go astray? She could let it hurt then. Enjoy the time between.

Because Sloan knew it could hurt worse. In the one and only way that she knew with utter certainty that it would hurt worse than this. If she married him, her children would be torn apart by divorce. Their lives would be turned upside down. Didn't children need stability? What kind of mother would she be, knowing that she was setting them up for that?

However, had it been just her...

But it wasn't. She didn't want it to be, really. She was thrilled to have her babies. Even if it meant taking responsibility and not letting herself have the time with Max that she otherwise would have.

The plot of the movie was hard for her to follow. Probably it wasn't actually complicated at all, but they were both out just for the sake of saying they could do it. The fact that it was their first real date was another matter entirely. Sloan felt the giggles starting in her chest and working their way up. It was all she could do to stifle them. The characters were sharing their first hot kiss so it seemed such the appropriate time to contemplate that she was on her first date with a man whose babies she had just had.

But it felt so much like a real date. The way her heart fluttered when his thumb rubbed across her palm. The way she looked up and caught him gazing at her during dinner with that 'new romance' kind of curiosity. But he was most likely wondering where his babies got their ears or the shape of their eyes. She had been guilty of looking at him the same way, too.

Although she couldn't quite entirely brush off her staring as maternal curiosity. Still, the shivers and the heart flutters, those were most like a real first date, even down to the wondering if her date possibly liked her back.

Sloan laughed in all the right places and let herself get sucked under by the feel of Max's skin against hers. And she waited for the big end scene. *They're fine. They're fine...* she repeated it in her brain as a mantra. Max's nervousness left her pretty sure he was thinking the same thing, too. Eventually the music reached a crescendo and they both popped up the second it was over. There was no need to see the credits or get stuck in the parking lot.

In the lobby, they turned and laughed together as they realized they were both doing the same thing, and Max had his cell phone by his ear the second they were clear of the theater.

"Hi, Mom.... Oh, good... No, we weren't worried at all. Just wanted to be sure that you were holding up all right... uh-huh.... real soon. Bye."

His smile made her smile. All was well and they would get back to another long night in the big easy chairs. Maybe he would scoot his around near hers again and she could wake up with her head resting on his shoulder again. She should enjoy the sensation of touching him while she could.

Too soon she would have to go. *Soon.*

CHAPTER 43

Max jerked awake, for a moment unaware of where he was and what had brought him here. But it seemed that he had been here so often and for so long that his surroundings gelled around him quickly. His surroundings included two screaming infants and Sloan, mussed, and confused, and jumping up half asleep like him to cradle the screaming babies.

Just as he was starting to wonder what could have set them off like that, he put all the discordant pieces together. His usually docile little ones were scared. So was everyone else in the Neonatal intensive care unit. The NICU was suddenly a hive of coordinated but frantic activity, with nurses and physicians running and grabbing sterile kits en route, as he scooped up Lindsay and watched Sloan gather Michael to her chest and start soft hushing noises. Sloan's soft voice couldn't drown out the shrieks and the buzzing or the calm terror of the nurses.

The NICU was about to lose a patient. In his heart of hearts, his first thought was *thank god it isn't mine*, and he pulled Lindsay just a little closer, careful only that he didn't crush her.

His second thought was a response to that first one. An old ingrained habit from his youth and his parents. He crossed himself and started speaking in a low voice. *Dear god, please let their baby be okay.* He had seen the curtains pushed aside. He knew the voice, even though he had never heard her scream before. Winnie Henderson. Baby Lance hadn't been doing well these last few days. *God, please let baby Lance be all right. He has parents who love him and desperately want him.*

Max rocked Lindsey against the pounding beat of his heart, unaware of anything except that he hadn't smushed her. He shifted the baby to one arm and reached out with the other to pull Sloan to him with Michael in between. The two infants still crying although not as harshly.

He continued to pray in the words of the Christian church of his childhood and the chants of spells he knew for health. He prayed and cast, both for the other family, about to fall apart, and in thankfulness for his own intact unit. All of his own were here in his arms now, and Sloan huddled into him. The frantic fear seemed interminable.

He kept chanting, low enough even Sloan couldn't hear the words of his spell over the beeping and buzzing and tears. The spell was continually blocked. Feeling his heart make a roll of dread in his chest, he tried chanting harder. There was only so much he could do without altar or herbs or stones, but it seemed none of that would matter. Throwing his spell out into the universe, he hoped it would help. However, what happened to Baby Lance was likely not anything Max was allowed to influence.

He didn't stop though. He kept trying, wondering if Sloan would figure out what he was saying, what he was doing. Eventually the buzzing was cut by random voices. By Winnie's terse pleas. By a doctor shoving his way into the mass, all around the incubator holding the tiny baby.

Max was suddenly uncomfortable, and his heart asked if it

was just a reaction to what was going on around him, before he realized that Sloan was struggling to get away from him. She was speaking—"Please, take Michael."—and holding the baby out to him. In spite of his confusion, he took the second bundle as she spoke again. "Gary isn't here." Then she turned and ran.

He curled his children into him and as Sloan approached Winnie he put the pieces together. Gary. Mr. Henderson. Winnie was alone. He could only watch as Sloan looped her arms around the woman. She was the only one to comfort the mother. The only non-medical staff. The only one of several parents sleeping nights in the NICU who got up to go to Winnie and hold her.

As Max looked around and took stock of the situation, he saw that he and Sloan were the only ones not so petrified of losing their own children. His own kids were gaining weight. Losing their preemie jaundice. Almost the largest kids in the ward. They expected to be released in a few days. But baby Lance, who had been a full two months early, wasn't as lucky.

Winnie and Sloan had made a huddle, curled into each other to the side of the action. He could almost hear her chanting to the sobbing mother. He could only imagine she was saying "It'll be okay, it'll be okay," even though he already knew there was nothing she could say or do that would change it.

After what felt like hours, the staff began to move away from baby Lance. His own heart stopped its regular, rapid pace to flutter with his nerves. Sloan led Winnie over to look at her baby, then he saw the mother collapse with relief against the incubator. Not even allowed to touch her tiny son.

Then Sloan was suddenly back in his arms. Max's shoulders and arms ached as though he had stood there for hours, but the feeling was likely only the result of tension. The ticking wall clock told him that it had truly been all of twelve minutes, but Sloan's voice was gravel in her throat.

When Max turned, he was startled to see his mother

standing just beyond the door with an aluminum pan grasped in hot mitts. Her usual bag of utensils and napkins slung over her shoulder. Not able to come any further into the ward with the food, she looked to Sloan, "Is Baby Lance going to be okay?"

Sloan nodded across the distance, "For now." And as she turned to look up at him he saw the tears that had stained her face. Her voice was almost inaudible. "We have to get out of here."

He leaned in to kiss her hair, all he was able to do with two infants tucked into his arms. "Just a few more days."

She nodded and buried her face into his chest. Just a few more days and they would be left alone with their children. In their house, miles from medical support staff. For the briefest of moments terror set in and he thought *screw the office, my Mom can move in*, but he shoved all those scary thoughts aside, grateful beyond words for all that he did have. Glad that he could take his babies home.

Max watched as his mother set down the casserole just beyond the double doors and scrubbed up before she came in assessing the situation. She reached out to take the babies out of his arms, seeing that it was preventing him from hugging Sloan back. As his mother turned away, cooing at the two tiny babies, he reached down and turned Sloan's face up to him, kissing her softly. It wasn't the time for slow, deep, soul kisses, though he wished it was.

"You made me so proud just now." He explained over the quizzical look that formed across her lovely features. "You were the only one to go to Winnie and help her out."

She shook her head. "I just felt that if it was me I would want..." She trailed off, then picked up the thread again, "When I saw that Gary wasn't there...Well, I'd have died if you weren't here..."

He kissed the top of her head, "You were brave and thoughtful..." *and I love you.* But he bit his tongue. Besides, his mother had put the babies down to sleep and turned the lights low when he hadn't been looking. Now she was out beyond the stainless steel doors again and was dishing up chicken and rice.

Max stood, with Sloan in his arms, rocking to a slow rhythm while his mother motioned to one of the nurses that the first plate was for a tearstained and grateful Winnie Henderson. Still he felt the physical metaphor as he let Sloan go out the door. She was only walking over to his mother as she motioned that she had served them up dinner with cold canned sodas just beyond the window. Max walked Sloan out of the NICU and sat down to eat, keeping an eye on his sleeping children through the large picture window.

There wasn't much conversation over the hot food tonight.

He couldn't keep from looking over at Winnie, who had eaten quickly though only when his mother reminded her to, and returned to staring into the incubator with baby Lance inside. Now the infant had even more wires and monitors than before. A quick look at Sloan told him she was shaken to her core. Lance had almost died.

After a while, his mother quietly packed up dinner and hugged them both goodnight. Max tugged Sloan back to the waiting easy chairs, scooting them together as quietly as possible, and sliding nearer the edge of the chair, in hopes that she would snuggle next to him again tonight. He pulled a blanket up over both of them, looping his arm around her as best he could.

Sloan had to see what they had together. But *when?*

CHAPTER 44

Sloan's heart went out to the woman, but she hugged Winnie Henderson good-bye and left her phone number in hopes that the woman might call. Michael tipped the scales at four pounds and twelve ounces yesterday, but they decided to all stay the extra night waiting for Lindsay to bulk up, not wanting to take one baby home and leave the other behind. All night, they woke her up and fed her, and finally this afternoon the nurse had weighed her again and she passed. The relief that washed over Sloan almost brought her to her knees, as did the expression on Max's face. She hadn't seen the deep fear that Lindsey wouldn't be released in time, until it passed and his face lost five years almost on the spot.

Sloan hadn't known it was possible to get out of a hospital so fast. She pestered the doctors to sign off on the babies before Lindsey wet her diaper and lost a precious ounce. She and Max dressed them in going home outfits as soon as the nurses took the last of the monitors off. Speaking to Winnie had eaten up a few of the anxious last moments waiting for the nurse to show them out. It wasn't as if she didn't know the way like the back of her hand.

Sloan sighed. *Home*. Finally. Her children had only been in the incubator for nine days, and neither had ever needed an IV. Thank god for that! Sloan didn't think she could have stood to watch even a skilled NICU nurse try to put another needle into one of her precious babies.

She hugged baby Michael to her chest as she draped a blanket over him for the walk out to the car. She felt Max beside her, his shoulder brushing against hers and his breath warm at her ear. "See, two babies leaving the hospital with us. You did it."

She had to laugh. "*I* didn't do it. Really you did. I wanted to eat cookies and work full time until they were born. Which was still supposed to be almost a month away."

They walked side by side down the hall. In the elevator, people congratulated them, and Sloan tried desperately not to be a rude mother who wouldn't show her kids to anyone. She did beam and say thank you. And she wished they were actually the happy family they appeared to be.

Finally, they reached the fresh air of the parking lot. Well, it wasn't really fresh, but it was outdoor air—the babies' first. She and Mom Summerland snuggled the little bundles close while Max went around to get the car. Then they all hovered while they tried to be certain that the babies were buckled right, and the head supports adjusted correctly. Sloan climbed into the back. Mom Summerland couldn't because she had mild arthritis. As the recipient of a C-section Sloan shouldn't drive, and Max needed to drive, because sitting in a car driven by his mother made him insane.

Luckily, he'd confessed that to her at the hospital before he let his mother chauffeur her back to the house the first time. It was the only thing that had stopped her from fleeing into his arms and announcing that his mother hated her and was trying to kill her.

Still, Max was still clearly nervous as the new driver of his infant children. He kept glancing into the review mirror and he hadn't even started the car yet. Instead of going, he climbed out and checked both the harnesses on the baby seats and then the locks that held the bases in, before climbing back in and buckling himself up.

"Max," She almost hollered, just to get through to him from the third row where she watched the babies in the middle.

"What?"

"Take a deep breath. You've been driving for years, and you've been driving these guys around for months now, back when they were still inside me." He couldn't have looked any tighter sprung. "If you don't relax I'm going to have to ask your Mom to drive."

With that Mom Summerland's hand reached across to him. "Sloan's right. I can drive if you need."

It was a sincere, heartfelt offer and Sloan stifled the giggle that threatened. It was all the impetus he needed and with a clenched "I'm fine," and a few deep breaths, he did his best to calm down. Still he shot her a look in the rearview mirror, begging for help, as though she was capable of giving it from the very back of the car. She buckled herself in and leaned in between the middle bucket seats the babies were strapped into. "You guys are so buckled up you look like you're going parachuting."

Two little deep blue sets of eyes blinked back at her. In the next year, they should outgrow these car seats that were now threatening to engulf them. She sighed. It was just so strange that they were here now.

They both had Max's ears, but the shape of Lindsay's eyes was definitely hers. Lindsay looked just like her own baby picture, and Sloan couldn't peel her eyes away. She felt the turns here in the back more than as a front seat passenger, and it was making her chest grow tighter and tighter with each curve they took. She tried not to look, but the bumps and bounces at last caused her to lift her head.

They were in Max's neighborhood, and she was in a state of confusion. Had she really believed he was just going to drop them all off at her condo, kiss the babies goodbye and go home with his Mom? But he had to. It was over. Her little interlude was finished. The babies were out of the hospital and she wasn't on bed-rest anymore and it was time to stop letting Max take care of her. She would have to go back to work soon. Since he'd brought them to his house, she would have to pack them up and leave now.

The garage door ground its way open, exposing the still neat parking spaces within. Max killed the engine and hopped out on one side while Mom Summerland did the same on the other. They unbuckled the babies and allowed Sloan to crawl out less than gracefully between the seats. She watched as they cuddled the babies close, suddenly feeling excluded. Despite the fact that she was the babies' mother, these two didn't need her.

For a moment she simply stopped and stared at their retreating backs as they gathered the things from the car. Her brain churned, thinking she didn't have the babies' bassinet set up in the condo yet. She had only stopped by briefly a few times to get some loose fitting clothing. What was she going to—

"—Sloan?" Max's head was tilted slightly, and he looked puzzled. He'd been speaking to her, she could tell. But he glanced to the side, and she followed what he was watching, her sight coming to rest on his mother holding out baby Lindsay. "Don't you want to show your daughter around her home?"

Sloan moved her jaw, but words wouldn't come. *This isn't her home.* But to a certain extent it was. Luckily, her arms did work, and her lips did manage a smile. Softly, her daughter was set into the cradle of her arms, and she followed Max woodenly through the door to the house. He smiled and announced all the rooms. "This is where you'll eat. This is where you'll play..."

She saw that all the shower gifts had been set up around the house in all the appropriate locations, and she began to get upset. Why hadn't any of them been set up at her place? She would need at least one baby swing.

Still zoned, she nearly panicked. They couldn't expect her to leave the babies here for a few days. She just wouldn't be able to do it. Right then, Michael started crying, a sound that rushed relief to every pore of her body. "He's hungry."

Thoughts flooded her mind as they swapped babies and she headed up the stairs to the master bedroom for some privacy. She was breastfeeding; the babies would have to stay with her pretty much all the time. She propped pillows and leaned back against the headboard, opening her shirt and getting the tiny boy situated.

Just as she started to relax a soft knock came at the door.

"Sloan?"

She jumped. "Just a minute!" She threw Michael's baby blanket over her exposed breast and took a breath. "All right."

Max opened the door, holding a wide-eyed Lindsay in the crook of his arm. "She got jealous."

She was safe. So she smiled. "I'll get to her next. Just set her down."

"No way." He came around and settled himself next to her on the bed as though he didn't need permission. Just as she started to open her mouth to protest, she realized he was right. He didn't. She was on *his* bed in *his* house... her mouth opened and the words tumbled out before her brain checked the wisdom of them. "Are you going to drive us back to my condo this evening?"

She saw the wave of shock and anger as it passed through him. She had expected him to barter or...or *something*, but not this fierce anger.

"*What*? You're staying here." He managed to calm down even as he spit out the words. "Sloan, I will *never* kick you guys out of here."

Wow, had she missed her mark. "It's not that I expect to get kicked out. It's just time for me to go home. You don't have to take care of me anymore. We need to work out a schedule."

"A *schedule?*" His face turned five shades of red again, but this time he stayed mad. "Are you *serious?*"

She blinked a few times and he continued.

"You *want* to go home with two preemies, all by yourself? You'll never sleep. To top it off, if you go, then when do I get them? A half hour here or there between feedings?"

She sighed. She was already stitched into this whole thing so tight and it would only get harder to extricate herself. "When they're six weeks old they can have a bottle, then they can stay here some of the time." It was reasonable.

"No way in hell." Obviously Max did not find her terms reasonable. "Sloan Ellis, you must have a new form of post-partum mental illness to think that you are going to be a single parent to premature twins by yourself for five weeks. You hardly slept at the hospital...You told the nurses that you had support at home. If not me, then who the hell were you talking about?"

She sniffed as Michael squirmed in her grasp. "I'll make it work, I'll be fine."

"Then you are even crazier if you think I am letting these two get away for that long. If you really miss your home, then we'll go live there." His voice was low, almost lethal. But it wasn't enough to stop her.

Her teeth clenched once before the dam broke. "Then when, Max? When do I stop living off your charity? When do we have separate lives?"

"Never!" He was standing over her now, and she couldn't even get up to face him down. "We are tied together by these children for the rest of our lives. You'd damn well better get used to it."

She felt the tears start down her cheeks, even as she saw his expression soften.

"I'm sorry." Her lip trembled, maiming the words. "I just don't want to traumatize them later when I have to move out. Sooner or later it has to happen. We'll have to make up a schedule and trade them off."

His jaw was stiff as he nestled Lindsey against Sloan's hip. "Not *now*. It doesn't have to happen *now*." With those words, he turned and closed the door behind him.

CHAPTER 45

Max blinked awake, certain he'd heard something, but it seemed he hadn't. Darkness swamped the house, letting only traces of the streetlights outside leech in through the still uncovered living room windows. The light bothered his eyes, but he refused to get window coverings and told his mother to keep her hands off his house. He wanted soft silly floral things that Sloan would pick out. Or sheers, right? She said he needed sheers, whatever sheers were.

God, he'd gone insane. His new life was completely unrecognizable from his old one. He was awake in the dark, although it was barely ten o'clock according to the TV console. He hadn't seen his friends in months. He was sleeping on his couch, imagining noises in his new house, and contemplating sheers. Max ran his fingers through his hair, most likely sticking it straight up.

There it was again.

That noise. Or just the thought that he had heard a noise.

Deciding to investigate only made sense. He was still awake at ten p.m. with clearly nothing better to do. He was also clearly still a brand new parent; he hadn't yet developed the need for self-preservation. The desire to be quiet and not wake a baby at all costs.

He tiptoed past the second bedroom, where he had first slept on his old full-size bed. His mother was sleeping soundly behind the tightly closed door. Always ready to be of any daytime help, she was a firm believer in the sanctity of the middle of the night.

It was a noise. The softest of whimpers. A baby. Without a thought, he turned the doorknob of the master bedroom and peeked inside, his eyes already adjusted to the deep shadows. Sloan, looking sleepy and good enough to eat wrapped tight in the blue bathrobe he had bought her, leaned over the bassinet and lifted out a whimpering Michael. Her voice was soft and low and made his blood warm, even though she was clearly talking to the baby. "Are you hungry?"

As she stood up straight, she spotted him, but didn't startle. "I've got it, you can go back to sleep." She faced away from him, as though nothing more could be said. Truth be told, he couldn't think of anything they needed from him, so he simply stayed propped in the door and watched. Then he saw that she was completely incapable of the simple act of climbing up onto the high bed with the baby in her arms.

She turned and spotted him still standing in the doorway, and whispered a small laugh. "Wow, I didn't know that you needed abs to lay on a bed. I'm a weakling."

Max got the feeling that he didn't belong there, standing in the doorway. He needed to be in the room with the three of them. He didn't think they really needed him, but maybe he could convince them they did. He scooped Michael from her, and tucked him, football like, into the crook of one elbow. Using his free hand to help Sloan scale the side of the bed, he then helped her rotate to reclining.

Within seconds, his usefulness waned as she held out her

arms, and he set the softly mewling baby in them, and tried not to stare as she set Michael to her breast.

Just before she looked up, Lindsay saved him. Missing her brother's heat, she cried out. Not the hungry little sounds that Michael had made. Her cry was a squall, angry and vengeful.

"Oh, baby. It's okay. Your turn is next." Max cradled her to his shoulder, thinking she would relent and pass back out.

But she didn't. She rebelled with an even deeper cry.

"My gosh, she sounds like someone is bathing a cat!" Sloan chuckled from behind him as he struggled to keep his attention away from Sloan's partially bared chest and on the infant.

"Are you wet?" He asked the baby as he rocked her, with one hand he reached into the fabric bin under the bassinette and pulled out the wipes, a diaper, and a changing pad. He carefully laid out each piece before attempting to lay little Lindsay on it. Then he rearranged the pieces once more, one handed. Then rearranged them again. He would get better at this, wouldn't he?

When, *finally*, he managed to get to the actual changing of the diaper, her little feet kicked and he had to grab her ankles, so she let out a tiny scream at the indignity of it all. Finally, he won the battle and she was in a clean diaper, with her jammies snapped back up. He put all the paraphernalia away then turned to the task of bundling her. He laid out the blankie and had his daughter wrapped into a tight burrito within fifteen seconds.

Lindsay calmed down and stared at him, making soft sounds and little sucking motions with her mouth. He stopped both with a binkie and looked up to find Sloan watching him with deep interest.

"You've gotten about fifty thousand times better at that."

He nodded and made a conscious decision to give it a shot. Sliding onto the bed next to her, he spoke the whole time, trying to filibuster any chances of her opposing. "Lindsay is hungry, too. You just tell me when you're ready and I'll swap with you."

Luckily Sloan didn't protest. A few minutes later, she

removed Michael and held him out to Max. In easy movements, they traded babies. As he was cuddling Michael and vowing not to move from his spot until Sloan specifically told him to, Max heard one deep breath from her. She was falling asleep again, in close enough proximity that he could feel her heat and the steady way she moved the air as she breathed.

He breathed easier beside her. The babies felt it, too. They stopped rustling and set about being calm and falling back to sleep. He had to stay here, in this bed with her. He would simply insinuate himself until she felt natural about it.

She had to stay here, too, in this house with him. He didn't want her to go. He *needed* her to stay. Hopefully one day she would feel that that, too, was a natural thing. For another moment, he thought again about casting spells on her, but his grandmother had drilled it into him—it was wrong to cast on people. There were few exceptions, Dylan Atterson being one of them. But he could get her to stay. Max could make it happen, but he didn't know how it would manifest and, in the end, it wasn't what he wanted. He wanted Sloan here because she wanted to be. And that he didn't know how to make happen.

CHAPTER 46

The papers in front of him held information in some foreign language. Or you would think they did, given his inability to follow the words. Max finally set it aside and flipped to another folder thinking he might have more luck. But of course he didn't, A.D.H.D. had set in. He almost laughed. Maybe what he really had was Sloan Deficit Disorder.

He was definitely facing an oncoming Sloan deficit. She was so desperate to get out of his house and get away from him. Of course, he'd reacted by trying to get even closer.

It sounded stupid, even to his ears. *Yeah, crowd her some more, that'll make her want you,* but he seemed not to be able to stop himself. He touched her when he could. Hugged her. Even put himself in the same room whenever possible. It had seemed to work. Well, part of it. They shared the master bed each night. They woke up as a pair and shuffled babies. Him changing diapers and her feeding them, and the two of them often fell asleep against each other, too. He loved waking up usually in the deep of night, Sloan asleep again, both of them passed out upright on the pillows propped against the wall. Her head was invariably on his shoulder and he could never make himself move.

Each night, she rolled in toward him. Each morning he woke up with her in his arms. And each morning she extracted herself as coldly and politely as she could. He knew he was being such an idiot to think there was something she might feel for him, but he wanted to believe so badly.

Max shook his head, as though that might actually straighten out his thoughts. It didn't. When he finally looked at his actual surroundings in the real world, he spotted Wil in the doorway. Jesus, he hadn't spent any time with Wil in months. Luckily his friend seemed to understand.

"Why are you here?"

Max didn't answer. It was a really good question on all levels. He'd been born to love Sloan, but apparently the same wasn't true for her. He was beginning to think he was doomed to love her from afar forever. At least he still recognized that was more than a bit melodramatic, and he didn't think that was what Wil was after anyway. So he answered with the obvious. "I'm not sure. I know I'm not accomplishing anything." He sank back into the leather chair, attempting to relax. It didn't quite work. "I've only been here two hours and I already miss them."

Wil nodded then closed the door behind himself. "Who? The babies or the hot blonde living with you?"

"D. All of the above." Max felt half of his mouth quirk. It always made him the slightest bit nervous that Wil could read him so well and didn't hesitate to speak what he saw.

"Is it going any better with the hot blonde?"

He opened his mouth, but no pat reply would come out. Finally, he found the thought he needed. "Do you remember Anne Marie?"

Wil nodded with a smile. "Yes, although I wasn't sure *you* did."

"She wanted this man, who would dote on her and tell her

how wonderful she was and hold her tight every night and miss her painfully when she was away. It seems that finally I have become that man." Max sighed, feeling the sound clench in his chest.

"But for a different woman."

"Yeah. A woman who clearly doesn't want that man. Who doesn't want *me*. Who doesn't seem to want *any* man." Max was grateful when Wil refrained from making a lesbian remark. "I have become a complete and total wuss. I am the definition of pussywhipped. And what's worse? I know it and *I don't care!* How sad is that?"

Wil nodded slowly. "What's actually sad is that she doesn't see what she's got."

Max felt the knife twist deep in his gut. Wil had been supposed to tell him to snap out of it. That he was fooling himself. That he didn't really feel that way. That he'd get over it, and he should just find a new woman. To buck up and take it like a real man. But Wil wasn't supposed to say *that*.

CHAPTER 47

Sloan smiled, although it wasn't a real smile. She faked it as well as she could. She tried to listen, but her own thoughts were rolling over Mom Summerland's words even before they entered her ears.

"Dear, you don't have to go back to work. Maternity leave is longer than that these days." The older hand covered her own with a small pat, as though that was all that was necessary to set the world to rights.

Sloan nodded the tight, polite nod that people did when they didn't really agree. "Yes, but I have bills to pay. I really need my paycheck."

"To pay for that condo that you aren't living in."

Okay. That snapped her eyes open. She knew she was unable to keep the shock from her face. When she reclaimed her tongue from where it was lying in her open jaw, she answered. "But I'm going back to that condo in a few weeks."

"Why?"

Wow. She couldn't believe that the sweet little lady who had brought casseroles to the hospital and held her tongue all this time was going to open fire and speak her mind now. But Sloan wouldn't cower. "Because that's where I live."

Max's mother still looked like the same kind-hearted woman, but she was wielding a knife-sharp brain and tongue behind that soft smile. "Well, Mr. Summerland and I don't like that these babies have parents who aren't married."

That at least, Sloan could at least agree with. "Neither do I." But she made the mistake of thinking that agreement would end the discussion. *Big mistake.*

"Then why aren't you married? I know that Maxwell has asked you and he says you keep turning him down. Is he lying to us?"

Sloan felt her teeth clench tight, not liking where this was going one bit. "No ma'am, he's not lying." *Why did his parents know this stuff?*

"If you want to be married, he's a great man. There's nothing wrong with him." Mrs. Summerland actually had the nerve to look offended. Of course, she did. Sloan had seen how much the woman loved her son. She knew he had faults and she admitted to them, but the sun still rose and set on 'her Maxwell.'

Sloan found herself stuck explaining something that she didn't even like to think about to herself and wouldn't you know it, neither of the babies was going to step in and help out with a scream or even a whimper. Sloan blinked at the scene around her. Two women at the table, sipping iced tea and enjoying the afternoon sunshine. The scene didn't show that she felt like a kitten facing a coyote. With a deep breath she answered as best she could. "Actually, there is one thing wrong with him—"

"What?"

"—he doesn't love me."

The last line felt like a punch in her gut as she spoke it out loud. But, while it shut Mrs. Summerland up, there was no victory in it. Just that tiny Titanic sinking in the middle of her chest. Sloan was forced to admit that some part of her was waiting for a response with her heart in her throat—that *but he's told me that he loves you.* It didn't come.

Mrs. Summerland nodded, and her claws retracted. "Are you sure?"

"Very." Finally, Sloan felt strong enough to look the woman in the eye. "In all the times he has asked me to marry him, he has tried every argument in the book: money, convenience, for the sake of the children. But in all those arguments he never once found it in him to even mention love. Not even that we might grow to love each other. Trust me. He doesn't."

Another deep breath, but this time it came from the other corner of the ring. It was low, almost inaudible and somewhat resigned. Still, Sloan caught it easily. "Good marriages have been built on less."

This time Sloan had the strength to make her answer loud and clear. "But *mine* won't be."

Just then, and too late by Sloan's book, Michael helped her out by letting loose an earsplitting wail. Hopping up to tend to him, she watched out of the corner of her eye as Mrs. Summerland wandered off to pack her things.

While Sloan was feeding Michael then Lindsay she thought through that last conversation. Maybe the older docile woman had found the chutzpah because it was her last day here. A last-ditch effort to not have bastard grandchildren.

The babies had turned three weeks old a few days ago. Max had gone back to work three half-days a week, and Sloan was cleared to drive, so she wasn't stuck in the house anymore.

Didn't anyone see that it bothered her, too, to not be married to the father of her babies? That her kids would get shuffled back and forth? But why was she supposed to throw away everything she believed in for a little convenience? A convenience that was going to be more inconvenient and ugly than anyone could imagine when he didn't fall in love with her. Or worse, when he *did* fall in love with someone else.

If it was just about her, Sloan would marry him in a heartbeat. Sure they would get divorced somewhere down the road when things went awry, but she could live with that. Half of all marriages ended up there anyway, and most of those were marriages where the couple went into it thinking they were going to stick it out forever. Sloan didn't delude herself that her 'yes' would lead to anything of the sort, but she still would have done it. *If* it had just been her, maybe, but she couldn't put children into that equation, not while knowing full well there was a divorce on the horizon.

She hated the track her mind was on, but it was running away with her thoughts. Wouldn't Max have lied and said he loved her? If he felt even just a little bit for her, wouldn't he have pulled that out to sway her? The man was a closer; he had to know that that phrase would likely reel her in, but he clearly couldn't bring himself to say it. Thank goodness he wasn't a liar. She truly was glad she knew. She might not like the fact, but she was relieved she hadn't been lied to. That she didn't marry into that lie, and one day several years from now look back at her wedding photos and realize that there was only one real smile in the picture. She would not be able to handle that, not with two kids who would be torn apart.

Tears were rolling down her cheeks and Sloan found herself grateful now that Mom Summerland had found the conversation just as distasteful as Sloan did. She'd gone off to pack, since she had to fly back tonight. They would all drive her to the airport this evening and then Sloan would get to claim her rightful spot in the passenger seat of the minivan. She realized that she must be hormonal to be thinking all these things and crying about it.

The house was quiet when she laid Lindsay back down to sleep. With soft steps, lest she get caught, she scrounged in the bottom of her suitcase for her things. Setting up on the dresser, as it was wood and the only thing available, she started a small spell to keep her children safe.

Though she wouldn't have thought it possible, fifteen minutes later she was even more frustrated than when she'd walked in. Was she simply not able to concentrate at all these days? Or was something truly wrong? She would have to ask Yasmin the next time she saw her cousin. Because, in spite of trying three times, in spite of thinking she had her focus back, in spite of using all her own items she'd brought from home, her spells disappeared as soon as she cast them.

Sloan would watch them form, then dissipate as quickly as they had come together. She tried re-casting them, thinking her slight spell could be built up into a full one, but it didn't work. Eventually, when they didn't build, when even little starter spells couldn't be made to work, Sloan pushed everything down into the back of her suitcase and called Yasmin.

There was no answer and Sloan tried to achieve the cross purposes of leaving her cousin a clear message while not being overheard. "My spells just don't work at all anymore. Can you cast some *safeties* on my children? Just so *someone* has?"

There wasn't much more to explain, Yasmin had heard it all before. They'd simply thought Sloan's skills would return when she wasn't pregnant anymore. Had her babies sucked all her skills away?

Full of questions she couldn't answer, Sloan crawled under the covers of the big fluffy master bed that smelled like Max. Sleep didn't come easily.

CHAPTER 48

M om Summerland made it to the airport on time, and Sloan had looked for, but hadn't detected, any animosity in the woman from their battle that afternoon. The babies fell asleep on the way home, and Sloan wondered if she would ever feel normal again.

She wanted to feel normal now. The babies had made it out of the hospital. She and Max had seen his mother off. They had their babies to themselves. This was, she thought, the normal course of action for most new parents. Except she was still a guest in his house and couldn't completely settle in.

Lindsay and Michael had probably fallen asleep because Sloan and Max had managed to not speak a single word to each other. By the time they were parked inside the garage and she unclicked her tiny daughter's car seat Sloan thought that "passed out cold" was a better description for the children. They didn't even bother to undo the seat harnesses, there was no point in waking such contented children. Sloan and Max just went single file to the bedroom and set the car seats facing each other so the babies would know they weren't alone when they woke up.

Max disappeared down the hall without a word and Sloan wandered back into the kitchen and fixed herself another glass of iced tea with a lemon wedge—a drink she was quickly getting addicted to. As she stood there, looking out onto the brief side yard, she tried to adjust. Her blank stare at the flowers climbing the fence between the yards didn't relieve her brain of any of the thoughts going through it. *Soon. Soon this would be the past and she could begin her new life.* Her own life.

She heard the footsteps in her ears, but not in her mind. Locked somewhere deep inside herself, she didn't acknowledge that she should pay attention or even look at him until she heard his voice behind her.

"I know I've asked you this before, but I would love for you to have this."

Slowly, she turned, blinking her eyes to bring her focus back here to the life in front of her. Max stood just a few feet away. He looked nervous, but kept his back straight. Clearly steeled for a response he wouldn't like, he held out the deep blue velvet box that held the engagement ring he had bought.

Again, Sloan was in an untenable situation. Him standing there in the kitchen, holding out the box, unopened even, wasn't the proposal she wanted. He wasn't the man she wanted. He was so very close. But Max wasn't really asking her to be his wife— his *real* wife, the one he would love and honor and everything that went with it. So Sloan did the only thing she could. She shook her head 'no.'

It didn't faze him and he kept talking. "I know you don't want to marry me."

Sloan bit her lip. He didn't know how wrong he was.

He wasn't really looking at her. "But I want you to have it. Maybe it shouldn't be an engagement ring. Maybe you even put it away for the kids' college fund. But I bought it for you and it's yours." He picked up her hand from where it hung limp at her side and tucked the box safely into her palm.

Even as she shook her head, he spoke again, "If you ever decide that you do want to marry me, all you'd have to do is put it on."

With that, he walked away, leaving her in the kitchen, her back to the window, the same blank stare on her face.

Then she got it together. Something slowly gelled inside her and she got angry. It was all she could do to keep from yelling and waking the babies, to keep from hurling the box at his back. *"Did your mother put you up to this?"*

He twirled around looking more than startled. "I—... I—... *No.*"

"Because she gave me an earful this afternoon about how it wasn't right that we aren't married." Sloan clutched the box with enough force that she feared she might dent it.

"I didn't know." His shrug was almost undetectable. "They don't approve. I can't change their beliefs."

"Oh, but you tell them all about how I'm telling you 'no'!" Her fury mounted. "Your mother seems to think I'm some slut who got knocked up but won't do the right thing. Or does she know about Chicago, too?"

He only managed to shake his head 'no' before she started in on him again.

"Why does she know that? *Why does she know any of this?*" This time she waited. And waited.

Finally, he spoke, now just as mad as she was. He almost shook, his hands were fisted at his sides, but he held them there. "My parents are religious. They don't think it's right to have a child out of wedlock. What was I supposed to do? Just never mention that they were going to have grandkids?"

She waited.

Max's teeth and muscles clenched. *At least he was showing some sort of emotion.* But the wry thought flitted away as he started up again. "They hounded me, and made *me* out to be the A-hole, so I finally told them that I *had* proposed and you said 'no.' That's all it was. Damn, I've got them on my case left and right, like it wasn't bad enough to have you keep turning me down."

Her voice was soft. "I'm not a deal, Max. You can't close me. Stop asking."

"That's exactly what I was just trying to do! To stop banging my head on this painful brick wall!" With that he stomped off.

She heard a door slam, then an engine start, and the grind and whine of the garage door slowly lifting on its chain. She didn't even think about stopping him. With her right hand, she reached out to the side to pick up her sweating iced tea glass from the counter. Staying where she was, she took a sip. As though the normal action would make her feel anywhere in the vicinity of normal.

Only after she heard the van drive away down the street did she even stop to realize that she still had a death hold on the little velvet box.

That was telling, wasn't it?

CHAPTER 49

Max drove around for hours. He wasted gas and time; it was easy enough to do in Los Angeles. He tried to wait out the overwhelming urge to cry or scream or just get himself into a good barroom fistfight. He did none of those things.

He didn't even let his brain wander, just remained blank, watching the streets go by and pushing back at the feelings that crowded him. Ultimately, he boxed them up and put them away in the far corners of his brain. Then he acted like the idiot he knew himself to be and went back that night for more punishment.

He hadn't ever slept in the guest bedroom. His mother had been there and by the time she vacated the space, he'd insinuated himself in the master bed, next to Sloan. Max almost didn't care that she didn't want him there. Or maybe she was just neutral about it. He was convenient. Two babies were a handful. Maybe she just wanted him to wake to the screaming sounds of infants the same as he did.

He woke up in the middle of the night with her. He changed babies, and handed them over to be fed, and snuggled them back in their bassinet when they were finished. He curled Sloan to him when she fell asleep and pretended not to notice when she would untangle herself as quickly as possible each morning.

After a few days, he moved the spare bed and furniture into the smallest room, leaving the new nursery clear so he could begin to paint it. He picked colors he thought Sloan would like —a soft, bricky red and a creamy yellow. He'd wound up asking a random woman at the paint counter what she liked, simply because she dressed like Sloan. He thought the choices would suit Sloan, but he didn't ask her what she wanted or what she thought of his choices. He just brought the paint home and closeted himself in the room whenever the babies were both asleep, determined to either get the nursery done or kill himself on paint fumes in the meantime.

He and Sloan lived a simple life where they didn't interact too much. He and Bernstein had another talk about how Bernstein was treating both of them. The man didn't like it, but it seemed someone high enough up had put a bug in his bonnet about gender inequality in his workplace. Somewhere along the way, they had cooked up an idea for new parents to work mostly from home and only come into the office two days a week. Sloan took Bernstein up on the offer and Max never said he'd been part of working it out. Next, Max finagled the deal for himself, too, setting his own schedule so he could be home on her days at work and in on the other three.

Sometimes, in the evening, they watched TV together when the babies slept, but they rarely said much to each other. They had excursions to the grocery store and the park. While the conversations were easy, they were limited to what kind of cheese to buy and whether or not they were low on milk. He considered getting a puppy, just so he wouldn't be so terribly lonely the first time she took the kids to her house. He convinced her to stay in his house another few weeks, because clearly he was a masochist.

He convinced her to let him take her sedan to work and that

she should drive the minivan while he was out. She didn't buy the "it's *our* car" argument, but he finally won her over with safety statistics. He sewed her into his life as seamlessly as possible.

His life was full.

But he was a hollow shell.

The babies penetrated the cold outer layer of him. Most no one else did, though. He laughed with his colleagues when he was in the office, but he didn't even have the slightest interest in joining them for drinks tonight. He wanted to hold his children, complement them on keeping their heads up. Watch them take delight in their own hands or his funny faces. Make real eye contact with the only two people in the world he could.

Mechanically, he stopped for each red light, started for each green, and sometime later pulled into the garage, not even realizing how he had gotten there. Pushing the gear into park, he guessed he'd lived here long enough, if this was where he went when he was on autopilot.

He tried to snap out of it as he turned off the car, but automatically he clicked the button to send the garage door down and made his way through the connecting door into the kitchen. But like a thick layer of sleep in a vivid dream, he just couldn't shake it. His mind registered the quiet house, and he knew the babies must be sound asleep. There was nothing but the sound of dusk falling and the normal creaks and twinges of an old house, as he walked through, just to locate Sloan, he told himself.

As he entered the hall he could make out the dulcet tones of her voice, but not what she was saying. He wasn't trying to eavesdrop, but he couldn't stop the magnetic pull he felt when he found that she wasn't in the bedroom, but in the office. His feet quietly followed her voice to just beyond the door. Max stopped there, not admitting to himself that he had tip-toed over and stayed out of sight on purpose.

Her gleeful laugh was vibrant and alive. He hadn't heard those sounds from her in weeks. Bands that had constricted his breathing loosened. It took just a moment to register that she was on the phone. It wasn't the words, it was the way she said them that held him there in thrall. She was vital and engaged. He took deep breaths, savoring the happy sounds of Sloan, and realized that she hadn't been really happy here in a while.

As he relaxed against the wall for the eavesdropping he couldn't help but do, the meanings of her phrases sank into him. His own body responded with the attraction that had always been there for this woman. The way she was happy made him happy. For the first time in weeks he could *feel*. Feel his heart beating and his blood pulsing.

Because he didn't know how to make her share that with him, he stole it from his place beyond the door.

"No Lisette!..." Her soft sigh sank even deeper into him, "I didn't move out. He talked me into another four weeks....Yes, I took them... Yeah, I can't believe it's been six weeks either... Oh, it was the funniest thing, Dr. Lee looked me in the eyes and made sure that I knew that it was okay for me and my husband to have sex. I just wanted to burst into hysterical laughter right there. I don't know how I kept it together.... No, like, real hysterics, crying and all that. I mean, we hardly even speak. It's just like being married, right?... well, not you... I'm sure you and Jeremy are all hot and heavy for each other all the time... . Oh yeah, I bet that six weeks after you have a kid is just hell for the both of you!..."

She kept talking, but he didn't hear it. He hadn't really taken in the rest of it after the word 'sex,' because all he could think about was *sex*. With her. The girl on the phone. Not the cold, distant one who lived with him. But this creature, the one that had always held chains to him. He ached with wanting her.

But she wouldn't give that to him. He stood up, breathing

deeply, and cautiously removed himself from the doorway. He didn't want to get caught here and upset her.

Max fixed himself a cold drink, but instead of calming him down it made him notice how he felt the chill slipping down him fully for the first time in weeks. When she finally emerged, she found him standing there, arms braced on the kitchen counter, forcing himself to breath evenly.

"Are you all right?" This wasn't the bright and vibrant Sloan that he'd heard through the door. This was the same Sloan she had been for weeks. She had the small, tight smile and the same controlled movements that were just a little too efficient.

When she said, "yes," he forced a nod that he wasn't certain she would believe, but it didn't really matter. He thought his blood would cool when this Sloan came back around. But it didn't.

Just knowing that she still existed in there was enough. Knowing he was headed for what was most likely serious trouble didn't stop him. That one shining beacon pulled him out across deep waters like a siren song—completely impossible to ignore.

So he waited, biding his time on autopilot. He quietly ate the dinner she made. He complimented her on it. Helped change babies. Fed a bottle to one while she nursed the other. Watched TV and even laughed in the right places. When she said she was going to bed he responded with his usual "I'll be up later." And he waited.

Max sat on the couch with the TV continuing to show programs he wasn't paying the slightest bit of attention to. He didn't dream or hope. His brain had simply tuned out and turned off while he waited for something he didn't dare let himself think. It was as though admitting what he wanted would jinx it in some fundamental way. Max wasn't taking even that chance.

By eleven thirty he couldn't wait any longer. He had planned to hold out until midnight. Surely, she must be asleep by now. He crept down the hallway of his own home, still not admitting to himself what he so desperately hoped for.

He slowly opened the door, heartbeat by heartbeat. It wouldn't do to have her wake now. If she roused and asked him what in the hell he was doing he would have to respond with *I'm being an idiot*, and he didn't intend to have to admit it.

Max had barely opened the door when he saw her. It made him pause where he was. Something about the way she was lying there with her eyes closed and her mouth just a little open. The covers were pulled halfway up her arms, and the sight made his heart catch in his throat. She was the one thing he had ever truly wanted but couldn't have. Others had learned about that kind of heartache at a younger age. Max had had to wait until he was thirty-six. It was a tough lesson however you faced it.

He forced himself to move, lest he wake her and have some explaining to do. As he slowly wound his way through the room to the bed, he realized that it was easier to be in love with her when she was asleep. Gone was the tightness of her features and the just shy of noticeable curtness in her voice.

She looked like she might open her eyes and smile. Tell him that she loved him and wanted to stay here forever. That was a pipe dream and he was learning that the hard way. But right now he had another dream and he was going to dream it at least for a little while.

Softly he lifted the edge of the covers and slid under beside her. He didn't stay still but went about his usual shuffling as he slid in at night. She made a little noise like she always did, and he calmed, waiting.

For twenty minutes, he lay there on the other side of the bed and thought to himself. About her. About the kids growing up and playing baseball in the backyard. Although he figured she had to feel the vibrations coming off him in waves, she didn't respond. She only settled down and went back into a deep sleep.

No matter how much he thought he might be able to have her while she was asleep, he couldn't do that. She had to be awake.

At last he rolled over to face her and began his assault. Slowly he gathered her into his arms, just like he did every night. It hadn't woken her then, and it didn't now. Instead of tucking her under his chin, he slipped down even with her and kissed her forehead. He softly pressed his lips to her eyes. Then her cheeks. He fluttered little kisses across her jaw and ears. She shuddered in her sleep and curled closer, accelerating his heartbeat and softening the fear that nipped at his heels.

His fingertips traced her long arms and then wound around her, trailing up her spine. With the patience of a saint he slowly traced each rib before sliding one large hand under her breast. Still mostly asleep, a soft moan escaped her. Without really touching her there, he brushed his lips against hers as he spoke in low, heated tones. "Baby. Just let me love you."

"Max." She dragged out his name like a woman who need him. "More."

She arched into his hand, adding to the pressure they both felt, and he heeded her command, finding he needed more, too —more of her, more from her. His fingers sought and finally found buttons he knew closed up the front of her gown. They only went down to her navel, but it was far enough. When he slipped his hand inside both her skin and her response were hot.

Sloan was breathing in tiny gasps and so was he. He wanted to take her now. But he also knew he couldn't do that. With his fingers walking along the soft skin at the top of her thigh, he gathered the flimsy gown, the one that had tormented him so many nights, up her leg. Max left it bunched there at her hip while he hooked a finger in her underwear and carefully, slowly dragged it down her legs.

Another light moan fought its way past her open lips, and Max had to stall himself and take a few deep breaths just to keep it together. But then he only tormented himself more by gently pushing her until she rolled acquiescingly onto her back. Her legs parted just from his hand touching her inner thigh.

"Ahhh!" Her voice, making that sound, was the beginning of the end.

His heart clenched as he lifted his mouth from where he wanted to devour her. "Sloan."

Her eyes were open now, although they didn't look to be seeing anything. So he spoke again. "Look at me."

Her face turned to his. Fully awake now, but she didn't speak. He needed her to speak, needed to know this was what she really wanted, too. "Sloan, say yes, you have to say yes."

"Yes." The sound dragged out of her, long and low, alert and needy. She pushed herself against his fingers, her eyes bright in the dark. His heart cracked open. *Yes.*

His fingers functioned of their own accord. There was no way he could stop the climb to where she opened for him and he found her hot and wet and ready for more.

While he stroked her, his mouth found another path, and he trailed wet kisses from her ear down her neck to the peak of one exposed breast. Her gaze came to focus on his face, although her soft lips had never shut and her breath still beat a rapid staccato in and out. She writhed, pressing herself more firmly against his fingers and making the tiny noises that were about to make him explode. He barely managed to hold himself back, and he asked again wanting desperately to hear her say it again. "I want you. Do you want me?"

A few breathy sighs. Her body moved against his. Her legs clasped around his hand, but he held still. Waiting.

And, finally, she spoke, "Yes."

That was enough for him, but she added in the same breathy voice, "Please."

The pain of holding his breath was released as he covered her exposed flesh with his body. His mouth found hers and mated with deep, frantic kisses driven equally by her tongue and lips. He removed his fingers and began to push into her.

Slowly he moved. In the sweetest of tortures, she raised her hips to meet him. In and out. Deeper and deeper, until, with a cry from both of them he buried himself all the way. For a few moments they fought, moving against each other as though trying to get further and further inside each other.

When she called his name, he exploded. The last thing he saw was her eyes, looking deep into his soul.

He couldn't see, couldn't think, couldn't remember his own name for a few minutes. God, she could make the world spin. When his arms began to give out, he rolled both of them to the side, tucking her into his arms.

She fit so well. There was nothing in the known universe that compared to having her like this, curling into him, adjusting her head against his shoulder. She didn't say any of the things he expected. *What were you doing? How dare you?* She didn't get up and leave.

That alone provided the most joy to him. He desperately wished for the energy to reach across her to the bedside table where the little blue velvet box rested, untouched. But he didn't have the energy to risk another rejection, not now when he had most of what he wanted. The rest would have to wait. He would take it one step at a time. The first step had been huge, and it sapped him of the power to try for more. He wasn't likely going to find it anytime soon.

Happier than he had been in what seemed like eons, he finally slipped off to sleep.

He smelled her and felt her pressed against him. The dream

and the reality mixing in his brain becoming harder and harder to distinguish. He spent the night with a smile on his face and Sloan in his arms.

But when he woke up he was alone in the bed.

Alone and cursing himself.

CHAPTER 50

"I t's okay if I stay out until this evening?" Sloan was a bundle of nerves, but Max simply looked at her like she was nuts.

"You asked me that last week, and I said it was fine. I don't want you driving while you're all hypnotized or something." He waved a hand at her, motioning her to get out the door. "Besides, the kids and I will just have fun at the park without you."

She kissed two tiny heads with little blinking eyes and went out the door. Her lungs were tight. She was early and she was bold-faced lying to him. But hypnosis was about relaxing, so she figured claiming the extra time to unwind would make sense.

She did need the time to relax. She was afraid that if she couldn't relax it wouldn't work, and she desperately needed this spell to work. Maybe she should call an acupuncturist or a masseuse just to get her ready for her spellwork. Though she'd cast safeties and more on herself, it wasn't that often that she had spells cast on her by other people. When it had happened in the past, it hadn't been important. Megan had given her a taste of Megan's own psychic ability for a while, once. But had it not worked, Sloan wouldn't have felt she missed out on much.

Today, it mattered. More than anything. Spells worked best with focus and she was more scattered than she'd ever been.

She'd bolted from Max's arms Tuesday morning, dressed as quietly as possible, and abandoned him with the babies. She was being a bad mother, but she knew they were safe and loved with him, and she'd been in no shape to care for an infant.

Her first order of business, after faking a few 'hello's as she entered the building, was to lock her door and close the blinds and call Rae. She had wailed into the phone. *I slept with him again! Again!* Through tears and sobs she had explained the whole thing.

Then she pushed herself through the worst part—that he must have known he could do it. She'd thought she was being clear—they should stay away from each other. But he had pushed through that 'I just want you to have this' scene and handed her the engagement ring to torture herself with. Then he had climbed into bed, easily seducing her in the middle of the night, knowing that she would be willing. And she had been. So willing.

Every time she got mad at him, he would tell her something personal about herself. Some secret she had confessed in Chicago. He said that he had told her things, too, but she had no idea what they might even be. She didn't remember a damn thing from that night.

Sloan had hung up with Rae, feeling only a little better because Rae set her on a course of action. She had scoured the family Book of Shadows and had finally found something that dealt with repressed memories—or at least memories. When the spell had been written they hadn't used that term. But what Sloan had stuffed down all week was now boiling to the surface.

She had lied to Max. She'd been truthful about going out, but she'd said that it was about losing the baby weight. Boy, was it not.

Parking in front of her condo, she climbed the steps and let herself inside. The place was as humid as a wet blanket and felt just as linty, probably from being unoccupied for so long. So she cranked the air and pulled a caffeine free Coke from the fridge. It was one of only three food items in here. Glancing around, she wondered if the place looked as empty as it felt.

So she plopped on the sofa and tried to stay still to beat the heat. She tried to focus on makeup tips from the latest issue of Glamour, but decided she was probably better off with Parents Magazine now. Not that it would make a difference. Her brain continued to wander off without her, and she wasn't certain it would come back. Scenes from Tuesday night reared in her mind. He'd said he wanted her. He'd made her say it, too—made certain that she wasn't taken advantage of. She hadn't been, not the way her heart had been pounding, and the way she had writhed in his arms, how he had just touched her and she had woken up wanting him inside her.

Sloan was polishing off a second Coke as the doorbell rang. She jumped, then swore softly under her breath. She had just calmed herself down too. But her nerves switched into overdrive.

When she opened the door she found Yasmin on the front steps. Immediately, she was pulled into a quick hug that did more to calm her nerves than anything else had.

"Did you just spell me?" Sloan asked as she pulled back.

"Yes, you needed it." Yasmin offered only a smile and she stepped around Sloan to walk through the unit. "Too hot. You want better air?"

"Yes." *There was a spell for that?* She watched as Yasmin took a deep breath, muttered something under her breath and then looked up and snapped both fingers skyward as she whooshed out the breath she held.

Sloan watched Yasmin work, rearranging the place. She suddenly felt frumpy next to her cousin's cute jeans and loose top. Yasmin didn't seem to notice that Sloan wasn't quite back in her jeans yet, but the doorbell rang again and Sloan jumped to answer it.

Megan hugged her, too, another short, fierce embrace that once again calmed Sloan down. "Don't worry. Yasmin's baby is four months ahead of yours. And you had two. You'll be back in your jeans in no time."

Sloan was starting to ask something, but Rae appeared in the doorway. "Don't ask. I didn't say anything to her." It was just Megan, both of them knew.

Rae was family; she didn't knock. Sloan decided it was time both the others had keys, too. They were clearly family if they could take their Saturday afternoon and evening away from their own families to help her solve a problem from getting herself drugged. Though she wasn't to blame, throwing herself at Dylan Atterson because she believed he was her Chicago Dream Man had not been her smartest move.

Within minutes, the air was cooler and they were set up with Sloan in the arm chair and the other three around the wood coffee table.

"No metal?" Yasmin asked.

"Peg construction," Sloan answered. She'd found it from a vendor on Melrose and was excited to finally have a fully wooden altar.

Megan and Yasmin started unpacking. Having been at the store themselves in the past few days, they'd simply grabbed what they needed. Sloan felt her nerves ratcheting up again.

Yasmin handed Sloan a small pad of paper and had her write down the full date that Sloan wanted to remember. That she had been in a hotel in Chicago. That she had been drugged.

Yasmin tried again to offer a disclaimer. "We haven't done anything like this before…"

Sloan didn't care. She had to try.

"Can you put in a little suggestion, too?" Sloan leaned forward, almost out of the chair, and decided to go for broke.

"Like what?" Megan frowned at her. They probably had their hands full, trying to get her to remember.

"Convince me to get over him?" *She could hope, right?*

"No. I could, but I won't." Yasmin shrugged. If you still want it in a week, maybe you can do it yourself. Even if you can't, I wouldn't want to do suggestions about the issue at hand until at least one week later. To give the person time to sort through what they found out." Then she smiled. "We can do other things, but I think we have a lot on the docket today."

"Lose my extra baby weight?" Sloan shrugged.

"That we can do." Yasmin laughed and gestured to her own jeans. Sloan grinned. *Should have known.*

CHAPTER 51

"Sloan, baby," Yasmin said in a soft voice.

Sloan didn't open her eyes, she was just supposed to sit there. Not that it mattered, with her skills of late, she wouldn't be able to help anyway.

"You've got spells on you."

"No, I don't," Sloan countered. "I've tried but they slide off."

"Like in class?" Yasmin prompted.

"Just like that." Sloan still didn't open her eyes. "Rae, did you do it?"

"I tried. I did do *safeties* on the babies and I tried one on you, but I got the impression it didn't work. I did a *healing* on you, too, but got the same result."

Sloan nodded. With her eyes closed she couldn't see what the three witches were doing or signaling to each other in front of her. Her shoulders tensed.

"Well, they're there," Yasmin sighed. "They aren't bad, they look neutral and positive, so nothing was done to you intending harm..." her voice trailed off and Sloan heard murmurings among the three.

Yasmin was clearly their leader here, as she announced, "Okay, first things first, get these spells off you."

"Wait." Sloan could hear the question in Yasmin's voice. "Can you cast on Megan? Have you tried to cast on anyone but yourself and the babies?"

"I don't remember."

When prompted, Sloan opened her eyes and—using the full altar in front of her—at Yasmin's bidding, cast a glamour on Megan.

"Holy shit! That worked. That was easy," Sloan gasped out as she looked at Megan's newly sleek and blond hair. It looked fully odd on Megan's half African-American face and Megan hopped up to laugh at herself in the hall mirror for the few minutes Sloan let the spell hold. Then she let it go and they all watched as Megan's hair returned to normal.

"Not ever going blond," Megan commented with a glint in her eye, "But that brings up something interesting. You could always cast on others, Sloan. You clearly still have it. You were just being a good witch and not casting on other people."

"Well, everyone I know that I would feel comfortable protecting is already a witch!" Sloan had never tried to look for other ways her power might still be intact. She had to admit it was a huge relief to know she hadn't lost her mojo.

"Okay, back to getting these spells off you. They're clearly blocking some of it," Yasmin announced and they all settled back in. It would likely be a long afternoon.

Ten minutes later, Sloan had sat through chanting she recognized and could have worked along with. They'd forbidden her from "helping" since she wasn't doing anything that worked anyway.

"Okay, open your eyes." They commanded of Sloan.

She felt as though she'd almost fallen asleep and it took a minute to get back to full focus. While everyone watched, curious, she tried another spell on herself.

She felt it take effect. "That worked!" The relief that poured through her was immense, a huge weight off her shoulders. "Oh, my God. Thank you."

They talked for a few minutes. While Sloan was happy that she was good to go again, they were all worried. Who could have done this? It wasn't a mean spell or truly harmful, but it had blocked Sloan.

"It could have been harmful had I needed my skills and not had them!" Sloan thought about how angry she would be had her babies suffered and she'd not been able to cast anything to at least help. She knew witchcraft wasn't always a cure. Sometimes the Universe just blocked something. Sometimes she could feel when that happened.

"Should we find out who did it?" Megan asked the group.

"First, we have to block it!" That was Yasmin, always the practical witch.

They all agreed, and Sloan sat back to have another spell cast on her with none of her own help. It was an odd feeling. They'd cast on each other in class a few times, but that had been when they were novices. Casting on each other often involved *glamours* and failed attempts. Now she sat in the middle of a coven of sorts. They had the power of three focused at her, and all were accomplished witches. Rae was the least accomplished of them, and she and Sloan had been blazing through the advanced class before Sloan had dropped out.

Rae was waiting for her sister to rejoin her before going back to class herself, but she'd been working. Sloan was the weakest witch at the table. So she felt this spell as it locked around her. When at last she opened her eyes, she said, "Lindsey and Michael, too."

This time, she participated and it was nearly dinner time before they finished all the work. Sloan felt bad, keeping them out, away from their own homes. "Thank you, guys. I can probably do the *memory* on my own now, right?"

She looked to Yasmin, who nodded, but responded more like a sister than a cousin. "You can. You have the skills, but are you sure you want to do this alone?"

Sloan was, and she nodded. Still, she felt the need to explain. "Max says we were crazy for each other. Everything he's said makes me feel like I've lost the most special night of my life, not the worst."

Still, they looked at her, but Sloan pushed on. "If it gets bad, I promise I'll call. But I think I'd like to do this alone. If it doesn't work, I may have to try again next weekend..." but next weekend felt so far away. She pushed her hopes higher, trying to stay positive and happy about the return of her skills.

"If it doesn't work," Yasmin added, "Try the *recover*. If that doesn't, maybe a generic *find* will work on lost memories." She reached out and grabbed Sloan's hand. "But you call us if you even just need to talk."

The women set up everything Sloan needed. A *recover* was not a simple spell, so they made sure she was ready before they left. Each left her with a fierce hug that she was pretty sure was also a small transfer of power. She was grateful—she could use it.

When at last she had the place to herself, she started casting the spell.

Even before she finished, memories started flooding her brain, nearly bringing her to her knees.

CHAPTER 52

S mall noises coaxed Max into the living room. Sloan was finally home. He'd been in the office while the babies slept and hadn't heard her come in, so he had no idea how long she'd been sitting there on the couch in the dark. As he made his way down the hall, Max could hear sighs from her. She must have gotten back late. His voice cut through the sounds she was quietly making, "Hypnosis wasn't all it was cracked up to be?"

"All that and more." He could barely make out the edges of her, but it was Sloan, and he didn't dare disturb the peace when she was talking to him.

At that moment he understood what he had missed and wondered how he could have mistaken the sounds. It was so clear now. "Are you crying?"

"Yes."

It only took that instant to find himself next to her on the couch and wrap her in his arms. No matter what she did or said, Sloan in pain was too much for him. "What happened? Are you all right?"

"Yes, I'm okay." Deep breath.

Though she said she was okay, it didn't sound like it to him. He waited and didn't get at all what he expected.

"Oh, Max. I messed *everything* up. I'm an idiot." She burrowed her face into his shirt. "I'm so, so sorry."

Her breath was warm on his chest through the fabric, her hair was silk under his fingertips. He wondered what he'd done for her to finally turn to him, to want him to hold her. He sighed himself, not really sure if he cared why she was curling into him while she was wide awake. "Shhh, it's okay."

"It's *not* okay. I'm sorry!" She practically wailed it, her fingers grabbing at him, finding purchase at the sides of his ribs. He felt hot tears smearing into his shirt and searing his skin underneath.

"Sorry for what?" She smelled like Sloan, and she felt like Sloan, and he wanted so much to just sit there and hold her, comfort her.

But she turned her face up to him. "I—I—....."

She couldn't find the words and turned away, her eyes looked heavenward as she searched for the ability to express herself. His hands disobeyed him, touching either side of her face and bringing her back to his gaze.

Even here in the dark of night, with tears streaking down her face, she was beautiful. The only thing he could think to do was kiss her. So he did.

His mouth sought and found hers. His lips brushed against hers, soft as the whispers he couldn't say. His breath was inhaled from hers, and he pressed more deeply against her, as though the way to her heart was in the touch of his tongue to hers. He held her, his fingers laced and locked into her hair, keeping her from pulling away and only in the distance of his thundering thoughts did he realize that she wasn't fighting him at all.

She kissed him back.

And his world came unspun.

Her hands traced his chest, her fingers raking against him

and stealing his breath. They brushed over buttons and, frustrated by the barrier of the shirt, she began working them through the tiny holes. Her fingers traced his skin as she revealed it, and at last they splayed wide across his chest, pushing his shirt off of him. With deft movements, he shucked the clinging sleeves and went to work on her shirt, at last peeling it down her arms.

Pants melted away. Underwear simply disappeared. She was clinging to him for dear life as he touched every part of her. She offered herself up to him, without him having to steal in during the night and wake her. Without him having to beg or convince. Or dream.

He tucked her under him while he tasted and felt and only began satisfying his cravings. When he needed the feeling of her around him, he pushed against her, thinking to lay her back along the cushions. But Sloan pushed back.

In his mind he knew this was the end. They were both naked on the couch, flesh to flesh, wanting and needing, but Sloan had surely come to her senses. He watched her mouth, plump from the minor abuse he had inflicted on it moments before, and wanted to do it again. But he waited for the word 'no' to form on those pretty pink lips. Somehow it didn't. His eyes traced the movement as her mouth got closer to him, only to lock onto his collarbone. Her tongue expertly traced the mark left by those lips. She tasted him like she was starving, her mouth and fingers sketching wide arcs over his skin and setting him to trembling against her touch. She found the underside of his jaw, his ear lobe, his shoulder. She bit him lightly there, proving to be more than he could take and he let out her name on a hoarse whisper as he pushed her down and drove into her. Right there on the couch. Beneath the wide windows that bore no sheers.

Again and again he pushed into her. And again and again she rose to meet him. Her hands grasped at him pulling him closer, even though his arms were wound vice-like around her, and he didn't think he could get closer or deeper inside her if he tried, but they both tried.

A noise ripped from his throat as he came. Moans came from deep inside her. Breathy *ahhhhs* that stole air from his lungs as she pulsed around him, prolonging his orgasm with hers.

He held her for a minute.

Then as he slowly gathered his senses, her voice came to him.

"Oh, God."

He froze. In that flash of time his veins froze solid. Her tone was all wrong. She couldn't.

But she did. "Max. I—...I didn't mean for that to happen, I was trying to—"

Somehow his voice found strength. He nearly yelled with the frustrations and heartache he had carried with him all these months. "I don't care what the hell you were trying to do."

He yanked his pants up from the chair where they had landed and stepped into them as he finally made the call himself. "You don't get to do it." He slid his arms into his shirt without giving a thought to the buttons. "Not again. You have walked out on me too many times, Sloan."

His socks were on, and his shoes were in view. "And to be sure, I am a class A idiot for allowing it, but not this time." He headed toward the door, keys in hand, his heart lost somewhere in the cushions of the couch. Damn, but he was seven hundred kinds of fool.

"Max!" She was still sitting on the edge of the sofa. Still naked. She looked shocked. *Good.*

"No, Sloan! Not this time." He wasn't sure how he said it. He heard the words from his mouth, and he meant them, but he left her there, staring after him, eyes wide. He was out the door, starting the car, peeling down the street in the dead of night before he knew what he was doing. Where he was going, he didn't know, but it was definitely going to be fast. Fast enough to forget the tears at the edge of her big blue eyes. Fast enough to leave behind the image of tousled blonde hair and the idea that he had some kind of prideful claim on it. Fast enough to race against the words that had been coming, the *you know that we can't do this* and the *this won't ever work* and every other version of *no* that she'd been getting ready to say. Fast enough to sweep the Sloan cobwebs from his brain and maybe, for once, think clearly.

He almost laughed out loud into the cold night at that. He hadn't thought clearly since the day he'd met her.

CHAPTER 53

S loan rocked babies, and she waited.
   Fed babies and waited.

She was a house prisoner without the minivan. Though her car was here, the car seats were clipped into the middle row of the car Max had taken. But then again, where would she go with her face tearstained like this? How would she leave not knowing when Max might come back? If he'd ever come back. It had been hours and felt like years.

She had tried to sleep, but it didn't work. Tried to read, but it failed to distract her. So she had wound up sitting on the couch watching out the back window, thinking she had been there so long she could see the grass grow.

When at last she heard the garage door open, she wanted to run to him. Fling open the door and bury herself in his heat, but she would be lucky if he even acknowledged her before he threw her things to the curb.

He had been so angry.

So she waited. Until he rounded the corner and looked at her. He ceased all movement, the midday sun backlighting him and making his expression difficult to see. But Sloan was certain it was hard as granite.

She steeled herself and spoke. "Where were you? It's been thirteen hours."

"Driving."

"Max, I'm so sorry, I—" Her heart leapt into her throat making it impossible to say all the things that needed to be said.

"Sloan, don't be sorry."

"But I—" It didn't matter because he turned his back to her, as though he was finished with this conversation, and he stalked off down the hallway.

Her mouth got ahead of her and blurted out the one thing she could think of. "I know about Chicago."

It worked. He stopped. He turned. "What are you talking about?"

Courage, Sloan she told herself and took a breath. She didn't like lying to him about how she'd done it, but they were barely seeing their past, let alone any future. "The hypnotist wasn't about losing weight. It was about digging up what I didn't remember."

He still didn't seem to care. His fists were perched on his hips. His voice was mocking. "And whatever did you find out?"

She couldn't look at him. "That you said you loved me." It was barely a whisper. She'd been so shocked to hear his voice saying those words as she relived that night in Chicago. In his hotel room, he'd told her he'd fallen like a rock the moment he saw her. He'd never said it again, but now... maybe she stood a chance. When he didn't speak, she looked up at him.

It seemed what she'd said didn't phase him in the slightest. He looked at her like she was the biggest fool on the planet to ever think she stood a chance with him.

"Of course, I love you! I'm an idiot." He raised his palms out to her then at the room around him, "Did you think I did all this just to get a live-in maid? Or curtains? Or make my parents happy?"

"Yes."

"Then you're an idiot, too, Sloan!" His voice was getting louder and hers was getting smaller.

"I've already admitted to that." She wished for a hole to crawl into, to lick her wounds or just curl up and die. But still she held out some tiny flickering of hope.

Max didn't. "Well that was a nice chat. I hope that hypnosis has made your life better." The sarcasm dripped from him in thick clumps. "But really, what does it change? You don't want to be here and you don't want me."

The hope flared inside her, giving power to her small voice. "But I *do* want to be here and I *do* want you."

"Could've fooled me!" With the sizzle of a wet wick, it died.

"I thought you were looking for a mother for your kids, a convenient family. You *never* said you loved me." Her voice and her heart cracked.

His shoulders slumped. "I said it until I was blue in the face, Sloan, what more do you want?"

"No." She shook her head. "You said it in Chicago, but never afterwards."

"Sloan, you thought I drugged you and maybe raped you. '*Oh, Sloan I love you, let's be a family*' seemed like the fastest route to a well-deserved jail sentence. You weren't interested in me before Chicago, and I was already pushing the boundaries of stalking, since you didn't love me back." He looked so defeated. "It wouldn't have changed anything." He turned again to walk away.

"Yes, it would have."

"Like what?"

"I would have said 'yes' when you asked me to marry you." Her heart wasn't beating anymore. It had been clear from the moment he had told her 'no more' and drove away that this reunion wasn't going to be the happy moment she had hoped for.

He sighed. "Sloan, I asked you a thousand times in a thousand different ways, and you said 'no' every single time. I don't know what you want from me."

"I want whatever you're willing to give."

From somewhere in his chest came a sound that would have been laughter if it hadn't teetered on a cliff of pain. It tore through her chest, that she had caused it, and his words told her she was right. "I would have given you everything. I tried to, again and again, and you kept pushing me away. I don't have anything left."

She nodded. Tears falling in earnest now. But Max just looked at her. Max who always leapt to take such good care of her, stood and watched her pain, and did nothing.

He was right. And so was she. He hadn't said the words 'I love you' since that night in Chicago. But he'd showed her in every gesture and every word. He'd taken care of her, held her when she was upset, caressed her and made her feel beautiful, soothed her when she worried. Even just last night on the couch, his hurt and anger had been because he'd loved her. And even then, she'd still been too afraid to look, to see what it might be. She'd been so scared of losing him that she hadn't seen that she already had him.

She wiped her own tears away and nodded. "If you ever decide that you do want to marry me, just ask. I'll say 'yes'. I promise."

He only offered a shrug. "You don't need me to ask you. You have the ring." And he stalked away.

She did have the ring! Nestled in its tiny box, sitting useless at her bedside. She tore down the hallway, afraid that it was gone, that something had happened to it. And grateful when she saw the dark velvet box, still there, untouched. By the time she got to it and then raced back out into the hallway, Max had disappeared. But he had to be here somewhere.

Her heart still pounding in her throat, making her gasp for breath, she threw open doors, unable to call to him. Finally, she found him, slipped under the covers of the guest bed. Not the master bed where he belonged. He was almost asleep, but she grabbed his hand and pressed the small box to his palm.

Her voice came out on ragged, wet sounds torn from her throat. "If you ever get the urge to ask me again, I'll say 'yes'. I understand if you don't want—"

"Marry me."

She smiled. "Yes!"

His eyes popped wide open. Then frowned at her. "No, Sloan."

Her breath sucked in, the pain ripping through her tearing apart every vital organ.

Pushing himself to sitting, he stared her down. "You were drugged that night. You've told me time and again that you weren't yourself." He sucked in a breath as if he needed fortification for what he was about to say.

Sloan tucked her hands together and tried to tame her wildly erratic heartbeat while she waited on him.

"When I kept asking you, I was convinced if you just said 'yes' you would come around and fall in love with me. The only time you ever said it was in Chicago. I want you more than I've ever wanted anyone. I *want* to marry you and spend the rest of my life with you. But it's not enough anymore just to be with you. I *need* to know if you could fall in love with me, too." He held the ring box tight in his fist, knuckles white and angry around it.

She nodded.

"You think you could love me back?" He stayed his ground, sitting rigid in front of her, trying to give nothing away. His face was stoic, but his eyes showed what her answer meant to him.

"The first time you touched me, my heart broke."

"What?" The sheltered expression slid off his face, replaced with the concern he always seemed to feel for her.

"When you shook my hand, I thought you were going to kiss my fingers instead, and I looked up at your face, startled. I think I fell in love with you right then." Her fingers twisted in her lap, remembering the moment, and how shattered she had felt right then, and so much of the time since that day. "And there was this woman sitting on your blanket, and she looked at me in a way that said you clearly belonged to her. And all I could think was that my soulmate was already with someone else."

"Really?"

She nodded, her eyes filling with tears.

He looked confused. "Then why did you keep saying 'no'?"

"Max, I never picked the right guys. Why should I believe that I had done a better job this time? Especially when your girlfriend was sitting right there?"

He smiled at her. For the first time in what seemed like forever the grin overtook his whole face. His eyes locked on hers, and she felt it deep in every bone. "You love me?"

She nodded, truly crying now. "Yes, more than anything."

Clearly, he still didn't fully believe her, but he popped the blue box open and took her left hand. She gasped when she saw the ring. It was gorgeous.

"What? You never peeked?"

"No. I thought... well, I thought all kinds of things. But never that you really wanted *me*. That ring seemed like everything I couldn't have. So I didn't look."

He slid it onto her fourth finger. "Sloan Jean Ellis, I have been in love with you from literally the first moment I saw you." He kissed her, his mouth melting into hers, stealing all thoughts from her brain. His tongue robbed her of breath, and yet stilled the tornado of hurt feelings that had whirled inside her all these months. She clung to him, pressed against him, knowing he was the change that she felt.

Then pushed her away as he stood up out of bed, still dressed. "Now go pack."

"Pack?"

"Yes, we're going to Vegas. On the next flight."

She inhaled. "Vegas?"

"Yes. So we can get married within the next twenty-four hours."

She must have looked confused because he continued. "If you ever want me to sleep a peaceful night again, you'll marry me A.S.A.P."

She took it all in for a moment.

But Max kept talking. "You can have the big wedding any time you want, with as many friends as you want. I won't breathe a word about Vegas. But I'm having a hard time believing this is real. You've run out on me too many times, and if it happens again I will burst into a million pieces. I need you."

"You're right. Let's go."

"Really?"

She had to laugh at him.

But he kept going. "You mean it? We'll live here? We'll be a real family? You'll hang curtains? We'll pick out paint?"

"Yes, to all of it. We'll put a swing set in the back yard and argue over who has to do the dishes. We'll gripe about socks on the floor, and wet towels, and empty toilet paper rolls. And I'll love you every minute of every day." She pulled his face down and kissed him, a new warmth settling deep inside her. This time she didn't fight it. "Now I have to pack. I think we can all be ready to go in about thirty minutes."

But he tugged her back for another kiss. This one deeper and longer. "Somehow we didn't wake those babies." His eyes danced with hot blue flames. "I'm certain that an hour or two will be soon enough."

CHAPTER 54

I n the end, they drove to Vegas in the minivan. It had taken all of five minutes to realize no one wanted to fly with two infants on the plane. With any luck, the car would rock the babies to sleep.

Sloan slept most of the way there too, since she hadn't slept the whole night Max had been out. Luckily, the time hadn't seemed to bother him or his stamina. They'd made love in the guest room so as not to wake the babies. The first time, they'd been successful. The second time, however, she was pretty sure they'd woken because she'd screamed Max's name so loud.

They'd fed babies, called a chapel in Vegas, then called their friends.

Though they were the first on the road, the others should get in before the ceremony. Max even called his parents. While Sloan didn't think they'd normally be ecstatic about a quickie Vegas wedding, they were more than thrilled to hop the next plane to Sin City and even begged them to hold the ceremony if the plane was late. Sloan had easily agreed. She also called Wil, but didn't tell Max.

Rae and Sam were hot on their heels, showing up as soon as

Sloan and Max checked into their room. In a short while, Rae was pushing the double stroller through the shops to help find a wedding dress. If she had to get married fast, Vegas was at least the place to do it. They found a gorgeous dress and it fit, though not the way Sloan wanted.

"I haven't lost the baby weight yet," she lamented as she stood in front of the mirror. "Maybe I can cast a glamour."

"Don't you dare!"

Rae's outburst startled her, and Sloan looked at her sister, confused.

"That man loves you. He is your Chicago Dream Man. You don't lie to him in any way." Her sister's eyes implored her. "If there's anything I've learned with Sam it's that we can't let anything come between us. That starts each time I want to hide something. Even something as simple as I bought another pair of shoes and I know it will drive him crazy. I tell him. I let it drive him crazy."

There was a heartbeat as Sloan took it all in. Rae's next words weren't what she expected though.

"Don't make him see anything other than the real you. You don't need *glamours*. I've seen the way he looks at you, and trust me, he's not seeing any baby weight. He just sees you. Don't mess with that!"

Sloan nodded at her sister's reflection in the mirror, but Rae had already ducked down to push fallen binkies back into tiny mouths. She fussed over blankets and Sloan heard, "Tell your mommy she looks beautiful."

Just then her phone buzzed with a text from Max that his parents had arrived and he was in his tux and ready. She called him, wanting—*needing*—to hear his voice. "Hi, Babe. Rae and the babies and I are on our way. Probably twenty minutes, maybe more if we hit traffic."

Wearing the dress out of the store, they headed for the limo Rae had rented her as a wedding present. Inside, she found bouquets and looked up at her sister, already wearing what she'd picked out as a maid of honor dress. With practiced hands, they buckled car seats into the back of the limo and Sloan was struck at the oddity of it all. Tucking her dress into the car and clutching her bouquet, she began her last ride as an unmarried woman. Her last ride before Max was well and truly hers.

They pulled up in front of the small beautiful chapel. While Max could have gotten them any one of the neon churches, he'd managed to find a pretty one. Rae pulled the babies out of the car and handed one car seat to Wil, who'd just pulled up with a carload of men Sloan knew as Max's friends. He hadn't seen them in a while, and she thought it was a great present. She smiled to Wil and whispered "thank you" as she gathered her dress and headed to the back of the chapel.

Ensconced in the bridal suite, she sat in the chair and laid her head back. It had been so long since the first night Max had proposed to her in Chicago. He'd said...

He'd said...

Sloan frowned. *It was gone.*

Her heart raced. Where had her memory gone? She searched for anything from Chicago but couldn't find it. Panicking now, she catalogued what she did remember. She'd been happy. So happy. She knew they'd made love, but she couldn't remember doing it. She knew he'd proposed, but all the images and the sounds and the feelings were gone.

Just then, Rae stepped into the room and saw her. "What's wrong?"

"I—" She started to explain, then said, "No. I need to tell Max."

"I'll get him."

Just like that, her sister was out the door, leaving Sloan alone with a growing horror in the pit of her stomach. His parents were religious. She was a witch. She was wearing silk underwear, a wedding dress, and spells. She couldn't marry him without telling him the truth. And she had to confess that she hadn't seen a hypnotist.

Max appeared in the doorway, a huge smile on his face until he saw her. She must look as frightened as she was. He could turn away right now. It would be legitimate. After all this, he should leave her for lying to him.

She started with the simplest thing. "I can't remember Chicago."

"What? You didn't ever remember it? You lied?" He still didn't seem angry.

Well, she might be about to blow that out of the water. "I did remember, but it's gone. And I did lie about something else."

She waited a beat, but saw he was waiting her out, his own expression wary. Good God, she'd put him through this so many times. So she just came clean.

"I didn't see a hypnotist. I called my friends and we cast a spell so I could remember. It must have worn off, though I didn't know it could." When he didn't say anything, she added one last line. "I want to remember it, but it's gone. I can't now."

He still didn't seem angry, just concerned. "You and your friends shouldn't play around with spells, Sloan. It can get very dangerous if you don't know what you're doing."

She shrugged. "We do know what we're doing. We're witches."

"What?" He was clearly startled by her admission.

So she said it again. "I'm a witch."

Max threw his head back and laughed. "Oh, my God."

That was not the reaction she'd expected. Frowning hard, she looked at him more closely. Nope, that was honest to God laughter. "It's not funny. It's what I am. I cast a spell on myself to remember Chicago, and now it's gone!"

He wiped real tears from the corners of his eyes. "I'm so sorry, Sloan. I countered that spell so it wouldn't work."

"What? Why would you counter my *recover*? And *how* would you do it?" *That took advanced witchcraft. Max...?*

He grinned before she could think it through. "My Grandma Summerland was a witch. She taught me and left me all her stuff."

"Summerland..." she let it trail off. Summerland was a common enough name, but a branch of the family was a well-known name in witchcraft on the new continent.

As soon as she said it, he whispered, "Ellis..." and nodded as he realized what they were doing. She was from a known witchcraft family, too.

"Why did you stop my spell?" she asked, still confused.

"In Chicago, Dylan Atterson gave you GHB but he also cast a spell on you. It was an evil double whammy."

"He's one, too?" She felt her hand go to her heart, this was getting bigger than she'd ever expected.

Max shook his head. "I finally believe him. He said he got it on the internet." He looked into the corner. "The first night, I had you close your eyes and hold things. That may be all you remember, but that was me taking his spell off you. I thought you were fully sober after that, because who would cast a spell *and* give you roofies? It's why I was so horrified the next morning. I thought I had taken care of everything."

Max paused, when Sloan nodded at him, he continued, telling her how he'd found more spells later, that he removed and blocked.

"*You're* the one who shut me down! I thought it was because I was pregnant!"

"I didn't stop you from casting on other people."

"I don't cast on other people!" she protested, realizing that Max had found it okay to cast on her. She would have to set a firm rule—

"Hey," He held his palms up to her. "I don't either. I only did it to remove spells that I believed you didn't know about. I did it because I thought someone had cast on you—"

"Yeah, *me!*" She protested.

He couldn't stifle his grin. "I promise I will not get in your way again."

"You cast on the babies." She found the words.

"*Safeties*, heath spells, just the usual for kids."

"Me, too." Though she'd thought they'd bounced right off. Maybe because the spell was already on them. From Max.

A knock came at the door and Max yelled to open it.

Wil poked his head in. "Are we going to have a wedding? I think the last few guests just arrived after getting caught in some traffic." He looked to Sloan, "Your sister said she thinks everyone is here."

Max reached out and took her hand. "Let's get this show on the road."

"Are you going to walk down the aisle with me?" She looked at his hand, her eyebrows rising with the question.

"No. That's for you. I'd better go get out front."

But he'd already seen the bride. Even so, there was no bad luck here. Nothing they couldn't counter with a little witchcraft. So Sloan stood at the back of the room, watching her groom make his way to the front. Tristan and Megan had just settled into a pew, nearly filling the tiny chapel intended for the smallest of weddings.

Max stopped with a hello and a frown. "Tristan, you're here...?"

Sloan spoke up from the back, "Tristan and his sister Delilah own a witchcraft shop on Vine Street. Along with my cousin, Yasmin." Sloan pointed them out in the pews, where Luke and Yasmin held their own infant.

Tristan laughed another hearty, joyful sound as he pulled Megan into a hug. Megan was laughing and hugging him back, too. Even Delilah and Brandon and their kids were there, all laughing. Sloan did not get the joke.

It was Delilah who managed to speak. "We all know Max. We just didn't know he was *your* Max. He's in the store all the time."

"It never occurred to me," Yasmin shook her head at it. "I mean, it's L.A. Why would the Max who comes into the store be your Max?"

The Max in question—now and forever *her* Max—turned and shrugged at her as if to say "who knew?" before taking his rightful place at the front of the church.

He'd probably bought the things to undo her spells from the shop. Thinking along those lines, Sloan called Megan to the back of the church as she was closest. "Can you undo the spell my beloved apparently cast on me before we get this shindig started? Can you do it without being obvious? I don't know what his parents know."

With a few deep breaths between them and some chanted words, Sloan felt the spell crack away and her memories of Chicago come back in full bloom. There it was. His proposal. The first time he said he loved her. Their first kiss.

As the music started playing, she looked up the aisle and walked toward Max. She'd done it. She'd played her cards too close to the heart for far too long, but she was okay. She had Max now and he had her.

They said their vows while her new family looked on. She and Rae had found Luke. Though their parents had died, they'd continued looking for him, and in finding their cousin, they'd found so much more.

She felt Max slip the ring on her finger and when the minister said they could kiss, she held back a little. What she wanted wasn't appropriate for the front of a church. She would have all the time in the world for that.

Rae and Sam were taking the twins for the night. Rae had

insisted, since they would be having their own in another eight months. As Sloan headed down the aisle with Max's hand firmly in her own, she smiled at her babies. They sat docilely on Rae and Sam's laps, small hands waving as her sister and brother-in-law moved them.

Their baby blue eyes twinkled and as Sloan stepped out into the night air, she realized something. "Max, our children are descended from two very powerful witchcraft lines!"

"Uh-oh," he responded, then laughed. "I guess we'll have to deal with their skills as they come up..."

Then, he swept her into the limo and a wide open future.

Thank you for reading! I love romances with real love and believable characters, and I hope you found all that in these pages. I want to fall in love right along with the characters, and I do, while I'm writing it.

About Savannah

I started writing when I was eight--I hand wrote an 80-page novella that I believed to be (adult) romantic suspense. I'm proud to say, I've gotten a lot better since then. I've grown up to be a nerd at heart! I love neuroscience and people watching, and if you look, you'll find some of that in each Savannah Kade book. Most days you'll find me in my office, looking out my window at a handful of the neighbor's cows, or watching my dogs or my cat roam the backyard.

Follow me, find me, ask me questions! I would love to hear from you.
www.SavannahKade.com
Savannah@SavannahKade.com